...hy Herman never disappoints. *Not By Chance* is a fitting end to ...Seaport series. Kathy isn't afraid to tackle the tough issues—race, ...try, meaning in life, and faith. I'll be looking forward to her future ...ls."

LYN COTE, AUTHOR OF THE WOMEN OF IVY MANOR SERIES

...here meaning and significance in life? Brandon Jones wants to ...w! Join him on an exciting and emotional journey through intol-...ce, prejudice, murder, and a lost love to find the answer."

...ORENA MCCOURTNEY, AUTHOR OF THE IVY MALONE MYSTERIES

"Herman's *Not By Chance* deals unflinchingly with murder, hatred, and racism. Yet her characters, in their own struggles, give us hope while showing what it means to love."

JANET BENREY, CO-AUTHOR OF HUMBLE PIE, DEAD AS A SCONE, AND THE FINAL CRUMPET

"*Not By Chance* is more than a good suspense novel. As you are pulled in to discover the who and the why behind a series of hate crimes, Kathy Herman takes you deeper still. With sensitivity and skill, she examines that age-old question, "What is God's purpose for our lives?" An unforgettable read on many levels."

ANN TATLOCK, CHRISTY AWARD-WINNING AUTHOR

"Kathy Herman is a master at weaving an entertaining storyline with essential biblical teaching. *Not By Chance* is not only a great read, it should be required reading for anyone who has ever dismissed the reality and devastation created by prejudice in the twenty-first century."

DEIDRE POOL, AUTHOR OF LOVING JESUS ANYWAY

"Kathy Herman's *Not By Chance* is a poignant reminder that we have been bought with a price—and we no longer plan our own course."

ANGELA HUNT, AUTHOR OF THE NOVELIST

"It takes a special author to weave a story that not only provides page-turning entertainment but also challenges us to examine our own motives and preconceptions. Kathy Herman has done just that in her latest title, *Not By Chance,* a compelling and thought-provoking read I highly recommend."

CAROL COX, AUTHOR OF *TICKET TO TOMORROW*

A SEAPORT SUSPENSE

BOOK FOUR

NOT BY
CHANCE

KATHY HERMAN

Multnomah® Publishers *Sisters, Oregon*

NOT BY CHANCE
published by Multnomah Publishers, Inc.

© 2006 by Kathy Herman
International Standard Book Number: 1-59052-490-X

Cover photo by JWH Design Services

The Holy Bible, New International Version
© 1973, 1984 by International Bible Society,
used by permission of Zondervan Publishing House

Multnomah is a trademark of Multnomah Publishers, Inc.,
and is registered in the U.S. Patent and Trademark Office.
The colophon is a trademark of Multnomah Publishers, Inc.

Printed in the United States of America

For information:
MULTNOMAH PUBLISHERS, INC.
601 N. LARCH STREET, SISTERS, OREGON 97759

Library of Congress Cataloging-in-Publication Data

Herman, Kathy.
 Not by chance : a novel / Kathy Herman.
   p. cm. -- (A Seaport suspense ; bk. 4)
 ISBN 1-59052-490-X
 I. Title. II. Series: Herman, Kathy. Seaport suspense ; bk. 4.
 PS3608.E762N67 2006
 813'.6--dc22

                              2006008721

06 07 08 09 10 11 12 — 10 9 8 7 6 5 4 3 2 1 0

To Him who is both the Giver and the Gift.

Acknowledgments

I owe a debt of gratitude to my editor, Rod Morris, who over the past five years has pored over the nearly one million words I have submitted in ten manuscripts and skillfully rearranged, revamped, corrected, or cut them—or made suggestions for revisions—which resulted in tighter story lines and a much more enjoyable read. Editors are often the unsung heroes. And as I finish out this second series, I'd like to say thanks, Rod, for being gentle enough to not discourage me, yet steadfast in leaving no sentence unturned. You always make me look better than I am.

I'd also like to thank my friend Paul David Houston, assistant district attorney, Nacogdoches County, Texas, for his valuable input regarding the handling of information leaks in police departments; and my buddy Will Ray, professional investigator, state of Oregon, for taking time to provide me input on forensic evidence and crime scene investigations.

I wish to extend my heartfelt thanks to my little sister and zealous prayer warrior, Pat Phillips, and to my newly formed online prayer team for your amazing support. How God is using you! Thanks also to Susie Killough, Judi Wieghat, Mark and Donna Skorheim, my friends at LifeWay Christian Store in Tyler, Texas, and everyone in my Bible study class and Sunday school class for your many prayers for my writing ministry. I have felt your prayers.

To those who read my books and those who sell them, thanks for encouraging me with e-mails and cards and personal testimonies about how God has used my words. He uses you to bless me more often than you know.

To my novelist friends in ChiLibris, thanks for sharing so generously from your collective storehouse of knowledge and experience. It's a privilege to be counted among you.

To the staff at Multnomah, whose commitment to honor God through the power of story is so very evident, thanks for the privilege of working with such dedicated professionals. Without your hard work, my books would never reach the shelves.

To my husband, Paul, whose encouragement never wavers, even when I doubt myself, thanks for always reminding me to look back over my shoulder at all the previous stories I've written and believe that somewhere in the quiet of my heart there lies another.

And to my heavenly Father from whom comes every good gift, thank You for entrusting me with the ability to write stories that bring people closer to You—for that is the desire of my heart and a privilege for which I am eternally grateful.

Prologue

H ey, Skunk!"

Caedmon Nash kept walking, trying to do what his mother had said and not react to the put-down he never got used to hearing and the bully who never tired of saying it.

"I told you to stay out of my neighborhood!"

Caedmon spun around in the middle of Shady Lane and glared at Abel Drummond and his jerky friends.

Abel took a step forward and shoved Caedmon in the chest. "You got a problem being called Skunk? 'Cause that's what you are. Black daddy. White mama. And you stink like—"

The other three seventh grade boys chimed in with every vulgar word for excrement Caedmon had ever heard.

"I don't *stink*," he finally said.

"Do, too." Abel's face wore a derisive grin. "Everybody knows skunks stink up every place they go. That's why we don't want you comin' in this neighborhood."

"It takes too long to go the other way. If I'm late gettin' home, I'll be in big trouble."

Abel snickered. "What's your hurry? We all know what your old lady's doin' when you're in school. I hear she likes them darkies so much she doesn't even charge 'em."

The other boys guffawed.

Caedmon felt his face turn hot, and it was all he could do not to grab Abel and hit him over and over the way he had imagined doing a hundred times. "Shut up! You don't even know what you're talking about." Caedmon started to walk away.

"You're not goin' anywhere till you pay the toll." Abel glanced back at the other boys. "Let's show the skunk what the price is for cuttin' through here."

Caedmon thought his heart would beat out of his chest. In the next instant he kicked Abel in the shin, then sprinted to the top of the hill, aware of footsteps pounding the pavement behind him.

He ran across the churchyard at First Methodist and out into the cemetery, then weaved his way through the maze of headstones, racing toward the far side of the tall hedge that formed a fence around the property. His eyes found the grave marked "Mills," and he cut in behind it, then dropped to his knees and crawled through an opening at the base of the shrubs, branches scraping his face and arms. He came out the other side, scrambled to his feet, and kept running.

Caedmon heard shouted racial slurs and looked over his shoulder, relieved to see no one chasing him. He stopped and hung his head, his hands on his knees, and tried to catch his breath. For once, he was glad to be the skinniest kid in the class.

"Don't matter what they say about us," his mother had said. "Just ignore 'em and mind your own business. We don't need no trouble."

Easy for her to say! She wasn't the one who had to listen to their put-downs and big fat lies. And what did she know about being laughed at and spit on and having her face shoved in the toilet? How he hated Abel and his stupid friends!

Caedmon shuffled across Harbor Street and over the railroad tracks toward the trailer park, his mind screaming with comebacks he wished he'd had the courage to say. He kicked a rock and sent it rolling into the culvert, feeling at the same time anger and sadness that his father wasn't around and he'd have to figure this out on his own.

Caedmon wet his fingers and wiped the bloody scratches on his arms. It wasn't fair that they could gang up on him and there was nothing he could do about it. Just as soon as he figured out a way to fight back, he would shut them all up—permanently!

1

Leave it to Beau to turn this into a competition!" Brandon Jones jumped up from the couch and stood leaning on the bookshelves in Kelsey Hartman's apartment, his hands in his pockets, his irritation turning to perspiration under his cashmere sweater.

Kelsey sank into the back of the leather couch. "He's just jealous. But it's not as though Beau Richards is the only one who wants to head up the South Atlantic Region. It's an enviable position."

"The job was *offered* to me, Kel. It's not as though I tried to ace him out."

"He'll get over it. Besides, you're the right choice for the job. You relate to people much better than he does." Kelsey got up and slid into Brandon's arms. "I'm so proud of you. I can hardly wait to tell Mother and Daddy that I'm marrying a regional vice president."

Regional vice president. Brandon imagined himself in a coat and tie, sitting around the boardroom table, sipping ice water and discussing the latest trends in women's fashions. "There's a lot to consider. The corporate office is a more structured environment than I'm used to."

"Just think what this could mean to our future. Once we're married, we could live nicely on your salary and bank mine. We'd have a healthy down payment for a house in no time. And I could stay home when we start having kids. It's an absolute blessing." Kelsey pushed back and looked up at him, her eyes probing. "What's wrong? You don't seem excited."

"It's a great opportunity, no question…but it'll mean putting in more hours. And a lot of Saturdays. That doesn't leave much time for recreation."

"For heaven's sake, it won't kill us to cut out some backpacking and rock climbing. And we can always work out at the gym to stay in shape. We're talking about securing your future—*our* future. I can't believe you're worried about all that."

"Well, it's the outdoor stuff that keeps me sane."

"Gee, thanks a lot." Kelsey wiggled out of his arms and flung open the balcony doors, then went outside and stood with her back to him, her arms folded.

"Honey, come back here. You know what I mean."

"Do I?"

Brandon walked up behind her and put his arms around her, his chin resting on her shoulder. "You're the love of my life. Without you, nothing else would matter to me."

"But it should. Why can't you be excited for yourself because you've been offered a well-deserved promotion?"

"I am. On one level."

"But…?"

"It'd be a huge adjustment spending my workday cooped up in an office, breathing recirculated air and connecting with nature from tinted windows overlooking downtown Raleigh."

"It's one of the best views in the city. And even if you have to work Saturdays, we'd have evenings together without the pressure of your having to leave town again."

"I know. But it's not like being on the road's been a hardship."

"I hate not seeing you five days in a row."

"We managed to fall in love, didn't we? From my perspective, the time we've spent together's been great."

"It has, but I would dread you being gone that much after we're married. This promotion would mean no more traveling. And you aren't that crazy about merchandising the stores anyway."

Brandon pulled her a little closer. "No, but it's allowed me freedom to set my own schedule. And there're things I look forward to on the road."

"Like what?"

"Well, like taking secondary highways through small communities and eating at hometown cafés…stopping at historical markers and scenic overlooks…driving toward the sunrise when the sky's orangey pink. Sometimes I have to pull over and watch. There've been times on the road when I've actually felt closer to God than when I'm in church."

"Which is just as well since you've missed the past three Sundays." Kelsey turned around in his arms and held his gaze for longer than he was comfortable. "You wouldn't even consider this promotion if we weren't engaged, would you?"

"We *are* engaged, so it's a moot point."

"Not really. What affects you affects me. You're Mr. Enthusiastic at work, and everyone thinks you're a company man. Are you?"

Brandon kissed the top of her head. "What kind of question is that? I've invested seven years at Mavis and Stein."

"Why do you have a totally different attitude about your work when we're alone?"

"What do you mean?"

"You're completely dispassionate about it—almost indifferent."

Brandon arched his eyebrows. "You've never once heard me complain about the company. It's just that dealing in women's apparel isn't my idea of something significant."

"Being a regional VP would certainly be *significant*. And the salary and benefits would be amazing. You'd be great at it."

"Tell that to Beau the blowhard."

"The real reason he's upset is because you can take it or leave it when he wants it so badly."

"Everyone wants something badly. I can't help it if he's had his eye on this promotion. But if I turn it down, we all know I'll never go any higher with the company."

"But is that the only reason you'd consider it? What is it *you* want badly?"

"To make you happy," he heard himself say.

"Well, this promotion would certainly do that. But only if you're enthused about it."

Brandon looked over her shoulder at the Raleigh skyline. "I will be, Kel. I just have to adjust my thinking. It was never really a goal of mine to be cooped up in an office all day."

"That's the second time you've used the words *cooped up*. If you didn't expect to work in an office, why did you get a business degree?"

"I don't know. Dad said it would open doors, and I just wanted to get through college. I started working in the catalog department because I needed a job, but I never actually chose this career. I just sort of eased into it. I kept telling myself it would grow on me, but it really hasn't."

"Why didn't you tell me this before? How are we supposed to set a wedding date before we know how much money we'll—"

"Shhh." Brandon gently put his finger to her lips. "Don't worry. I'm going to accept the promotion. I just need to adjust my thinking."

"Can you do that?"

He pulled her closer and avoided those questioning hazel eyes. "Sure. I can do anything for *us*." A giant snowflake fell on his sleeve, and then another and another. He looked up into the January sky, which seconds later became a swirling mass of white. "Come on. We'd better go in."

Kelsey linked her arm in his, her head against his shoulder, and went back in the apartment. "Just think, before this time next year, we could be married and living in our own home."

2

Ellen Jones watched the entire page vanish from the screen on her laptop and started frantically clicking keys in hopes that she hadn't done the unthinkable.

"Nooooo! Please be there! I'll never be able to remember what I wrote!"

She clicked on Documents and searched to see if she had saved her work. She hadn't.

Ellen threw back her head and let out a groan. Why did it seem as though this novel was begging not to be written?

She was suddenly aware of footsteps ascending the winding staircase and then her husband standing in the doorway of the widow's watch.

"Were you calling me?" Guy Jones said. "I heard you hollering but couldn't understand anything you were saying."

"I was scolding myself." Ellen turned off her laptop and closed it. "I can't believe I deleted an entire morning's work—all my brainstorming ideas gone, just like that."

"Maybe you saved them in the wrong file."

Ellen shook her head, fighting the emotion just beneath the surface. "I wasn't paying attention and hit the wrong button. I know better than not to save whatever I'm working on. My creativity's flat and I can't seem to focus."

"You're just trying too hard."

Ellen tapped her fingers on the desk and tried not to sound irritated. "You're the one who keeps pushing me to finish it."

"Only so you'll have a second manuscript ready to go when you get a contract on the first."

"I've been trying for almost three years, Counselor. No one's going to publish my manuscript. You've seen the stack of rejection letters. I'm not cut out to be a novelist."

Guy went over and pulled her to her feet, his arms around her. "Are you kidding? You're a writer to the core. We've just had a lot of family upheaval that's played havoc with the flow of creativity. Once you can get quiet inside, the words will come pouring out of you."

Ellen sighed. "It's hard to stay motivated when nothing happens."

"It will. How about me taking you to Gordy's for lunch?"

"I thought you had to work on your closing for next week's court case."

"I do, but I'm ready for a break. It's ten after eleven. Why don't we go now and avoid the rush?"

The phone rang, and Ellen reached down and picked up the receiver. "Hello."

"Hi, Mom."

Ellen looked at Guy, her eyebrows raised. "Well, if it isn't our long lost son, the one who never gets around to returning his messages."

"Yeah, sorry about that," Brandon Jones said. "I've had a lot going on."

"So have you thought any more about coming down over Labor Day? Surely even a vice president can squeeze in a long weekend with three months' advance notice."

"Actually, I was thinking of coming the day after tomorrow."

"Are you serious?" Ellen locked gazes with Guy.

"Yeah, it's been way too long. I thought I'd take some time off and head that way."

"I hope you're bringing Kelsey with you."

"Actually, I'm coming by myself. She's used all her vacation time."

"What a shame. We were looking forward to getting to know her better. Oh well, your father and I will take you any way we can get you. Do you need directions to the house?"

"No, I printed them off the Internet. Sounds easy. Listen, Mom, I need to take this other call. I should be there by noon, okay?"

"I can hardly wait! Your father will be ecstatic. Drive carefully."

"I will. See you soon."

Ellen hung up the phone. "Don't faint, but Brandon's coming to visit."

"I gathered that much. When?"

"He's driving and should be here by noon on Saturday. Can you believe it?"

"Did I hear right—he's not bringing Kelsey?"

"She's out of vacation time. But I got the feeling this is about number two son feeling guilty that he's never been to Seaport."

"Good. There's no excuse for losing touch with his grandfathers. And he's never laid eyes on either of Owen's kids. How long's he staying?"

"I forgot to ask. Goodness, I need to make a list and get to the grocery store. I'm sure he's expecting peach cobbler the minute he walks in the door." Ellen laughed, her heart suddenly light. "I've missed him so much. It's hard to believe our baby's a vice president and engaged to be married."

"Looks like the five years we spent prodding him through college is finally paying off." Guy smiled wryly. "But I want to spend time with the young lady who's got her hooks into him and make sure she's not after his money."

Ellen chuckled. "Will you stop? Kelsey's a lovely girl. I should probably call Owen and tell him his brother's coming."

"Try his cell number. He was driving to Pensacola today for a meeting."

Ellen dialed the number, trying to remember how long it had been since her two sons had seen each other. "I sure hope Owen and Hailey don't have plans for the weekend."

"Hello."

"Owen, it's Mom. You'll never guess who's coming to town."

Brandon Jones pulled down the metal door of the rented storage unit that was packed to the hilt with nearly everything he owned. He locked the padlock and glanced at the Raleigh skyline in the distance, then walked over to his yellow Nissan Xterra and climbed in the driver's seat, regretting last year's decision not to buy that classy little hybrid.

At least he had enough in savings to get him by for a while—as long as he didn't have to pay rent. *Rent.* How would his parents react when they realized that his coming for a visit was going to involve an extended stay?

Brandon was suddenly aware of a figure shuffling toward the car, the man's clothes filthy, his hair sticking out in all directions. His empty eyes matched the color of the dirt pile on the adjacent lot.

"Hey, buddy," the man said. "I'm going through a rough spell. Could you spare some change?"

So you can blow it on booze? I don't think so. "Uh, sorry. I haven't got any cash on me."

The man looked at him as if he'd been expecting that response and kept on walking, his shoulders slumped.

Brandon watched him for half a minute, then opened the door and stepped out of the car and cupped his hands around his mouth. "Hey, Mister. I'm headed over to Jake's Café. I could buy you lunch."

Brandon unfolded his arms and took them off the table so the waitress could set a double cheeseburger and fries in front of him.

The unkempt stranger who identified himself as "just Gary" had ordered a turkey breast sandwich, cottage cheese, and a glass of milk and had said very little on the drive over or in the twenty minutes they had waited for their order.

"Will there be anything else?" the waitress asked.

"This ought to do it," Brandon said.

Gary grabbed half his sandwich and took several huge bites before he began to chew, his cheeks puffed out like a chipmunk's. It sounded as though he mumbled a thank-you as he reached for the glass of milk.

Brandon stole several well-spaced glances at Gary's face, careful not to be too obvious. He guessed him to be in his mid- to late fifties and wondered what kind of sob story the guy had tucked away to justify his circumstances. He didn't ask.

The two men ate in awkward silence.

When Gary finished, he wiped his mouth with the napkin and started to get up. "Thanks. I really appreciate it."

"You want another sandwich? Dessert? Something else?"

Gary held his gaze, those piercing brown eyes seeming to size him up. "I wouldn't mind a cup of coffee."

"Why don't you have dessert, too? I'm going to have a piece of pie, and I hate eating alone."

"All right."

Brandon motioned to the waitress to come to the table. "We both want dessert. I'll have pecan pie and coffee with cream."

"Same here."

"Okay, then," the waitress said. "I'll be right back."

Gary folded his dirty hands on the table and looked out the window. "I haven't had pecan pie in a long time. My mom's was the best."

"Mine makes the best peach cobbler in the northern hemisphere."

There was that uncomfortable silence again. Brandon looked around the café and noticed a few people were whispering and looking over at his lunch guest.

"Never eaten with a homeless guy before?" Gary asked.

"No, I guess I haven't."

"People always stare. I'm used to it. Looks like you're pretty successful. Nice SUV."

"Yeah, too bad it's not paid for. I'm between jobs at the moment."

"Laid off?"

"No, I quit. The pressure got to me."

Gary lifted his eyebrows and didn't say anything.

"I'm sure that probably sounds foolish to you, considering your circumstances. But I know it was the right decision." Brandon hated that he sounded defensive. "It's suffocating being in an office all day."

"Yeah, why suffer in a temperature-controlled environment just to have money when you can get free room and board in the great outdoors?"

Brandon took a sip of ice water, surprised by Gary's sarcastic tone and wondering what kind of response the man expected to a comment like that. He was relieved when the waitress brought their dessert and coffee and set it on the table.

"Anything else?" she asked.

Brandon glanced over at Gary. "You want a sandwich to go?"

"Okay, sure. Peanut butter and jelly would be good."

Brandon reached in his pocket and pulled out his credit card and handed it to the waitress. "Add the PBJ to my bill, and we're done."

"All right, sir. I'll be right back."

Brandon's eyes followed her until she walked through the swinging doors. He was aware that Gary had started talking again, his mouth full of pecan pie.

"I'm not lazy, in case that's what you're thinking."

"Look, man, I'm not judging you. I'm not exactly batting a thousand either. I've got to face my parents and tell them I just turned my back on what they consider the opportunity of a lifetime." Brandon took a bite of pie and washed it down with coffee. "So why *aren't* you working?"

"People always think it's because I'm either lazy or a drunk. Actually, I'm just crazy."

"You don't seem crazy to me."

Gary laughed and then laughed louder. "Of course, I am. I'm nuttier than a fruitcake. Everyone knows people *choose* to be homeless, and no one in his right mind would want to live this way."

Brandon shifted in his chair, aware of people staring. "That doesn't mean you're crazy. You must have a reason. Explain it to me. I'd like to understand."

Gary looked down at his plate and said in a hushed voice, "No one's ever cared to understand."

"Then let me be the first."

Several seconds passed in silence, and then Gary said, "I was a detective once. Vice. Can you believe it?"

"Sure. Why not?"

"I was good, too. Investigated dozens of cases and got a lot of losers put behind bars. But I got sick and tired of seeing the bad side of people day in and day out. After a few years, I got burned out and quit. Never could get motivated to do anything else. My wife divorced me and took the kids, and I set out to find the meaning of life. I figured there must be a reason for all this insanity." Gary reached across the table with his eyes. "But I always came up empty. Far as I can tell, we're born, the strong prey on the weak, we get old, we die. Seems pretty pointless."

"You don't believe in God?"

Gary snickered. "If there is a God, He's sleeping on the job—at least the God the Salvation Army keeps trying to sell me."

The waitress walked over to the table and handed Brandon the credit card receipt. "You gentlemen come again."

Gary stood and picked up the to go box the waitress had set on the table. "Well, this *gentleman* is heading out. Thanks for helping me out, Brandon. Really, I mean that. You seem like a nice kid. Hope you find whatever it is you're looking for."

"Thanks."

Gary took a few steps toward the door and then stopped and glanced over his shoulder. "By the way, if you ever figure out what the heck life is about, would you come tell me? I'm living under the Twelfth Street Bridge."

3

Brandon Jones drove into the Seaport city limits and was instantly taken with the huge live oaks and stately old homes that graced either side of Seminole Boulevard. He glanced up at the spurts of sunlight that shot through the canopy of branches as the car moved beneath and decided that Seaport looked more like Raleigh than the Florida he had envisioned.

His stomach rumbled and reminded him that he had skipped breakfast, trusting that his mother had planned a feast for Saturday's lunch. He wondered how long Gary had held off before eating the peanut butter and jelly sandwich.

Brandon glanced down at the directions he had printed off the Internet and pulled into the right lane and turned onto Seaport Parkway. He spotted a florist shop, and a pang of loneliness reminded him that Kelsey wasn't with him and never would be. He wanted to buy his mother a dozen long-stemmed roses but thought that seemed extravagant for a son out of a job.

He saw a Publix grocery store up ahead and pulled into the parking lot. He went inside and quickly cruised the aisles until he found a refrigerator case of floral arrangements. He removed a bouquet of white daisies and took them to the express lane, gave the clerk seven dollars, then went out to his car.

He sat for a moment, all too aware that he hadn't resolved in his mind when he should tell his parents the truth about his circumstances. He turned the air conditioner on high and pulled out of the parking lot onto Seaport Boulevard, then made a left on Beach Shore Drive. He still had a few blocks to decide.

Ellen Jones set the last water goble t on the table and stood back and admired how nice everything looked.

"Brandon may not care that you used your china and crystal," Guy Jones said, his arm around her shoulder, "but this looks great. And your lunch smells wonderful."

"I just want him to feel welcome."

"Which is more than he deserves." Owen Jones stood in the doorway and popped a green olive into his mouth. "Why are you making such a big deal over a son who's never there when you need him?"

"Your brother's had a lot going on in his life," Ellen said.

"Oh, and we haven't? Where was Brandon when Daniel was born? Or when Annie and I had to deal with Tim's suicide? Or when you had to deal with Granddad's Alzheimer's and Papa's hip surgery? Or when Dad was threatened after his secretary got mixed up with that drug dealer? I'm the one who's been there for you, and prodigal boy gets the fatted calf."

"Your mother's pot roast hardly qualifies as the fatted calf," Guy said. "But as long as you brought up the prodigal, maybe you should take another look at his bitter older brother."

"I'm not bitter," Owen said. "I just don't understand why you're going all out when Brandon doesn't lift a finger to help you."

Ellen studied her firstborn's face for a moment and then said, "Honey, we love you boys because you're our sons, not because of what you do or don't do. Your father and I have expressed how grateful we are for all the ways you've helped us. Our excitement to see Brandon doesn't diminish our gratitude or our love for you. I thought you knew that."

"Yeah, I do. Sorry."

"He's here!" Hailey Jones hollered from the living room.

Ellen untied her apron and tossed it on the kitchen counter. She hurried out the front door and down the steps and threw her arms around Brandon and held him for several seconds. "I'm so glad to see you."

"These are for you," he said, handing her the bouquet of white daisies.

"Oh, how nice. Thank you, honey. They'll look lovely on the table. Did you have any trouble finding the house?"

"Not at all."

Guy shook Brandon's hand and then put one arm around him and pulled him close. "Great to see you, son."

Owen punched Brandon on the arm. "Hey, Pip-squeak. It's about time you showed your sorry face."

"Yeah, it's been too long." Brandon reached over and hugged Hailey. "Hello, beautiful."

"Hello yourself. But let me show you *beautiful*." She turned and motioned for a small boy and girl to come stand next to her. "This is Daniel. And this is Annie."

Brandon squatted and looked into the faces of the children whose pictures he carried in his wallet. "Oh, my goodness. You're even bigger than I thought!"

"I'm five years old," Annie Jones said proudly. "And my bwother, Daniel, is two, and he's not potty twained yet. We have a wiener dog named Snickers and a owange cat named Stwipey, and I might get a gerbil when I'm six. Do you got any pets?"

"No, but I can't wait to see yours. Do you know who I am?"

Annie gave a firm nod. "You're my daddy's bwother. Your name is Uncle Bwandon."

"That's right. Does your brother talk?" He reached over and tickled Daniel in the ribs and evoked a giggle.

"A little, but he's shy. Mama says I can't talk for him or he will never learn to use his words."

Brandon brushed the blond curls out of Annie's face. "You're pretty like your mama."

"My real mama got dead in a car cwash, and my new mama wanted to take care of me, so I got adopted."

"Yes, I knew that," Brandon said. "You are a very special young lady."

Annie held out a long blond ringlet. "I got curly hair and blue eyes like Gwandma. And painted toenails, but not lipstick or maxcara."

Brandon looked over at his mother and smiled. "And I'll bet Grandma just eats all this up."

"Every chance I get," Ellen said. "Are you hungry? Lunch is ready anytime."

"You kidding? I've been thinking about your cooking all the way from Raleigh."

Ellen linked arms with him. "Come on, then. I made all your favorites: pot roast with carrots and potatoes, broccoli and cheese casserole, homemade sourdough rolls, and peach cobbler for dessert."

Brandon smiled. "I've died and gone to heaven."

"After we eat lunch," Annie said, "can me and Daniel show Uncle Bwandon the playhouse Gwandpa made us? And how we do somersaults?"

Owen lifted Annie and held her on his hip. "Princess, your Uncle Brandon's been driving a long time. Why don't we let him rest a while?"

"I've waited a long time to see these kids," Brandon said. "Feed me and I'm game for anything."

Brandon ate the last bite of his second helping of peach cobbler and pushed away his bowl. "Everything was unbelievable, Mom. I get so tired of grilled chicken, grilled shrimp, grilled burgers, grilled *everything*. I know it's supposed to be better for you, but I love old-fashioned home cooking."

"Doesn't Kelsey cook for you?" Owen asked.

"Kind of hard when she works all day."

"Is she going to keep working after you're married?"

"Kel can work as long as she wants to."

Owen put his elbows on the table and leaned forward. "So are you ever going to set a date? You've been engaged six months."

Brandon manufactured a smile and hoped it looked real. "You'll be the first to know. Enough about me and Kelsey. Tell me how it feels to be the CFO of Global Communications."

"Great," Owen said, "now that we're operating in the black again. It was a real challenge getting it turned around, and I think I've finally earned the respect of the board. At least the chairman doesn't call me sonny anymore."

"Did he really do that?"

Owen grinned. "No, but I'm sure he was thinking it."

Brandon looked over at his dad. "Is it satisfying to be a law partner after all those years in private practice?"

"Oh, I'm loving every minute of it," Guy said. "I think winning the Brinkmont case hooked me for life. Brent's put me on some really big cases, and I never run out of challenges. I've finally got a legal secretary who's as good as Kinsey was. Her name's Rachel. Whatever we're paying her, it's not enough."

"I feel the same way about mine," Owen said.

Brandon patted his mother's hand. "You're awfully quiet. How's the novel writing coming?"

"So-so. I can't seem to finish the second one, and it's hard to stay motivated since I've yet to get a contract on the first."

"You'll find a publisher," Guy said. "Just takes determination."

Ellen half-smiled. "Talent helps. So tell us how it feels to be a vice president?"

Brandon laid his napkin on the table and stood. "We've got plenty of time to talk business. I want to see this widow's watch where Mom's been writing her books—and the rest of the house, too."

He felt a tug on the bottom of his shirt and looked down and saw two clear blue eyes framed with blond curls.

"I'll show you where Gwandma wites," Annie said. "It's up the winding stairs, and you hafta be careful so you don't twip. Come on." She took his hand. "It's a vewy special place, and we're not allowed to eat cookies up there."

Brandon put his fist to his mouth in jest. "No cookies?"

Annie shook her head. "Gwandma says the cwunching is iwigating."

"Well, we wouldn't want to *irrigate* Grandma, now would we?" He winked at his mother and let Annie lead him up the winding stairs and away from the questions just waiting to be asked.

Brandon sat out on the veranda, listening to the peaceful sounds of night and thinking back on the events of the day. He decided it had been surprisingly enjoyable. At least he had managed to talk around the family's questions and hadn't out-and-out lied.

His thoughts turned to Annie and Daniel, and he realized he was smiling. Annie had dominated his attention much of the afternoon with her continual chatter and desire to show him every conceivable thing she had learned to do—everything from cartwheels and somersaults to riding her bicycle with training wheels to singing a seemingly endless medley of songs, complete with hand motions.

At one point when she was marching to "Father Abraham" and delighting all the adults, Daniel got a big red ball and set it in the grass. He rolled it to Brandon and said emphatically, "*My* turn."

"You asleep?"

Brandon glanced up at the doorway and saw his mother's silhouette. "No. Come sit with me. I was just thinking about what a great day it was."

"Indeed. You were really the hit."

"Yeah, Annie and Daniel are great. It's fun being Uncle Brandon."

Ellen sat in the wicker rocker opposite his. "Have you decided how long you're going to stay? I'm sure it's not easy being away from Kelsey."

"Why don't we play it by ear?"

"Anything in particular you want to do tomorrow?"

"I'd like to go down to the beach in the morning and watch the sunrise. I haven't done that since you and Dad sent me to Cozumel after I graduated from college."

"In that case, why don't we all go to late church so you won't have to rush back? We won't have to leave until 10:45—that is, assuming you want to go with us."

"Yeah, sure, Mom. Count me in."

"Anything else you want to do while you're here?"

"Spend some quality time with each of you. I can't believe how much I've missed. You said Granddad's Alzheimer's might keep him from recognizing me, but I want to see him anyway. And also visit with Papa. He must think I don't care about him anymore."

"Oh, honey, he remembers being young. I'm sure he understands how busy you are."

Brandon shook his head. "Don't make excuses for me, Mom. If I didn't have time, I should've *made* time."

"Well, your father and I know how hard it was for you to leave Kelsey right now and come here to see everyone. We really appreciate the sacrifice."

Brandon looked up at a smattering of stars between the tree branches and wondered what his folks would think of his *sacrifice* when they found out he didn't have anywhere else to go.

4

When Pastor Peter Crawford ended his Sunday sermon, Brandon Jones rose with the congregation of Crossroads Bible Church as they started singing "Great Is Thy Faithfulness."

He leaned over and put lips to his father's ear. "Where's the men's room?"

"Go out to the foyer and turn right. You'll see it down the hall."

Brandon left the sanctuary and headed straight for the nearest exit. He pushed open the heavy wooden door and was hit with a blast of moist, hot air that scattered the papers on the visitor information table.

He jogged down the front steps and spotted a stand of leafy trees on the commercial property to the left of the parking lot. He went over and leaned against the thickest tree trunk, glad for the shade and breeze and thinking how childish it was to hide. But how else could he avoid having to put on a whopper of a performance when the pastor and all his parents' friends asked questions about his job or his engagement?

If only he had told his parents the truth! He had almost mustered the courage to talk to them before they went to bed but decided the bad news might keep them awake all night. And he couldn't quite bring himself to break the news at breakfast. Or on the way to church.

He was suddenly aware that the music had stopped and people were starting to trickle out of the church. A young couple exited the church and came down the steps, hand in hand, the woman's long dark hair much like Kelsey's. The familiarity in their laughter evoked a twinge of jealousy in Brandon and seemed a cruel reminder that he wasn't going to get married. Or take his bride on a honeymoon. Or live happily ever after.

Guy Jones came out the big wooden doors and stood next to one of the round white pillars. He shaded his eyes with his hand and looked out toward his Mercedes, then went back inside.

Brandon decided he might as well get it over with. He reached in his pocket, took out his cell phone, and hit the autodial.

"Hello."

"Dad, it's Brandon."

"We've been looking all over for you! Where'd you go?"

"I'm outside. Sorry I disappeared, but I had a good reason."

"Is something wrong?"

"You could say that. I have something to tell you and Mom that I should've told you yesterday. But this isn't a good time to meet your friends."

"Your mom has them all corralled here in the foyer. What am I supposed to say?"

"That I'm not feeling well, which is the truth."

Guy Jones exhaled into the receiver. "All right. Give us a few minutes, and we'll meet you at the car."

"You *what*!"

Brandon winced at the tone of his father's voice, glad that he'd opted to break the news in a public place and confident that none of the other customers at Gordy's Crab Shack could hear the conversation above the drone.

"Son, how could you be so irresponsible and shortsighted?" Guy sat back in his chair. "You just threw away the past seven years and jeopardized your financial future."

"I've been a good employee. I'm sure the company will give me a good job reference."

Guy shook his head. "Don't count on it. I'm sure they didn't appreciate a vice president leaving with only two weeks' notice. Companies need more time to fill those kinds of positions."

"It's not as though I left them high and dry. They have capable people they can promote from within."

"Well, they promoted *you*. Do you realize what you just threw away?"

"I know exactly what I threw away."

"You didn't even give it six months, for crying out loud. What was so unbearable that you couldn't tough it out?"

Brandon squeezed a slice of lemon, then pushed it down into his iced tea with a straw. "Dad, I'm not like you and Owen. I don't function well in an office."

"Then why didn't you just ask for your old job back? Merchandising the stores seemed to agree with you."

"Only because I psyched myself up. The reason I lasted as long as I did was because I enjoyed the driving." *And didn't want to disappoint you.* "Even if they'd let me have my old job back, I never would have gone any higher with the company. It was better to get out."

"Then I suggest you get out there and find something else. You'll be darned lucky to find another position that good without a master's degree."

"Have you got a résumé?" Ellen said.

"I can put one together, but I doubt it'll be all that helpful since I want to make a career change."

Guy's eyes locked on to Brandon's. "You're just going to throw all that work experience down the drain?"

Brandon took his index finger and drew a line through the condensation on his glass. "I want to do something significant, Dad. Gearing my life around women's apparel just doesn't do it for me."

"Well, you'd better figure out what *does* do it for you before your savings runs out. We won't charge you to stay with us, but don't expect a nickel more."

"I won't. I've got enough to cover my car expenses and incidentals till I find something else."

Ellen reached over and touched his hand. "What does Kelsey think of all this?"

Brandon pushed out the words he'd practiced all the way from Raleigh. "She postponed the wedding…permanently." He stared at his glass for what seemed an eternity. *Somebody say something.*

"She broke the engagement?" Ellen finally said.

"Yeah."

Guy shook his head from side to side. "You've made some bad choices, but this takes the cake!"

"All I did was resign from something I hated," Brandon said. "People do that every day."

"Not without having another job."

"I have money in savings. I'll find another job."

"Well, you won't find another Kelsey!"

"Breaking up wasn't *my* choice. She, of all people, should've understood how I was feeling."

Guy's eyebrows met in the middle. "What about how she was feeling? Ever think of that? No clearheaded woman wants to commit her future to a guy she can't count on."

"That's completely unfair! I worked my tail off for seven years! I just got tired of being where I don't belong."

"You always think you don't belong. You said the same thing the entire five years we pushed you through college, but you finally got your business degree, didn't you? The key is commitment. If you want to be married, you're going to have to stop thinking about yourself first!"

"Shhhh." Ellen glanced around the room. "Why don't we continue this discussion at home?"

"I'm starved," Guy said. "I don't want to leave yet."

"Then at least lower your voices."

Guy paused and looked down at his hands and then at Brandon. "You'd better be thinking about how to win Kelsey back."

"I'd do almost anything to get her back—except spend my life working at something I hate."

"I'll never understand why the job wasn't good enough for you."

Brandon sighed. "Dad, it's not a question of the job being good enough for me, or even of me being good enough for the job. I want to do something significant. If I'm going to work five or six days a week until I'm sixty-five, I'd like to feel as though I've made a contribution to something more significant than women's fashion."

"Supporting a wife and children isn't significant?"

"Of course it is, but I'm talking about—"

"Yourself! It all boils down to what *you* want. Too bad about everyone else."

Brandon bit his lip, thinking he could argue with his father all day and still never be heard. He glanced despairingly at his mother and over her shoulder saw an attractive African-American woman approaching the table.

"Hello, Joneses. Is this who I think it is?" the woman said, her dark eyes round and playful.

Ellen nodded. "This is our youngest son, Brandon."

"Well, I'm pleased to finally make your acquaintance. I'm Weezie Taylor, the assistant manager."

Brandon reached up and shook her hand. "Nice to meet you." *Please don't ask questions.*

Weezie folded her arms, her weight resting on one hip, and seemed to be studying his face. Finally, she let out a robust, contagious laugh. "Whooeeeee, I'm relieved to see his head's just the right size. The way you've been braggin' about him, I thought it might be all puffed up."

Brandon smiled in spite of himself. "Can't believe half of what they tell you."

"Well, one thing I believe is they're awfully proud of you."

The waitress who'd taken their order came and stood at the head of the table, balancing a large platter. "Okay, I've got two orders of spicy grilled shrimp and a combo platter."

"Better let me scoot out of the way," Weezie said. "Real nice meetin' you, Brandon. Hope you'll come in again while you're here."

"Thanks. I'm sure I will."

Brandon was aware of the waitress placing the combo platter in front of him and the silence coming from the other side of the table, but his eyes followed Weezie Taylor, whose clowning had evoked hearty laughter from some customers who had just been seated. "Is she always like that?"

Ellen nodded. "She's a real character. I'm afraid I did go on and on about you the other day. I'm sorry if her comment embarrassed you. She meant it as a compliment."

Ellen sat on the couch knitting a sweater, painfully aware that Guy had hardly said a word since they left Gordy's.

"If you're trying to teach Brandon a lesson, this isn't the way to do it."

"All I'm trying to *do*," Guy said, "is come to grips with the fact that our son just threw away the best career opportunity he may ever get."

"I understand you feel that way. But Brandon certainly weighed the pros and cons. He's a very bright young man."

Guy lifted his eyebrows. "He's intelligent. I'm not so sure he's all that bright. The kid had it made, Ellen."

"Well, obviously he didn't think so."

"I just wish he would've come to me first."

"What would you have told him?" Ellen set her knitting in her lap.

"I would've told him that when all is said and done, every job has its up and downs, that he should look for the positive aspects and be grateful for a good salary and benefits. Most people work the same number of hours for a lot less."

"He knows that. I don't think it's about the money."

"That's because he's never been the head of a household. At some point money needs to be a key factor."

"Well, it'll be interesting to see what kind of career path he wants to try. He's only thirty. It's not as though he has to have his entire life nailed down tomorrow." Ellen heard footsteps coming toward the living room.

Brandon appeared in the doorway, dressed in swimming trunks and a T-shirt, a rolled-up towel in his hand. "I think I'll go down to the beach for a while."

"All right, honey," she said. "Dinner will be ready around six."

"You need me to stop at the store?"

"No, I've got everything I need. Thanks."

"Okay, see you later."

Ellen waited until she heard the front door close, then looked over at Guy. "I realize fathers handle sons differently than mothers do, but I fail to see the value of your shutting Brandon out. He knows you're disappointed in him. Isn't that enough?"

"It won't hurt him to sweat a little. He made a bad decision, and I'm certainly not going to mollycoddle him. The kid's expectations are way too lofty."

"Because he wants to find significance in his work?"

"If he'd had the right perspective, he would've found significance right where he was…and he'd still be engaged to Kelsey."

Ellen looked down and began knitting again. "Don't you think it's a good idea to understand where he's coming from before we decide how he should or shouldn't feel?"

"I totally understand where he's coming from, and he needs to get his head out of the clouds and realize that opportunities like the one he just threw away don't come along every day."

Ellen bit her lip and wondered if her already wounded son could hold his own if the conflict with his father turned into an all out battle.

5

On Monday morning, Gordy Jameson pushed open the door of Gordy's Crab Shack and held it until his wife was inside, aware that the lights were already on.

"Weezie must be here," Pam Jameson said.

"She's *always* here. I don't think the woman ever sleeps."

"I heard that."

Gordy turned and saw Weezie Taylor sitting in a booth, papers spread out in front of her. "You're not scheduled till two. You're supposed to be relaxin'."

"That's exactly what I'm doin'. I just compared the first five months' figures to last year's." Her smile stole her face. "Sales are up 32 percent—7 percent higher than my already ambitious projection. Whooeeeeeee, I'm good!" She got up and danced in a circle, then gave him a high five.

Gordy smiled and winked at Pam.

Weezie moved over and put her arm around Pam's shoulder. "This sweet wife of yours earned us a whoppin' 187 percent increase in dessert sales!"

"Goodness," Pam said. "No wonder I've been busy."

"Girlfriend, you've been more than *busy*. You keep this up and we'll have to start sellin' your pies to the supermarkets. Move over, Mrs. Smith!" Weezie put her hand to her forehead. "I can see it all now, Pam's Blue Ribbon Pies—six mouthwaterin' choices now available in the frozen food section of your local Publix store."

"Hold your horses," Gordy said. "It's all we can do to keep up with the business we've got. We know Pam makes the tastiest pies in the panhandle, so let's capitalize on that to bring in new customers. Forget the grocery store notion. It's never gonna happen."

"Never say never!" Weezie's hearty laugh resonated throughout the room. "Weezie the wise and wonderful is always lookin' for new opportunities."

Gordy chuckled. "Why don't you take all that creative energy outta here till your shift starts? Go shoppin' or run errands or somethin'—whatever it is you women do when you're not tryin' to take over the world."

"Think big, I always say."

"Well, for now you just keep thinkin' smart."

Pam glanced at her watch. "Guess I should go fire up the oven if we're going to have fresh pies for the lunch crowd."

"I may as well help since I'm already here," Weezie said.

"Absolutely not." Gordy gently nudged Weezie toward the door. "Pam and I can handle things. Go enjoy a few hours to yourself. Why don't you take advantage of this cool front and go walk the beach or somethin'?"

Brandon Jones lay in the sand and watched a flock of pelicans soaring, their wings gleaming when they turned toward the sun. The sound of the surf on the sand had a lulling effect, and his thoughts kept drifting to Kelsey and the things about her he missed: the flowery scent of her hair, her warm lips and cold nose, her creative mind, the way she seemed to purr when she ate chocolate, her shameless crying at movies. His mind raced through one scenario after another until he pictured her working at her desk in the marketing department. He wondered if the regional vice president position had been filled—and if Kelsey would be able to handle working at the corporate office now that he was gone.

Gone. That sounded so distant. And final. He had hoped that coming to Seaport and immersing himself in the beauty of the gulf coast would bring a reprieve from the pressure. But his father's reaction proved even more negative than he had imagined, and he wondered how long he could endure living under his parents' roof. Not that he had a choice.

"Brandon?"

He turned toward the woman's voice, his hand shading his eyes.

"Aren't you Weezie from the crab shack?"

"Uh-huh. I was gettin' my toes wet and saw you over here. Didn't want you to think I was ignorin' you."

"Sorry, I didn't see you. I was lost in thought."

"Well, don't let me bother you. I just wanted to say hello."

Brandon sat up. "You don't have to run off. I wouldn't mind company."

"I expect you're lonesome for that sweet fiancée of yours. Your folks can't say enough nice about her."

"Uh, actually…we sort of broke up."

Weezie dropped down in the sand and sat facing him, a sheepish look on her face. "Sorry. I'm always stickin' my foot in my mouth."

"No, it's all right. My folks didn't even know till yesterday. In fact, that's what we were discussing when you came over to the table." Brandon looked out across the gulf and spotted a cruise ship on the horizon. "You may as well know I resigned my position at the apparel company, so I'm between jobs, too. Unfortunately, I'm anything but the boy wonder my parents were bragging about."

"I'm sure they're thrilled to see you."

"Yeah, till I told them I don't have a fiancée or a job and need a place to stay till I get my life together."

"Baby, parents don't stop wantin' to see their kids because they're goin' through some stuff."

"Do you have children?"

Weezie shook her head. "My Joshua was killed in a huntin' accident before we ever had kids."

"Well…I assure you my folks are deeply disappointed in me, especially Dad."

"I have a feelin' they're more disappointed *for* you than in you."

Brandon decided not to tell her what he really thought.

Weezie leaned back on her palms and tilted her face up, her eyes closed. "Sun feels good. Only supposed to get to eighty today."

"I thought Florida was hot in June."

"Hang around. You'll be beggin' for mercy. This is just a cool spell, so enjoy it while it lasts."

Weezie's dark skin looked almost bronze in the sunlight. Brandon noticed she was wearing a silver cross ring on her left hand. "How long since Joshua's accident?"

"Twelve years, God bless him. And not a day goes by that I don't think of him. I'm sure the Lord had His reasons for callin' him home, but it sure did leave a hole in my heart. Never have met a man who could hold a candle to him either."

"How long were you married?"

Weezie opened her eyes. "Four years, three weeks, and two days. Wouldn't trade one minute of it."

"I don't think you ever really get over losing someone you love."

"Well, I know I'll see him again in heaven, and that helps a lot. In the meantime, I'm not lettin' any moss grow under my feet."

"It's obvious you like your job."

Weezie nodded. "Love it. But I loved it when I was a waitress, too. Sometimes I miss the people contact, so I go out on the floor and mingle with the customers just to stay pumped." She chuckled. "It's fun kiddin' around with folks and gettin' to know them. That way we all have a good time."

"I didn't realize you were a waitress before. How long have you worked there?"

"Twelve years. I started after Joshua died. I waited tables for nine, then three years ago, Gordy up and promoted me to assistant manager, just like that. Coulda bowled me over with a feather. Hard to believe I actually get paid to do what I love doin'."

"How cool. I've never had a job I really liked. Must be great."

Weezie lifted her eyebrows. "Come on, an educated kid like you...*never*?"

"Well, not since I graduated from college and went to work for Mavis and Stein. I started out in catalog sales, then got promoted to assistant director of advertising, then director of merchandising, and most recently to regional vice president. I don't know what's wrong with me. There're plenty of people who'd die for a career like that. It left me feeling empty."

"What would you like to do?"

"I don't know. Something significant. I'd like what I do to make a difference."

"A difference *how*?"

Brandon exhaled. "I don't know exactly, but I want more from my job than just a paycheck and benefits. I want to make a positive difference in people's lives. Am I just totally out in left field?"

Weezie eyes grew wide and she held his gaze. "I guess that depends on who you've got coachin' your team. Ouch!" She winced and grabbed the back of her head. "Somethin' whacked me."

Brandon looked behind her in the sand and picked up a smooth stone not much smaller than a golf ball. He sprang to his feet and glanced in every direction. He didn't see anyone, just an outcropping of tall, jagged rocks several yards behind her. "Wait here."

He trudged over to the rock formation and walked around behind it. He heard what sounded like a loose rock falling, then something heavy fell on him and knocked him to the ground. He was aware of someone breathing, then felt a hard blow to his ribs. He lay still for several seconds, and when he was sure the assailant was gone, he got up and ran out in the open to see which direction he had fled.

About fifty yards down the beach, he saw what appeared to be a kid about twelve or thirteen running toward the public pier, sand kicking up behind his heels.

Brandon started chasing him, anger pushing him as fast as he could go, but he quickly realized the effort was futile. He finally stopped and watched the kid get smaller and smaller until he finally blended into the beach and disappeared. He was aware of Weezie standing next to him.

"You okay?" she said.

"Yeah. You?"

She held out two red fingertips. "Bleedin' a little. No serious harm done."

"That little punk could've really hurt you! Why would he do something like that?"

"Maybe it was an accident."

"No way," Brandon said. "He jumped me and kicked me in the ribs, then took off. Sorry I couldn't catch him, but he had too big a head start."

"You sure you're all right?"

Brandon nodded. "But I'd sure like to find out who the little twerp was and what his problem is."

At ten minutes past two, Gordy sat Weezie in his office and handed her an ice pack. "Hold this on your head. I can't believe you haven't had a doctor look at that."

"Will you stop bein' a mother hen?" Weezie said. "It's just a surface wound. I've got work to do."

"Just sit still for twenty minutes and keep the ice on it. Will Seevers is sending one of his officers over here to talk to you."

"About what—some mixed up kid who probably writes cuss words on buildings and tramples people's flower beds?"

"He hit you in the head with a rock, Weezie. What if he'd hit your eye? And he kicked the Jones boy in the ribs. So stop tryin' to make like it was nothin'. You need to file a police report."

"What can the police do when neither of us saw his face?"

"Well, I don't think you should just let it go. As long as he's still out there, he could hurt someone else. The kid could be a time bomb ready to blow."

Weezie rolled her eyes. "And you thought *I* was the drama queen."

"Okay, so I'm a little overprotective."

"A little?"

"You're like family, for cryin' out loud. I take this kinda thing personally."

"I know you do," Weezie said softly, giving his arm a gentle squeeze. "And I appreciate that about you. But there's no reason to go frettin' over a random act by some troubled kid."

There was a soft knock at the door, and then Pam walked in with Officer Jack Rutgers.

Gordy went over to the door and extended his hand. "Hey, Jack. Thanks for comin'."

"No problem. The chief said you called about Weezie being attacked on the beach."

Gordy glanced over at Weezie and felt the heat flood his face. "Well, *attacked* may have been a little strong. Some kid hit her in the head with a rock. But the little creep also jumped Ellen Jones's son and kicked him in the ribs before he ran off."

"Are you injured?" Jack said to Weezie.

"Nothin' serious. A little cut. A little swelling."

"Little?" Gordy's eyebrows scrunched. "She has a goose egg on the back of her head."

"Tell me exactly what happened," Jack said.

Weezie described what had happened, then said, "I got a glimpse of the boy when he came out from behind the rocks, but I never did get a look at his face. Looked to me like he was middle school age. Tanned. Skinny. Hair was curly and kinda bleached out. Had on denim cutoffs and a white T-shirt. Ran like a rabbit."

"Did you notice his shoes?"

"Some kind of high-top athletic shoes like all the kids are wearin'. Black, I think."

"Did he say anything?"

"No."

"Do you remember anything else?"

"Nothing's comin' to mind."

Jack wrote something on his clipboard. "Any idea why the kid would do this?"

"Can't imagine."

"Okay." Jack rose to his feet. "I'll get a statement from the Joneses' son, too. Maybe he has something to add."

6

Brandon Jones stood at the front door of his parents' house and watched Officer Jack Rutgers walk back to his squad car and drive off.

"I wasn't very helpful," he said to his mother. "They'll never catch that kid based on what Weezie and I told them."

"If he keeps acting out, they might," Ellen Jones said.

"Well, let's hope he doesn't *really* hurt someone in the meantime…the little creep."

Ellen put her hand on his back and rubbed gently. "It's hard to know what causes a young person to want to hurt someone. He's probably been hurt himself. We should pray for him."

Brandon shut the door and turned around and saw compassion in his mother's eyes. "Yeah, you're right. I never would've thought of it."

"I'm sorry this added to your stress."

"Don't worry, it's nothing compared to Dad giving me the cold shoulder."

"Your father just needs time to assimilate your circumstances. Since he doesn't see you that often, it's easy to forget you've grown up and are capable of making decisions on your own. Right or wrong, he has your best interests at heart."

"I'll take your word for it, but I don't think Dad and I are ever going to see eye-to-eye on this one. I tried it his way for seven years. Now I need to figure it out on my own."

"Why don't we go to the kitchen and talk?" Ellen said. "How about some oatmeal raisin cookies? I baked them fresh this morning."

"Annie said we're not allowed to have cookies because the

crunching *irrigates* you." He grinned at his mother, then followed her down the hall and into the kitchen.

She arranged a plate of cookies and set it on the breakfast bar. "Crunch to your heart's content. It's only irritating when I'm trying to write and nothing's happening."

"It's taking you a lot longer to write your second novel."

Ellen bit into a cookie. "Maybe it's all the emotional upheaval of the past couple years, but I've lost interest."

"Then why are you doing it?"

Ellen got up and went to the refrigerator, her back to him. "You want some milk?"

"Sure," Brandon said. "So tell me again about Dad's work schedule."

"He leaves for the office in Tallahassee at the crack of dawn on Mondays and gets home around dinnertime on Wednesdays. The rest of the week he works out of his office here at the house." Her pensive blue eyes seemed to study him. "You'll have as much privacy as you want. You're the first person to stay on the second floor, and half the time we forget it's even there."

"Thanks, Mom. It'll be better for all of us if I stay out of Dad's way."

Gordy Jameson stood behind the front counter at the crab shack, changing the cash register tape and chuckling at the dialogue between Weezie and Pam as they arranged pies in the glass case. A blast of warm air distracted him, and he looked up and saw Police Chief Will Seevers coming in the front door.

"I didn't expect to see you on a Monday," Gordy said.

Will stepped over to the counter. "Can we talk in your office?"

"Yeah, sure. I'm done out here."

Gordy closed the register and locked it, then headed down the hallway to his office. He flipped the light switch. "Want somethin' to drink?"

"No, I can't stay. This is business."

Gordy straddled a folding chair and rested his arms on the back. "What's up?"

"Isn't Weezie a volunteer at the People's Clinic?"

"Yeah, every Saturday morning. Why?"

Will sat in the chair opposite Gordy. "In less than a week, three clinic volunteers have filed police reports. Last Wednesday a nurse reported her tires slashed in the clinic parking lot; on Friday a pediatrician reported the back window and lights on his Lexus were busted out; and today Weezie reported the rock throwing incident."

"You think the same kid did all that?"

Will shrugged. "I can't take him out of the picture, but I can't imagine what would motivate an adolescent to target clinic volunteers."

"Does seem weird. Maybe the vandalizin' had nothin' to do with them workin' at the clinic. And maybe the incident with Weezie had nothin' to do with the other two."

"That's a lot of maybes, Gordy. All I know for sure is that all three incidents involved volunteers at the clinic, and all three volunteers were African-American."

Gordy studied Will's face for a moment. "Wait a minute…are you thinkin' this was a racial thing?"

"I don't have enough to form an opinion. But right now I can't think of any other reason why someone would single out three blacks. Nothing they're doing at the clinic should raise any objections. Kinda hard to argue with free medical care for anyone who needs it when it isn't costing the taxpayers a penny. These three incidents seem personal to me, like someone's got an ax to grind."

"How come I haven't read about any of this in the paper?"

"We kept it quiet, Gordy. We thought we were dealing with a vandal and didn't want the clinic to start losing volunteers. After the second incident, I assigned an officer to cruise the parking lot, and we haven't had any more trouble there. But the thing with Weezie bugs me because the MO changed, and I want to know if we're dealing with the same punk. I sure wish I could talk to that kid who got away."

"Yeah, that's two of us."

Will stood. "Okay, I'm going to talk to the clinic founders and the volunteers and give them a heads-up. I'll talk to Weezie on my way out and Brandon Jones before the day's over. This might not amount to anything. But I want whoever did this to know that the police are on it and it won't be tolerated."

At four-thirty that afternoon, Brandon was standing in the dormer of his parents' home, looking out at the lush trees and shrubs and flowers that graced the front yard, his thoughts consumed with Kelsey.

A squad car pulled up, and he wondered if the police had found the boy. Brandon jogged down the stairs and out to the entry hall just as the doorbell rang.

"Mom, the police are back." Brandon opened the door, surprised not to see Officer Rutgers, but an older officer with great-looking glasses and a receding hairline.

"I'm Police Chief Will Seevers. Are you Brandon?"

"Yes, sir. Did you find the kid?"

"No, we haven't. But I wanted to fill you in on the latest—your mother, too, if she's here."

"I am." Ellen walked toward the door, drying her hands with a kitchen towel. "Come in, Will."

"I can't stay. I just wanted to make you aware of something."

Brandon listened as the chief explained about the two incidents at the clinic.

"What happened to Weezie may have nothing at all to do with the other two cases," Will said. "But since these crimes were committed against African-Americans who all volunteer at the same clinic, my antenna's up."

"You really think it could be racial?" Ellen said.

"*Could* is the operative word here. We don't know anything more than what I just told the two of you. I wanted you to be informed."

"Wish I would've caught the kid," Brandon said. "At least you'd have a starting point."

"Well, we're seeing a pattern emerge. Maybe we can nip this in the bud."

"Let's hope so," Ellen said. "Thanks for stopping by, Will."

"No problem. Say hello to Guy."

Brandon waited until Chief Seevers went down the front steps, then turned around and looked at his mother. "You call the police chief by his first name?"

"We've become good friends. Don't forget, your father worked on a committee with him during the planning phase of the People's Clinic. But our family has certainly had more than our share of needing his attention."

"Yeah, I guess you have. Sorry I wasn't around."

"Well, you're here now and right in the thick of things." Ellen lifted her eyebrows. "I'm beginning to think this family is a crisis magnet."

"I'm not sold on the racial motive. If that boy had a serious problem with blacks, he'd be doing a lot worse than throwing rocks and would probably be running with a pack of thuglets."

"Thuglets?" Ellen said. "Now that's a descriptive word I'm sure I won't find in *Webster's*."

"No, but it's a fitting word for adolescents who are dangerous. I don't sense this boy is in that camp."

"How can you possibly know that?"

Brandon smiled and took Ellen's arm. "Because I'm intuitive like my mother."

7

Just after eleven on Monday night, Brandon Jones sat on the back deck of Gordy's Crab Shack, gazing up at the starry sky and aware of the staff inside scurrying to clean up after closing.

Weezie Taylor came outside and set a limeade in front of him on the table. "Might as well drink this, or it's gonna get thrown out."

"Thanks. I don't know what you guys put in these, but they're great."

"It's Gordy's mother's recipe. Been the same since his folks started this place almost sixty years ago."

"They still own it?"

Weezie pulled up a chair and sat. "No, they've passed on. Gordy's kept the place pretty much the same."

"I can see why. Great food, quaint atmosphere. I'm partial to this back deck. I love being close to the water."

"Me too," she said. "But lots of folks prefer air-conditioning this time of year."

"When the sun's hot maybe. But it's beautiful out here tonight." Brandon took a sip of the limeade. "You off now?"

"Yeah, I need to lock up. We're about finished closin' out."

"So does working late like this mess up your time clock?"

"Not really. I usually go home and wind down for two or three hours before I go to bed. Don't really need a lot of sleep. I'm one of those high-energy people. So what was it you wanted to talk to me about?"

"Chief Seevers came by late this afternoon and told me about the vandalism at the clinic. Said what happened on the beach might be related and could've been racially motivated. I just wondered what you thought about that."

Weezie swatted the air. "I've got more important things to think about."

"Seems pretty important to me."

"This is the first time you've been around it, am I right?"

"Yeah, I guess so."

"Well, believe me, this kinda stuff happens all the time."

"So you're just going to blow it off?"

Weezie leaned closer, her elbows on the table. "What do you think I should do?"

"I don't know."

"That's just it, neither do I. What I'm *not* gonna do is waste time stewin' over some mixed up kid who may have thrown a rock at me because I'm black. But regardless of why he did it, it's his problem. I'm not makin' it mine."

Brandon traced the rim of his glass with his finger. "Did you get the sense it was racially motivated? I mean, why didn't the kid say something when he kicked me? Or shout some racial slur when he knew neither of us could catch him?"

"I've felt all along that the police are makin' too much of it. But the vandalism at the clinic sure does concern me."

"Well, hopefully the police will get to the bottom of it. I just wanted to stop by and check on you before you left for the night. How are you feeling?"

"I'm fine, other than this lump on the back of my head's sore."

"Did you see a doctor?"

Weezie nodded. "Gordy insisted. The doctor cleaned it, but it didn't need stitches. You're the one who oughta be sore."

"Yeah, I'm feeling it tonight." Brandon glanced at his watch. "As long as you're going to be up for a few hours, you want to go get coffee or something?"

"Sure, that sounds good. There's a neat little all-night coffee shop not far from here."

Ellen Jones turned off the eleven o'clock news just as the phone rang.

"Hello, Guy."

"Hi, honey," Guy Jones said. "Sorry I didn't call earlier. I've been running all day."

"Did you get your deposition?" she asked.

"No, I'm driving up to Valdosta early in the morning. It shouldn't take long to get it. I have a three-thirty meeting back here with the partners."

"Sounds hectic."

"The drive should be relaxing. I'm actually looking forward to it. So what've you been up to? Has Brandon been enlightened in his search for a career path with a deeper purpose?"

"That was uncalled for."

"Sorry, I still can't believe what he walked away from. The kid would've been making six figures by this time next year."

"Well, something happened today that distracted him from all that." Ellen told Guy about Weezie getting hit in the head with a rock and about Will Seevers stopping by the house to tell of the vandalism at the People's Clinic and a possible connection.

"For crying out loud, can't anyone in this family stay out of the news?"

Ellen drew her legs up on the couch. "Will's kept it out of the papers. He was afraid it might discourage people from volunteering at the clinic."

"Good thinking. So Brandon and Weezie are okay?"

"His ribs are sore, and she has a bump on her head. Nothing serious."

"What was Brandon doing on the beach with her anyway?"

"They both just happened to be there this morning. Weezie recognized him and they talked for a while, and that's when she was hit with the rock."

"And Will thinks it could've been racially motivated?"

Ellen took her finger and traced the flower pattern on the couch. "He made it clear he's not sure, but Brandon doesn't think it was."

"And he thinks this because…?"

"Just a feeling."

"Oh, well that's a good reason. What does Weezie say?"

"I haven't talked to her. Brandon went down to Gordy's to try to catch her before she goes home for the night."

Brandon sat at the table by the front window at Java's Coffee Shop, Weezie across from him, the aroma of vanilla lattes bringing back memories of Raleigh. "You come here often?"

Weezie shook her head. "Every now and then to read the paper and have my morning coffee. But truthfully, I don't enjoy comin' by myself. I'm just too much of a people person."

"Then how do you stand living alone?" Brandon said.

"For some reason that doesn't bother me. Home is the one place I still feel close to Joshua. But I've never been able to sit by myself in a room full of people without feelin' lonesome."

"Yeah, I can relate to that. Pretty hard to get motivated to do anything without Kelsey."

"Any chance you'll get back together?"

"I doubt it. She wants stability, and I can't give her that right now. Besides, if I change careers midstream, I'll be lucky to make half of what I was making at Mavis and Stein. I doubt she'd settle for that."

"She will if she loves you."

"That's certainly in question. I never thought she'd break off the engagement."

"Well, give it time, baby. Bein' apart just might bring you back together."

Brandon reached in his shirt pocket and took out some packets of Advil. "You want something for pain?"

"Almost forgot about it till you asked. Head's throbbin' a little, but I'm okay. Sorry your ribs are botherin' you."

Brandon popped the tablets in his mouth and took a big gulp of water. "I hope the little beast broke his toe."

"I imagine someone already broke his spirit."

"You sound like my mom. Aren't you at least annoyed?"

"I was. I let it go."

"Just like that?"

"It's easier the quicker you do it."

Brandon wiped the cinnamon off the rim of his mug. "You said earlier that this kind of thing happens all the time. Have you been targeted before because you're black?"

"No one's ever attacked me or my property, but I've been stared at, laughed at, and put down plenty of times. Can't even repeat some of the names I've been called. The highway patrol's pulled me over for no real reason, other than to be sure I'm not doin' something criminal. Sometimes white folks get waited on before I do." Weezie folded her hands on the table. "I've had to learn that it's not who you are but *whose* you are that matters."

Brandon glanced up at her. "What do you mean?"

"I'm a child of God Almighty. Anything someone does to me, they do to Him and will have to answer for it someday. That's the Lord's business. Mine is to love people and be a reflection of Him. And that doesn't leave any room for feelin' sorry for myself or gettin' back at people."

"What an amazing attitude. Have you always been this positive?"

Weezie let out a robust laugh that caused a couple across the room to look up. "Heavens, no! I used to have a chip on my shoulder the size of Mount Rushmore. Joshua's love whittled it away some. And when I finally accepted the Lord Jesus into my heart and realized that I'm a King's kid and don't need to prove nothin' to nobody, the chip went away." She took a sip and wiped the froth off her lip with a napkin. "Never has come back."

"Because you stopped being bitter?"

"Yeah, and I've also stopped bein' hung up about whether my ancestors came from Africa or whether they were slaves. The way I see it, where I came from doesn't matter as much as where I'm gonna end up for eternity. It's bein' His that gives me value, and nobody can take that from me."

Brandon sat for a few moments and considered Weezie's words.

"Did I say somethin' that offended you?" she said.

"Not at all. I've just never known anyone who talks about stuff like this. There's a lot to think about. You want another latte?"

"Don't mind if I do. I forgot how much I like 'em."

Brandon started to get up and walk to the order counter when a loud knock on the window startled him. He glanced outside and saw a handful of guys scratching their ribs and laughing.

"What's with the *Planet of the Apes* routine? You know these guys?"

Weezie shook her head. "They probably came out of that bar down on the corner. Just ignore 'em."

"Come on, let's move to another table."

"No, they're leavin'," Weezie said. "Mercy me, I sure hope they have a designated driver."

Brandon opened the front door and stepped inside, surprised that his mother had not set the security alarm. He walked softly out to the kitchen and flipped the light switch, then reached in the refrigerator and got a bottle of water.

"I didn't think you'd be this late." His mother's voice had that woe-is-me edge to it.

Brandon turned to the doorway where she stood in her bathrobe, her eyes at half-mast. "I asked you not to wait up."

"I couldn't sleep," Ellen Jones said. "I was worried about you. Do you realize it's after two?"

"It never occurred to me you'd be awake or I'd have called to let you know where I was. After Weezie got off work, we went over to Java's and talked."

"How is she?"

"Fine. Actually, better than fine. She has a great attitude. Mom, go back to bed. We can talk in the morning."

"All right, honey. I'll set the security alarm."

"No, I'll do it. But I'm going to sit outside for a while and try to wind down. I've had way too much coffee."

"Okay. Good night."

"Good night, Mom."

Brandon turned out the kitchen light and opened the French doors and went out onto the veranda. He sat in his mother's wicker rocker and let the cool sea breeze wash over him, his mind replaying his conversation with Weezie Taylor. She was a remarkable person, and her talking about spiritual things had made him hungry for more.

The sound of glass breaking shattered the silence. Brandon opened his eyes and sat pin-drop still, his heart pounding, and listened intently until he heard the sound again.

He jumped up and went inside and pulled back the drapes in the living room. Out in the driveway he could barely make out the figure of a man smashing the windows on the Xterra with what appeared to be a baseball bat.

Brandon pushed open the front door and went out on the porch and shouted, "Hey, what do you think you're doing?"

Brandon ran down the steps and out to his SUV, aware of two doors slamming on a dark, late-model truck parked across the street. The truck sped away to the end of the block, its tires squealing as it turned the corner.

Brandon walked around the car and threw his hands in the air, furious that every window had been shattered. Who would do this and why? His mind flashed back to those jerks outside Java's, and suddenly he had an uneasy feeling about Weezie.

He ran back in the house and quickly flipped the pages of the phone book and read down the list of Taylors, but found no Weezie. What was Weezie a nickname for? Louise? Eloise? He looked for both first names and found neither.

He picked up his parents' address book and scanned all the Ts and didn't see a Taylor. He slammed the book shut, his mind racing with frightening scenarios, and hurried down the hall to his mother's bedroom.

8

Gordy Jameson listened to the answering machine pick up at Weezie's house and waited until he heard the beep.

"Weezie, it's Gordy. If you're home, pick up! This is an emergency! Ellen called, and some bozos smashed the windows on Brandon's car and may be headed to your place! Be sure your doors are locked! The police are on the way!" He slammed down the receiver and looked at Pam. "Somethin's wrong. Why didn't she answer?"

Pam Jameson squeezed his hand. "Don't assume the worst. She's probably sound asleep."

"I'm driving over there. Call Ellen and Brandon and tell them what's going on."

"At least give the police time to get there. What can you do? You don't have anything to protect Weezie or yourself with."

Gordy buttoned his shirt and tucked it in his shorts, then grabbed his car keys off the dresser and kissed Pam on the cheek. "I'll call you when I know something."

He went out the front door and got in his car and headed for Weezie's place, aware that he was driving much too fast.

Just this side of Old Seaport, he turned onto Hawkins Highway and was blinded by the high beams of an oncoming vehicle. He flicked his lights off and on, but the vehicle whizzed by him without dimming the headlights, which just added to his anxiety.

Gordy drove another couple miles, then slowed as he passed the old-fashioned Mobil gas station and his headlights illuminated the red, white, and blue mailbox with the name Taylor painted on the side.

He turned in the gravel drive and snaked through the piney

woods about a quarter mile till he reached the small blue house with hummingbird feeders hanging from the eaves. The house was dark, and he didn't see Weezie's Toyota. He left his car lights on and ran up on the stoop and pounded the front door several times with his fist.

"Weezie, it's Gordy!"

He banged on the door again and called her name and waited for what seemed an eternity, then ran around to her bedroom window and knocked on the glass. He cupped his hands around his eyes and looked in. The warm glow of a night-light revealed that her bed was still made.

Gordy walked back to his car, wondering where she could be at three in the morning. Brandon said he had walked her out to her car and waited until she was locked in and on the road before he left Java's.

Gordy saw colored lights flashing in the trees and then a squad car coming up the drive. He waved his hands in the air, and the driver pulled up next to him and rolled down the window.

Gordy bent down and saw two officers he didn't recognize. "I'm Gordy Jameson, the one who called. I knocked on the door and Weezie didn't answer, so I looked in her bedroom window. Her bed hasn't been slept in."

"Maybe she stopped somewhere on the way home," the officer said.

"She told Brandon she was goin' home. Somethin's not right."

"Okay, but don't jump to conclusions. The morons that smashed Mr. Jones's windows may not pose any threat to Ms. Taylor. Wait here and we'll take a look around."

Gordy leaned against the car, his arms folded, and watched the officers move around the house, shining their flashlights in the windows. They disappeared for a few minutes behind the house and then walked back to where Gordy was standing.

"We didn't find anything suspicious," the tallest officer said. "We'll sit out here for a while and see if anyone shows up and then check back periodically. Are you sure there's no place Ms. Taylor might have gone for the night—a family member's? A boyfriend?"

"No one that I can think of. I'll go by the crab shack and see if maybe she's there." Gordy wrote his cell number on the back of his business card and handed it to the officer. "I'd appreciate a call if you find her. Weezie's worked for me for a long time. She's like family."

Brandon sat with his mother in the living room, waiting for the officers to finish making their report on his car and hoping for word that Weezie had made it home safely.

The phone rang, and Ellen jumped up and walked into the kitchen. "Hello… How strange… I don't know either… Sure, hold on."

Ellen walked back into the living room, the cordless phone in her hand. "It's Gordy. He just left Weezie's house, and she's not there."

Brandon took the phone and didn't miss the apprehension in his mother's eyes. "I can't believe she's not home, Gordy. It's been over an hour and a half since we left Java's."

"Are you sure Weezie was goin' straight home?"

"I assumed so. She said she was so hyped from the caffeine that she'd probably be up all night canning green beans. Are you sure she wasn't there? Maybe she didn't hear you at the door."

"The place is dark and her car's not there. The curtains were open, and I could see her bed's still made. The police looked around and didn't see anything suspicious. I'm gonna go by the crab shack and see if she decided to work late, but I've got a bad feelin' about this."

"That's two of us." Brandon glanced up at the police officer who appeared in the doorway. "If she's not at work, call back and I'll ride with you and help you look. I think the police are about done here."

"Thanks, I just might do that."

The police officer waited until Brandon handed Ellen the phone, then walked over and gave him a piece of paper. "I found this on the front seat."

Brandon read the words written in red marker: *Stay away from the black widow or we'll step on both of you!!!*

"Nothing like getting right to the point," the officer said.

"Why would anybody care if I talk to Weezie?"

"Maybe someone thinks you're doing more than talking."

"Well, we're not. But it's nobody's business what Weezie and I do together!"

The officer sat on the couch across from Brandon and Ellen, his hands clasped between his knees. "At least two people decided to make it their business. Any idea who?"

Brandon combed his hands through his hair. "Not unless they were with those drunk guys who knocked on the window at Java's. There were five or six of them who stood outside, scratching their ribs and making ape noises. It was really disgusting."

"Were they white?"

Brandon nodded.

"Didn't it seem to you that their actions were intended to be demeaning to Ms. Taylor?"

"I just thought they were drunk and obnoxious."

"Would you know them if you saw them again?"

"I doubt it. I was trying to ignore them. But I'm sure they were white."

"How old?"

"I don't know—old enough to know better."

Brandon got up and stood behind the love seat, his hands on his mother's shoulders. "I thought this kind of stuff died out in the sixties. I can't believe I'm being targeted for talking to a black lady, and she's being targeted just because she's black."

"So there's no physical relationship between you two?"

Brandon rolled his eyes. "We went to Java's to talk about what happened on the beach this morning—period. You wouldn't even be asking me that question if Weezie were white."

"I'm sorry if the question's offensive, but it's relevant considering the note. Where have you been seen with her?"

"Just at the beach and Java's."

"And at Gordy's," Ellen said, "while you were waiting for her to get off work."

"Right."

The officer wrote something on a notepad and looked at Brandon. "Did you talk to Ms. Taylor at Gordy's?"

"Off and on. She came over to the table a few times and sat for a minute."

"Did you notice anyone eyeing you?"

"No, but I wasn't paying attention either."

"How long were you there?" the officer said.

"From a quarter to ten until we left for Java's just after eleven. We each drove our own car."

"Anybody at Java's stand out besides the drunk guys?"

"Not really. There were a few couples there, and some kids studying. They hardly seemed to notice us. Well, once when Weezie laughed, a couple looked over at us and smiled. That's about it."

"Do you think this is related to the vandalism at the clinic?" Ellen said.

"If it is, ma'am, we'll have to connect the dots. Your son's the only Caucasian that's been targeted, and he's not a volunteer."

Gordy pulled into the empty parking lot and looked across the pier at the front of Gordy's Crab Shack and saw only the security lights on. He picked up his cell phone and pressed the autodial.

"Hello."

"Pam, darlin', it's me. Weezie wasn't home. I left the police out there and drove back to the crab shack to see if maybe she was workin'. She's not here either."

"I'm really getting scared, Gordy. Where could she have gone?"

"She could've had car trouble or somethin'. I'm gonna check the gas stations, convenience stores, all-night diners—places like that."

"Shouldn't someone file a missing person report?"

"It's probably too soon for that. Brandon Jones offered to help me look for her. I may stop by Ellen's in a little while and pick him up."

"Call me the minute you know something."

"I will."

Just as a hint of pink began to appear on the horizon, Gordy fumbled to get the key in the lock, then slowly pushed open the front door of his house, hoping Pam had fallen asleep.

"Gordy! Did you find her?" Pam jumped up from the couch and hurried to the door.

He shook his head and went over to his recliner and flopped in it. "I'm worried somethin's happened to her. The guys who busted out Brandon's windows also left a threatening note with a strong racial overtone."

"And you didn't call and tell me?"

"Nothin' you could do." Gordy told her about the note the police officer had found in the front seat of Brandon's SUV and about the incident with the drunk guys at Java's.

Pam sat in his lap, her arms around his neck. "Seems odd they would've smashed Brandon's car windows, knowing he might figure they did it and describe them to the police."

"He doesn't remember what they looked like. Shoot, he doesn't even know how many there were."

"They don't know that."

"Good point." Gordy rubbed the stubble on his chin. "I feel so helpless. Brandon and I looked everywhere we could think of."

"You need to rest a few hours," Pam said. "We may have to work a double shift."

Gordy willed away the emotion that tightened his throat. "I can't rest till I know where she is. I think I better give Will a call."

Pam followed him to the kitchen, and he dialed Will Seevers's home number.

"Hello."

"Margaret, it's Gordy. I know it's early, but is Will up?"

"Yes, he's reading the newspaper. Hang on."

Gordy reached over and took Pam's hand and squeezed it.

"Hey there," Will said. "How come you're up already?"

Gordy rattled off a detailed account of the worst night he could remember since Jenny died. "I have a bad feelin' about this."

"For heaven's sake, Gordy, why didn't you call me sooner? I would've helped you look."

"Why spoil your sleep? You couldn't have done anything more than your officers were already doin'. Plus, I really thought we might find her."

"Listen, I'll get dressed and go down to the station right now. Give me time to read the police report and talk to Al Backus. He's investigating the vandalism at the clinic, and I want him in on it. Why don't you meet us at my office in an hour?"

"Okay, Will. Thanks."

Gordy hung up the phone and told Pam everything Will had said. "I can't sit here for an hour and do nothin'. I think I'll drive out to Weezie's place again and look around before I go down to the police station."

"I'm sure the officers would've called if she'd come home."

Gordy kissed Pam's hand. "Maybe it's just therapy for me, but I've gotta feel like I'm doin' somethin'."

Gordy turned down Hawkins Highway and headed for Weezie's place, his mind replaying the scene at Java's just the way Brandon Jones had described it to him. The behavior of those bozos seemed too blatant not to be related to Weezie's disappearance.

Gordy slowed the car as he approached a curve and noticed that the guardrail had been knocked out. He pulled onto the shoulder and got out of the car and walked over to the edge. At the bottom of the embankment was a red car.

He angled his way down the steep incline, weeds clawing at his bare legs, his heart threatening to pound out of his chest. As he got closer, he saw it was a Toyota Corolla and recognized the fish emblem on the back window.

He ran up to the driver's side door and yanked it open and saw that Weezie's eyes were closed and there were cuts and bruises on her face. He shook her arm. "Weezie, it's Gordy! Can you hear me? Weezie!"

Her eyes opened, and she blinked sleepily. "I hear you fine. Why are you hollerin'?"

"Are you hurt?"

"I don't think so. It was one bumpy ride, but thank the Lord the car landed upright. I couldn't see in the dark to climb back up the hill, so I just sat tight waitin' for morning and must've fallen asleep. How'd you know to look for me?"

"Somebody smashed the windows in Brandon's SUV last night and left a threatening note. He thought it might've been those jerks you saw down at Java's and was worried they might've followed you. Ellen called me and I called you, and when you didn't pick up, I sent the police out there. It's a long story, but when you never showed up, I feared the worst. So what happened?"

"Came close to bein' the worst. I was singin' my gospel music, and all of a sudden in my rearview mirror I saw headlights coming at me real fast. I thought they were gonna pass me, but the car started bumpin' me in the rear, then sped up and pushed me so fast I lost control on that curve. Had one heck of a ride down that hill." Weezie's eyes filled with tears. "I prayed they'd just keep on goin'. Guess they did."

"Could you tell who was in the car?"

She shook her head. "Too much light in my eyes, but I guarantee you it was no kid this time."

"I'll call an ambulance. You shouldn't try to climb back up that hill."

"Get me out of here first, and we'll see. I really don't think I'm hurt."

9

Police Chief Will Seevers sat at the table in his office with Investigator Al Backus and went over the police report and the statement Brandon Jones had given the responding officers.

"The threat's a bad deal," Al said, "but at least now we know there's definitely something racial going on."

"I sure don't like the implication." Will set the report on his desk and looked at his watch. "I wonder what's keeping Gordy?"

"You want me to hang around and wait for him or start knocking on doors?"

The receptionist's voice came over the intercom. "Chief, your friend Gordy is here to see you. He said to tell you he's got Ms. Taylor with him."

Will looked at Al, his eyebrows raised. "Great! Send them on down."

"That's a load off," Al said. "I wonder where she was."

A minute later, Gordy Jameson and Weezie Taylor walked into the office.

"Boy, are we glad to see you," Will said. "Sit down. You want some coffee or water or orange juice or something?"

Gordy shook his head, the circles under his eyes matching the color of the wrinkled shirt he was wearing.

"Orange juice sounds awful good," Weezie said.

"I'll get it." Al got up and took a can of orange juice out of Will's mini refrigerator and handed it to Weezie.

"Wanna know where I found her?" Gordy said. "At the bottom of an embankment! Those good-for-nothin' beer-guzzlin' racists ran her car off the road and just left her there. She could've died for all they cared!"

Will was thinking he hadn't seen Gordy that mad since high school, when some football players had assaulted a mentally challenged girl and their wealthy parents got the charges dropped. "Weezie, why don't you tell us exactly what happened."

Will listened carefully as she recounted her ordeal.

Al leaned forward, his elbows on his knees. "You said the headlights behind you were blinding. If you could still see the lights when the vehicle was on your tail, then it must've been considerably higher than your Corolla."

Weezie nodded. "I'd say that's right. But I never got a look at it or whoever was in it. I'm just praisin' the Lord they didn't climb down that embankment to make sure I was dead."

"If they intended to kill you," Al said, "they probably would have. This feels like harassment that went too far, like maybe they were trying to teach you a lesson for being involved with a white man."

Weezie looked at Al, her eyebrows furrowed. "You can forget *involved*. We were havin' coffee in a public place. If you're thinkin' what I think you're thinkin', you're way off base."

"Are you saying there's nothing going on between you and Brandon Jones?"

Weezie's eyes moved from Al to Will to Gordy and then back to Al. "If you mean some kind of romantic relationship, that's exactly what I'm saying. Mercy me, I can't believe you even have to ask."

"Sorry, but it's important," Al said. "The threatening note implies that the two of you are involved."

Gordy sighed. "So what's she supposed to do, hang a disclaimer around her neck?"

Weezie reached over and touched Gordy's arm. "Now I want the three of you to listen to me real good: I am *not* sexually involved with Brandon Jones—or with any man. Whoever wrote that note is a small-minded bigot with an active imagination."

Brandon Jones thought he heard a phone ringing and opened his eyes, and for several seconds couldn't remember where he was. He saw the crown molding and blue striped wallpaper and remembered he was in the guest room at his parents' home—and that Weezie was missing.

He sat up on the side of the bed and combed his hands through his hair, wondering if the police had found her and what the next step would be if they hadn't.

He heard a knock at the door. "Come in."

Ellen Jones opened the door and sat on the side of the bed next to him. "Good news: Gordy found Weezie, and she's okay."

"Thank, God. I've been praying like nuts. Where was she?"

Brandon listened as his mother told how Weezie had been run off the road and had spent the night in her car.

"Gordy's wife, Pam, is taking her to the doctor this morning," Ellen said. "But as far as anyone can tell, she's not hurt, other than some cuts and bruises."

"It infuriates me that anyone would lash out this way. I wish I had memorized every detail of those creeps down at Java's instead of ignoring them. I wonder if Weezie remembers anything specific?"

"I don't know. Chief Seevers is sending someone over to talk to you. They're trying to piece together the details, but they're thinking vandalism at the clinic may have been done by the same men."

Brandon shook his head. "I thought the People's Clinic was supposed to bring people together."

"It has," Ellen said. "But there're always a few who seek to undermine what others are working so hard to build."

"They're doing a whole lot more than undermining." Brandon stood and stretched. "I guess I'd better go call the insurance company before the police get here. My comp coverage should take care of the car windows without me having to pay a deductible. At least I hope so. Maybe I'll stop by later and see how Weezie's doing."

"Honey, it might be a good idea for you to stay close to the house for a while—at least until the police can get a handle on who's doing this."

"What you really mean is I should stay away from Weezie."

He thought his mother's face turned pink. "It seems wise," she said. "Just until the police figure this out. I think you need to take the threat seriously."

"I'm not caving in to these creeps. They're not going to tell me who I can associate with and who I can't."

"I understand how you feel, son, but this is one time when you need to put the principle aside in the interest of safety."

Brandon exhaled. "So we just do what they say or else? If we give in to those tactics, we're playing right into their hands."

"Only until the police figure it out."

"And what if they don't?"

Will Seevers sat with Al Backus at the table in his office and reread each of the vandalism reports. He took off his glasses and took a sip of coffee. "No DNA. No fingerprints. No witnesses."

"Ah, but we've got a chip of wood from the bat used on the pediatrician's Lexus." Al smiled wryly. "A Louisville Slugger."

"I wonder how many millions of those are out there?"

"Probably just one with this chunk of wood missing. Maybe we'll get some evidence from last night's smash fest at the Joneses' that will link these cases together."

"I sure hope so, Al. When this hits the news, the NAACP will camp on our doorstep till we make an arrest. In the meantime, the clinic will probably lose volunteers."

"Maybe that's what these clowns are hoping for."

"Makes no sense. What beef could they have with the clinic?" Will held out his hand. "Give me that page with Weezie's comments about the guys at Java's." Will took the paper and reread it.

It was dark outside Java's, but I saw several white guys, maybe as many as six, come up to the window. They started making ape gestures and laughing. They seemed drunk to me. I think they were dressed in shorts and T-shirts. One wore a Florida Marlins ball cap. They looked about my age, but I only got a glimpse. That's all I can recall.

Will handed the page back to Al. "Go talk to Brandon Jones and see if he can add anything to what Weezie remembers. Then head for the bars in the same vicinity as Java's, and see if one of the bartenders remembers a half dozen guys getting out of hand. I know the description we have is pretty generic, but maybe it'll lead to something.

Gordy stood at the door of the crab shack, welcoming lunch customers and wondering why Pam wasn't back yet from taking Weezie to the doctor.

Eddie Drummond walked across the pier and over to Gordy and patted him on the back. "Me and the guys missed you at lunch yesterday. Where were you?"

"I had stuff to do, Eddie."

"You gonna join us today?"

"Sorry, I can't. Pam's out and I need to keep things runnin'."

"She sick?"

Gordy heard a familiar whistle. He looked up and waved to Captain Jack, glad for the distraction. "Hope you brought your appetite," he said to Eddie. "Today's special is fried shrimp."

"Man, I'm starved. My mouth's been watering for Pam's triple berry pie half the morning."

"Well, we've got plenty of that."

Captain Jack walked over to them and flashed a toothy grin. "You eatin' with us today, Gordy?"

"Nah, I'm a little short-staffed again today."

"Rats! You're the only one that can keep Drummond straight."

"Me?" Eddie said. "You're the liberal. You're twisted so far to the left that not even a chiropractor could straighten you out." Eddie laughed and put up his fists and threw a few imaginary punches.

"I'd expect that kind of comment from a radical, right-wing Limbaugh lover such as yourself."

Gordy smiled and shook his head. "You two. Come on, I'll seat you out back. I'm sure Adam will be here shortly. Good thing, too. Sounds like you could use a referee."

Gordy stood talking to a group of ladies sitting in booth three when he spotted Pam and Weezie going into the kitchen.

"Thanks for decidin' to try Gordy's today. I hope you enjoy your lunch." He counted out five dessert coupons and placed them on the table. "Dessert's on me. Might wanna try the fruit pies. My wife makes 'em from her mother's blue ribbon recipes."

He went into the kitchen and walked over to Pam and Weezie. "So what'd the doctor say?"

"He thinks I'm fine," Weezie said. "I'm sore is all. The cuts and bruises don't amount to anything."

"Well, that's good news. But you're not workin' today."

"Why not?"

"You just spent a terrifying night in your car, prayin' whoever pushed you over the edge didn't come back to finish the job. I'd say you could use a break."

Weezie shook her head. "I don't want a break. I want to forget it and go on."

"You can forget it tomorrow. Today you need to rest."

"But I'd rather work."

"You're not invincible, woman. You need to get quiet inside and let your body rest and your emotions calm down."

"Who says I'm not calm?"

Gordy reached out and touched her arm. "Weezie…you need to rest."

"And just how am I supposed to rest knowin' those guys are still out there? I feel safe here at work."

Gordy glanced at Pam and read her eyes. "That's why you're movin' in with us for a while."

"I'll do no such thing!"

"Why not? We've got an extra bedroom and bathroom off the kitchen. You'll have privacy, and we'll feel much better knowin' you're all right."

Pam nodded. "It's a good idea, Weezie. The police will get these guys, but until they do, come stay with us. We love you. You're family."

Weezie's eyes brimmed with tears. "Yeah, I guess we are at that."

"Pam, darlin', how about you keepin' an eye on things here, and I'll run Weezie out to her house so she can get whatever she needs?"

"You don't have to go with me," Weezie said.

"Well, I'm not lettin' you go by yourself. And I don't want you and Pam out there alone either. Let's give it another thirty minutes till the lunch traffic dies down and then head out there."

"Come on, Weezie," Pam said. "You can help me roll out the pie crusts. We've got some whopping June sales figures to shoot for."

Gordy went out in the main dining room just as Eddie Drummond came in from the back deck. "Did you get enough to eat, Eddie?"

"Yeah, the shrimp was great, but that triple berry pie is to die for. Tell Pam I said so, okay?"

"Yeah, sure."

"So what's wrong with Pam? You said she was sick."

"I didn't say that, Eddie. I said she was out."

"Doing what?"

"Takin' care of personal business."

"In other words, none of *my* business. I get it."

At four thirty that afternoon, Will Seevers picked up his phone to call Al Backus just as Al waltzed into his office and flopped in the chair.

"Man, I'm beat," Al said.

"How'd you guys do?"

"Brandon Jones didn't have anything to add to Weezie's description of the guys at Java's. So we went barhopping and tracked down the bartenders who were working last night. Had to get a couple of them out of bed. They didn't remember any group of customers that stood out more than another. All the joints tend to be crowded and rowdy in the summer with the influx of college kids."

"I'm sure you mentioned our suspects might be older, maybe forty, give or take?"

"Yeah, but that didn't trigger anything. Neither did the ball cap. Maybe our suspects didn't come out of a bar. Maybe they were just passing by Java's and saw a black woman and a white man sitting together and decided to have a little fun. We don't know that these guys had cars or that they followed Brandon and Weezie."

Will wadded up an old phone message and tossed it in the trash. "No, but it doesn't ring true that a group of guys that age would be roaming the streets that late at night. They probably work. My guess is they'd been in at least one of those bars and were walking back to their cars."

"Maybe so, but the bartenders at Mikey's, The Cove, Flamingo's, Rounder's, and Big John's gave us zip."

Will leaned back in his chair, his hands behind his head. "If our suspects were behaving like jerks when Weezie and Brandon saw them, maybe they annoyed someone else, too. Are there any all-night businesses in that part of town?"

"Yeah, a diner around the corner from Java's and a convenience store down the block."

"I want you to go back and see if anyone working the night shift remembers them. See if they have surveillance cameras. Maybe that'll give us something."

10

After dinner, Brandon Jones made a phone call and talked for several minutes. After he hung up, he sensed his mother standing in the kitchen doorway.

"That was Weezie on the phone," he said. "She went to the doctor, and other than soreness and cuts and bruises, she's fine. She also wanted us to know that Gordy and Pam insisted she move in with them for a while, so that's where she is."

"Good," Ellen said. "I thought you were going to work on your résumé this evening."

"You don't seem very concerned about Weezie."

"You said she's fine. I think now it would be good if you focus on getting your own life moving forward."

"I am, but I can't blow off what's happened in just one day."

"No, but I think it would be best if you heed the threat and stay away from her."

"You really expect me to do that just because a bunch of racist punks told me to? Would you?"

Ellen sighed. "You're not equipped to fight these men. This is one time when you should just walk away."

"You *never* backed down from a threat when you were working for the newspaper."

"Yes, and it's a wonder I lived to tell about it."

"So you'd have done things differently?"

"Don't change the subject. There's no reason for you to further antagonize whoever did this by continuing to associate with Weezie, especially since you hardly know her."

Brandon sat at the breakfast bar and folded his hands. "It's surprising how quickly you get to know a person when you've gone through something together. Weezie and I had a great conversation last night that I'd like to continue. She's really spiritual. Did you know that?"

"I'm aware she's a believer."

"I'm telling you, Mom, she has her act together. It's incredible how secure she seems with who she is. I feel like I should be taking notes when I'm with her. In fact, I got more out of listening to her than I ever did in Bible study… Why are you frowning? I thought you'd be glad that I'm getting interested in spiritual things."

His mother's eyes seemed to search his for longer than he was comfortable, and finally she said, "Yes, but one-on-one spiritual mentoring between people of the opposite gender is never ideal, especially when you're vulnerable."

"Why not?"

"Because it would be easy to develop an emotional attachment to Weezie, and her to you. I don't think it's wise to put either of you in that position."

"What do you mean by emotional attachment?"

"People who bare their souls to one another often experience emotional intimacy. That's not the kind of relationship you need to have with Weezie."

Brandon threw his hands up. "You're worried I might end up involved with a *black* woman, is that it?"

"Don't put words in my mouth! My concern goes way beyond race or hormones or the fact that she's ten years older than you." Ellen sat on the stool next to him and said nothing for a few moments. "Son, you *are* vulnerable whether you realize it or not. Your ego's taken a huge hit, and your life seems empty at the moment. It's only natural to want to fill the void. But you can't trust your feelings right now."

Brandon exhaled. "Thanks for your vote of confidence."

"I have every confidence in you. In fact, I believe you and Kelsey might still have a future. But I also know you're aching to be loved and accepted and comforted. Weezie's a precious person, but don't look to her to fill that void."

"Mom, we had *coffee*. Get a grip!"

"I know you think I'm out in left field, but I'd be negligent if I didn't caution you before you get into something you might regret later."

"Okay, I've been cautioned. You can stop worrying. You did your maternal duty."

There was a long moment of silence, and Brandon hated that he had sounded so flippant.

"At least think about what I've said." Ellen rose to her feet. "Your father will be home tomorrow night. Expect him to be vocal about this, too."

Will Seevers walked out of the police station and glanced up at city hall across the street, its white clock tower ablaze in the evening sun. He walked over to reserved parking and started to get in his car when he saw Al Backus jogging over to him.

"Glad I caught you before you left," Al said. "We talked to the managers and employees who were working last night at the convenience store and the all-night diner. No one remembers a group of unruly guys fitting the description Weezie and Brandon gave us. The convenience store owner was more than happy to give us the surveillance tapes, but I don't think they're going to tell us anything."

"All right. I've got officers patrolling the area, and they'll have their eyes peeled for these clowns. Try to get some rest. I held an impromptu with reporters earlier, and WRGL News ran the short version at six, so you can bet it'll be spit shined at eleven. I expect the cable channels to jump on it like fleas on a hound dog."

"I hate this," Al said. "We got such positive media coverage when the clinic opened, and now we're right back to dealing with hate crimes. So much for our glowing example to the rest of the country."

Will glanced up again at city hall. "Let's not lose our perspective. The clinic's a *big* success, and people of different races and religions *are* working together for a common good. We just need to find these spoilers and figure out what their beef is before they end up killing someone."

Brandon sat in the living room with his mother, waiting for the eleven o'clock news to come on, painfully aware that his mother hadn't said anything to him since their unpleasant discussion earlier in the evening.

"Mom, I'm sorry if I sounded disrespectful a while ago. I didn't mean to. I guess I'm a little touchy right now. So much has happened, and sometimes I think I'm never going to feel normal again."

"You will. It's just going to take some time to figure things out."

Brandon took the TV off mute just as the news came on.

"Good evening. This is Shannon Pate."

"And I'm Stephen Rounds. Welcome to *Regional News at Eleven*. Police Chief Will Seevers held an impromptu press conference with reporters late this afternoon, following a rash of crimes that began last Wednesday with vandalism at the People's Clinic and escalated early this morning to what appears to be attempted murder. Police have reason to believe these crimes were racially motivated. Jared Downing is reporting live from the People's Clinic. Jared, tell us what you know."

"Stephen, last Wednesday evening around 6:15, Rochelle Thomas, an African-American nurse who volunteers here at the People's Clinic, called police and reported that the tires on her car had been slashed in the parking lot.

"Then at 5:30 p.m. on Friday, Dr. MacKenzie Irwin, an African-American pediatrician, called police and reported that the rear window and taillights of his vehicle had been smashed in the parking lot. After this second incident, Police Chief Seevers authorized a stronger police presence in the vicinity of the clinic, and there hasn't been any more vandalism here.

"However, this morning around 1:15, *another* African-American clinic volunteer, RuWeeza Taylor, and her Caucasian companion, Brandon Jones of Raleigh, were harassed by as many as a half dozen middle-aged Caucasian men who stood outside the front window of Java's Coffee Shop on West Sunset Drive, seemingly drunk and making racially offensive gestures at Ms. Taylor. The couple ignored the men, and they left.

"Now, Stephen, this is where it turns dangerous. Just after 2:00 a.m., Taylor and Jones left Java's in separate vehicles. About thirty minutes after Jones arrived at his parents' home, where he's visiting, he heard glass shattering and discovered a man smashing the windows on his SUV with what appeared to be a baseball bat. Jones ran outside and shouted at the man, who then fled the scene with at least one companion in a late-model dark blue or black truck.

"Jones told police that his instincts told him to alert Ms. Taylor, and when she failed to answer the phone, police officers were dispatched to her residence and found the house dark and no sign of her car on the property.

"What transpired after that isn't yet clear, but we do know Ms. Taylor was found by her employer just after dawn, not seriously harmed and sitting in her car at the bottom of an embankment not far from her home. She later told police that she had been forced off the road by another vehicle around 2:15 this morning.

"Now, Stephen, here's another odd twist to this case. Taylor and Jones had filed a police report earlier yesterday morning after an incident on Seaport Beach. Ms. Taylor was hit in the head with a golf-ball-sized rock, which apparently had been thrown by a boy of about twelve or thirteen, who ran away before either Taylor or Jones could see his face.

"Police Chief Seevers declined to comment on any suspects or the motive for the attacks, citing the ongoing investigation. However, he did emphasize that Seaport has zero tolerance for hate crimes and that his department will do everything in its power to bring the perpetrators to justice.

"Though it was obvious the chief chose his words carefully, I don't think there can be any doubt these were hate crimes. So far, none of the victims has agreed to comment on the record for fear of retaliation.

"I spoke with about a dozen people from the African-American community, and all declined to go on camera or to be quoted. I can tell you that each expressed grave concern that these chilling incidents might be the resurgence of racial violence, the likes of which this town hasn't seen since the 1960s. This is Jared Downing reporting live from the People's Clinic. Back to you, Stephen."

"Thanks, Jared. We're going to keep a close watch as this investigation continues and will keep our viewers informed with up-to-the-minute coverage.

"In other news tonight…"

Brandon got up and handed his mother the remote. "I'm going upstairs to read. I can't believe none of the victims will talk to the media. I should've talked to that reporter who called."

"There was nothing to be gained by it. The media knows what happened, and it's better if your face isn't in the news."

"What difference does it make, Mom? Whoever made the threat already knows where I'm living."

"Don't remind me."

Ellen turned off the TV after the news and sat by the phone. She grabbed it on the first ring. "Did you watch the news?"

"I certainly did," Guy Jones said. "I noticed Will didn't tell the press about the threat Brandon got. I figured he would withhold some key detail only those responsible would know about. So how's Brandon handling it?"

"He doesn't seem scared enough to suit me. Says he's not going to stay away from Weezie just because a bunch of racist thugs told him to."

"That's indignation talking. He's smarter than that."

"He's smart, but I question how rationally he's able to look at the situation. He's already put poor Weezie on some kind of a spiritual pedestal. All he needs is to get emotionally entangled and further complicate his life." Ellen told Guy about her caution to Brandon and about his terse response. "Obviously it didn't sit well with him that his mother offered advice he didn't want and didn't ask for."

"But you're right. I'll reinforce it when I get home. Any scuttlebutt on how all this might affect the volunteer situation at the clinic?"

"Not yet, but I'm sure African-Americans will rethink their involvement. What a shame." Ellen fiddled with the satin pocket on her bathrobe. "I haven't said anything to anybody else, but I have my doubts that what happened to Brandon and Weezie was even related to what happened at the clinic. It just doesn't jibe. Unless they were followed from Gordy's to Java's, which doesn't seem likely, how would the men who harassed them even know Weezie was a volunteer? And the incident on the beach seems stranger than ever now."

"Yeah, good point. I don't know, honey. But you can bet Will Seevers will be under the gun to find out."

11

William Seevers sat in his recliner rereading Tuesday's sport's page, aware of the mantel clock striking midnight. "Are you ever coming to bed?" Margaret Seevers stood in the doorway in her nightgown, her hairdo flat on one side.

"I would just toss and turn and keep you awake," Will said. "I'm still pretty wired."

Margaret came in and sat on the couch, her hand over her mouth to capture a yawn. "You're worried the racial thing is serious, aren't you?"

"I don't know enough yet to worry. But it bothers me that the incidents at the clinic are so different from those that happened to Weezie, not to mention Ellen and Guy's son. We might be dealing with different perps, which is actually more upsetting. I'd prefer we be able to pin down one motive and one set of suspects and go after them. But all we've got to go on is a generic description of some drunk, middle-aged white guys, an adolescent whose face was never seen, and a goon with a ball bat and at least one buddy driving a dark blue or black truck. The only thing that makes sense to me is that these crimes were racially motivated, but that conclusion is based more on the threatening note in Brandon Jones's car than anything else. I mean, face it—the vandalism at the clinic could've been random and have nothing at all to do with race. But throw Weezie in the mix, and the possibility can't be ignored. I'm bracing myself for the NAACP to be at my door in the morning demanding justice."

"Well, you want justice, too. Tell them that."

"Trust me, they'll want it faster than I can supply it. I just hope we get some solid leads before this thing really does turn deadly."

Gordy Jameson lay in bed, listening to the sound of the surf. He wondered if Weezie was comfortable in the back bedroom and hoped she'd been able to fall asleep okay.

He rolled over and kissed Pam on the cheek, then slipped into a pair of cutoffs and went out the sliding glass door to the patio. He lay in a chaise lounge, his hands behind his head, and gazed up at a gazillion sparkling diamonds spilled across black velvet. The majesty of the heavens was something he could count on to be there—like God Himself—and he couldn't remember a time when he wasn't awed by it. He decided he could use a little awe about now.

Though fatigue had settled deep in his bones, he wasn't sleepy. His mind kept replaying the events of the past couple days. It was upsetting enough that someone had run Weezie off the road and just left her there, but it was equally frightening that someone would threaten a white man merely because he dared to have coffee and conversation with a black woman. And what kind of losers would intimidate volunteers who were helping the needy of the community?

Gordy sighed. These racists were still out there, contaminating the city with their hate and plotting their next move. They could be his neighbors. His customers. Anyone he passed on the street.

Brandon Jones sat out on the veranda, his eyes closed, his hands wrapped around a cold glass of lemonade, and listened to the crickets. He wished he had thought to bring his camping gear when he left Raleigh. At least if living with his parents became unbearable, he would've had the option to find a campground and pitch a tent. He dreaded his father returning home tomorrow night and what his presence might do to the already tense mood in the house.

How could his mother think he would let something develop between Weezie and him? He was still in love with Kelsey and wasn't looking for anything other than stimulating conversation. Weezie was an amazing person with a unique outlook on life. Whatever it was she had discovered, he wanted it for himself, and he couldn't let his mother's hang-up keep him from pursuing it.

He took a sip of lemonade and let his mind drift to the unpleasant events of last night: the drunk guys at Java's…shattering glass…the threatening note…Weezie missing…driving around with Gordy…coming back empty-handed. It all seemed surreal. He knew Weezie'd had a brush with death, but none of it had really sunk in yet. Not even the threat.

Stay away from the black widow or we'll step on both of you!

He repeated the phrase several times in his mind. Why didn't he feel afraid? Or mad? Or even defiant? All he felt was numb.

12

Gordy Jameson sat out on the back deck of the crab shack, his eyes closed and his face tilted up to the bluebird sky. Wednesday morning's sun melted over his face, and he felt himself drifting off to sleep when Billy Lewis's voice startled him.

"Mister G, I am fin-ished now," Billy said. "I did an ex-cel-lent job."

Gordy opened his eyes and saw Billy standing over him, a row of crooked teeth exposed by the proud smile that stretched his cheeks.

"That was fast." Gordy shaded his eyes and glanced around the deck, not surprised to see every table and umbrella clean and bright. "Good job, Billy. I can always count on you."

Billy pointed to the scruffy-looking pelicans that lined the railing. "I do not think the pel-i-cans will stay away."

"Don't worry. The little beggars won't hang around long if nobody feeds them." Gordy got up and put his hand on Billy's shoulder. "You headin' out?"

Billy nodded. "I am need-ed at church."

"Oh, that's right. You're gettin' ready for that big flea market to raise money for the unwed mothers' home."

"I can help, Mister G."

"I know you can." Gordy reached in his wallet and took out two twenty-dollar bills and handed them to Billy. "Since I'll be workin' and won't make it by, let me donate to the cause."

Billy's smile took over his face. "Thank you, Mister G. I will give this to Pas-tor Craw-ford."

"You're welcome. Say hello to that sweet wife of yours."

"Okay."

Gordy stood for a moment looking out at the gulf, wishing he could take advantage of the cooler weather and take Pam deep-sea fishing. He glanced over at the pelicans perched on the railing and six pairs of pleading eyes and chuckled. "Forget it, fellas. All I need is you hangin' around here, pesterin' the lunch crowd."

He glanced at his watch and walked back inside and saw Weezie talking with a couple of waitresses. He waited until she was finished and then walked over to her. "Why are you here so early?"

"Because if I wait till two, I'm gonna go out of my mind. There's nothin' to do at your house except watch TV. The place doesn't even need to be cleaned."

"I don't want you cleanin' our house," Gordy said. "You're a guest."

"I know that, but I only have one gear when I'm awake, and that's forward. I need to be busy doin' somethin'."

"All right. Why don't you help Pam in the kitchen and keep an eye on things during the lunch rush. The guys have been on my case to eat with them."

"Go do it." Her smile was a bright half-moon. "I can handle this lunch crowd with one hand tied behind me. Step aside and watch Weezie the wise and wonderful do her magic. We might actually *make* money on dessert today."

"Geeze, RuWeeze, I don't know how I survived all these years in this business without you."

"Aw, you did fine on your own. Goal settin' keeps me pumped." Weezie put her hand on her hip and held his gaze for what seemed an inordinate amount of time.

"What is it?" Gordy said.

"You haven't told the staff that I'm the RuWeeza Taylor that got run off the road, have you?"

"I don't see any reason why anybody besides Pam and me needs to know, unless you wanna tell them. But somebody's bound to make the connection."

"Maybe not. It's not like these cuts and bruises show up that much on my dark skin. I sure don't wanna get stuck talkin' to customers about it."

"I doubt you're going to be able to avoid the media."

"Well, I don't want any part of keepin' the racial tension stirred up. We're dealin' with some bad apples, but it's a small number. People need to keep the right perspective and not go off half-cocked."

"I'm with you," Gordy said, "but you'd better brace yourself. It won't take the media long to find out where you work, and it's gonna be next to impossible to keep from talkin' about it."

Brandon Jones pushed the newspaper aside and took a sip of coffee just as his mother walked into the kitchen.

"I guess you read the front page?" Ellen said.

"They made the situation sound as bad as that dragging death that happened in Texas. That should draw every civil rights advocate in the known world down here. No way am I getting in the middle of this."

Ellen sat on the stool next to him, her eyes full of understanding. "Brandon, you're in it whether you want to be or not. I know I said I didn't want you to talk to the media, but you're probably going to have to make a statement of some kind."

"I just wish I could get my hands on whoever did this!"

"Will Seevers will get them. Meanwhile, expect the media to be relentless and in your face. You're not going to escape it. I wasn't going to say anything till you had your coffee, but reporters from the *North Coast Messenger* and WRGL News have already called this morning and left messages for you to call them back."

"I'm not saying anything till I talk to Weezie and find out what she's saying to the media."

Ellen bit her lip and didn't say anything.

"Mom, I can't just ignore her. Anything either of us says will affect the other. You know the media's not going to separate what happened to the two of us. They're already referring to us as a couple—which I'm sure just thrills you to death."

"I don't care what people think, Brandon. That's not the issue with me. I'm worried that something you do or say might cause who-ever made the threat to act on it. Obviously *someone* thought you were a couple."

"Yeah, and I resent having to pop their bubble just to save my neck. Who are they to dictate to me who I can or can't hang with?"

"I suggest you pick your fights," Ellen said. "If you and Weezie were romantically involved, then I might understand you being stubborn about this. But since you're not, why not dispel the myth and get these racists to back off?"

Brandon held his mother's gaze and could tell that she understood it was a matter of principle.

Ellen looked down and exhaled. "Why couldn't you be more like your father?"

Will Seevers stood outside the door to the police station, wrapping up a press conference with the media and representatives of the NAACP. He glanced at his watch but didn't look at the time. "I'll take one more question, and then I need to get back to work."

A familiar blond woman raised her hand and started speaking without being called on. "I'm Valerie Mink Hodges with the *North Coast Messenger.*"

What's she doing back here? Will thought.

"Chief Seevers, it's one thing to prosecute the offenders if and when you arrest them; it's another to prevent these hate crimes from happening in the first place. What kind of protection, if any, can African-Americans expect from your department?"

"As I've already stated, we've increased the police presence at the People's Clinic and also in the area around Java's Coffee Shop. But until we establish some sort of pattern, there isn't much we can do other than encourage the citizens of Seaport to be vigilant and report any violence, threats, or anything that even looks suspicious. Let's don't jump to the conclusion that we have a widespread hate crime problem going on here. We need to find whoever's doing this and get them off the street. Thank you, that's all the time—"

"Sir," Valerie continued, "since Hurricane Katrina, scores of African-American families have settled here. Isn't it possible that some people resent the sudden increase in the minority population?"

"Anything's possible, Ms. Hodges, but we've been doing just fine getting these families integrated into the community. I'm not going to speculate in that regard. I'm interested in getting the *facts*."

"Well, it *is* a fact that a number of African-American volunteers at the clinic are hurricane evacuees who've settled here.'"

"It's also a fact that most are not," Will said, "including the nurse and doctor whose vehicles were vandalized. Like I said, let's not jump to conclusions. That's all the questions I have time for right now. If you'll excuse me, I need to get back to work."

Will turned and walked back into the police station, Investigator Al Backus on his heels.

"That broad's a real pain," Al said. "I didn't realize she was working for the *Messenger*. She must be living somewhere in the tri-counties now."

"The minute she opened her mouth I realized she was the reporter from Biloxi who ha d it in for Ross Hamilton. What did we do to deserve her twice in a lifetime?"

"Beats me. Maybe she got bored reporting about Katrina reconstruction efforts."

"Couldn't she just go after FEMA or something?" Will went in his office and flipped the light switch, then sat at his desk. "I don't want anyone in this department talking to her except me. Shift gears for a minute. Did the NAACP seem satisfied with my answers?"

"The only thing they're ever satisfied with is results."

Will glanced out the window. "Fair enough. Then at least we're on the same page."

Gordy sat at a round umbrella table with Captain Jack, Eddie Drummond, and Adam Spalding, finishing his lunch and enjoying the conversation.

"By the way, Gordo," Eddie said. "I had my radio on in the shop this morning. Heard your buddy, the police chief, talking to the media. Remember that Biloxi reporter, Valerie something-or-other, the one who went after Ross Hamilton? She's working for the *Messenger* now."

Gordy lifted his eyebrows. "Swell. The last thing we need is her stirrin' up trouble."

"In case you hadn't noticed, we've *already* got trouble."

Adam took his straw and pushed the lime slice down into his

glass. "You suppose the group of guys that harassed that couple at Java's decided to split up and follow the two of them home? There's no way those incidents were isolated."

"I have a theory," Eddie said. "I think they left one of the bars three sheets to the wind and spotted a white man with a black woman. They decided to have a little fun, and it got out of hand."

Gordy felt his neck get hot. "Well, their *little fun* terrorized that woman and could've gotten her killed. What they did was criminal."

"I know," Eddie said. "All I'm saying is they could be ordinary guys who got drunk and made a big mistake. People can do dumb things when they're drunk."

Gordy swatted the air. "You could pour a pint of Scotch down me, and I wouldn't try to hurt someone. There's somethin' real wrong with anybody who could run someone off the road, tanked or not."

"With all due respect, Gordo, I have a lot more experience with boozers than you do."

"Eddie's absolutely right." Adam nudged Gordy with his elbow. "We humbly bow to your deep understanding of barroom behavior gained over years of experience at The Cove with your beer-guzzling buddies."

"Go ahead and laugh, but I *have* learned a lot by watching people!"

Adam leaned forward, his arms folded on the table, a grin on his face. "I think Eddie knows who went after that couple."

"I do not."

"You sure?"

"Sure I'm sure. I'm just saying that people do stupid things when they're drunk that they'd never do when they're sober. Criminy, stop twisting everything!"

"Take it easy. I'm just razzing you." Adam reached in the muffin basket and took out a hush puppy. "You suppose these same guys were drunk in the middle of the day when they slit the nurse's tires or when they smashed the taillights and back window out of the doctor's car?"

"The cops aren't even sure it was the same guys," Eddie said.

"Give 'em time." Gordy tipped his glass and crunched an ice

cube. "Will Seevers'll connect the dots and make sure these cowards get what they deserve. As far as I'm concerned, he can lock 'em up and throw away the key."

"What's Weezie think about all this?" Captain said.

"Uh-oh, that reminds me…" Gordy pushed back his chair and stood. "I was supposed to read the job descriptions she's been workin' on. We're meetin' in an hour. I'll see you fellas later."

Brandon Jones waited until his mother's car backed out of the driveway and then dialed Gordy's home phone number and got only the answering machine. He hung up and dialed the number for the restaurant.

"Gordy's Crab Shack, this is Weezie."

"Oh good, it's you. This is Brandon. Have you got a couple minutes for me to run something by you?"

"Sure, I'm not officially here till two. What's up?"

"Reporters from the newspaper *and* the TV station called and left messages. I didn't want to comment until after I talked to you. I just wondered what you've been saying to the media. For some reason, I haven't heard anything."

"That's because I haven't been approached yet," Weezie said. "They can't reach me at home and must not know where I work. Gordy says it won't take 'em long to find me. But no one at the clinic's gonna give out my personal information."

"The media must've gotten my parents' address off the police report. What do you think I should say?"

"What do you wanna say?"

Brandon exhaled. "Part of me wants to give them the cold shoulder and not let them use me. And part of me wants to use them to send a message to those imbeciles who ran you off the road and smashed my windows."

"What kind of message?"

"That the Civil War ended over 140 years ago and they need to get over their penny-ante prejudice or move to another country!"

"Oh, well that'd show them," Weezie said. "They're liable to slip a white sheet over their heads and burn a cross in your folks' yard."

"Okay, so it's a little inflammatory. That brings me back to my original question: What do you think I should say?"

"I can't tell you what to say. You have to be true to yourself."

"Then tell me what you're planning to say."

There was a long moment of silence, and then Weezie finally said, "You might not agree with it. Most people won't."

"Just tell me."

"All right. I'm gonna say that it's up to the courts to dole out justice, but that I've forgiven whoever ran me off the road and asked the Lord to bless them."

"Why in the world would you ask God to *bless* them?"

"Because the Bible says to do good to those who hate us, bless those who curse us, and pray for those who mistreat us."

Brandon sat back in his chair and tried to absorb what Weezie had just said. "There's no way I could do that."

"Well, I couldn't either if I let myself dwell on what happened."

"I don't understand how you can you just blow off that these guys treated you as if you were nothing more than a bug on the highway, just because you're black!"

"Baby, I know who I am—and it has nothin' to do with color and everything to do with who I belong to. I already told you that. Look, I don't expect people to get it. Most will think I'm a coward for not speakin' out. Some African-Americans will make a fuss that if I let these white men intimidate me, it'll open the door to more hate crimes. It's not what *they* think but what God thinks that matters. And He says to love my enemies."

"Would you actually say that to a reporter?"

"Only if I felt God nudgin' me to. But I know what I'm *not* gonna do and that's get manipulated by anyone who's usin' what's goin' on here to pit blacks against whites. That kind of talk never goes anywhere positive."

"You can't deny there's a problem here."

"There's always been a problem here, but I've seen how far African-Americans have come. Change takes time and evolves over generations. I'm not gonna forget all that because a handful of drunk racists decide to act on their stupidity. There's already enough racial tension on both sides."

"I know that, but it's blacks who are under attack at the moment."

Weezie laughed. "Did you up and change colors on me?"

"I'm black by association. And I can tell you I don't like being discriminated against one bit. I can't believe you're not demanding justice."

"Makin' demands might get us hired, but it doesn't get us heard—and it sure doesn't earn us respect. The way I see it, the way to be respected is to act respectably even when the other side doesn't. And that's what I plan to do. Hold on just a minute…"

It sounded as though Weezie put her hand over the receiver and was talking to someone else.

"Brandon, I'm sorry. I've gotta go meet with Gordy before I start my shift."

"I still don't know what to say to the media."

"Just say what's on your heart. You'll do fine."

13

On Wednesday evening, Brandon Jones sat at the breakfast bar, working on his résumé and enjoying the aroma of whatever it was his mother had put in the oven. The kitchen door opened, and his father came in from the garage, carrying a small leather suitcase and a garment bag.

"Hi, Dad."

"Hi, yourself." Guy Jones set the bags on a barstool. "I'm gone all of three days, and you're front page news."

Brandon half-smiled. "Runs in the family."

"I'm glad you weren't hurt. Your mom's kept me up on things, and I've been following the story in the Tallahassee newspaper and on TV. So is your insurance company going to pay to have your windows replaced?"

"Yeah, my car's down at Seaport Auto Glass. I should get it back tomorrow."

Ellen Jones came into the kitchen wearing a pink sundress, a flowery fragrance wafting under Brandon's nose as she passed.

"Welcome home, Counselor." Ellen put her arms around Guy's neck and kissed him.

"Mmm…what perfume are you wearing?" Guy said.

"I don't recall the name. Some free sample that came with the cosmetics I bought today."

"I think I'd like to have the name of that one. So did you make any progress on your novel this week?"

Ellen shook her head. "Too many distractions. Owen, Hailey, and the kids are coming for dinner, and we're having your favorite: herb chicken, cornbread dressing, and fresh asparagus spears. I've got burgers and macaroni and cheese for the kids, and Annie wants you to grill their burgers and wear that funny chef hat she and Daniel got you for Christmas."

Guy chuckled. "I can't believe the things I agree to do for those kids."

"Oh, you love it, *Gwandpa*."

"So Brandon, have you thought any more about where you want to send your résumé?"

"Not really, Dad. It's been crazy around here."

The room was quiet for several agonizing seconds, and then Guy patted him on the back and said, "Yeah, I suppose it has. Okay, I'm going to change my clothes. Ellen, what time are the kids coming?"

"Six thirty."

Brandon sat at the dining room table hoping the dinner discussion wouldn't be centered on him. He glanced over at Owen and Hailey and thought they looked liked the happiest couple on the planet. Suddenly, the wound where Kelsey's heart had been pulled away from his felt as if it were open and bleeding again.

"Well, little brother," Owen Jones said, "how does it feel to be named on the front page? Seems to be a rite of passage for this family."

Brandon broke a roll in two and began to butter it. "I would've much rather remained the odd man out, thanks."

"The media's been calling all day to talk to him," Ellen said.

Brandon glanced at his dad out of the corner of his eye. "I'm not all that eager to be quoted. I just don't think I can avoid it if I want any peace. Next thing I know, they'll be at the front door."

"Yeah," Owen said, "they were a real pain after you-know-who did you-know-what."

Annie Jones gave a firm nod. "When my first daddy shot hisself in the head."

Ellen put her napkin to her mouth and then said, "So much for using discretion. Truthfully, Owen, the media wasn't all that relentless with you. They reported the news, but they did respect your privacy and didn't exploit the situation with Annie."

"Sure. But they didn't back off until *after* they laid out my private business."

Ellen shrugged. "At least it was short-lived. I'm not sure this story is going to fade away as quickly, thanks to Valerie Hodges. After the questions she fired at Will Seevers today…I'm sure people are wondering about a lot of things."

"That's not necessarily bad," Guy said. "She brought up a valid point about the hurricane evacuees that probably needs to be addressed."

"They haven't posed a problem," Ellen said.

"How do you know?"

"Because I worked at the shelter and saw volunteers come out in droves. They helped get these families back on their feet. Most have homes now and are working."

"*Seven hundred* of them," Guy said. "Do you see any of them in our neighborhood?"

"Well, no, but—"

"Wouldn't you agree it's much easier to deal with poverty in a controlled environment where you don't have to confront the long-term effects and can feel good about helping?"

"That's a little cold," Ellen said. "A lot of us worked long and hard to ease the suffering. We genuinely cared."

"I know, and I don't mean to minimize what you did. It was heartwarming. But those seven hundred evacuees are now living somewhere in this city, and not everyone is excited to see the African-American community get bigger."

"We've been able to absorb these neighbors without it being a problem. Other cities have, too."

"Have they?" Guy said.

Ellen sighed. "What is your point?"

"I want you to look at this objectively, honey. It's one thing to volunteer your time to help people who are hurting and disadvantaged; it's another to welcome them permanently into your neighborhood. It's certainly not out of the question that adding seven hundred evacuees to our community could've sparked racial tension, or least contributed to it."

"Yes, but the root of the problem is prejudice."

"I don't believe most whites nowadays separate themselves from blacks just because of the color of their skin," Guy said. "People are afraid of what poverty has done to the black community, especially the soaring crime rate. Since they don't know how to deal with it and don't want it to spread to their own neighborhoods, they blame it on the black culture and do nothing. But poverty is the biggest culprit. We're starting to see a huge spike in crime in Hispanic neighborhoods, too. And we've always had problems in poor white communities."

"Then why don't we fix the poverty as long as we're pouring billions into rebuilding after Katrina?" Hailey Jones said. "It would be worth spending whatever it takes to stop it."

Guy shook his head. "It's complicated. People who've been taught to think one way don't just suddenly change because they're given everything they need. Education is vital, and it has to start with the young so they'll be equipped to pursue their dreams. Without it, they're doomed to the same cycle of poverty as their parents."

Ellen exhaled. "You're right. I guess it is complicated. But whatever our differences, we're all part of the human family, and there's no excuse for hate crimes."

"I couldn't agree with you more, honey. I'm just saying that we need to look beyond skin color and confront some of the tangible issues. Until we do, we'll never turn it around."

Brandon started to say something and then hesitated and then decided just to say it. "Mom, you worked at the shelter for months and made friends with a lot of African-Americans. Did you respect them?"

"Of course. I treated each one with dignity."

"I didn't ask how you treated them," Brandon said. "I want to know how you felt when you did it. Didn't you feel superior—just a little?"

Ellen stared at him blankly. "I don't think so. Why would I?"

"Because you're white upper-middle class and have never had to ask for anything?"

"That's precisely why I wanted to help," Ellen said.

"I know. But be honest—didn't it make you feel good that you were in control of the situation and weren't one of them?"

"I certainly didn't want to be an evacuee living in a shelter."

"But how would you feel about being black?"

"Brandon, where are you going with this?" Guy said.

"I just think we should be honest with ourselves. Given the choice, would any of us around this table choose to be black?"

There was a long moment of silence, and Brandon looked from person to person. His niece was the only one smiling.

"I like black," Annie said proudly. "My bestest friend is Shayla. She's my nanny. And my favorite candy in the *whole* world is licorice!"

Brandon smiled at Annie and lifted his eyebrows. "Anyone else brave enough to tackle this one?"

"What about you?" Owen said. "Would you choose to be black?"

Brandon sat quietly for several seconds, his hands folded on the table. "I don't think so."

"Why not?"

"I'm not sure. I need to think about it. But when I figure out why, maybe I'll understand some of this racial stuff a whole lot better."

Police Chief Will Seevers sat at his desk, staring at nothing and wishing he could turn back the clock to his twenty-fifth wedding anniversary trip to Barbados. He closed his eyes and could almost feel the balmy breeze brush over Margaret and him as they lay side by side on chaise lounges, the blue-green waters of the Caribbean just a few yards away.

A knock at the door brought him back to the moment.

"Come in."

Al Backus came in and flopped in a chair. "The media is getting antsy. You should probably give them *something*."

"I already did," Will said. "They can wait till I have something new."

"The NAACP is making a lot of noise, and a couple cable networks are out there doing interviews."

"I don't care if the governor is out there! I'm not commenting again until I have more to say than the scratches on the rear of Ms. Taylor's car are consistent in height with the front bumper of a pickup truck. I wish they'd all back off and give us room to do our job. It's not as though we're sitting around here twiddling our thumbs."

"I've got my two best detectives working the bars tonight," Al said. "Maybe all this media hype will work in our favor and someone will remember something and decide to talk."

Will got up and looked out the window, his hands in his pockets. "Hard to fault the black community for being nervous, but all we need is the media feeding the false notion that the cops aren't doing enough."

"Then you'd better go out there and tell them yourself," Al said. "Because that's exactly what's happening."

14

I n the wee hours of Thursday morning, Will Seevers sat in his recliner thumbing through a travel magazine and thinking about the negative press he had gotten on the eleven o'clock news. He tossed the magazine on the end table, took his cell phone off his belt clip, and pressed the autodial.

"Sanders."

"Detective Sanders, it's Chief Seevers. You and Botts having any luck?"

"We may be on to something," Wade Sanders said. "About ten thirty we went into Big John's and started asking questions. It seemed like a dead end until we approached a Caucasian woman sitting at the bar. She looked about thirty-five, give or take. Told us she hangs out there six nights a week and knows all the regulars. She was a real Chatty Cathy until we asked if she remembered seeing a rowdy group of guys in there Monday night."

"How'd she respond?"

"She didn't. Went right into diversion mode," Sanders said. "Started acting drunk and was all over us. Said she couldn't resist any man who carried a badge. Botts and I are convinced it was an act."

"Did you ask her to answer the question?"

"Yes, sir, but she started giggling, and we couldn't get a straight answer out of her. She was drawing too much attention to us, so we went outside for a few minutes. When we went back in, she was gone. We never saw her leave. She must've slipped out the back door. The bartender said he noticed she borrowed a couple's cell phone and placed a call right after we left."

Will pulled the lever on his recliner and leaned back. "Does the bartender know her name?"

"Jessica Ziegler. Says she's in there every night but isn't much of a drinker. He lets her hang out at the bar because she attracts the guys and it's good for business."

"Does he know where she lives? Works?"

"Thinks she's the bookkeeper at an auto parts store over on Grant Street. We'll check it out tomorrow."

"Any idea who the couple was whose phone she borrowed?"

"No. The bartender didn't recognize them as regulars, and they paid cash so he doesn't have a credit card receipt. He did say that Jessica always comes in alone and leaves the bar with a different guy on a regular basis."

"Any chance she's a pro?"

"Not according to the bartender. Apparently she confides in him, mostly about her insecurities. You know, how ugly she feels, how fat she is, stuff like that. Makes no sense because she's a decent looking gal. Says he can't remember her ever talking about anything other than herself."

"Okay, Detective. See if this Jessica leads us anywhere."

"We will, sir."

Will disconnected the call and went out to the kitchen. He took a carton of Dutch Chocolate ice cream out of the freezer and got a spoon out of the drawer. He could feel Margaret's presence and was thinking the woman could hear a fly crawl up the wall.

"You promised you weren't going to snack on high fat foods," Margaret said, suppressing a yawn.

"Honey, why aren't you asleep instead of trying to be my conscience?"

Margaret smiled, her eyes still not fully open, and put her arms around his neck. "Because I love you and would like to keep you around a few more years. The doctor said your cholesterol is too high."

"I know. I'm working on it."

"I can see how hard you're working." She took the carton of ice cream out of his hands and put it back in the freezer, then reached in the pantry and took out a green box. "Here, try these instead."

"What are they?"

"Fat-free devil's food cookies. They're good."

Will rolled his eyes. "Yeah, chocolate-flavored cardboard."

Margaret reached in the box and put a cookie to his lips.

"Mmm...not bad. Do I get milk, or is that on the no list?"

"Skim milk's fine." Margaret poured him a glass and set it on the table, then sat in the chair across from him. "Maybe you should ask the doctor to give you something to help you sleep."

"I'm fine. You know how I get when a case is working on me."

"I do. That's why I suggested you take something. How are you going to do justice to this investigation if you're exhausted?"

"The same way I've done it for twenty years."

Margaret put her hand on his. "You're not a kid anymore, Will. You've got to start taking better care of yourself."

Will felt his phone vibrate and took it off his belt clip. "Sorry, honey. I need to take this."

"Will Seevers."

"Chief, it's Jack Rutgers. I'm over at Mt. Zion Holiness Church at Ninth and Duncan—the church with that big wooden cross outside."

"And...?"

"The cross is burning. Someone from the media's already here and doing a live broadcast."

"Let me guess. Someone torched it?"

"Yep, with kerosene. Sorry to mess up a good night's sleep, but I thought you'd want to know. Backup should be here any second."

"Thanks, Jack. I'm on my way."

Brandon Jones ambled along the surf on Seaport Beach, the gentle waves of the gulf crawling up on the sand and turning to suds under his bare feet.

How he longed to be with Kelsey, to talk with her about the events of the past few days. He had dialed her cell number half a dozen times and then hung up, certain that another rejection would be harder to bear than just allowing himself to miss her.

He wondered if the Raleigh newspaper and TV stations had mentioned him by name, and if she would even make the connection. He still hadn't decided what he was going to say to the reporters who left messages on his parents' answering machine. Tonight it was all he could do just to ponder the question he had posed to his family and was still struggling with himself.

Until this week, he would have argued vehemently that this country had moved beyond the racial injustice that scarred its history. It was unconscionable to him that he had been threatened for no reason other than being with a black woman. It was the first time in his life that he had experienced racial discrimination, and he was both angry and a little scared. A part of him wanted the chance to sound off, but how wise was it to open up with the media? What if whoever did it came after him—or Weezie—again?

He heard sirens off in the distance and tuned them out with an imaginary mute button, determined not to let anything distort the sounds of the wind and the sea. He trudged over to the warm, dry sand and lay on his back, his arms behind his head. He marveled at the explosion of stars across the heavens and allowed the majesty to consume him. In moments like these, he had no doubt that there was a God and that Jesus lived in his heart.

So why was he still overwhelmed by life's disappointments and pain? Where was the peace he was supposed to feel? And the joy—whatever that was?

Gary's words came rushing back to him.

If you ever figure out what the heck life is about, would you come tell me? I'm living under the Twelfth Street Bridge.

Brandon breathed in and exhaled audibly. He doubted anyone knew the answer.

Will turned onto Duncan Street and pulled his squad car in front of Mt. Zion Holiness Church and saw a small group of people standing on the sidewalk. He got out of the car and ran to the yellow crime scene tape, then ducked under it and went over to where Jack Rutgers was standing.

"Any of these bystanders see anything?"

"Nobody's talking right now," Jack said. "They're all scared. You *know* what they're thinking."

Will folded his arms and studied the smoldering cross. "Forget it.

Seaport hasn't seen Klan activity since the seventies."

"Maybe not, but I promise you those reporters over there are going to play it up for all it's worth."

Will lifted his eyebrows. "Count on it."

A middle-aged African-American man stood on the other side of the crime scene tape waving his hand as if to get someone's attention.

Will walked over to him. "I'm Chief Seevers. Did you want to say something?"

"Yeah, I heard one of those reporters say that the people who did this were wearin' white hoods. That's not true. They were all covered up in dark clothes. I was sittin' over there on my porch steps havin' a smoke when a pickup stopped in front of the church. A couple of guys jumped out and disappeared in the dark. I thought maybe a drug deal was goin' down. I didn't want any trouble. A few minutes later, that cross was on fire. The guys ran back to the truck and beat it outta here."

"Were they white?" Will said.

"What do *you* think?"

"I'd prefer to stick with the facts. Did you see their faces?"

"Nah, but they were white. Judgin' by the way they ran, they must've been about my age."

"Did you get the license number?"

The man shook his head. "I couldn't see much. I'm sure the truck was dark, though. Might've been a Ford."

"Did they say anything?"

"You kiddin'? They were too busy laughin'."

"Can you show me who it was that gave the media the wrong information?"

"I never did see. I just heard the reporters discussin' it. Man, talk like that could start a race war. I got a wife and kids. I don't want trouble in this neighborhood."

"I'll need your name and address in case we need to ask you more information."

"Name's Joseph Lewis. I live over there in that green house—904 Duncan."

Will was aware of a hand on his shoulder and then Jack speaking just above a whisper. "Chief, dispatch just reported a front window smashed at Obadiah's Barbecue over on Kirby. That's just five blocks from here. All available units are headed that way."

Will paused and shook his head from side to side. "It's going to be a long night."

Ellen Jones went into the bathroom and got a drink of water and then crawled back in bed. She watched the ceiling fan go around and around and then turned over on her side and saw Guy's dark eyes looking at her.

"Sorry if I'm keeping you awake."

"Why are you letting Brandon's question torment you?" he said.

"It's not his question that's tormenting me; it's my answer. I *don't* want to be black. There, I said it, and now I feel perfectly wretched." She pulled the covers up over her head.

"Since neither of us can sleep, at least tell me how you came to that conclusion." Guy pulled the covers off her head and tucked them gently around her neck.

"Because African-Americans are not treated equally, no matter how much we say they are."

"The laws are in place, honey."

"And we both know that forcing people to fulfill the law is legalistic and cold." Ellen sighed. "I had honestly never imagined myself as a black woman before tonight. No matter how much I'd like to convince myself otherwise, my life would be much more difficult if I were. Whites like to think that African-Americans can rise above their circumstances and become anything they choose, but it's easier said than done, especially if you have limited finances and no one to encourage you."

"But *you* did it," Guy said. "When your father didn't support your desire to go to college, you got loans, you worked, and you went. That wasn't easy."

"No, but not everyone's a self-starter. And even among those that are, African-Americans have it harder."

"Do you know that for a fact? Where's your supporting evidence?"

"Stop thinking like an attorney for a minute and just let yourself *feel*."

"I'm not very good at that."

"I know, but it's a valuable exercise. Be honest with yourself. How would you feel about being black?"

"Ellen, what's the point of all this?"

She looked deep into his eyes. "The point, Counselor, is to flesh out the truth and admit to ourselves that equality doesn't come just because the law says it has to."

"It's certainly a good start."

"Maybe so, but we both know I'm not going to find many white people who would honestly choose to be black. Don't you find that rather telling?"

"Not at one thirty in the morning."

Ellen poked him in the chest. "You're the one who wanted me to talk, Counselor."

"Okay, I admit I don't especially want to be black either. But my reason is based on social and economic disadvantages, not prejudice. I think I can be objective about it."

"So can I, but being objective doesn't *change* anything. I mean, if white Americans balk at the thought of being African-American, isn't that a pretty good indicator that we still haven't resolved the equality issue?"

"Honey, none of this is new."

"I know. But now it's become personal."

Will got out of his squad car and stood in front of Obadiah's Barbecue, which was illuminated by the headlights of two police cruisers. He saw broken glass all over the ground and a jagged, gaping hole where the front window had been.

Jack Rutgers motioned to him. "Chief, come take a look at this."

Will went over and stood next to Jack and saw the image of a burning cross on the outside of the door. "Is it *painted* on there?"

"Yeah. Looks like even the Klan is cutting back on expenses."

Will shook his head. "The KKK is too arrogant to change its signature. Somebody's messing with us." Will moved closer and examined the artwork. "It's not completely dry. Did dispatch say who called it in?"

"The caller was male and wouldn't give his name."

"Probably because he did it," Will said. "What are the odds that anyone else would've been down here to notice that broken window? It's pitch-black on this block, and everything shuts down after 8:00 p.m."

"Obadiah's has been here as long as I can remember," Jack said. "My dad used to bring me here after every ball game when I was a kid. I think the same black fella still owns it. He must be ancient now."

"Well, let's hope he's not too scared to hang on to it after this."

Will glanced over at the officers gathering evidence and taking pictures and noticed that the two media vans that had been at the church were now parked across the street.

"Jack, check and see if dispatch can get the caller's phone number. I'll go try to keep those reporters from turning back the clock to the sixties."

15

Brandon Jones awakened to the sound of muffled voices and remembered he was in the guest bedroom at his parents' home. He saw sunlight coming through the crack in the drapes and glanced at the clock. It was ten after nine. He hadn't left the beach until almost four.

He sat up on the side of the bed and combed his hands through his hair. Just before he fell asleep, he had decided that today he would talk to the press, walk over to Seaport Auto Glass and pick up his car, and then spend the afternoon visiting his grandfathers.

Brandon got up and stepped into the shower and let the warm water relax his tight muscles. He was acutely aware that he was going to have to confront his job situation even though he was no closer to finding a career direction than when he arrived here. He would gladly take a summer job waiting tables just for something to do, but knew he would have to deal with his father's reaction and didn't know if he had the energy or the self-confidence.

He put on khakis and a green polo shirt and went downstairs to the kitchen, glad to see two bran muffins and a thermos of hot coffee waiting for him on the breakfast bar with a note:

Brandon,

Your dad's working in his study all day today. I'm going down to the beach to watch the sunrise and then stopping at Mina Tehrani's to take her some bran muffins and visit for a while. You need to watch CNN headline news <u>before</u> you return the calls to the media. There were more racial incidents in Seaport last night.

Love, Mom

Brandon glanced at his watch and grabbed a muffin and a cup of coffee, then went in the living room and turned on the TV. *Headline News* was already half over, and he wondered if he had missed whatever it was his mother wanted him to see.

"…The same insurgent group claimed responsibility for a car bomb that exploded outside Kirkuk, killing four Iraqi soldiers and six U.S. marines and injuring thirteen civilians, including three-year-old twin boys. This is the fourth insurgent attack this month.

"Authorities in Seaport, Florida, still have made no arrests following a rash of attacks against African-Americans in that town. Police have received numerous reports of slashed tires and smashed car windows, and one report by an African-American female, who told police her car was forced off the road and down an embankment.

"And in the predawn hours this morning, police were dispatched to the Mt. Zion Holiness Church, where a tall wooden cross, which has been displayed for years on the front lawn of the church property, had been set ablaze. A short time later, police were dispatched to Obadiah's Barbecue five blocks from the church, where the plate glass window had been smashed and a burning cross painted on the front door.

"Seaport Police Chief Will Seevers told CNN that he does not believe the racial attacks are the work of the Ku Klux Klan, which has not been active there since the seventies. But he also acknowledged that his department has made no arrests, which is drawing criticism from leaders in the African-American community and the NAACP, who allege that the police department is not taking the attacks seriously enough.

"In London today, members of Parliament voted to…"

Brandon turned off the TV and walked down the hall to the study and knocked on the door.

"Dad, could I talk to you for a minute?"

"Sure, come in."

Brandon went inside and sat in the chair next to his father's desk. "I just watched *Headlines News* and heard about the racial stuff that happened last night. This is getting ridiculous. How'd you and Mom find out about it?"

"Will asked Gordy to call and fill us in. He wants you and Weezie and the clinic volunteers to be extra careful till he can get to the bottom of what's going on."

Brandon looked out the window and shook his head. "I thought cross burning was a thing of the past."

"I think we all did. Gordy said Will thinks it's a few troublemakers trying to ride the Klan's coattails."

"It's really sick. I guess I need to say something and get the media off my back. I'm supposed to pick my car up today. I think I'll take the afternoon and go see Granddad and Papa."

"Papa will be thrilled to see you. But Granddad won't know you."

"Yeah, Mom filled me in. I'm really sorry I wasn't here to help you guys when you were dealing with all that. I can't go back, but I'm ready to make it right."

"Good." Guy put down his pen and took off his reading glasses. "Have you finished fine-tuning your résumé?"

"More or less."

"I've been a little hard on you lately, and I want you to know that I'll help you any way I can. But I really think you need to make finding a new career path your number one priority."

"I will. I'm just burned out right now, and it's hard to think about going back to work. I'm not sure you can understand what that's like. All you've ever done is practice law, and you love it."

"That's true. But I do know how stressful it is to struggle with finances. Your mother and I did our share of that while I was in law school. It concerns me that you'll probably have to take a huge cut in salary at a time when you should be preparing to get married and start a family."

"Well, thanks to Kelsey that's not going to happen."

"I wouldn't write off that relationship just yet. She might be receptive after you get your feet on the ground again." His father's eyes seemed to search his. "Your mother said you've been seeing a lot of Weezie lately."

Brandon closed his eyes and shook his head. "What is it with everyone? First the police, then Mom, and now you. I've seen Weezie all of three times and always in a public place. She's smart and wise and has a refreshing perspective on things I'm interested in right now.

I enjoy listening to her. There's absolutely nothing wrong with that."

"All right. But *someone* obviously thinks there is—enough to threaten you."

"So I'm expected to sever all ties with Weezie just because some racist boneheads say I have to and because Mom's afraid it might lead to some kind of emotional intimacy I don't even understand?"

"No one expects you to sever ties with her, son. But it doesn't seem prudent to pursue a friendship with her either."

"All I want is to discover why the woman is so content with her life. She's got the best outlook of anyone I know. I can learn a lot from her."

Guy arched his eyebrows. "Not if you're dead."

Gordy Jameson sat at an umbrella table on the back deck of the crab shack eating lunch with Eddie Drummond, Captain Jack, and Adam Spalding. The racial tension in town was big news, and that's all the guys had talked about since they arrived.

"Wouldn't surprise *me* if the Klan was doing this," Eddie said. "Could be that a second generation feels the same way about blacks as their parents did."

Captain popped a hush puppy into his mouth. "But why lash out at blacks now after the race situation has steadily improved since the sixties?"

"Not everything's improved," Adam said. "The percentage of crimes committed by blacks is disproportionate and on the rise. And the majority of the poor in this country are African-American. That creates a lot of tension on both sides."

Eddie rolled his eyes. "It's their own fault they can't get ahead. Everyone knows they have a lousy work ethic."

"That's so ignorant," Gordy said. "Weezie's the best employee I've ever had, hands down. All she needed was a chance."

Adam nodded. "That's right."

"Okay, rich boy," Eddie said. "Then why don't you take some of your bazillion bucks and create some 'chances' just for blacks?"

"My family's companies have created hundreds of thousands of jobs, Eddie. And I'm sure many of them went to African-Americans.

You might want to knock that chip off your shoulder. You're always bellyaching about the rich, but do you know anyone who's working for a poor man?"

Eddie dismissed him with a wave of his hand. "I wonder how Weezie feels about what's happening. Sometimes I almost forget she's black. Too bad they're not all like her."

"On the other hand, I'm sure blacks are grateful that all whites aren't like *you*." Captain laughed and pitched at ice cube at Eddie.

Gordy took a sip of limeade and wondered what the conversation would be like at lunch tomorrow after the guys had seen Weezie on the evening news.

Brandon shut the door on his Xterra and walked in the front entrance of Sea Gate, the assisted living facility where his paternal grandfather lived. He walked past the fountain in the courtyard and down the hall to room 107. He stood outside the open door and knocked gently. What if his grandfather was angry that he hadn't been in touch for so long? Maybe he should have called first.

Roland Jones looked up from his easy chair, his lenses thicker and his gray hair thinner than the last time Brandon had seen him.

"Papa, it's me, Brandon."

The old man stared blankly for a couple seconds, then said, "Well, for heaven's sake…I—I almost didn't recognize you. Guy said you were coming to visit, but I didn't know you were already here."

Brandon went in the room and squatted next to the easy chair and covered his grandfather's bony hand with his own. "I'm sorry I haven't been in touch for a while. It's great to see you."

"Well, same here. Stand up and let me get a good look at you."

Brandon stood up straight and took a big step backward. "Can you believe I'm thirty? Not exactly the skinny little kid you used to take hiking on Mount Reagan, eh?"

"Doesn't seem all that long ago," Roland said. "I guess you're still living in Raleigh and engaged to that sweet young lady Guy and Ellen are so crazy about?"

"Actually I'm not." Brandon sat on the side of the bed, his hands clasped between his knees, and explained that he had quit his job, that the wedding was off, and that he had moved in with his parents until he could decide what he wanted to do with his life.

"Sounds like an awful lot to think about all at the same time," Roland said.

"Well, now you know what I've been doing. Tell me about this place. Seems really nice."

"It's grown on me quite a bit. I've got my group of cronies to play cards with and a few that still enjoy chess. I'm big on news and sports, so I stay busy. I feel real bad about Lawrence, though. I hear he doesn't know your folks anymore."

"Yeah, his Alzheimer's has gotten bad. I'm going to stop by and see him later… Papa, you said you're big on news. Have you been keeping up with the racial stuff that's going on?"

"Actually, our TV's been in the shop for a few days. I think they got it back today, but I haven't been down to the rec room to watch anything. I listened to the ball game on the radio this afternoon."

Brandon smiled. "Those Marlins are sure hot."

"Yeah, eight wins in a row and still going strong. Your brother's become quite a fan."

"That's what I heard. Papa, listen…I need to give you a heads-up about some things because you're liable to see me on the news."

Roland's wiry white eyebrows met in the middle. "You in trouble?"

"No. Not with the law, anyway." He told his grandfather everything that had happened from the time Weezie got hit in the head with a rock until he finally spoke with the media just a few hours ago.

"Good heavens, boy. I know Weezie. I've eaten at Gordy's with your folks a number of times. This is downright criminal, that's all there is to it."

"I'm sure WRGL News is going to run at least part of what I told them at six and eleven. Not exactly my idea of a television debut."

Roland shook his head from side to side. "Hard to believe there's still people around with that kind of hate. I don't suppose I ever told you, but way back when, the KKK had a chapter in our town. In fact, your grandmother and I knew a couple Klansmen personally."

"You did?"

"Oh, sure. One was a neighbor—a fireman, actually. The other owned the corner drugstore. We never felt the same about them after we found out. But in those days, it was dangerous to be an enemy of the Klan, so most people stayed out of their way. They did their dirty work in secret anyway, so we didn't hear all that much. But there was a lynching once—a colored man accused of raping a white nurse at the hospital. Our neighbor was arrested along with a few other Klansmen, but they never stood trial for his murder. I was just grateful they didn't try to hire me to represent them because I know I couldn't have done that."

"The police chief doesn't think the Klan is active here anymore."

"He might be surprised what goes on behind closed doors. They're a sneaky lot. That's for sure."

"I just wish I could remember what those guys at Java's looked like. I'm not even sure I'd know them if I saw them again."

"Well, let's hope you don't."

Will Seevers sat at the table in his office, going through all the files related to the case. He heard a knock at the door and looked up just as Al Backus walked in, his five o'clock shadow almost as dark as the circles under his eyes.

"Okay, we paid Jessica Ziegler a visit at her work," Al said. "If she knows something, she's putting on a good act. She volunteered to let us check out her phone records, and there's nothing suspicious on there. The woman bent over backward to cooperate." Al pulled out a chair and sat across from Will. "Only one thing doesn't jibe: She denied placing a phone call after Sanders and Botts left the bar last night. She says the bartender must've had her mixed up with someone else, that she went to the ladies' room and then went out the back entrance with some one-night stand named Joey."

"Did Joey confirm that?"

"No. Jessica didn't ask his last name and says he left around 6:30 this morning. None of the neighbors remember seeing her come home or the guy leave."

"So all we've really got thus far is a small chunk of wood from the Louisville Slugger and the threatening note that our handwriting analyst thinks was written by an arrogant, angry, and potentially violent perp."

"Who's right-handed and has a badly chipped ball bat or a buddy who does. And possibly drives a dark blue or black late-model truck."

Will leaned back in his chair, his arms folded across his chest. "I've never known a racist who could keep from shooting off his mouth. I want you to keep working the bars—talk to more of the regular customers and see if that leads anywhere. It might be a dead end, but it's the only thing we've got. I'm thinking it's time for me to call in a favor and get Sheriff Martin to loan us a couple of deputies. Frankly, it'd be nice not to be the only law enforcement official being slammed in the media."

16

B randon Jones jumped up from the couch and went across the
hall to the kitchen door. "Mom, the news is coming on."

"Okay, I'll be right there." Ellen Jones dried her hands
and went into the living room and sat on the couch next to Guy.

"Good evening, I'm Stephen Rounds."

"And I'm Shannon Pate. Welcome to *Regional News at Six*. Seaport
police still have made no arrests this evening after a string of frightening attacks have left the African-American community reeling. If
there was any doubt that the incidents were racially motivated, last
night's cross burning at the oldest black church in the city should
remove all doubt…"

Brandon's mind wandered back to this afternoon's interview with
WRGL News, and he tried to remember what he had said. What if
the reporter took his comments out of context? Or his parents didn't
approve of what he said? Or the guy who smashed his car windows
decided to come at him again and do something worse?

"…Earlier today, WRGL reporter Jared Downing met with two of
the victims, RuWeeza Taylor of Seaport and Brandon Jones of Raleigh,
who agreed to be interviewed on camera."

Brandon grabbed the remote and turned up the sound. "Jared
Downing never mentioned he interviewed Weezie."

"Shannon, we reported earlier in the week that these two friends
were at Java's Coffee Shop around 1:15 a.m. Tuesday and were harassed by half a dozen Caucasian males making racially inappropriate
gestures at Ms. Taylor. The men left almost as quickly as they had
appeared. And just after 2:00 a.m., Mr. Jones and Ms. Taylor parted
company and left Java's in separate vehicles, unaware that each had
been followed…"

The scene switched to Weezie, and it looked to Brandon as if she might have been sitting in a booth at the crab shack, but the menus had been removed and it was difficult to tell.

"RuWeeza, we've heard about your terrifying experience of seeing those headlights closing in on you from behind. What did you think was happening?"

"At first I thought the vehicle was gonna pass me. But the second it hit my bumper, I knew I was in trouble and there wasn't anything I could do. The next thing I knew, the vehicle sped up and forced my car off the road and straight down an embankment."

"What was going through your mind?"

"I can't remember thinkin' anything till I hit bottom. Then I was prayin' that whoever did it would just keep on goin' and not come back lookin' for me. I stayed in my car because I knew I'd never be able to climb up that steep hill in the dark."

"How long before you were found?"

"Four hours."

"What were you thinking about all that time?"

"I was rackin' my brain, tryin' to figure out who'd wanna hurt me, but I really didn't know. Finally I just sang hymns till I got sleepy. The Lord was with me."

"How did you react when you learned the incident was racially motivated?"

"I was sad. And sorry for whoever did it. Must be awful to be swallowed up with hate. To me, that's worse than what happened to me."

"But aren't you angry that someone had such little regard for your life?"

"I was. I let it go."

"It doesn't matter to you anymore?"

"Sure it matters. But I won't let this thing eat at me till I get bitter. I had no choice about what was done to me, but it's totally my choice how I respond to it. I've forgiven whoever did it and asked the Lord to bless him and change his heart. I was at peace before this happened, and I'm not gonna let this thing rob me of that."

"You have an amazing attitude considering the harrowing ordeal you've just been through. I'm not sure many victims of a hate crime would be willing to forgive so readily."

"Well, it's what the Bible teaches and what I believe."

The camera switched back to Jared Downing live.

"Shannon, I also spoke with Brandon Jones of Raleigh who's here visiting his parents. After Brandon parted company with RuWeeza at Java's, he drove back to his parents' home. About thirty minutes later, he heard glass breaking and ran outside and saw a man smashing his car windows with what appeared to be a baseball bat…"

The scene switched to Brandon sitting on the front steps of his parents' home.

"Brandon, what went through your mind when you saw the man smashing your car windows?"

"I had this uneasy feeling it might be one of the guys who'd harassed us at Java's earlier. Since I'm just visiting here and hardly know anyone, that's the only thing that made sense."

"So you think you were targeted because you were with a black woman?"

"Yes, that's exactly what I think, especially after what happened to RuWeeza."

"Are you angry?"

"You bet I am. She could've been killed. And it's unconscionable that in twenty-first-century America either of us were victimized just for having coffee with someone of a different race and gender."

"Are you satisfied that the police are doing everything they can to find out who did this?"

"Absolutely."

"Are you aware of the mounting criticism that suggests otherwise?"

"Yes, but I don't want the police pressured into arresting the wrong person just because the public wants someone held accountable. What good is an arrest if justice isn't served?"

"What would you like to say to the man who smashed your car windows?"

"Nothing. There's no way to reason with a racist."

"How has this changed you, Brandon—or has it?"

"It definitely *will*, though I'm still trying to process the whole thing. I can tell you that being a victim was an experience I don't care to repeat. And it's caused me to do some soul-searching about the times I've blown off the black community's allegations of racism.

Until you're the victim, it's easy to believe racism isn't a problem."

"I appreciate you talking with me, Brandon. You've given us something to think about.

"So there you have it from the perspective of two of the victims of these attacks. And it doesn't appear this issue is going to go away anytime soon. This is Jared Downing. Back to you, Shannon."

"Thanks, Jared. We'll keep our fingers on the pulse of this story and bring our viewers new developments as they happen.

"In Tallahassee today, legislators—"

Guy turned off the TV and turned to Brandon. "You did a good job, son."

"Thanks. It sounded better than I thought it would. Jared cut out a lot. I admire what Weezie said about forgiving the guy, but I'm just not there yet."

"I doubt if many people are," Ellen said. "It was helpful to hear what you *both* had to say. Come on, dinner's ready. I'm anxious to hear about your visit with Papa and Granddad."

Will Seevers turned off the TV in his office and sat staring out the window at the live oaks in front of city hall. He was vaguely aware of a knock at the door and then Gordy Jameson standing in front of his desk.

"I was on my way home and saw your car was still here," Gordy said. "What happened to Margaret's meat loaf night?"

"It's still on. I told her I'd be a little late. I wanted to catch the six o'clock news first and see if I needed to say anything to the media before I leave."

"And do you?"

Will shook his head. "Weezie and Brandon both did a good job. I don't need to add anything."

"I haven't had a chance to watch the news yet, but I was there when Jared Downing interviewed Weezie this morning. Other than her soundin' more forgivin' than those bozos deserve, I thought she came across well."

"Frankly, what she had to say may have let some of the steam out of the racial pressure that's building up. The NAACP is crazed over the cross burning incident. I need all the help I can get to keep the black community from panicking."

Gordy went over to the window. "The crowd's bigger than it was last night."

"Yep. And everyone out there wants the case solved *yesterday*."

"Have you got any solid evidence?"

"Only that at least two guys in a black pickup are involved in at least *some* of what's going on. But nothing about last night's episodes is consistent with the Klan's MO, even though that seems to be what they want people to think."

"Could it be some kinda rival gang statement, what with graffiti painted on the door and all?"

"This was not graffiti, Gordy. The image didn't have symbols, threats, names, numbers, or territory indicators. Besides, most of the gang activity has moved over to Port Smyth." Will sighed. "So who the heck's doing this, and what's their game?"

Gordy came over and put his hand on Will's shoulder. "Why don't you go home and enjoy dinner with your family? Get your mind off this stuff for a few hours. It's gonna be here tomorrow."

"Yeah, I know. It's hard to shift gears with all the unknowns sitting on my gut."

Brandon took a second helping of his mother's shrimp pasta and passed the serving bowl to his father. "I'll tell you one thing, I was impressed with how alert Papa was."

"Yeah, he doesn't miss a trick," Guy said. "Sounds like you had a great visit. I thought for sure I had told you that your grandparents knew some KKK members way back."

Brandon shrugged. "If you did, I don't remember it. Anyhow, it was interesting visiting with him, and he seemed as glad to see me as I was to see him."

"Of course he was," Ellen said. "Thanks for taking the time to stop by and see Granddad, too. I'm sorry it was disappointing, but I did forewarn you."

"I'm glad I went. It's really a nice facility, and they seem to be taking good care of him. He asked where *Ellie* was. I never heard him call you that before."

Ellen smiled faintly, a faraway look in her eyes. "He did when I was a little girl. Sometimes he thinks Annie is Ellie because she looks so much like I did. But he can't seem to put any of our names and faces together in the present tense."

The phone rang.

"I'll get it." Brandon pushed back his chair and went out to the kitchen. "Hello."

"Hey, little brother."

"Hi, Owen. What's up?"

"Saw you on the news. Thanks for not embarrassing the family."

Brandon chuckled. "Miracles never cease. But as far as I'm concerned, if I never say another word on camera, it'll be too soon."

"Yeah, I hear that. Listen, I have another reason for calling. A friend of mine in Kansas City is the CEO of a high-end children's clothing company and is looking for a branch sales manager. I'd be glad to put in a good word for you."

"That's really nice of you, but I'm looking into some things on my own."

"Pays seventy grand plus bonuses. Terrific benefits. Some traveling. I'm sure I could get you an interview. And Kansas City has some really beautiful neighborhoods. You ever been there?"

"No, I'm sure it's great. Thanks for offering, but like I said, I'm looking into some things on my own."

"Really, what?"

Brandon felt hot all over, and the inside of his mouth felt like cotton. "I'm sort of searching for a new career path, Owen. Didn't Dad tell you?"

"No. I guess he skipped that part. So what do you want to do?"

"I don't know yet, but I don't want to be in top management or in the apparel industry."

"Are you nuts? You were practically making six figures."

"Money's not my first concern." He could almost hear Owen smirking. "I don't expect you to understand where I'm coming from because you love your job. I mean, it's great that you get paid big bucks to do what you love. But I got paid big bucks to do what I hated, and it wasn't worth it."

"What was so horrible about it?"

"Lots of things, not the least of which was being confined to an office."

"Well, that eliminates most white-collar jobs. I guess you could always go to trade school. Kind of late in the game to start over, though."

"I already feel like a Class A loser because I don't know what I want to do. And I know Dad thinks I'm a big failure, so say what you have to say and get it over with."

"Hey, I'm not going to hassle you. It's your life. I just know you may never get another opportunity like the one you walked away from."

"Yeah, I know that, Owen. But guess what? I don't miss it and won't go back—not for any amount of money. I'm burned out. Fried. Finished. Do you get that?"

"Take it easy. I didn't mean to upset you. Maybe you should go talk to someone. Burnout can be serious."

"I don't need a shrink." Brandon put his hand on the back of his neck and rolled his head in a circle. "All I've done since I got here is deal with all this racial stuff. I need fresh air and time to think. I could kick myself for not bringing my backpacking and camping gear."

"I wish I had it to lend you. The only outdoor sport I'm into is golf, and you hate golf."

"I don't hate it. I just can't hit the hole."

Owen chuckled. "Neither can I."

There was a long moment of dead air.

"Brandon, listen…I'm here if you need me, okay? I promise not to hassle you. Let me know if there's anything I can do. I'm serious about that. I know I razz you a lot, but I have a lot of respect for what you accomplished at Mavis and Stein—even more so now that I know you didn't even enjoy what you were doing. There's no way I'm going to fault you after you gave it all you had. You're no loser."

Brandon blinked the stinging from his eyes. "Uh, listen, I need to get back to the table. We're in the middle of dinner. I'll talk to you soon, okay?"

"Yeah, hang in there. You'll get it all figured out."

17

On Friday morning, Brandon Jones left his parents' house at first light and walked down the hill to Seaport Beach. He sat cross-legged in the sand and listened to the gentle whoosh of the waves and the shrill peeping of sandpipers scurrying along the soggy sand in search of breakfast.

He slowly filled his lungs with damp, salty air and held it for a few seconds. How he wished he could pick up the remote and put this scene on pause and rest as long as he wanted. Why did life have to be so complicated? What was the purpose of all this beauty if the demands of life didn't allow people time to enjoy it?

Off to the east, he noticed the sky was starting to look orangey pink. Soon the sun would be up, and the pace of life would increase to fast-forward. What was the point? Did God put people here just to grow up, get a job, raise a family, and leave some sort of legacy for their kids? If so, what did that mean for those who never married or never had kids? Or people who were crippled or sick or unable to contribute anything at all? Things certainly didn't seem equal.

"Hi, you."

Brandon looked up and saw his mother standing there, dressed in jogging clothes and running shoes. "I'm surprised you can get cranked up to go running this early."

Ellen Jones smiled. "If my only motivation was exercising, I'd probably procrastinate. But watching the sun come up surrounded by all this beauty puts me in an attitude of praise like nothing else. I can hardly stand to miss a day."

"I know what you mean. Sometimes seeing something beautiful in nature makes me feel closer to God than when I'm in church. Why is that?"

"Maybe because the Creator's fingerprints are all over it." Ellen dropped down in the sand next to him. "You've always had an affinity with nature, even when you were little. You spent nearly every summer night camped out in the backyard in spite of the mosquitoes and the heat and the fact that your brother abandoned the pup tent for the comfort of his air-conditioned room."

Brandon chuckled. "Owen wasn't about to admit he was afraid of the dark or that the skunk that sprayed the neighbor's beagle might crawl in his sleeping bag. I wonder whatever happened to the journal I kept?"

"It's in the cedar chest."

"I'd like to look through it sometime. Wow, would you look at that sky? I can't believe more people don't come out here to see this."

"Remember the time you and I watched the sunrise in Colorado?"

"I do. We were on vacation and had rented a cabin by some mountain stream."

Ellen nodded. "Guy and Owen slept in, but you and I climbed up on that big boulder and huddled together under a wool blanket. We drank hot chocolate and waited for the sun to come up. The entire mountain turned hot pink before our very eyes. I'd never seen anything like it before."

"Yeah, I remember when I told Owen about it, he made some comment about pink being a girl's color. He and I have never looked at things the same way."

Brandon lifted his eyes and was silenced by the beauty of the sunrise. He watched until the sun had cleared the horizon and then turned to his mother. "Is that not cool?"

"Yes, *way* cool, I'd say."

Brandon chuckled to himself at how funny that sounded coming from her. He sensed she was meditating, so he sat quietly for a few minutes and just enjoyed the closeness.

Finally she patted his knee. "Well, I've invaded your space long enough. I guess I'll go run my three miles before it gets hot."

"Mom...can I ask you a personal question?"

"Sure."

"Do you consider yourself happy?"

She paused and then turned to him. "If you mean content, yes. If you mean void of sadness, no."

"What do you have to be sad about?"

"Oh, honey, everyone has sad things to contend with. It makes me sad that Granddad can't remember and can't communicate anymore. I'm sad that Owen and Annie still have flashbacks of Tim's suicide. I'm sad that my neighbor has cancer and my friend had a miscarriage. I'm sad that you and Kelsey broke up and that you and Weezie and the others were victims of racism. I could go on and on."

"How can you say you're content if all that's weighing on you?"

"Well, for one thing, I have many blessings, too, and I try not to dwell on things that disappoint me. But I also have a deep sense of knowing that I'm loved by God and part of His plan and that nothing can separate me from Him—ever." Ellen held his gaze and seemed to be probing his thoughts. "Brandon, why don't you tell me what's really behind that question?"

"I don't feel like I really belong anywhere."

"Of course you do. You're a loved and valued member of the family. And you're part of God's family for all eternity. You can't *belong* any more than that."

Brandon sighed. "I know all that with my head, but my heart feels empty. I miss Kelsey so much. I don't have any sense of direction and don't even know where to begin looking for it. It's as though my life is pointless."

"It's hard to see clearly when you're grieving. But God has a plan for your life. And just because you've lost your bearings doesn't mean you're off course. In fact, I firmly believe God has planned even the storms we go through."

"That's not encouraging."

"It is if you realize He's reshaping your character for something He planned for you to accomplish even before you were born."

"Before I was born? Where'd you come up with that?"

"Ephesians 2:10 tells us that believers are God's workmanship, created in Christ Jesus to do good works that God prepared *in advance* for us to do. I find that extremely encouraging."

"How am I supposed to know what those good works are?"

His mother reached over and put her hand on his. "I'm not sure you are. I think our job as believers is to empty ourselves of our own wants and desires and let God fill us with more of His. We start by studying His Word and walking with Him day by day. I think it's in that process of being transformed that we become pliable and useful for His purposes."

Brandon looked out across the rippled waters of the gulf. "It sounds so hard. You know I don't understand all that."

"All you really need to understand is that God wants to fill your emptiness with Himself. This seems like a perfect time to let Him teach you what that means."

"How do I do that?"

"Why don't you ask Him?"

Gordy Jameson stood at the front counter at the crab shack, changing the register tape. He felt a blast of warm, moist air and looked up into the face of Weezie Taylor.

"What are you doin' here so early?"

"I can't stay alone in that house another minute with all that junk food screamin' at me from the pantry. You know how hard I worked to get back in shape. Boredom is hazardous to my well-being."

"So's goin' home right now. You can't close at night and then come back here in the morning and start workin' again. You need some relaxation. Can't you just hang out at our place and watch soap operas or somethin'?"

Weezie put her hand on her hip. "You think soap operas are re-laxin'? I'll have you know there's not a single commandment that has not been broken right there on camera. It's like peekin' in on Sodom and Gomorrah, only with commercial breaks. If I wasn't black, I'd surely be red in the face. You know what I'm sayin'?"

Gordy threw his hands up. "All right, Weezie, spare me the drama. You can stay."

"Thank you."

"We've got a group of twenty-four comin' in at seven. Go take inventory and order us some fresh fish. Make sure we've got plenty of shrimp and crab, too."

Weezie nodded. "I'll work on the scheduling, too, and then help with the lunch crowd so you can eat with the fellas."

"All right. By the way, you haven't said much about your interview yesterday. Pam and I thought it was good."

"Thanks. I sure hope no one misinterprets what I said, because what's happened *does* matter, and I hope Will Seevers gets whoever's doin' it off the street. I'm just not gonna allow it to consume me."

"I think that came through loud and clear." Gordy lifted his eyebrows. "Have you thought about how you're gonna answer questions around here? I'm sure lots of our customers recognized you on the news."

"I'm not rehearsin' any pat answers. I'll just tell the truth. But I hope the talk dies down quickly so I can stop thinkin' about it and get back to my life and my own house."

Gordy put his hand on his heart. "I'm crushed that you wanna leave us."

Weezie laughed. "We both know that's not true, but you're sweet to say so. I've really appreciated you and Pam takin' me in for a few days."

"Well, you know you're welcome to stay as long as you want."

"Thanks. Let's see how things go in the next day or two."

Will Seevers sat on a wrought-iron bench in Bougainvillea Park, glad to have evaded the media and thinking about how little evidence his department had gathered. One lousy wood chip and a threatening note with no fingerprints. He took a bite of his sub sandwich and resisted the urge to call Margaret and boast that there were only six grams of fat in it. He felt his phone vibrate and took it off his belt clip. "Seevers."

"It's me," Al Backus said. "The lab says the brand of paint used on the door could've been purchased at almost any store that carries art supplies. We're checking around town. Maybe our perp bought his paint recently and something about him stood out like a sore thumb."

"I could handle a break like that."

"Also, the tire tracks in front of the church are consistent with tires that come standard on two different models of Ford trucks in 2005 and 2006. We're now in the process of determining if any of those makes and models in dark blue and black are registered to convicted felons. It's a long shot, but you never know. It might lead somewhere."

"Okay, Al. Keep digging."

Will put his phone back on the clip and took another bite of his sandwich. He couldn't get Jessica Ziegler out of his mind. Why was the bartender so sure she had placed a call on a borrowed cell phone and Jessica so adamant that he was wrong? It was possible she was telling the truth, but the bartenders he had known were sticklers for detail.

Will's phone vibrated again. "Will Seevers."

"Chief, it's Jack Rutgers. Thought you ought to know that I responded to a vandalism call from the Mt. Zion Holiness Church. The pastor reported that someone spray-painted two big Ws on the front lawn where the cross was torched. Must've happened sometime last night. I got pictures and samples of the paint and a cast of one partial shoe print that was clear as a bell in the wet dirt. Looks like an athletic shoe."

"Anybody see anything?"

"No. I talked to several neighbors, including Joseph Lewis, the neighbor who saw the two perps who set the cross on fire. He didn't see or hear anything unusual last night. Says he's a light sleeper and would've heard a vehicle pull up."

"Might've been a bunch of kids messing with our crime scene."

"Could be, but looks like they've been busy."

"What do you mean?"

"I just pulled up in front of Obadiah's Barbecue. Wanna guess what's spray-painted on the taped up window?"

18

Will Seevers stuffed the last of a Snickers bar into his mouth and stepped over to the window in his office. He looked out at the growing media presence and NAACP supporters in front of city hall and squinted until he could make out the words on one of the protest signs: *Blacks beware—Cops don't care.* He wadded up the empty candy bar wrapper and threw it at the trash can and missed.

His cell phone rang, and he took it off his belt clip. "Seevers."

"Chief, it's Al Backus. We've been to each of the crime scenes, and you're not going to believe how busy our perp's been. I'm a couple blocks from the station and was checking to see if you're back."

"Yeah, I'm in my office."

"Great. I'll bring you the pictures. Be there in ten."

Will disconnected the call and sat at his desk, thinking that unless Al was one step closer to making an arrest, the press was going to make mincemeat of the department's investigation. His mind raced through all the details still dangling. What he wouldn't give to be able to tie up some loose ends.

He glanced at his watch and then dialed his home number.

"Hello."

"Hi, honey. How's your day going?"

"Oh, fine," Margaret Seevers said. "I've been running errands and am about to tackle the laundry. Meagan called a few minutes ago, absolutely giddy. She got picked to play Liesl in *The Sound of Music* at the Summer Civic Theatre."

"That's terrific! Why don't we take her to Sudsy's to celebrate? We haven't done that in a while."

"Sudsy's?" There was a smile in Margaret's voice.

"Something wrong with that?"

"Will, she's fifteen. She wouldn't be caught dead in that place anymore. Why don't we take her to the mall and let her pick out some fun accessories or something? She's had her eye on a really cute designer watch at Baldwin's."

"Yeah, okay. You're probably right. It's so hard to accept that she's not a little girl anymore. I don't want her to grow up so fast."

"Me either. So how's the investigation coming?"

Will looked up and saw Al Backus standing in the doorway with a manila envelope in his hand and motioned for him to come in.

"Uh, we had a new development this morning. Listen, honey, Al just walked in and I need to go. Turn on WRGL at four. I'm doing a press conference outside city hall. That'll catch you up on what's going on."

"Okay, Chief. Go get 'em. I'm making low-fat chicken and dumplings for dinner. Come hungry."

"Great, then I'll still have a reason to live if I blow the news conference. See you around six thirty. I love you."

"Love you, too."

Will hung up the phone and walked over and sat at the table where Al had laid out several rows of photographs.

"Okay," Al said. "Here's what we know. All the Ws we found were written in white spray paint and appeared in duplicate. Though the size and placement of the letters varied from location to location, the style didn't, so we're probably looking at a single writer. The letters don't fit the profile of gang graffiti since there's no symbolic language or territory distinction. My guess is they're initials of some kind—either an individual's or a group's.

Al pointed to the set of photos at the top. "These show the front lawn of Mt. Zion Holiness Church. The two Ws are each approximately four feet in height and about the same in width. This next set shows the window on the barbecue joint; the letters are considerably smaller, though the style's consistent. This third set shows the letters painted on the roadway at the site where Weezie Taylor's car was forced off. The fourth set of letters was painted on the newly repaired back window of Brandon Jones's SUV. The fifth set was painted on the back window of the doctor's Lexus. And the sixth set was painted on the right front tire of the nurse's car."

Will shook his head. "So somebody actually went back *after* the fact and left his signature at each crime scene? How do we know it's not some kind of stunt?"

"We don't. But whoever did it knew exactly where to put the letters, right down to the exact spot where Weezie Taylor was forced off the road. We never released the exact location."

"Anybody could've seen the downed guardrail. Did you check her home?"

"Yeah. We didn't find any letters painted on the house."

Will rested his elbows on the table, his chin on his palms, and let his eyes move across the line of photographs showing the two Ws at each crime scene. "Al, when you finish compiling your list of felons who've registered a black or dark blue Ford truck fitting the profile, be sure to note whether any of them have Ws for initials."

"Don't worry, I'm already on it."

Gordy hung up the phone and went out to the dining room, where Weezie was schmoozing with customers. He smiled at the sound of her laughter and realized how much he had missed it during the past couple days. He waited until he could make eye contact with her and then nodded a couple times toward his office. When she gave a slight nod in return, Gordy went back into his office and sat at his desk.

About a minute later, Weezie came in and pulled a chair next to his. "What's up?"

"Will just called, and there's been a weird development."

Gordy relayed to Weezie every detail Will had given him concerning the two Ws that had been painted at each crime scene, including on the highway where her car had been forced off. "I know you're anxious to go home, but this thing isn't over."

"But it's a good sign that no Ws got painted on my house. I doubt whoever ran me off the road even knows where I live."

"You can't be sure of that."

"Well, whoever's doin' this hasn't bothered any of the victims again, other than to mark his territory like some arrogant lion struttin' his stuff."

Gordy folded his hands on the desk and looked intently at her, his eyebrows scrunched. "Weezie, I want you to stay with me and Pam until Will gets these scumbags. I know you feel uprooted and all, but you're safe with us. You'd be takin' a risk goin' home, and I wouldn't sleep a wink worryin' about you being alone out there. If you won't do it for yourself, do it for me. Please?"

"You're makin' it hard to say no."

"Only because I care about you. Shoot, Weezie, you're the closest thing to a sister I've ever had. I doubt this place would even be here if you hadn't held it together. You got me through a very rocky time after Jenny died. And as far as I'm concerned, you're family. Pam feels the same way."

"You've both been awful good to me."

"Then whaddya say we change our shifts around? I'll work late a few nights and give you a chance to hang out with Pam. That way you won't be workin' day *and* night. I promise to get all the junk food out of the house so you won't be tempted to fall off the wagon. I'll even dump what's left of my peach ice cream down the disposal."

Weezie's eyes widened. "You haven't gone a day without peach ice cream since I've known you. I can't believe you'd be willin' to change your entire routine just to get me to stay at your place."

"Well, I'm not gonna be worth a hoot if somethin' happens to you."

Weezie reached over and squeezed his hand. "Well then, I guess we'd better stick together through this thing."

Brandon Jones walked in his parents' house and slammed the front door hard enough to rattle the crystal teardrops on the chandelier in the entry hall. He cringed when he heard his father's footsteps coming down the hall and realized it was too late to walk the other way.

"I know you're disgusted about your car," Guy Jones said, "but don't take it out on the house."

"Sorry…I told Papa I'd come see him this afternoon, but I'm sure as heck not driving my car with that creep's initials on it! The police asked me not to remove the paint until they get back to me—which, of course, they haven't done. I'm so sick of being at the mercy of everyone else! I just want my life back."

Guy lifted his eyebrows. "Then why don't you start sending out your résumé? The sooner you're gainfully employed, the sooner you can be independent again. Owen mentioned that someone he knew in Kansas City was looking for a branch sales manager. Did he talk to you about it?"

"Yeah, he did."

"And...?"

"It's not what I'm looking for." Brandon tried to relax the frown he could feel tightening his forehead. "Dad, please don't make me defend myself. I've never been this burned out before, and I need time to clear my head and figure some things out."

"And just how much time do you think you can you afford to take?"

"I don't know. But I'll tell you what I can't afford to do, and that's make another career decision to please everyone else!" *I can't believe I just said that.*

"What are you talking about?"

"Nothing. Forget it. I need to go move those plants Mom asked me to set outside."

Guy put his hand on Brandon's shoulder and held him back. "I asked you a question. Are you implying that you went to work for Mavis and Stein just because your mother and I wanted you to?"

"It doesn't matter. That was a long time ago."

"I think it does, and you still haven't answered my question."

Brandon turned around, his hands in his pockets, and stared at his shoes. "Look, Dad, I had no idea what I wanted to do with my life when I graduated from college. I needed a job and going to work for M and S in catalog sales earned me a paycheck. That was my choice, but..."

"But *what*? Finish your sentence."

Brandon lifted his eyes and looked at his dad, and the words just seemed to spill out of his mouth. "But each time I got offered a promotion, I felt pressured to either accept it or live with the awful worthlessness I feel anytime I don't measure up to your expectations! So I chose the path of least resistance, but I can't do it anymore! I just can't."

Guy stared at him for a few seconds. "I'm not a mind reader, Brandon. I had no idea you had those feelings! Why didn't you come talk to me?"

"And say what—that I felt like a complete failure? I already knew what your gauge of success was, and taking on more responsibility so I could make bigger decisions and earn bigger bucks didn't do it for me! I tried to tell you a dozen ways, but you never listened!" Brandon paused and let the emotion pass and then said, "I shouldn't be talking to you about this when I'm upset about the car. This isn't coming out right."

"Or maybe you're finally mad enough to get honest with me!"

Brandon stood with his eyes fixed on his father's face, unable to find his voice and aware of footsteps moving briskly in their direction.

"What's going on in here?" Ellen Jones said. "I could hear you two shouting clear out on the veranda."

"It's okay, honey." Guy put his hand on Ellen's shoulder. "Why don't you give Brandon and me a little space? This is between the two of us."

"Hardly," Ellen said. "I'm sure the whole neighborhood can hear you. I suggest you stop this conversation until you can speak in a civil tone and before you say something you'll regret."

Too late for that, Brandon thought.

An awkward silence descended on the three of them, and Brandon was aware of the ticking of the cuckoo clock in the kitchen and the wild pounding of his own heart.

"All right," Guy finally said. "I've got work to do. But I intend to finish this conversation before the end of the day."

Will Seevers stood at the microphone in front of city hall with Al Backus on one side of him and Sheriff Martin on the other, satisfied that he had given a complete and accurate accounting of where the investigation currently stood. "I'll be glad to answer a few questions." He pointed to a young man with dark glasses.

"Lyle Zimmer with the *Miami Herald*. Sir, it's now been ten days since this rash of racial attacks began, and you've been unable to make a single arrest. Why haven't you asked the FBI to assist you in this case?"

"Because we have no reason to believe that any of the crimes in question were committed by persons outside this community, much less outside the state. And my department, assisted by the Beacon County Sheriff's Department, is already doing absolutely everything possible to solve the case. I don't believe that bringing in another branch of law enforcement will hasten our ability to make an arrest." Will pointed to a redheaded lady waving a pen. "Yes…"

"Maggie Stephens, the *Pensacola Monitor*. I know this has been asked before, but I'd like to pose the question to you again in light of recent developments. Do you think the racial tension in Seaport has anything to do with the fact that hundreds of evacuees from Hurricane Katrina decided to stay here permanently?"

"I do not." Will pointed to a middle-aged African-American man with a neatly trimmed beard.

"Brian Scone, the *Tallahassee Democrat*. Sir, the black community has repeatedly accused your department of not taking these crimes seriously enough. What is your response to that? And would you have handled the case differently if your victims were white?"

"Let me remind you that one of our victims *is* white. The Seaport Police Department does not exhibit racial bias in dealing with victims. As for how seriously we're looking at this case: We eat, drink, and sleep with it. We're not going to let up until the person or persons responsible are brought to justice." Will pointed to a woman in a yellow dress, but the woman next to her took a step forward, and his heart sank when he realized who it was.

"Valerie Mink Hodges, the *North Coast Messenger*. Is it true that the Caucasian victim to whom you just made reference received a threat of bodily harm in the form of a note left on the front seat of his vehicle?"

"I'm not going to comment on what we have or don't have in the way of evidence while the investigation is ongoing." *How the heck did she hear about that?*

Valerie waved a piece of paper in the air. "Sir, I have a photocopy of that handwritten note. It most certainly is a threat, obviously intended to intimidate Mr. Jones from having any further contact with

Ms. Taylor. Why did you withhold this information? Don't people have the right to know if racial threats are being made? What else are you hiding from us?"

Will felt his face and neck get hot and tried not to frown or show any reaction. *She's bluffing. There's no way she got her hands on that note.* "Ms. Hodges, let me reiterate that I'm not going to comment on what we have or don't have in the way of evidence." Will pointed to a man in a striped shirt, but Valerie wouldn't stop talking.

"Chief Seevers, you said in an interview just two days ago that we shouldn't jump to the conclusion that we have a widespread hate crime problem going on here, but this kind of threat would seem to imply otherwise, don't you think?"

"The key word, Ms. Hodges, was *widespread*, and I still don't believe that's the case. Now let's move on and let someone else ask a question."

"Excuse me, but I'm not quite finished."

"Yes, Madam, I'm quite sure you *are*."

19

Will Seevers yanked open the side door of the police station and stormed down the hallway, Al Backus on his heels. He went into his office and flipped the light switch. "Shut the door and sit down."

Will paced in front of the window for a couple minutes, his mind shouting the angry words he hoped to be able to say to whoever had leaked the information about the note. Finally he went over to the desk and brought his fist down on it. "I want the name of every person who had access to that note when it was in your possession, Al. And that means anyone who handled the file or even went near your desk or breathed the same air!"

"You don't think for a minute that I—"

"No. If I didn't think I could trust you, I'd just as soon pack it up." Will hung his head, both palms on the desk, and shook his head. "If Valerie Hodges has a copy of the note, she won't waste any time publishing the contents. We already know this woman doesn't care whose toes she steps on. I want you to go talk to her and see if she's bluffing. Maybe she knows the gist of the note but not the actual wording. Find out."

Al rose to his feet. "Okay, let me get to the bottom of this. I'm as steamed about this as you are."

"I'm not sure that's possible."

"Before I go talk to that loudmouthed reporter, I'll check with the evidence officer and see if the note was ever signed out."

"We both know that's unlikely." Will leaned against the front of his desk, his arms folded tightly across his chest. "If Hodges prints the contents of that note, somebody's head is going to roll. I won't stand for anyone undermining the integrity of this department!"

"Maybe we don't have a leak. She might've gotten Weezie Taylor or Brandon Jones to tell her about the note. You know how sneaky and persuasive she is."

"Well, get out there and find out. I don't want any more surprises!"

Brandon Jones lay on the bed in the guest room at his parents' home, dreading the thought of another confrontation with his dad. He wondered if things could ever be the same between them after this.

Brandon heard footsteps coming up the stairs, and he sat up on the side of the bed, his heart racing. A few seconds later, his father appeared in the doorway.

"May I come in?" Guy said.

"Yeah, sure."

Guy stepped over the pair of khakis on the floor and sat in the overstuffed chair. "I'm sorry I raised my voice earlier. I'm not used to you talking to me in that tone."

"I know, Dad. I'm sorry, too. I'm feeling a little pushed and just went off. That's not what I wanted to happen."

"Well, I'm glad it did." Guy made a tent with his fingers. "We've been avoiding each other since I got home from Tallahassee, and I would much rather us get brutally honest and cut the game playing. Postponing confrontation is not usually my style anyway, but I haven't really known what else to say to you. I made it clear how I feel about your circumstances."

"Then why are you here?"

"Because I realized earlier that you hadn't made it clear to me how *you* felt. I had no idea you accepted those promotions merely because if you didn't, you would feel worthless for not living up to my expectations. Would you mind pointing out what I ever said or did to make you believe I thought you were worthless?"

Brandon stared at his hands. "It wasn't so much what you said as it was the look on your face. It just made me feel bad about myself. I can't explain it any better than that."

"You and your mother have a habit of letting your *feelings* determine your reality. I assure you, I've never once in my life thought you were worthless."

"Well, if you didn't before, I'm sure you do now."

Guy combed his hands through his hair. "Brandon, I don't think you're worthless. I think you're making a poor decision. There's a huge difference. My job as your father is to offer you wise counsel and steer you in what I see as the right direction. To do less wouldn't be loving, regardless of how much we disagree."

There's no way he's going to admit it, Brandon thought.

Guy sat forward in the chair, his hands clasped between his knees. "We're not going to resolve this if you clam up. Frankly, I was more comfortable with the conversation when you were good and mad. At least you were honest."

"And you think *you're* being completely honest?"

"Of course."

"You keep talking as if the choices I've made haven't affected how you look at me. I think you're kidding yourself."

Guy shook his head. "Will you stop trying to decide how I think? You're my son. I love you. I'm proud of the person you are, regardless of your circumstances."

"Then why did you give me the silent treatment after I told you I quit my job?"

"I was disappointed for you."

"Why? I was relieved."

"Maybe so, but I couldn't just ignore the amazing opportunity you walked away from, not to mention Kelsey. Look, I'm not saying I don't have high hopes for you, but your worth as my son isn't based on what I want you to be or not be."

"Then what *is* my worth based on, Dad? Because as long as I can remember, you've shut me out when I disappoint you. It always felt to me like your way of manipulating me into performing up to your standard. But I just can't do it anymore. I need to discover my own sense of self-worth."

Guy nodded. "That's something we agree on. So what's your plan?"

"I'm too burned out to know what I want to do, and it's not smart to jump into something before my heart's in it with me. I need some time to think it through."

"So you're just going to lie on the beach and meditate?"

Brandon threw his hands up. "Dad, that's exactly the attitude I'm talking about! You use sarcasm as a put-down." He paused and waited until the emotion passed. "I need the freedom to make my own decisions and even my own mistakes. I know you love me. But I want your respect, and I don't have it."

"I never said that."

"Okay, then go ahead and tell me how much you respect me."

Guy shifted his weight, his eyebrows furrowed.

"You can't say it because you don't."

"Son, I respect your sensitivity and strong character. You're much like your mother. I don't always understand your feelings, but I have a lot of respect for the fine person you've become. But I also respect ambition and hard work and results. I can't pretend I don't. I suppose that kind of respect *is* earned."

"So all I'm asking is that you allow me the space to earn your respect my way. As long as you're on my case to do it your way, we're going to have this conflict."

Guy sat quietly for a few moments, turning his wedding band on his finger and seeming to ponder Brandon's words. "All right. I'll work at being an encourager and not telling you what to do. If I slip up, you may have to remind me. Fair enough?"

The doorbell rang.

Brandon turned and craned his neck to see out the dormer window. "There's a squad car parked out front."

"Really?" Guy got up and stood with his palms on the windowsill. "That's not Will's car. I wonder what's going on." He turned to Brandon. "So are we okay now?"

"Yeah, Dad. We're cool."

"All right then. Let's go see what the police are doing here."

Brandon followed his dad down the stairs and out to the entry hall, where his mom was talking with a police officer he didn't recognize and whom she didn't seem particularly fond of.

"Investigator Backus," Guy said, "what brings you here? Has there been a break in the case?"

"Nothing yet, but there was a new development earlier today.

The chief held a press conference this afternoon, and Valerie Hodges, a reporter from the *Messenger*, questioned the chief about whether the police found a threatening note."

"How'd she know about that?" Brandon said. "The police told Weezie and me not to tell anyone."

Backus's bushy eyebrows met in the middle. "So you didn't talk to her?"

"No way. Besides, Mom said she's unethical."

"Yeah, that's one way to put it. Are you sure you didn't mention this to anyone else?"

"Absolutely. Mom and Dad and I talked about it among ourselves, but we haven't even told my brother and his wife."

Al looked at Ellen and then Guy. "I have to ask. Did you tell anyone?"

"Of course not," they answered at the same time.

"Have you asked Weezie?" Guy said.

"I just left Gordy's. Ms. Taylor said she hasn't told anyone except Mr. and Mrs. Jameson, and they haven't said a word to anybody about it."

"How else could the reporter know about it?" Brandon said.

Guy looked knowingly at Investigator Backus. "Sounds like there may be a leak in the police department."

Will walked into Gordy's Crab Shack and worked his way through the crowd of people waiting to be served. He looked around the dining room until he spotted Weezie Taylor talking to some customers being seated for dinner. He waited until she left the table and then walked over to her.

"Hi, Weezie. Is Gordy working tonight?"

"No, but I think he's still here. Try his office."

Will went down the hallway and stopped at the first door and saw Gordy working at his desk. "You busy?"

"Not too," Gordy said. "Did you stop by for takeout?"

"No, but I should probably take something home in case Margaret's *low-fat* chicken and dumplings are a disaster."

"Now that she's a skinny Minnie she's tryin' to whip you into shape, eh?"

"There's more to it than that. The doctor said my cholesterol's high, so the woman's on a mission to keep as many fat grams as possible out of my food and off my taste buds. Ain't love grand?"

Gordy chuckled. "Tell her not to talk to Pam, will you? So what's up?"

"Did you see this afternoon's press conference?"

Gordy shook his head. "I didn't know about it. But Al came by and told us that Valerie Hodges said on camera that she had a copy of the note you found on Brandon's front seat. He asked if Weezie or Pam or I had told anybody about the note. Of course, we didn't. We understood why you withheld it from the media, and we respected that."

"Yeah, well, she got to someone. And if it wasn't you, Pam, or Weezie or any of the Joneses, then someone in the department leaked the information."

"That stinks," Gordy said.

"Yeah, it does, and I'm not stopping till I find out who it is."

"Any suspicions?"

"Not really. I'm sure Al wouldn't do it. And I can't imagine Jack Rutgers or any of the detectives would either. But I'm sure as heck going to find out."

"Any breakthroughs on who might have gone back and spray-painted the Ws at the crime scenes?"

"No, but the Ws in the text of the threatening note and the Ws at the crime scenes look similar and may well have been written by the same person. The analyst says the way he forms his letters indicates he could be arrogant and angry and potentially violent. My hunch is that he's one of the guys who harassed Weezie and Brandon."

"Did someone in the bars remember a group of loudmouths on Monday night?"

"No. One female patron down at Big John's acted weird when a couple of my detectives questioned her about it, but it didn't lead anywhere. If those guys who harassed Weezie came out of one of the bars, somebody's bound to remember them. We just have to keep talking to the folks that frequent those places. Sheriff Martin loaned us a couple deputies to help."

"Is there somethin' I can do for you, Will? You came down here for a reason."

"I wanted to vent a little before I go home. But I also wanted to tell you some great news: Meagan got picked to be in *The Sound of Music*."

A grin spread slowly across Gordy's face. "Didn't I tell you the kid was a natural? What part did she get?"

"Liesl, the oldest von Trapp daughter."

"Hot dog! That's means she'll get to sing a solo. I can't wait to tell Pam. Aren't you glad I prodded her into it?"

"Yeah, thanks. She listens to you. I just hope I can put a lid on this case long enough to get excited with her. Right now my mind is consumed with all the loose ends. I could use a little closure."

20

Ellen Jones sat in bed, a pillow propped behind her, and watched the antics of three hummingbirds fighting each other for the feeder that hung outside her window. A cardinal was perched at the end of a live oak branch, his red chest puffed out, his melodious song seemingly intended for an audience of One.

She was suddenly aware of footsteps and whistling moving in her direction, and then Guy breezed through the doorway, carrying a breakfast tray.

"Here you go, honey." Guy Jones set the tray across her lap and kissed the top of her head. "Happy Saturday. Don't burn yourself on the icing. I just took these beauties out of the oven."

"Mmm." Ellen closed her eyes and savored the aromas of Guy's homemade cinnamon rolls and Starbucks breakfast blend coffee.

She opened her eyes and leaned down and took a whiff of the single red rose in the porcelain vase. "I'm not sure I'd know what to do if we didn't start our Saturdays this way."

"Me either. I love spoiling you." Guy crawled over to his side of the bed. "By the way, Brandon just got back from the beach. He's going to drive around town this morning and get a feel for the layout, which says to me he's decided to stay with us a while."

"I'm glad the two of you are finally speaking."

"Yeah, we're fine. Sometimes I forget how sensitive he is. It kills me that he stuck it out with Mavis and Stein just because he didn't want to disappoint me. Guess I really need to work on my communication skills. So what's with this dream you had about Valerie Hodges? You were talking a blue streak at three this morning, but I wasn't awake enough to catch it all."

Ellen blew on her coffee and took a sip. "It was more like a nightmare. I've already forgotten most of it, but I remember that she made up some story about Brandon, and the FBI came and took him away. I'm sure it was born out of my subconscious loathing for the woman's lack of professional ethics."

"Guess your run-in with her over the Hamilton case has left a bad taste in your mouth."

"It's more than that. She doesn't care whose boat she rocks as long as making waves gets her noticed. If she has a copy of the note, there's no doubt in my mind she'll disclose what's in it."

"Well, don't get too hung up about it. Whether she does or doesn't isn't going to impede Will's investigation. Keeping the note quiet was just a safeguard in case someone made a false confession. Odds are that won't happen."

"But who does Valerie think she is, going behind his back and getting someone inside the department to reveal information the police chief didn't want out there?"

"You don't have any proof that she did that. The source might've come to her."

Ellen rolled her eyes and took a bite of cinnamon roll. "Why don't we talk about something else, Counselor?"

"Honey, I don't like the way Valerie operates either. So put on your newspaperwoman's hat for a minute and tell me what you would've done if you were frustrated that the police hadn't made an arrest and were convinced that the police chief was withholding information from the public."

"I would've made myself a nuisance until I was allowed to confront the police chief one-on-one. I've certainly done that before." Ellen glanced over at him and smiled wryly. "I would've done plenty of nosing around, too. But I never would've revealed sensitive information in a press conference just to draw attention to myself. That's the only reason she did it, you know. She couldn't care less whether the police solve this case or not. She's using them to get attention. That's what motivates her."

"Okay, but how would you as a reporter have handled it if someone in the police department had told you about the note?"

"At the very least, I'd have exhausted every effort to contact

Brandon and Weezie to find out what they had to say about it. But I'd also make sure the police chief knew that I had obtained sensitive information, and I'd insist on meeting with him privately to discuss it."

"What if after you told him what you knew, he denied it?"

Ellen licked her sticky fingers and took a sip of coffee. "That would be pretty hard for him to do after I showed him a photocopy of the note. But I'd give him a chance to talk me out of going public with it. I'd want to know his reason for withholding the information. If his explanation convinced me it was better for the case that the information not be released, I'd probably agree not to print it."

"Well, I guess that's what makes you more of a professional."

"*Made*, Counselor. That's all in the past. I'll tell you one thing, after finding out about the Ws spray-painted at the crime scenes, I'd have made a beeline for the newspaper archives and started researching the history of hate crimes in this area. The perp used those initials for a reason. It's as though he's daring us to find out what they mean."

Guy chuckled. "I wish you could see your face."

"Why?"

"You're all aglow. Just like you used to be when you were following a big case. I can almost see the adrenaline pumping through your veins."

Ellen smiled. "Really?"

Guy tilted her chin up and looked into her eyes. "Honey, why don't you amuse yourself and try beating Valerie at her own game? You'd find it satisfying to get involved in fleshing out the facts, wouldn't you?"

"Sure, but it's too time intensive if I have any hope of ever getting this second novel written."

"So take a sabbatical. Your writing's not going well at the moment anyway."

"That's an understatement. I've written two worse-than-mediocre chapters in the past six months."

Guy put his hand on hers and seemed to be mulling something over in his mind. Finally he said, "Ellen, have I been pushing you too hard? After listening to Brandon, I'm beginning to wonder if I do that with everyone."

"You've been a great encourager…but, yes, you tend to push me pretty hard. I think you're more interested in me being a novelist than I am."

"Ouch. I was afraid of that. Why didn't you say something?"

"I did, in a roundabout way. But I don't think I wanted to admit it to myself until recently. Listening to Brandon air his frustration made me more aware of my own. Don't get me wrong. I enjoyed writing the first novel, partly because I needed a new direction after I left the newspaper and partly because it gave me a forum to vent my feelings about the gossip that surrounded the Hamilton case. But it's not very good, and we're kidding ourselves to think anyone's ever going to publish it. I don't even care anymore." Ellen turned to him. "The truth is, I'm much more drawn to the drama of real life. I love the craziness of the newsroom and scrambling to make deadlines. I love the sound of the presses and the smell of the ink and the feel of a not-quite-dry newspaper. Sometimes it's all I can do not to call Margie just so I can hear the noise in the background and picture my old office. I'm sure this must be disappointing for you to hear, but it feels good to finally get honest with myself."

"I think deep down I knew," Guy said. "I only asked you to quit your job as editor of the *Daily News* because you'd had one too many brushes with enemies. I thought getting you out of that environment and moving to Seaport would keep you safe."

Ellen laughed. "Well, that backfired. Each member of our family has taken turns being a news item since we moved here."

"Ironic, isn't it?"

"Very." Ellen squeezed his hand, her mind reeling with possibilities. "Are you serious about me playing reporter just for fun?"

"Why not?"

Ellen smiled without meaning to. "Yes, why not?"

Brandon Jones drove under the thick, leafy tree branches that covered Seaport Parkway and admired the grand old houses that graced either side. He stopped at a red light and looked at the map the man at the service station had drawn him. People's Drive was about twelve blocks farther.

The light changed and he continued on, trying not to be irritated by the paint film on his back window. The turpentine had removed the two Ws, but it hadn't gotten rid of all the smears.

He passed by the florist shop he had seen when he first arrived and was reminded again of how lost he felt without Kelsey. He wondered how she was spending her Saturday and if she had found someone else to go rock climbing with.

He crossed Seminole Boulevard and continued on, surprised that this side of Seaport Parkway had almost no trees. As far as he could see on either side of the road were retail shops. He spotted People's Drive up ahead. He pulled into the left turn lane, then onto People's Drive, surprised that the scenery changed again. The asphalt on the road looked fresh, and young palm trees lined both sides of the street. Directly in front of him, about a block away, was an attractive white stucco building with red Bahamas shutters and a red tile roof.

The road ended at the parking lot, and Brandon was surprised to see about a dozen cars, including Weezie's red Corolla.

He pulled into a parking space and turned off the motor, thinking how impressive the facility was. He had envisioned something drab and basic.

He walked up the sidewalk toward the front entrance and noticed hundreds of tiny shoe prints in the cement. Out front, in the middle of a flower garden, stood a life-size bronze statue of two young men, each with his arm around the other. Brandon read the plaque:

IN MEMORY OF DARYOUSH FASSIH AND ISAAC KOHLER
May the people of Seaport henceforth join hands
in friendship and mutual respect

Brandon was surprised by the emotion that came over him at the tragic loss that had inspired the construction of the clinic. His parents had told him about the senseless deaths of these Muslim and Jewish teenagers, but the bronze figures were so lifelike, he almost expected them to start talking.

He opened the big wooden door and walked over to the glass

window and saw Weezie Taylor typing some forms. A smile spread across her face, and she slid open the glass window.

"Mercy me, what're you doin' over here?" Weezie said.

Brandon shrugged. "I was in the neighborhood—on purpose. I decided to take a tour of the city and see where things are. It's not as though I've had a chance to do that before now."

"Did you get the paint off your car windows?"

"More or less. Listen, don't let me keep you from doing whatever you need to. I just wanted to drop in and see what the place looks like."

"Well, don't miss the waitin' area. See those beautiful blue and white tiles—2,837 of them? Each one is signed by someone who lent a hand puttin' this place together. I'm tellin' you, it was somethin' to see. Black, white, brown, Muslim, Jew, Christian, atheist—it didn't matter. All that mattered was that we were all gettin' along and were committed to keepin' it that way."

"Pretty impressive. So anyone who needs medical care can get it here?"

"Medical and dental—and at no cost. The foundation is providin' everything, and the help is all volunteer."

"Amazing."

Weezie nodded. "Sure wish I knew why anybody would wanna sabotage it."

"What time do you get off?" Brandon said.

"Noon. I start my shift at Gordy's at two."

"Do you want to have lunch with me before you go to work?"

Weezie got up and walked over to the sliding glass window, her arms folded on the sill. "It's probably not the smartest move for you to be seen with me right now."

"I'm not worried about it, but I'll understand completely if you don't want to."

"Now don't be puttin' words in my mouth. What'd you have in mind?"

"I saw a really cool looking place down on the beach. Looks like they had tables up on the roof. It was Topsy's or something like that. At Sixth and Beachcombers."

"Yeah, Topper's."

"Is it any good?"

"Too good, I'm afraid. We may not be able to get in that place at noon on a Saturday."

"How about if I go early and save you a place."

Weezie smiled. "Sounds like a deal."

Will Seevers sat in his recliner reading the sports page and thinking how delicious Margaret's Egg Beaters Spanish omelet had been.

"What time do you want us to take Meagan shopping?" Margaret Seevers turned the page of her magazine. "I need to run over to the church and deliver a sack of nonperishables for the food pantry."

"She won't be out of bed until noon, right?"

Margaret smiled. "At the earliest. Then it'll take another hour for her to decide what to wear and how to fix her hair in case she runs into anybody she knows. Why don't we shoot for two or three, and we can have dinner at Gordy's afterward?"

"Sounds like a plan. I'm sure Meagan can hardly wait to talk to him about getting picked for *The Sound of Music*. You're really going to let me eat at Gordy's?"

"Sure, just pick something grilled instead of fried, and substitute low-fat cottage cheese for the potato. Skip dessert and have fruit instead."

"Mmm, I can hardly wait." Will looked over at her, the corners of his mouth twitching.

Margaret turned another page of the magazine just as the phone rang. She reached over and picked it up. "Hello... May I tell him who's calling...? Please hold for a just minute." She put her hand over the receiver. "It's the editor of the *North Coast Messenger*."

Will winced and took the phone. "Will Seevers."

"Hello, Chief, it's Robert Adkins. As a courtesy, I wanted to give you an opportunity to comment on the threatening note that Valerie Hodges made reference to at your press conference yesterday afternoon. We're preparing to print the contents of the note on the front page of tomorrow's newspaper."

"I already said I'm not going to comment on what we have or don't have in the way of evidence while the investigation is ongoing."

"With all due respect, Chief, let's forgo the formal statement and get real. It's pointless to deny the note exists. I have a photocopy in my hand. 'Stay away from the black widow or we'll step on both of you.' That sounds like a substantial racial threat that the public deserves to know about. What are you hiding?"

"Off the record?" Will said.

"All right."

"I'm not hiding anything the public needs to know. And you're well aware that it's customary for the police to withhold some element of a crime in order to ensure we get the real perps. It would've been nice had you come to me before Hodges opened her mouth at the press conference and blew it for us. I don't know how she managed to weasel her way into my department, but I'm not going to give her the satisfaction of verifying information she had no right to. So on the record: I'm not going to comment on what we have or don't have in the way of evidence while the investigation is ongoing. Have a nice day, *Bob*."

Will handed the phone to Margaret, his temples throbbing. "I can't wait to get my hand on whoever leaked that note."

Will's cell phone vibrated on the end table, and Margaret jumped, her hand over her heart.

"Sorry, honey. I hate having to take this, but I need to." He reached for the phone. "Seevers."

"Chief, it's Jack Rutgers. I hate to spoil your Saturday morning, but we've got another situation. A 911 call came in from an Angel Phelps at the Harbor Street trailer park. She just discovered two white *W*s spray-painted on the side of her trailer. The 911 operator said she was pretty upset. I don't have all the details, but I know she's Caucasian. Her twelve-year-old son is biracial, and somebody stole his bicycle and roughed him up."

Will leaned his head back and exhaled loudly. "Just what we needed. Okay, Jack, give me the address. I'll meet you over there. I want to talk to them myself."

21

Will Seevers pulled his squad car within inches of Jack Rutgers's taillights and turned off the motor. He looked up at the two Ws spray-painted on the yellow trailer parked in space J-9. He couldn't tell by looking if the Ws matched the others.

He got out of the car and walked past a small group of neighbors, he assumed, all asking questions at the same time. The only distinctive voice was that of a tattooed African-American man in overalls and no shirt whose complaint against the police department ended with a string of obscenities aimed at Will.

Will bristled but continued walking past the crowd and up the wooden steps to the front door, convinced that nothing he could say was going to dispel the man's misguided opinion of how he was handling the case.

A cute bleach-blond in tight jeans and a pink tank top opened the door. She appeared to be about thirty, give or take. "I'm Angel Phelps. Are you Chief Seevers?"

"Yes, ma'am."

"Come in. My son and the other officer are in the livin' room."

Will followed Angel into a wood-paneled room where a boy sat on the couch, bruises on his face and arms and a Band-Aid over one eyebrow. His skin was light brown and his hair a mass of sun-bleached curls. *Handsome kid*, Will thought.

Jack Rutgers came over and stood next to Will. "The boy's name is Caedmon Nash. I told him who you were and what we would be doing."

"If you're wonderin' why his name's different from mine," Angel said, "it's because I took back my maiden name when I divorced his good-for-nothin' father."

"Anything else I should know?" Will said.

"Just that my son's a good kid, and there was no cause for anybody to rough him up like that."

Will nodded. "Okay, let's go see if we can find out who did it." Will went over and extended his hand to the boy. "Caedmon, I'm Chief Seevers."

"I go by Cade."

"All right, Cade. I'm sure you're aware there have been some racial problems in town. It's the job of the police to figure out who's doing it and why. I'd like you to tell us what happened to you last night."

Cade tapped his fingers on the arm of the couch and didn't look up. "I was out ridin' my bike. It was almost nine, and I was supposed to be in by dark. I was pushin' my bike across the tracks to come into the park, and all of a sudden some guys came up behind me and started punchin' me over and over. Then they grabbed my bike and left."

"How many were there?"

"Four."

"Did you see any of their faces?"

Cade shook his head.

"You must've seen them from behind as they were leaving."

"They were white. Much taller and older than me."

"Do you remember what they were wearing?"

"I think they had on shorts, but I'm not sure."

"Did they say anything?"

Caedmon glanced up at his mother and then at his hands. "I don't remember."

"Young man, you tell these officers the truth," Angel said. "Those punks didn't take your bike without sayin' *somethin'*."

"I don't remember, okay?" Caedmon glared at his mother.

"Well, you'd better! Whoever painted those Ws on the house wasn't just playin' around! These are dangerous people! Racists! Do you get that?"

"Ms. Phelps, why don't you tell me what you remember," Will said.

Angel sat on the couch next to the boy, her hands on her knees. "Cade came stormin' in here just after nine, madder than I've ever seen him. He was swearin' and kickin' things. Said some guys roughed him up and stole his bike. I started to call 911, but he begged me not to. He said he knew how to get his bike back, and if I got the police involved it would just make things worse. I think someone's bullyin' him, but he won't talk to me about it."

Will moved his eyes to Caedmon. "Is that what went down?"

"I told you I don't know who they were."

"Then why'd you tell your mother you knew how to get your bike back?"

Caedmon shrugged. "I just said that so she wouldn't call the cops. I already felt like a wuss without havin' to admit to you I couldn't even defend myself."

Will studied the boy's face and decided he wasn't telling everything he knew. "Those Ws painted on your house are the same initials that have been used to mark each of the recent hate crime scenes. Do you realize that?"

"I guess."

"Cade, if you know who did this, you need to be brave and tell us before these guys hurt someone else. Did they threaten you?"

"I told you, I don't remember them sayin' anything."

Will looked over at Angel. "When did you discover the letters on the house?"

"About eight this morning when my next-door neighbor knocked on the door and told me. I was shocked. Someone must've done it during the night, but I never heard nothin'."

"Have you ever received a racial threat of any kind?" Will said.

Angel arched her eyebrows. "My son's biracial. People give me nasty looks and make snide remarks all the time. Sometimes they whisper behind my back. But no one's ever threatened me."

"What about you, Cade? Has anyone ever threatened you?"

"Why would they? I'm only twelve."

And a lot more transparent than you think. Will rose to his feet.

"Okay, I'm going to let Officer Rutgers take it from here. If you think of anything else, I want you to call the station." Will gave them his business card and glanced over at Jack. "Can I talk to you for a minute?"

Will walked to the entry hall, Jack on his heels. "Bag the clothes Cade was wearing during the attack and gather as much evidence as you can here and at the scene. See if any of the neighbors heard or saw anything."

"It's obvious the kid's holding out on us," Jack said.

"Well, before we lean too hard on him, let's see if these Ws match what we have on file."

Brandon Jones sat at a small umbrella table at Topper's Grill, watching a young man down on the beach juggling bowling pins. He glanced at his watch and wondered how much longer the waitress would allow him to occupy a table without ordering anything besides a Coke.

He looked up, relieved when he saw Weezie Taylor walking toward him.

"Sorry I took so long," she said. "I would've called you if I'd had your cell number. One of the doctors had to leave early and deliver a baby, and we got real busy. I couldn't leave till we got everybody worked in."

"That's okay. I'm glad you're here." He handed her a menu. "Tell me what's good. I'm starved."

"Oh, I *love* the potato skins smothered in sour cream and chives." A grin stole her face. "I can make a meal out of just those."

"That good, eh?"

"The sweet potato skins are even better. I think I might have those because I'm off fat food right now, and they taste good without sour cream. But Topper's is famous for havin' every kind of juicy burger you can think of. And their Santa Fe Chicken is out of this world. And the Oriental Salad is somethin' else. Surf and Turf's to die for. Shoot, there's nothin' on here that isn't good."

Brandon laughed. "Keep talking like that, and they may offer you a job. You eat here often?"

"Every couple weeks or so I come over here with my sister-in-law Shayla."

"Shayla…where have I heard that name?"

"She's Annie and Daniel's nanny."

"Oh yeah, that's right. Annie said that Shayla was her *bestest friend*."

"That little blondie is somethin' else," Weezie said. "Shayla loves those kids. It's been a gift from God workin' there."

"I think it's mutual."

The waitress walked over to the table. "Are you ready to order now?"

"I'll have the sweet potato skins," Weezie said. "Hold the sour cream. And a Diet Coke."

"I'll have a double jalapeno burger, potato skins on the side, and a lemonade."

"Thanks. I'll be right back with your drinks."

Brandon folded his hands on the table and looked at the bustling activity on the beach. A group of young people had put up a net and were playing volleyball. "This town is hopping this time of year."

"It's gettin' to be that way all year-round. I don't know what the population is now, but we're growin' way too fast to suit me. Seems like a new motel or restaurant or shop opens every week."

"Well, I hope they're hiring. I need a summer job while I'm trying to figure things out, and I'm sure it's too late to get a lifeguard position."

Weezie was quiet for a few moments and seemed to be pondering something. "You like kids?"

"I love kids. Why?"

"The same foundation that funds the People's Clinic is sponsorin' a three-week summer camp for disadvantaged kids, and one of the counselors had to back out because his mother took sick. Camp starts next week, and they're freakin' because they've got kids signed up and need more help."

"What age group?" Brandon said.

"Boys eleven to thirteen."

"I don't have much experience with boys that age."

Weezie laughed. "You were one. Can't get any more experienced than that."

"Actually, I went to camp every summer until I started high school. And after that, I worked as a camp counselor nearly every summer till I graduated from college."

"Well, there you go. You've already been trained. It pays two hundred a week, and you get food and lodging."

"I thought all the work at the clinic is done by volunteers."

Weezie nodded. "It is, but like I said, this is a separate outreach. The tuition, operatin' expenses, and salaries for the three-week camp session are bein' funded by the foundation. If this first session at Camp Piney Woods goes the way everyone's hopin' it will, they'll expand the program next summer."

"Where's the camp located?"

"North of town. It's an old Boy Scout facility that's been renovated." Weezie took a sip of Diet Coke and looked at him over the top of her glass. "Listen, camp starts in a week. If you think you might be interested, you should contact Dr. Tehrani right away."

"Is his first name Ali?"

"Uh-huh. Your folks know him. He started the foundation that funds the clinic, and he's takin' care of the hiring. I think his only requirement is a willing heart."

"I remember what a positive impact camp had on me. I'd sure like to find out more."

Will Seevers sat at the table in his office, looking at the photographs of the letters spray-painted on Ms. Phelps's mobile home and comparing them to the letters found at the other crime scenes.

Al Backus came through the doorway and joined him at the table.

"Thanks for coming in, Al. I wouldn't disrupt your Saturday, but this is important."

"No problem," Al said. "I doubt we're going to get an entire weekend off till this thing is solved. So whaddya think?"

Will handed the photos to Al. "These shots were taken at Angel

Phelps's place. And those on the table were taken at the other crime scenes. You tell me."

Al examined the photos in his hand, and then looked down at those on the table. "Not even close."

"Yeah, that's what I thought. No way were these letters written by the same perp."

"So where does that leave us?"

"I want to know who roughed up Caedmon Nash and stole his bicycle and what persuaded them to copy the MO. The mother thinks someone is bullying the kid, but Jack and I couldn't get a straight answer out of him. For all we know, whoever did it might know who's responsible for the rest of these crimes."

"Or it's a bunch of schoolmates who saw it on the news and thought it would be fun to do," Al said.

"Maybe. But Cade Nash is biracial. Maybe he's being harassed and won't talk because he's afraid."

"What kind of relationship does he have with his mother?"

"It's hard to tell with an adolescent, but it seemed strained to me. The kid's father isn't in the picture, and whatever's going on he's not sharing with his mother."

"You want me to talk to him?" Al grinned smugly. "I'll bet I can get him to talk."

"Actually, I don't think he's going to give it up unless we lean on him, and he's the victim here. The kid's been through enough. I don't want him interrogated." Will leaned back in his chair, his hands behind his head. "Cade told his mother that he knew how to get his bike back, but if she got the police involved, it would just make things worse. So here's what I want you to do…"

22

Ellen Jones sat on the couch with Guy, waiting for the six o'clock news to come on and mulling over the events of the day. "I really enjoyed the stroll on the beach this afternoon."

"Me too," Guy Jones said. "And I'm glad Brandon came home looking a little more lighthearted. My talk with him yesterday must've done some good."

"It hurts me that he's been carrying around all those feelings and never even told us."

"Well, I've got to learn to be more sensitive and make sure the lines of communication are open." Guy held out the remote and pressed the mute button.

"Good evening, this is Shannon Pate."

"And I'm Stephen Rounds. Welcome to *Regional News at Six*. Seaport police are stunned today after still *another* racial incident, this one involving a juvenile at the Harbor Street Mobile Home Village on the city's east side. Jared Downing is on the scene tonight and has the story. Jared…"

"Stephen, police responded to a 911 call just after eight this morning from Angel Phelps, who lives with her son in this mobile home park behind me. Phelps made the 911 call after a neighbor knocked on her door and informed her that two white Ws had been spray-painted on the front of her mobile home. Phelps told police that an incident last night involving her twelve-year-old biracial son might have precipitated the act of vandalism.

"Phelps said that her son, whose name is being withheld at her request, told her he was pushing his bicycle across these railroad tracks around nine last night when four youths allegedly came up behind him and started punching him and then stole his bicycle. He came home immediately afterward and told his mother what had happened, but it's unclear at this hour why she didn't report the incident to police until this morning.

"Police Chief Will Seevers told reporters late this afternoon that a chemical analysis of the paint and close examination of the letters spray-painted on Phelps's mobile home indicated they were *inconsistent* with those found at the other crime scenes. The chief declined to comment on whether the suspects in this case have been linked to the previous hate crimes, citing the ongoing investigation.

"So for now, no arrests have been made in any of the hate crimes, and people in the black community are wondering why. This is Jared Downing. Back to you, Stephen."

"Thanks, Jared. This rash of racial incidents gets more interesting by the hour. You can be sure we'll follow this story closely in the days ahead. In other news tonight…"

Ellen's mind was reeling with questions. Was it a group of young people who had gone back and painted the Ws at the crimes scenes just for fun? Was it one of the youths that assaulted Ms. Phelps's son who threw the rock at Weezie and kicked Brandon in the ribs?

Ellen was aware that a commercial had come on and Guy was talking.

"I suppose your mind is already processing all this," he said.

Ellen turned to him, a smile tugging at the corners of her mouth. "You know me too well. I don't know if I'm going to last until Monday. I'm dying to figure out the significance of the two Ws. I've already made a diagram of all the facts that have been released to the media, and I can hardly wait to go down to the newspaper and dig into the archives. But you realize that I may not discover anything at all."

"That'd be a first."

"Not really, and this is a long shot. Could be that the perp is simply using his initials and there's nothing intriguing at all about this."

Guy lifted his eyebrows. "Oh, I have a feeling you'll make it intriguing, one way or the other."

Brandon walked along the surf on Seaport Beach, enjoying the sensation of breaking waves turning to foam and washing up over his feet.

A warm, moist wind blew out of the south, and the hair tickling his ear reminded him he needed a haircut.

This was the first relaxing day he'd had since he arrived in Seaport. His leisurely drive around town left him even more impressed than he had expected to be. There was so much beauty here, not just the white sandy beaches and the endless blue waters of the gulf, but also the lush parks, towering live oaks, wide avenues, and beautiful old mansions.

His favorite stop of the day had been the red and gray lighthouse out on the point. He had sat on the grassy hill overlooking the gulf and spotted dozens of dolphins in the distance, shooting up out of the glistening water and twisting and turning in perfect harmony as if they had been performing at SeaWorld. It was there that missing Kelsey had seemed almost more than he could bear. Even the wonders of nature couldn't salve the nagging ache that reminded him every waking moment that he had lost not only her, but all sense of direction as well.

His mother's words came rushing back to him. *Just because you've lost your bearings doesn't mean you're off course. In fact, I firmly believe God has planned even the storms we go through.*

Brandon wasn't sure if he liked that or not, but it was easier to accept than the idea that life had indiscriminately dealt him a hand that he was supposed to play the best he could.

He thought about Gary begging on the street and wondered if the guy's search to find the meaning of life had been sincere or if he had gotten exactly what he had expected to find all along.

God, I sure don't want to end up like him. I choose to believe there's a Master plan, but I need You to show me where I fit.

The sun had disappeared behind a billowy gray cloud, and a fan of white rays shone down on the water and spotlighted a single sailboat on the horizon. Brandon slowed his pace and then stopped, his hands deep in his pockets, and drank in the splendor. A peace he'd never known before seemed to melt over him.

He walked over to the dry sand and sat, then took out his cell phone and the piece of paper with Dr. Tehrani's phone number.

Will Seevers sat in his recliner, thumbing through a travel magazine and wondering if he had sent Al Backus out on nothing more than a wild goose chase. It was after 10:00 p.m., and he hadn't heard back from Al.

"You're tapping your foot again," Margaret Seevers said.

"Sorry."

Will's phone vibrated and he grabbed it off the table. "Seevers."

"You were right," Al Backus said. "As soon as it got dark, Cade snuck out of the house and led us right to the culprit's door—a kid named Abel Drummond. Drummond's dad got him to finger the other three boys involved. All neighbor kids, all classmates of Cade's. We rounded them up and are bringing them in now. You wanna be in on this?"

"You bet. Have you talked to Cade and his mother?"

"Yeah, I'll fill you in when I see you. It's gonna be fun watching these little punks squirm. I expected at least one set of parents to call a lawyer, but all of them seemed eager to cooperate. Each boy admitted taking part in stealing Cade Nash's bicycle. I'll get them to admit to the spray-painting and whatever else they've been up to."

"Okay, Al. I'll be there in fifteen minutes."

He disconnected the call and pushed down the lever on his recliner and rose to his feet. "At least something worked. Cade led us to the kids who stole his bike. Al's bringing all four of them in. Maybe the pressure will ease up a little when the public finds out we're on top of this one."

Margaret closed the novel she was reading. "I'd play it up for all it's worth if I were you."

Will stood on the other side of the two-way mirror and watched Al Backus begin his interrogation of Abel Drummond, who was seated with his parents on the opposite side of the table. Will was surprised when he recognized the boy's father as one of Gordy's lunch buddies.

"I understand you waived your son's rights to a lawyer?" Al said.

Eddie Drummond gave a slight nod and avoided eye contact. "Me and the missus want to cooperate any way we can. Abel did wrong. No one's saying he didn't. But I don't think we need to make a federal case out of it either. My boy's never been in trouble before."

Al folded his hands on the table and looked intently at Abel. "Tell me what happened tonight when Cade Nash rang your doorbell."

"He said he wanted his bike back. So I took him out to the garage and gave it to him."

"Just like that?" Al lifted his eyebrows.

"Yeah. If he told you different, he's a liar."

"How'd you get the bike?"

Abel glanced over at his dad.

"Don't look at me," Eddie said. "You look the investigator in the eye and tell him the truth."

Abel's feet jiggled under the table. "What did Cade tell you?"

"Never mind Cade. I'm interested in hearing *your* version."

"Okay. Me, Reese, Dakota, and Josh went out messin' around after dinner. We played some video games down at Shooter's and then got frozen custard and walked home and saw Cade cuttin' through our neighborhood."

"Did you say something to him?"

"Yeah, we told the skunk he was trespassin'."

"Skunk?"

"Yeah, his old lady's white and his old man's a nig…he's a darky. So we call him skunk. We don't want his kind stinkin' up our street. He knows better. He was askin' for it."

Eddie looked at Abel and threw his hands in the air. "I can't believe this! I didn't teach you to treat people that way."

"Oh yeah, Dad, act like you never say anything against blacks. That's all you talk about when you get home from work! The blacks won't do this. The blacks won't do that. How lazy they are. And how stupid they talk."

"That's not true!"

"Hold it!" Al said. "I want Abel to tell me what happened in his own words. Mr. Drummond, you need to keep quiet. Let's stick to the subject." He looked at Abel. "What do you mean *he was asking for it*?"

"We've chased him out of the neighborhood lots of times. He only comes back to dare us. He's lookin' for a fight."

"So after you told Cade he was trespassing, what did he do?"

"He flipped us off, so we started hittin' him. But he went berserk and started screamin' and kickin' and bitin'. We were afraid someone would·hear us, so we let him go, and he took off runnin'. We agreed that I'd keep his bike in my garage. I mean he left it on the street. It's not like we stole it. I was surprised he came lookin' for it. I didn't think he had the guts."

"What did he say when he came to the door."

"He just said, 'Gimme my bike.' So I did. My dad was standing right there. He heard the whole thing."

"Mr. Drummond, is that how you remember it?"

Eddie nodded. "I didn't know anything about the bike till then. Abel was supposed to be home at nine last night, and he showed up at ten after. I warned him if it happened again, he'd be grounded."

"Okay, what happened next?" Al said to Abel.

"I watched music DVDs for a while, ate some popcorn, and then went to bed."

Al leaned forward on his arms and got close to Abel's face. "Don't mess with me. I already know what happened. What time did you leave the house?"

"I didn't. I went to bed."

"Where'd you get the spray paint—was it yours, or did one of your buddies bring it?"

"I don't know anything about any spray paint."

"Sure you do. What time'd you sneak out of the house?"

"I told you, I was home all night. We have a security system. Go ahead, ask my parents. They'll tell you I was there."

"I set the alarm myself," Mrs. Drummond said. "I'm a very light sleeper. There's no way that alarm could've been disarmed without me hearing it."

Al looked intently at Abel. "Have you talked to or seen any of the other boys since last night?"

"Yeah, we hung out for a while this afternoon."

"So which one of them spray-painted the Ws on Cade's mobile home?"

"None of us spray-painted anything."

"Yeah, well, think again. Lying will just buy you time in juvenile detention. Then again, maybe you're ready to leave home for a while."

Abel looked at his dad and then at Al. "I don't know anything. I swear."

"Come on, you think I'm an idiot? You rolled a biracial kid and took his bike, and you expect me to believe those Ws, which are identical to the ones painted at all the other hate crime scenes, just magically appeared on Cade's house?"

"Believe whatever you want, but I don't know anything about it."

"Come on, Abel. Stop playing games. We both know you did it, don't we?"

Abel shook his head. "Why do you keep asking me the same question when I already told you I don't know anything about any spray-painting?"

Al leaned forward, his elbow on the table. "Because I don't believe you. Somebody's harassing African-Americans and leaving those initials behind. Maybe you're involved in those other crimes, too."

"No, I swear!"

"Maybe you know who is. Maybe you're just trying to be like them."

"No, I'm not." Abel looked pleadingly at his dad. "I don't know who did it."

"You actually expect me to believe that you and your bully friends roughed up Cade, agreed that you would keep his bicycle in *your* garage, then all went home and stayed in for the night like good little Boy Scouts?"

"That's what happened."

"Wanna know what I think happened? I think you were so proud of yourself for roughing up Cade and stealing his bike that you spray-painted the Ws on his house to show off like the other perps. Why don't you just admit it and get it off your chest. The judge will go easy on you if you cooperate."

"I'm not gonna say I did somethin' I didn't."

Al folded his arms across his chest and leaned back in his chair.

"Tell me what you boys talked about today when you got together."

"Just stuff."

"Did this *stuff* include Cade Nash?"

"Yeah, we had a laugh about the bike and figured the skunk was worried about where it was."

Al leaned forward, his elbows on the table, his face close to Abel's. "His name's *Cade*. I don't want to hear you use any other name for him from now on. Is that understood?"

"Whatever."

Eddie grabbed his son's shirtsleeve and pulled him close. "*Whatever*? That's how you answer an officer of the law? You show some respect and cut the attitude or you're gonna find yourself locked up! This is not a joke! You're in real trouble."

Abel nodded, his eyes wide, his cheeks flushed. "Okay, sorry."

"Do I need to get my son a lawyer?" Eddie said.

"Only if you think he has something to hide."

"I don't," Abel said. "I'm telling the truth. Honest!"

"Honest?" Al rose to his feet, his palms on the table, and looked intently at Abel. "I don't think you know the meaning of the word *honest*!"

Detective Wade Sanders entered the room with calculated precision and walked over to Al and grabbed his arm. "Take it easy, Al. Why don't you go cool off and let me talk to Abel?"

"Yeah, okay," Al mumbled.

Wade turned to the Drummonds, a pleasant expression on his face. "I'm Detective Sanders. Can I get you something to drink?"

Will stepped back from the two-way mirror and waited for Al to come out of the interrogation room and over to where he was standing.

"What do you think?" Al said.

"I think you have too much fun playing the role of bad cop."

Al grinned. "My specialty. I don't know that I believe him, but I primed the pump. Let's see if Sanders can get him to spill anything. I'm going to go work on the kid Sanders was talking to."

Will glanced at his watch and realized it was almost midnight. So much for an enjoyable weekend with his family.

Just after 2:00 a.m., Will stuffed the last low-fat potato chip into his mouth and crushed the bag and threw it in the trash.

He heard footsteps coming down the hall and then saw Al Backus breeze through the doorway and collapse in a chair. "Sanders, Botts, Peters, and I took a crack at each of these kids. I don't think they did the spray-painting."

"If not them, then who? And why? I don't need any more loose ends to keep me up at night!"

Al exhaled. "Me either, but I can't find a crack in what they told us. If I push much harder, they're going to lawyer up. They each gave us the same story about what happened last night, right down to their long-term harassment of Cade. But they all played dumber than dirt when it came to owning up to the spray-painting. Each set of parents backed up their kid's alibi, and it's a long shot that Abel Drummond disarmed the security system without his mother hearing it. They didn't do it, Chief. We're gonna have to look for another explanation."

"But why would anyone else paint the Ws on the mobile home?" Will got up and paced. "It would've made perfect sense if the boys had done it, but if that's not the case, then what the heck are we looking at?"

23

On Sunday morning after church, Brandon Jones dutifully followed his parents to the fellowship hall and put on his most pleasant face in anticipation of finally meeting their friends. He didn't know which subject he most dreaded having to address: the job he'd quit, the fiancée he no longer had, the hate crimes that had thrust him into the news—or the threatening note that had been recounted on the front page of this morning's newspaper.

He filled a Styrofoam cup with coffee and blew on it, then took a sip, aware of an elderly woman with painted eyebrows and jet-black hair moving purposefully toward him.

"You're Brandon Jones," the woman said. "I recognize you from your pictures. You favor your mother, especially those blue eyes and that gorgeous curly hair. I'm Blanche Davis. I live on the corner of Live Oak Place, down from your folks—the gray two-story with the white Bahamas shutters."

Brandon nodded and held out his hand. "I know exactly which house that is. Very pleased to meet you, Ms. Davis."

"Oh, honey, call me Blanche. Everybody does." She patted the top of her head. "You'll have to excuse this silly wig, but the chemo's made me a dead ringer for Kojak. I'm afraid I'd scare you all to death if I didn't slap this old thing on before I left the house. Listen, I'm sorry about everything that's happened to you and Weezie. What a mess. I want you to know you've been in my prayers. So where're your folks?" Blanche glanced over at the coffee pot and waved to Ellen.

A few seconds later, Ellen Jones came over and put her arms around Blanche. "How are you feeling?"

"A little weak but not bad considering. Oh, look." Blanche raised her hand in the air. "Yoo-hoo, Julie…Ross… Come meet Brandon."

A thirtysomething couple with a cute little redheaded girl about Annie's age came over and stood next to Blanche.

The man offered Brandon his hand. "Hi, I'm Ross Hamilton. And this is my wife, Julie, and our daughter, Sarah Beth."

"Nice to finally meet you. Mom's told me a lot about you." He looked down at Sarah Beth and smiled "And especially *you*."

Sarah Beth's eyes lit up. "You're Annie's Uncle Brandon. She said you give the funnest piggyback rides in the *whoooole* world."

"She did, huh?"

A husky young man with a crew cut and baggy trousers and a plain woman wearing too-big eyeglasses and a purple dress walked up and stood next to Guy, childlike grins on their faces.

Guy Jones put his hand on Brandon's shoulder. "Son, I want you to meet some very special friends of ours, Billy and Lisa Lewis."

Brandon reached out to shake their hands, thinking this must be the couple his mother had written Bible study lessons for. "Really nice to meet you, Billy. You too, Lisa."

"We are very hap-py to make your ac-quain-tance," Billy said, smiling with satisfaction as if he had recited a line from Shakespeare. "Did you like our church ser-vice to-day?"

Brandon nodded. "I did. And Pastor Crawford's sermon was great."

For the next few minutes his parents and their friends talked among themselves, sharing personal tidbits from the past week. Blanche had one more round of chemo to go, and the doctors were pleased with her progress. Julie was feeling good and getting over the sadness of her miscarriage. Billy and Lisa passed around a new picture of Lydia and Samuel, their Compassion children from Uganda.

Brandon was touched by the closeness of this diverse and unlikely group of friends, but other people were slowly working their way toward him, and he was nervous that with each new introduction, the conversation might lead to subjects he would just as soon avoid.

He squatted next to Sarah Beth. "How would you like one of my famous piggyback rides?"

She jumped up and down and clapped her hands. "Yes!"

Brandon looked at Ross. "Okay with you?"

"Yeah, sure."

Brandon turned around and let Sarah Beth climb onto his back, then stood up and headed down the hallway.

Brandon sat with his parents at a corner table in Gordy's Crab Shack, his plate piled high with samplings from the Sunday buffet. "I'm glad you aren't irritated that I used Sarah Beth as an excuse to exit gracefully. Things were going so well that I didn't want the conversation to turn to stuff I don't want to talk about."

"That's okay," Ellen said. "You met the people I really wanted you to meet."

"They seem nice. It's hard to believe the crazy history you all have with each other."

Ellen broke a roll in half and buttered it. "Well, that's probably why we're close. God seems to use dire circumstances to make friends out of people we would otherwise choose to pass by. The People's Clinic is living proof of that."

"Speaking of the clinic," Brandon said, "I'm meeting with your friend Dr. Tehrani this afternoon."

Guy stopped chewing. "Really? What for?"

"His foundation is sponsoring a summer camp for disadvantaged kids, and they need a camp counselor for the adolescent boys. I'd like to apply for the job. I like kids. I love the outdoors. I've worked in a camp setting. And I need a job that won't drain me till I can get over this burnout. Seems perfect."

"Isn't it a volunteer position?"

"No, it's a separate deal from the clinic. It pays two hundred a week, plus lodging and meals."

Guy didn't say anything.

"Dad, I know this isn't easy for you, but I'd really like to do this. Helping disadvantaged kids is certainly a good thing, and it's just for three weeks. I've asked God to direct my steps, and since He's not going to come down and draw me a map, I have to start somewhere."

"Wouldn't it be wise to start with your education, son? Somehow

I don't think summer camp is God's answer for your life."

Brandon was sure his mother kicked his father under the table.

"I don't either, but it's a temporary solution that will allow me to contribute something while I'm figuring things out." Brandon took a sip of limeade. "Plus I'll be out of your hair."

"You're not in our hair," Ellen said.

"Yes, I am, and you know it. You guys have been great, but you don't need an adult son sponging off you. This camp position seems like an answer to prayer. It starts Saturday."

Guy took a bite of his baked potato and didn't say anything.

"Seems like a good idea to me," Ellen said. "By the end of the three weeks, you should have some idea what you want to pursue."

"That's what I'm praying for." Brandon moved his eyes to his dad. "Will you please say something? You promised to be an encourager."

"I know, but this feels wrong to me. I'm afraid you'll get complacent and not try to push yourself at all."

Brandon took a bite of what appeared to be a fried oyster. "I can't afford to get complacent. But I can't afford to jump into the wrong thing again either. Frankly, working out in the fresh air sounds great right now."

Guy laid down his fork and looked at Brandon. "This insistence you have that working in an office makes you feel confined…that seems like a phobia you need to work out in therapy instead of something you let define your career choices. Keep it up and you're going to talk yourself right out of that college degree and into a hard hat."

"Dad, I don't need a shrink. I think I felt trapped by *what* I was doing, not so much *where* I was doing it. Does that make sense?"

"Yes, but that's not what you said the first time we talked about this."

"Well, I'm starting to understand some things better. Until yesterday, I hadn't had one day since I arrived here that wasn't a hassle. It's hard to clear your head with all that going on. I'm not so sure being in an office is the problem. I just need to find significance in what I do."

Guy took a sip of iced tea. "So how did you find out about the camp job?"

"Weezie told me. I stopped by the clinic on my self-guided city tour yesterday, and we had lunch at Topper's. Great place. You ever eaten there?"

His mother turned to his father and sighed loudly.

"I know you guys are worried about me being seen in public with Weezie, but we've decided not to let the threat intimidate us."

"Would it have been so difficult to choose an out-of-the-way place instead of Topper's?" Ellen said. "You might as well have painted a target on yourselves. For all you know, the people who threatened you are watching."

Brandon shook his head. "I made a lot of stops yesterday, and no one was following me."

"Well, now that the content of the note is officially *out there*, I suggest you reconsider."

"And do what? Cower at home and let these guys win? My friendship with Weezie is purely platonic, but it's nobody's business, and I'm not going to be intimidated into staying away from her."

"It's beyond me that you would take such a risk when you hardly know her."

"Why? You hardly knew Dr. Tehrani's wife, yet you refused to cut ties with her even when the terrorist threat was high and the FBI came knocking on your door."

"This is completely different."

"How?"

"I didn't want Mina to think all Christians hate Muslims."

"Okay. And I don't want Weezie to think all whites hate blacks."

"She knows better than that."

"I'm sure Mrs. Tehrani did, too. But you wanted your support to be tangible, right?"

"Yes, but *I* wasn't threatened," Ellen said.

"With all due respect, Mom, your marriage was. Yet you chose to stand with Mrs. Tehrani even when Dad objected. Don't get me wrong. I'm not criticizing what you did. I understand it was a matter of principle and that you and Dad worked it out. I'm just making a point."

Ellen picked up her fork, her face flushed, and started poking at her salad.

Will Seevers heard a car door slam and tossed the newspaper on the end table. A few seconds later, the front door opened and his daughter walked across the entry hall and into the family room, then sat in his lap, her arms around his neck.

"Hi, Daddy," Meagan Seevers said. "Did you get enough sleep? Mom says you're working too hard."

"I'm fine, honey. How was church?"

"Good. We prayed that you'll find the racists soon."

"Wonderful. I need all the help I can get."

Margaret Seevers came in the family room and stood in front of his chair. "I wasn't sure if you'd be up yet, but I brought you a seafood salad from Gordy's. I put in the fridge."

"Thanks, that sounds good. Sorry I missed church today, but I didn't get to bed till four."

Meagan kissed her dad on the cheek. "I've gotta go practice my lines. See you later."

"Okay, honey." Will looked up at Margaret, then reached out and took her hands. "You look stunning in that pink dress. I would've been proud to have you on my arm this morning. I hate it when police business preempts church and everything else that's really more important."

"After twenty-plus years of this, I just go with the flow." Margaret smiled. "Actually, Meagan and I had some real quality mother/daughter time over lunch at Gordy's. On the way out, we ran into Guy and Ellen and their son. What a nice looking young man."

"Yeah, he is."

Margaret sat on the arm of the chair and was quiet for a few moments and then said, "I guess you saw the front page of the paper?"

"Yeah. I'm going to look under every rock till I find out who leaked that note. I expect Valerie Hodges to stoop to that, but not the people who work for me."

Margaret patted his knee. "I know. So what happened with the boys last night? Did you get them to confess to the spray-painting?"

"I wish." Will relayed to Margaret everything that had happened during the interrogations. "Their stories all matched up, which actually complicates things. We've been viewing the Ws as the perp's signature. Obviously that isn't what happened here, and we have no idea who else would've done it or why."

"Maybe some other kids in the trailer park got the idea from seeing it on the news and decided to scare Cade and his mother. I'm sure everyone knows he's biracial."

Will nodded. "We thought of that. Al's got a team going door-to-door, talking to everyone who lives in the trailer park. But there's a racially diverse group of residents there, and it seems unlikely that anyone would single out Ms. Phelps or her son like those other punks did. Oh, I forgot to tell you—one of the *punks* is Eddie Drummond's son."

"Gordy's friend Eddie?"

"Yeah, after the boys got into a scuffle and Cade ran off, Eddie's son Abel stashed the bicycle in his garage."

"Does Gordy know?"

"I doubt it. None of the boys names were released since they're all minors. I'll call Gordy later and give him a heads-up. This Drummond kid's a real smart aleck like his father. But I have to say, Eddie was extremely cooperative and totally appalled at the racial slurs that came out of his kid's mouth. Al and the other detectives grilled these boys hard, but there weren't any inconsistencies in their stories."

"Who were the other boys?"

"Reese Raynor, Josh Hall, Dakota Williams. All between twelve and thirteen. None as cocky as Abel Drummond. Dakota had a spark of defiance in his eye that turned to tears when Al got tough. Josh shook during the entire interrogation, and I was half expecting him to wet his pants. Reese reacted the least and his answers were the shortest, but he kept looking apologetically at his father like he knew he was going to get it when he got home. Let's just hope the parents were horrified enough to ride herd on those kids so it doesn't happen again."

"What happens to them now?"

"We turned it over to juvy. The boys'll get a big slap on the wrist and that's about it. None of them have any priors."

"Will, they beat on a kid and stole his bicycle."

"Kids have been bullying other kids since the beginning of time, honey."

"But these boys are half-grown racists. If someone doesn't straighten them out, what will they be like ten years from now?"

Will exhaled. "I'm sure the judge will give them a serious talking-to. But nothing's going to happen to them unless they step out of line again. Right now I want us to focus on finding out who painted those letters on the mobile home. If there's a link to the other cases, we need to find it."

24

Brandon Jones pulled into the parking lot at the People's Clinic and saw a black Lexus parked near the door. He turned off the car motor and sat for a moment, suddenly not so sure this was what he should do. What if he didn't like dealing with adolescent boys? What if taking this job drove a wedge between him and his dad? What if his dad was right and he became complacent and stopped trying to push himself?

Brandon sighed. *Lord, if You want me to do this, please make the door swing wide open. All I need is another mistake to have to apologize for.*

He got out of the car and walked up to the entrance and found it unlocked. He stepped inside and looked around the lobby, then walked up to the glass window and rang the bell.

A few seconds later, he heard footsteps, and then a man with dark hair, kind eyes, and a thick salt-and-pepper mustache appeared in the doorway and extended his hand.

"Hello, Brandon. Ali Tehrani."

"Nice to meet you," Brandon said. "My parents speak highly of you."

Ali smiled. "Your parents are very kind. Please, come sit with me in the office, and we will talk."

Brandon followed Ali down a short hallway and into a functionally furnished wood-paneled office with light blue carpeting.

"Please, make yourself comfortable," Ali said. "Would you like some coffee?"

"No, thanks," Brandon said. "I'm fine."

"Weezie told me I should hire you on the spot. She's been singing your praises."

"She has, has she?"

"Indeed. So you have experience with camp?"

Brandon smiled. "I went to camp every summer when I was a kid, and then worked as a camp counselor when I was in high school and college. I like kids. I enjoy just about every outdoor sport: baseball, football, basketball, soccer, swimming, biking, whitewater rafting, backpacking, rock climbing—you name it, I've probably done it. I'm also a certified lifeguard and am certified in CPR."

"That's impressive. Too bad I already hired a camp director."

"All I'm looking for is a summer job while I contemplate a new career path."

"Yes, Weezie told me of your circumstances."

Circumstances? That word always sounded so nebulous.

Ali made a tent with his fingers. "I would be delighted to have someone of your caliber working with these boys. Most of them have never set foot inside a camp before, and I really want it to be a great experience. I think Weezie told you that we just completed the renovation at Piney Woods, and this is our first camp session. Truthfully, it's a dry run. I think we've got everything covered, but I'd feel a whole lot better having someone with your experience and maturity on staff. Did Weezie tell you the job pays two hundred dollars a week?"

Brandon nodded. "It sounds like just what I'm looking for right now."

"I'll need you to fill out the application, and I am requiring everyone who will be working with these kids to take a drug test and submit to a background check. Is this acceptable to you?"

"Absolutely."

"Camp starts this coming Saturday. But I'd like to introduce you to the other staff and start your training as soon as possible. When could you be available?"

"About five minutes ago. Point me in the right direction, and I'll pack my gear and head that way."

A smile stole Ali's face, and his eyes laughed. "Splendid. Brandon, I am continually amazed at how things work out. Yesterday I was losing sleep over this unexpected vacancy—and now here you are, ready and willing to help. And so much more than I had hoped for."

That's confirmation if I ever heard it, Brandon thought. *Thank You, Lord.*

Ali reached into a folder on his desk. "Let me show you pictures of the facilities and a layout of the property, then we'll go over the job description and agenda."

On Sunday afternoon, Will Seevers sat at the table in his office, fuming about the leak in his department and going over every detail of the hate crime cases. He heard footsteps coming down the hall and looked up just as Al Backus marched through the doorway, his eyebrows furrowed, the line across his forehead deep.

"I'd love to give that big mouth reporter a piece of my mind," Al said, "but I wouldn't want her to report that I was guilty of conduct unbecoming an officer." Al flashed a derisive grin.

"Forget Valerie Hodges. I'm more interested in finding out who leaked the information. I know you're spread thin, but I want somebody's head on a platter. No one is going to disrespect this department on my watch and get away with it."

"That's why I'm here instead of home watching the ball game. Before I leave, I'll have a report on your desk, including the names of every person who had access to the note. I also brought you a list of convicted felons driving black and dark blue 2005 and 2006 Ford trucks equipped with standard tires that match the rubber we found on the street in front of the church."

Will took the report from Al and read down the list of names. "None of them have Ws for initials."

"No, but look at the fourth name down: Mick Beasley, Caucasian male, age forty-six, Seaport address. Did twelve years for aggravated assault. Was released from prison in 1999. Sanders and Botts paid him a visit at that address last night and again this afternoon, but he wasn't home. The truck wasn't parked in the driveway, and several newspapers were piled up out front. He may be away for the weekend. We'll stay on it. None of the other felons listed live within fifty miles of here."

Will handed the list back to Al. "Go talk to Jessica Ziegler again. Show her Beasley's picture and see if she knows him."

"The lady hasn't exactly been forthcoming."

"So draw it out of her. Make her think you have reason to believe she knows him. Gauge her reaction carefully, Al. Something about her bothers me."

"All right. We'll show Beasley's picture around the art stores, too. Maybe someone will recognize him and remember him buying paint. The partial footprint analysis suggests a size eleven Performa running shoe. Wouldn't it be sweet if Beasley were wearing them when we catch up to him? So, anything jumping out at you from the files?"

Will took off his glasses and rubbed his eyes. "Yeah, I'm bothered about the Ws we found on the trailer. When's the last time you remember seeing a copycat crime signature where no crime was committed?"

"Never. It's bugging me, too. But I just don't think those boys did it."

"That's the only thing that makes sense."

Al pulled out a chair and straddled it, his arms folded on the back. "Not necessarily. What if Cade did it to draw attention to what was happening to him? He knew his mother would call the police when she saw the Ws, and he'd be forced to admit what's been going on. Maybe it was his way of crying out for help."

"Only he didn't cry out; he lied. My guess is he was ashamed— not just for being bullied, but for why he was being bullied. I can only imagine how hard it must be for him. The whites consider him black, and the blacks consider him white. For some reason, he hasn't found a close friend in either world. That's a heavy sentence for a twelve-year-old."

"Yeah, well his mother should've thought about that before she jumped into bed with a black man."

"She was married to him, Al."

"Her name's different than the kid's."

"She took back her maiden name when she divorced Cade's father."

"If you ask me, having a kid of mixed race is cruel and unfair."

"Well, I didn't ask you, and you need to stay objective. I'm trying to fight racism. I don't need it in my own department."

"You telling me you think it's okay to saddle a kid with all that?"

"It doesn't matter what I think. Our job is to protect every citizen in this town."

"You've gotta wonder why a good-looking woman like Angel Phelps would marry a black man."

"Maybe she loved him, Al. Ever think of that? Keep talking this way, and you're going to find yourself back in sensitivity training."

"Come on, Chief, it's just you and me here. Let's take off the masks and be honest with each other. I know you're wondering the same thing."

Will put his glasses back on and opened another file. "There're only two things I'm wondering at the moment: who spray-painted the mobile home, and who leaked the note to Valerie Hodges."

Ellen sat at her desk in the widow's watch, studying the facts she had gathered from the newspaper, radio, and TV regarding each of the hate crimes. There was a knock at the door, and she saw Brandon standing there.

"Hi. Come in."

"This is such a cool room, Mom. All this glass almost makes you feel as if you're outside."

"I know. I love it up here."

Brandon went over and stood in the glass alcove, his hands in his pockets. "I'll bet you can see a hundred miles from here. I don't know how you get any writing done."

Ellen laughed. "Obviously, I don't. Did you meet with Ali?"

"Yeah, I did."

"And?"

"I got the job. He wants me to go ahead and get the drug test tomorrow and then move out to the camp tomorrow night and begin orientation so I'll be up to speed by Saturday."

"Have you told your father?"

"No, he's taking a nap." Brandon pulled up a chair next to Ellen's and sat. "It's so ironic. I used to spend more money taking a few buyers out to lunch than I'll be making in an entire week at the camp. But I'm actually excited about going. It seems like God opened the door for this, though it feels weird saying that since it's such a small thing."

"But in God's economy, you never know which experiences will prove invaluable down the road. And you'll be safer out at the camp where you won't be as easy to find—at least until Will figures out who threatened you."

Brandon's eyes seemed to search hers. "I didn't mean to hurt your feelings at lunch. I didn't know how else to make the point about my relationship with Weezie other than to compare it to yours with Mrs. Tehrani."

"Well, you were right. It was hard to see another point of view when I was the one standing my ground. Actually, worrying about you has helped me to understand the times your father was at his wit's end when I held fast to a principle, even when it put me in danger."

"I'm doing everything I can to be safe. But it seems wrong to ignore Weezie just because some racists told me to."

"I understand. Unfortunately, that doesn't lessen my concern."

"Well, you won't have to worry about it for the next few weeks." Brandon gazed out the window and appeared to be studying the frigate bird soaring overhead. "The other morning when we watched the sun come up, you said that our job as believers is to empty ourselves of our own desires and let God fill us with His. I've thought about that a lot, and that's what I want, even though I don't have a clue how to do it. So I asked God to show me. And I started reading the Bible again. I figured the one in the nightstand was strategically placed for my benefit."

Ellen smiled. "Smart boy. Why don't you take it with you to camp?"

"Thanks, I will. I guess if God wants to reshape my character for some purpose only He knows, He'll get it through my thick head eventually, right?"

Ellen reached over and touched his arm. "I don't see you as thickheaded, but as principled, softhearted, and willing. That's the kind of person God can mold into whatever He desires. Just let Him. You don't have to understand the whole process."

"But I want to understand it. Don't you think that at thirty years old I should have my act together or at least know where I'm headed? Instead, I feel more in the dark than I have my whole life."

"Honey, sometimes it's only after we've been blinded that we can appreciate how glorious it is to walk in the light. Think about the apostle Paul on the road to Damascus. God blinded him in order to change his entire perspective. And once his sight was restored, he did amazing things for God."

Brandon lifted his eyebrows. "I'd settle for a meaningful job."

"Maybe God wants to show you that with the right perspective, any job can be meaningful."

"Now you sound like Dad."

"I just want you to be open to whatever the Lord wants you to learn at camp. I know from experience that God doesn't waste anything in the process of growing us."

"All right." Brandon looked at his watch. "I think I'll run over and see Papa before dinner. It'll be almost a month before I'll have a chance to see him again. Go ahead and tell Dad I got the job. I'll be home by six."

Gordy Jameson sat in his office, looking over the staff schedule Weezie had made up, when he sensed someone standing in the doorway and looked up.

"Can I talk to you about something?" Will Seevers said.

Gordy laid the schedule on his desk. "Yeah, sure. Come in and pull up a chair. You here havin' dinner with Margaret and Meagan?"

"No, I just left the station. It's been a wild weekend."

"Bet you're peeved the *Messenger* printed the contents of the note."

"Not half as peeved as I am about someone in my department leaking the information. But that's not why I'm here. You're aware that we picked up four juveniles for allegedly attacking a biracial kid and stealing his bicycle?"

"Yeah."

"Well, just between you and me, one of the little punks was Eddie Drummond's boy, Abel."

Gordy stared blankly at Will and realized he was serious. "Abel? Did he confess?"

"Oh, yeah." Will gave Gordy a quick overview of the interrogation and the racial slurs that came out of Abel's mouth. "Eddie was beside himself. He acted like he'd never heard the kid talk that way before."

"He's never mentioned it. As far as I know, he's never had any trouble with Abel."

"Well, the kid's only twelve. Maybe it's just now coming out. But kids don't teach themselves to hate." Will's gaze was intense. "Is Eddie a racist?"

"Do you really think I could be friends with him if he was? Every now and then he rags on a couple of African-Americans he works with…says they're lazy. But that's about it. He loves Weezie."

"Everybody loves Weezie."

"Yeah, except that racist slimeball that ran her off the road."

Will nodded. "Well, Abel Drummond is getting it from somewhere. Let's hope Eddie is smart enough to reprogram the kid's thinking before he ends up in real trouble. I just thought I'd give you a heads-up in case the subject came up over lunch. You can't let on like I said anything to you."

"I wouldn't. But I doubt Eddie'll talk about somethin' that personal with the guys."

"Well, if he seems down in the mouth, you might want to take him aside and see if he'll open up. Seriously, Gordy, his kid's headed for trouble if someone doesn't change the course he's on. If I were Eddie, I'd be proactive about it."

"You talkin' about a shrink?"

"I doubt counseling will fix him. I think he's got to see it modeled at home. And from the outbursts I heard during the interrogation, I doubt that's happening. Eddie may not see himself as a racist, but his ragging on those guys down at work has made a big impression on Abel—not to mention whatever else he may have said. We both know Eddie's no altar boy. His jumping to conclusions about Ross Hamilton proved he doesn't exercise the best judgment in the world. He's impulsive and opinionated. Add that to prejudiced, and you've got a very bad example for a young boy."

"Aw, I've had my run-ins with Eddie, but he's not a bad guy. And I sure don't think he's a racist."

"Well, his son is, Gordy. And Eddie'd better be finding out why."

25

Brandon Jones opened the door to his parents' home and was hit with the delicious aroma of something spicy. He went to the kitchen and saw his mother stirring a pot on the stove and his father sitting at the breakfast bar, reading the Sunday paper.

"What smells so good?" Brandon said.

Ellen turned around. "Shrimp Creole. I hope you're hungry. I made enough for an army."

"Yeah, I'm starved."

"You're not going to get fed like that at camp," Guy said.

"That's for sure. So Mom told you Dr. Tehrani hired me?"

"Yes, and I called Ali and talked to him myself."

"Why did you do that?"

Guy looked over the top of the newspaper. "I was just curious about the camp. I knew the board had purchased the facility and voted to go forward with it, but I hadn't taken much of an interest in it."

"And you wanted Dr. Tehrani to be sure that your son was out of there in three weeks? Is that it?"

"I told you why I called him. Don't try to turn it into something it wasn't."

"Dad, I'm not a kid. You don't need to go behind me and make sure I did everything right. Do you know how embarrassing that is?"

"I assure you, that's not what happened."

"Did the two of you talk about me?"

"Eventually, sure. Ali went on and on about you, and I just reinforced what he said. There's no doubt in my mind that you're much more than he ever bargained for. Hiring you will probably be the best two hundred a week he's ever spent…"

There's a but *in there somewhere*, Brandon thought.

"But you and I both know this job won't lead anywhere. If I thought it would get you moving in the right direction, I'd pay you two hundred dollars a week to look for a real job."

"I don't want your money, Dad! I want the freedom to make my own choices! I thought we were on the same page. It's been forty-eight hours since you promised to be an encourager and not tell me what to do, and we've already disagreed twice on this issue."

Guy held up his palms. "Okay. I just think you're making a mistake to postpone your job hunt for an entire month. The longer you put it off, the harder it's going to be."

"It's not as though I'm lazy." Brandon let out a sigh of exasperation. "I'm not going to defend my reasoning anymore."

"Well, maybe after three weeks of rubbing elbows with poor, disadvantaged kids, you'll feel differently about the career you just threw away."

"No, I won't. I'll never regret leaving Mavis and Stein, only that I didn't do it sooner. I was a square peg in a round hole. That doesn't make me inferior to you or Mom or Owen or anybody else who happened to land in the right career the first go-around!"

"Of course it doesn't," Ellen said. "Your father doesn't think that."

"Honey, I can speak for myself." Guy folded the newspaper and set it aside. "I see so much potential in you, son. My biggest fear is that you'll settle for being less than you can be."

"But that's exactly what I felt I was doing in the corporate world. I'm after more, not less. But my measuring stick for what that is differs from yours."

"Ah, therein lies the rub."

Ellen came over and began kneading Guy's shoulders, almost as if to signal a truce. "How was your visit with Papa?" she said to Brandon.

"Good. I told him what I'm doing, and that started a discussion about some of our camping adventures with him and Grandma when Owen and I were kids. We had a really great visit and then took a walk around the place, and he introduced me to some of his cronies.

I hope I'm as sharp as those guys if I make it to their age."

"Don't we all," Ellen said. "Okay, I need about ten minutes, and then dinner will be ready."

Brandon glanced in the dining room and saw the table was already set. "Unless you need me to do something, I'll go start my laundry. I'd like to be packed in the morning before I go take the drug test and get a haircut."

Brandon lingered for a few seconds, wishing his dad would say something positive. Finally, he turned and left the kitchen, his resolve surprisingly unaffected by his dad's lack of support.

Brandon walked into Gordy's Crab Shack at a quarter to nine and saw Weezie talking with some customers occupying the first booth. He flashed her a smile of recognition and then followed the waitress out to the back deck.

Brandon took a seat at a table next to the wood railing. "I'm just going to have dessert and coffee. I'd like a piece of triple berry pie, warm, with a double scoop of vanilla ice cream. Cream with the coffee, please."

The waitress winked at him. "Good choice. I'll bring that right out to you."

Brandon noticed there were no customers except for a couple sitting on the other side of the deck. He wondered why it wasn't busier, and then remembered that Gordy's closed at nine on Sunday nights.

The door opened. Weezie stepped outside and walked over to the table and gave him a hug. "I'm thrilled you got the job."

"Yeah, me too. Thanks for putting in a good word."

"You didn't need *my* help." Weezie let out a hearty laugh. "You're more qualified than the man they hired to run the place. Whoooee, they're gettin' a deal!"

"Think so, huh?"

"I know so. When do you leave?"

"Tomorrow afternoon. I was hoping we could visit a while after you get off tonight—if you're not busy, that is."

"Okay. I'll let Gordy and Pam know. If I don't show up at their house ten minutes after I get off, they'll send the cavalry out lookin' for me. Why don't we just visit out here on the deck? I've got half a pitcher of limeade that's just gonna get thrown out if somebody doesn't drink it."

Brandon nodded. "Sounds great. I ordered pie and coffee. That should keep me occupied till you get off."

"Shouldn't take long to close out with all the people I've got workin' tonight. Sure is pleasant out here. The humidity must be down."

"Hard to believe that this time tomorrow night I'll be at camp. I suppose it'd get old after a while, but right now it sounds like a fun way to break up the intensity."

"I know." She patted his hand. "You relax and enjoy your dessert. See you in a bit."

Weezie went over and held the door for the two people at the other table who were leaving, and the waitress who was coming out with Brandon's pie and coffee.

The waitress walked over to him and set his order on the table. "Can I get you anything else?"

"No, this is great. Thanks."

"All right. Enjoy."

Brandon took a sip of coffee and then a bite of warm berry pie topped with a dab of ice cream. He savored the taste for a moment and let his senses take in the sound of the waves and the smell of the salt air and the last vestiges of the sunset still visible on the horizon. He thought about his dad and knew that he would be going to bed soon and leaving for Tallahassee first thing in the morning. Guilt clawed at his conscience for having avoided him after dinner.

Brandon took out his cell phone and started to key in his parents' phone number, but he couldn't make himself complete the call. If he mentioned where he was, it would only aggravate an already tense situation. He turned off his phone and put it back in his pocket, acutely aware that the only one who ever called him on it was Kelsey.

He felt an unexpected surge of emotion. It had been nearly a month since he'd kissed her or held her or even seen her. He couldn't imagine living with this aching vacuum indefinitely and hoped that working at the camp would at least break the cycle of self-pity. He knew from experience that he wouldn't have time to think about himself once he took responsibility for the boys entrusted to his care.

A brisk evening breeze blew off the gulf and tousled his hair. He pondered the complexity of his circumstances and how odd it was to feel at the same time both free and lost. He finished the pie and coffee, the glass-covered candles on the tables burning brighter as the scenery slowly disappeared under a cloak of darkness.

He was aware of the door opening and Weezie approaching the table with a pitcher and two glasses. "Sorry it took so long, but the busboy accidentally toppled a whole rack of pies, and we had a huge mess to clean up." Weezie's laugh resounded in the quiet. "You should've seen us in there scramblin' to get that sticky pie filling up off the kitchen floor. Poor Pam's gonna need help peelin' apples in the mornin'. We've used up all the pies in the freezer."

"Heck of a way to start a Monday."

"No kiddin'. Good thing she's as laid-back as Gordy." Weezie picked up the pitcher and filled Brandon's glass with limeade and then her own. "So tomorrow you disappear into the woods and we don't see you again for three weeks."

"Almost four, since camp doesn't start till Saturday."

"It's gonna be good for you. I hope your dad's okay with it."

Brandon took a sip of limeade and wiped his upper lip. "Not really. His idea of giving me freedom is to lay a guilt trip on me and let me do whatever I want with it."

"Oh, give him time. Sometimes dads think they've gotta fix everything."

"You think I need fixing?"

Weezie patted his hand. "Baby, we all need fixin', but only the One who made us knows how to do it. Sometimes dads push a little hard, but it's usually because they love their kids and wanna see them happy."

"Well, I'd be a lot happier if my dad would just give me room to breathe."

"Be glad he cares. I'd have given anything just to *know* my daddy. He ran off when I was five."

"I'm sorry. Bet that was tough."

Weezie nodded. "Mama had to work two jobs to keep a roof over our heads. I didn't get to see a lot of her and practically raised myself. I was angry, bitter, headstrong—and up to no good much of the time. I resented that my dad wrote me off."

"I remember you saying you used to have a chip on your shoulder, but it's hard for me to imagine you that way."

"Well, believe it. I was a hellion."

"In what way?"

Weezie's eyes grew wide. "When I was in grade school, I broke all the rules. I guess negative attention was better than nothin'. When I was in middle school, I started runnin' with a rough crowd—drinkin', smokin' pot, and shopliftin' clothes and shoes and music tapes. It's a wonder I never got caught and thrown in jail. Mama was beside herself but too busy workin' to ride herd on me. When I got into high school, I started lookin' for love and attention in all the wrong places." Weezie waved her hand. "Why am I tellin' you this? It's all history now, thank the Lord."

"But that's exactly why it interests me. Somewhere along the line you must've undergone some kind of dramatic change."

"Not till I got tired of the pit I was in. I'm sad to say I got an abortion when I was fifteen. Never did tell Mama, but the guilt haunted me."

"Is that what finally changed you?" Brandon said.

"Actually, it started with an old-fashioned tent revival I wanted no part of. One of Mama's friends was married to the preacher and invited us to come. Mama thought if I got religion, maybe I'd straighten out, so she dragged me there. I'd already made up my mind that I didn't want anything to do with a God who let me feel like an orphan. So I sat in that big ol' revival tent and pretended to be listenin', but I wasn't.

"Then all of a sudden the preacher looked right at me and pointed his finger. I'll never forget what he said: '*You* were no accident. God's crazy about you. He has plans to prosper you and not harm you. Plans to give you hope and a future. He created you to do something important—something not even angels get to do.' Well, for a black kid from the poor side of town who felt like a nobody, that was exciting—till he said what it was."

Gordy Jameson sat at the kitchen table, looking at the Sunday sports page and not really seeing anything.

"You've been awfully quiet tonight." Pam Jameson slid a three-by-five card into the plastic sleeve of her recipe book. "Did Will's dropping by the crab shack have anything to do with it?"

"Yeah, he let me in on some police business that's botherin' me."

"Can you share it?"

Gordy reached over and took her hand. "Will told me on the q.t., so it has to stay between you and me. You know those four youths who got hauled in for muggin' the biracial kid and stealin' his bike? One of them was Abel Drummond."

"Oh, my. Eddie and Melody must be beside themselves."

"That's not the worst of it. Will said Abel was the ringleader and that he's a racist. The kid's twelve, for cryin' out loud." Gordy relayed to Pam everything Will had told him about the tone of the interview and the racial slurs that came out of Abel's mouth. "Will believes the kid's headed for trouble unless someone reprograms his thinking. He's hopin' Eddie will bring it up with me so I can encourage him to get help."

"Won't the judge demand it?"

"I doubt it. Will says the juvy system is already bustin' at the seams. All Abel's technically guilty of is bullyin' another twelve-year-old. The boys didn't really steal the bike. The kid ran off and left it. Abel took the bike home and kept it in the garage; and when the kid came lookin' for it, he handed it over without a fight. But Will thinks Abel is a disaster waitin' to happen."

"Are you willing to get into this with Eddie?"

"I don't know. But it's out of the question unless he brings it up because it's confidential police business. Somethin' else is buggin' me. Will said Abel didn't learn to hate blacks on his own and asked if Eddie's a racist. He said Abel went off on Eddie and accused him of always sayin' how lazy blacks are and how stupid they talk. I told Will there's no way I'd be friends with Eddie if he were a racist, but now I'm wonderin' if I'm bein' naive. Maybe Eddie cleans up his act around me because he knows I'd throw him out if he started talkin' that way."

Pam squeezed his hand. "That's good, isn't it?"

"Not if he's puttin' down blacks everywhere else and people know he's my friend. I don't wanna be guilty by association."

Brandon leaned forward on his elbows. "So what did the preacher say?"

"That God made us so we can show the world what His love looks like." Weezie arched her eyebrows. "Of course, my heart sank lower than my knees because I was sure God was cruel and uncaring and didn't love *me* at all. I went home more depressed than when I came. I went right on makin' bad choices and bouncin' from one man's bed to another, but the preacher's words wouldn't leave me alone. I knew I was missin' somethin'."

"So what finally happened to turn you around?"

Weezie smiled warmly. "Not what, *who*: Joshua Taylor. I met him at my cousin's wedding and was taken with him from the start, even if he did talk about the Lord like He was standin' right next to us. I'd never been around anybody like that."

"So Joshua was a pastor?"

"No, he was a mechanic down at Amos's Auto Repair. But he was somethin' special, I'll tell you that. Never once made a move on me, if you know what I mean. Joshua treated me like a lady, and pretty soon I started actin' like one. I couldn't get over how kind and carin' he was with everybody. Why, he'd give you the shirt off his back if you needed it. He was always lookin' out for other people before he gave a thought to himself. And I was intrigued by the way he talked about God as if he actually knew Him. It finally dawned on me that Joshua was a livin', breathin' example of what that preacher had talked about all those years ago. When I could actually see what God's love looked like in another person, I started wantin' it for myself."

Brandon took his finger and erased the water ring on the table. "So the preacher's words finally made sense to you?"

"They sure did. And the day I finally gave my heart to Jesus, I caught a glimpse of myself in the mirror. Instead of seein' that bitter, stubborn, rebellious black kid that gave up on herself, I saw the face of a woman filled with purpose and hope and a future. I saw eyes burnin' with the love of God. And I knew down deep inside that the Lord Almighty, the Creator of the universe, was livin' in *me*, Weezie Taylor. And He was crazy about me. And He was gonna let me do somethin' angels don't get to do: show Him off to the whole world. And you know the best part of all? None of my awful sinnin' had changed His mind a lick. He had this planned long before I gave Him a thought! He was just waitin' for me to step into my dancin' shoes!" Weezie jumped up and turned in a circle, her arms in the air. "Whoooeee, somebody say hallelujah!"

Brandon laughed without meaning to and realized how much he longed for the passion he saw in her.

Weezie dropped into the chair and let out a robust laugh. "You probably think I'm some kinda nutcase."

"Not at all. I'm enjoying this. Go on."

"Where was I...? Oh, yeah, the day I got baptized Joshua gave me a Bible. I opened it every chance I got and couldn't seem to get enough. Since then my life's goal has been to show people what God's love looks like by lettin' Him transform me into the image of His Son. I figured there's no higher callin' than that, whether you're runnin' the White House or cleanin' toilets." Weezie swatted the air. "Listen to me goin' on and on. I need to put a sock in this mouth of mine and listen to what it was you came down here to talk to me about."

Brandon couldn't stop the smile that stretched his cheeks. "I just wanted a pep talk. I'd say you've more than covered it."

26

Ellen Jones sat out on the veranda as a pink tint spread across the Monday morning sky, her mind cataloging all the facts she knew about the hate crimes in anticipation of digging into the archives of the *North Coast Messenger.*

"Here's your coffee, honey." Guy Jones set a tray on the side table and kissed her on the cheek. "I've got to run. The partners are meeting at ten, and I have some prep work to do. Thanks for getting my suit from the cleaners."

"You're welcome."

Guy stood next to her for several seconds, seemingly lost in thought, and then said, "I guess I'll see Brandon in four weeks. Would it have hurt him to say good-bye?"

"He probably got busy preparing to leave for camp and lost track of time. I doubt he remembered you have to leave for Tallahassee at the crack of dawn."

"I'm sure he's counting on me thinking that."

Ellen gently wrapped her fingers around Guy's wrist. "You two really have made a breakthrough. It may not seem like it this morning, but being honest with you was a big step for Brandon. He isn't feeling good about himself right now, and any hint of disapproval probably makes him revert to hiding his feelings."

"Well, I can't pretend to approve of something I don't."

"No, but once you've given him your opinion, you can let him make his own choices and support his right to see things differently."

"I thought I did that."

Ellen gave his arm a squeeze and let go. "Offering to pay him two hundred dollars a week to get a *real* job isn't exactly the kind of support I had in mind."

Guy looked at her sheepishly. "I probably should've had girls. Maybe I wouldn't feel compelled to push so hard."

"Maybe you just need to get behind whatever it is he wants to do and then give him a push of support."

"Another month of being out of the workforce and he'll have less confidence than ever. He's just postponing the inevitable. He's going to regret it."

"Then allow him to figure it out on his own. He may have to take a few detours before he can find the right path."

"That's the hardest thing in the world for me to do."

Ellen looked up into his eyes. "I know. But it's what he needs most from you."

"What if he can't get it together? What if he blows any chance of ever making something of himself?"

"Well, you can't do it for him. And pushing him a direction he doesn't want to go will only drive another wedge between you."

Guy exhaled loudly and put his hand on her shoulder. "You're right. I just don't want Brandon to struggle financially for the rest of his life."

"I don't either. But we need to leave the situation in the Lord's hands and let Him work it out. You know as well as I do that God has a purpose for everything. Truthfully, I'd rather see him pinch pennies with a smile on his face than rake in a fortune with a ball and chain around his heart."

Will Seevers flipped the light switch in his office and set a cup of Starbucks coffee on his desk, aware of footsteps behind him.

"I didn't think you'd be here till eight," Al Backus said.

"It's not like I'm getting much sleep these days. Thanks for leaving me the list of people who had access to the note. Anyone in particular stand out to you?"

Al shook his head. "Not really. I trust every detective I work with. We're tight. I can't imagine any of them leaking information."

"What about secretaries? File clerks? Maintenance people?"

Al folded his arms across his chest. "I don't know. I pretty much kept the file locked up."

"*Pretty* much?"

Al's face suddenly looked flushed. "Things were crazy around here when we got hit with all that racial stuff all at once. I don't remember ever being careless with the file, but I didn't lock it up every time I went to the men's room or went down the hall to get a Coke. I'm positive it was locked up at night or anytime I left the building."

"So whoever leaked it could've gotten their hands on it sometime when you were here?"

"That's all I can figure. The evidence officer said it was never signed out."

"Then I suggest you rake your people over the coals one by one and get someone to admit it. I want that leak, Al. I can't run this department with an employee who's undermining what we're trying to do here!"

"I'll get with each person on the list before the day's over. I won't stop digging till I've got your man."

Will gave a firm nod. "That's more like it. By the way, have you caught up with Mick Beasley or Jessica Ziegler?"

"No, Beasley's still not home. The neighbors don't know where he is. I've got a couple detectives who plan to pay Ms. Ziegler a visit at work this morning and show her Beasley's photo."

"Good."

Will's cell phone vibrated. "Don't go away…" Will took the phone off his belt clip. "Will Seevers."

"Chief, it's Jack Rutgers. We've got a big problem."

Brandon Jones turned over on his side and let his eyes focus on the bright sunlight filtering through the tree branches. His dad should be long gone by now. He wished he'd had the courage to make peace with his dad before he left for Tallahassee but decided even silence was better than fighting with him before they parted ways for a month.

Brandon sat up on the side of the bed and rubbed his hands through his hair, the faint aroma of coffee wafting under his nose. He glanced at the clock and saw that it was almost nine.

He heard the hallway door open and footsteps coming up the

stairs. Seconds later his mother stood in the doorway. "Oh, good, you're awake."

"Yeah, just. I didn't mean to sleep so late. Is Dad gone?"

"He left at six. He was hoping you'd at least say good-bye before you went off to camp."

"I thought he'd be glad to get rid of me."

Ellen sat on the side of the bed next to Brandon. "Your father's not the enemy. He really does want what's best for you."

"Yeah, as long as what I want lines up with what *he* wants."

"Be patient. He really is trying. So what's your plan today?"

"I'm already packed. I need to go take the drug test and get a haircut. And I need to get batteries for my digital camera. Maybe pick up some sunscreen and insect repellent. I may swing by and see Papa again on my way out."

"Are you sure you packed *everything*?"

Brandon studied her face and then smiled. "I didn't forget the Bible."

"Good." Ellen patted his knee. "I left two freshly baked muffins and a thermos of coffee for you on the breakfast bar. And a ham-and-cheese on rye in the fridge. After that, you're at the mercy of the camp cook."

"You going somewhere?"

His mother nodded, her face animated. "Down to the newspaper building to dig through the archives. I'd like to pursue something."

"What's that?"

"I'd like to see if I can find a past connection to the Ws."

"Does Dad know?"

"Actually, he suggested it. He thinks I'd enjoy beating Valerie Hodges at her own game."

"You would, wouldn't you?"

"Definitely."

"I thought Dad was dead set on you staying out of the newspaper business and writing novels."

Ellen sighed. "Well, both of us finally realized it's not who I am. I love the real life drama of the newsroom."

"What if your novel gets published?"

"That can't happen now. Every manuscript I sent out has been rejected, and I'm done pursuing a publisher. It was a great release for all my feelings about the gossip surrounding the Hamilton case, but I've totally lost interest. I'm ready to accept that it was a fun project but not what I want to spend my life doing. I'm a journalist, Brandon. You can take the newspaperwoman out of the newsroom, but you can't take the—"

"Newsroom out of the newspaperwoman." Brandon laughed and put his arms around his mother. "I'm so glad. You seem much happier than you were when I first came here."

"I am."

"You going to try to find a job with the newspaper?"

"I don't know. I'll take it a step at a time."

"Yeah, that's what I'm trying to do."

"Before we leave, I just wanted to reassure you that since God opened the door for you to work at the camp, He'll be with you on the other side of the threshold. He uses every experience to grow us. So while you're there, listen intently. He often speaks softly and in ways you're not expecting."

Brandon nodded.

Ellen took his hand and held it tightly. "I also wanted to say that I'm proud of the person you are and have every confidence that you'll find your niche. Remember, I'm rooting for you and praying for you—and dearly love you."

"I love you, too." Brandon blinked the stinging from his eyes and rested for a moment in the comfort of his mother's affirmation.

Will Seevers barreled down a gravel road that wound through the piney woods near Old Seaport. He spotted a clearing up ahead and the flashing lights of several police vehicles and a fire truck. He passed the sign for Victory Chapel and saw two white Ws spray-painted over the name. He pulled up behind another squad car and surveyed the smoldering remains of the old wooden church. Will got out of his car, Al Backus on his heels, and walked over to Jack Rutgers, aware that the coroner had just pulled up. "Fill me in."

The blood seemed to have drained from Jack's face, and he hesitated a moment and then said, "We aren't sure yet how this went down, but there are seven charred bodies in what appears to be a parsonage attached to the back of the church. We think it might be the pastor and his family."

"Good grief. Who called it in?"

"The 911 operator said the call came in less than thirty minutes ago from what sounded to her like a middle-aged Caucasian male. He wouldn't give his name."

Will folded his arms across his chest, his pulse racing faster than his mind. "Could've been someone who happened upon the scene and was afraid to get involved."

"Or the spokesman for the dirtbags who actually set the fire," Al said, "and made sure the victims were ashes before drawing attention to their handiwork. They probably picked this place because there's nothing else out here."

"Any tire tracks?"

Jack nodded. "Yeah, and some footprints. CSI is on the way."

Will looked up and saw the fire marshal walking in his direction.

"There's no doubt it's arson," the marshal said. "I can't be sure exactly what happened till we take a closer look. But based on what I've seen, my best guess is that the entire exterior of the building was soaked with gasoline, and then a torch or a Molotov cocktail was tossed in through a broken window in the front of the church. That's where the fire started. This old building was tinderbox."

"Can you tell if whoever was in there tried to get out?"

"Doesn't appear so. Probably slept through it and died of smoke inhalation. I doubt they ever knew it happened. Looks like five of the victims were children. Man, I hope you get these creeps—and soon."

Will stood with his eyes fixed on the charred ruins, his heart pounding and his mind screaming with the implications. "Come on, Al. Let's take a look inside and then call an emergency meeting with Sheriff Martin. When this hits the news, we're liable to have a riot on our hands."

27

L ater that morning Police Chief Will Seevers sat at the table in his office with Al Backus and Sheriff Hank Martin.

"I called us together because we need to plan our response to this latest attack," Will said. "I've already contacted the FBI and ATF, and agents are on the way. We need to act quickly to keep the black community's outrage from getting out of control. Plus, this thing's going to draw national attention. Every prominent black leader will speak out—and I doubt any of it will reflect kindly on the Seaport PD. We need all the law enforcement help we can get to show the public we're committed to getting whoever's doing this."

Hank nodded. "I also think it's time you put me or some other African-American out there in front of the cameras. We have a better understanding of the fear that's got a grip on the black community. People are done listenin' to what they perceive as the indifference of white cops." He looked at Will. "Believe me, *I* know you're workin' your tail off to solve this. But after what happened at that church, I assure you the black community isn't gonna sit back and wait for justice unless they believe it can really happen. Hearin' from a brother might go a long way in preventing things from gettin' out of hand."

"Good point. Any thoughts, Al?"

"We should also request assistance from the Port Smyth PD. We need to have a strong police presence ASAP."

"If rioting breaks out, even that won't give us enough manpower. Let's hope we don't have to ask the governor to call in the National Guard." Will sat back in his chair and stared out the window. "I still can't believe this thing escalated from smashed windows and slashed tires to the senseless murder of seven."

Will heard the receptionist's voice on the intercom. "Chief,

Special Agent Bryce Moore of the FBI has arrived."

"All right. Bring him down to my office." Will turned to Al and Hank, his eyebrows arched. "If this is a bad dream, I hope I wake up soon."

Gordy Jameson heard footsteps coming down the hallway and turned off the radio in his office.

"You wanted to see me?" Weezie Taylor said.

"Yeah, why don't you close the door behind you?"

Weezie closed the door and sat in the chair next to his desk. "What's up?"

Gordy looked into her round dark eyes, his heart heavy. "I've got some really bad news. There's been a fire at Victory Chapel. I'm sorry, but your pastor and his family didn't make it."

"Didn't make it? You mean…you mean they're all *dead*?"

"There were seven victims."

Weezie's eyes turned to dark pools, her chin quivering. "How'd it happen?"

"Arson. And possibly murder. Two white Ws were spray-painted on the big sign out front. Will just called and wanted me to tell you before you heard it from someone else. It's all over the news."

Weezie rocked back and forth, her arms folded across her chest, tears trickling down her cheeks. "Lord, give me grace. Give me grace. Give me grace…" Finally she put her head in her hands and wept.

Gordy slipped his arm around her shoulder and sat silently, wondering if Will would be able to keep the peace after this.

Brandon Jones pulled up in front of a two-story log building at Camp Piney Woods and turned off the motor. He got out and let his eyes move across the grounds, the scent of pine taking him back to his boyhood days in Baxter.

He walked up to the entrance and went inside and was immediately greeted by a tan, well-built guy with sun-bleached hair who looked to be about twenty-five.

"Hi, I'm Dax Barnes, the camp director."

"Brandon Jones." He offered Dax his hand and felt surprisingly old. "Dr. Tehrani hired me to work as a counselor and told me to come out here this afternoon and begin orientation."

"Yeah, I've been expecting you. Your background's impressive. I've worked at camps since I was a teenager, but never with anybody from the corporate world."

"Well, I'm just a Boy Scout at heart." Brandon winked.

"Great. The seven boys you'll be working with are between eleven and thirteen. All from disadvantaged homes. None have been to camp before. So if you're nervous about doing things just right, don't be. Whatever we're able to offer them will be a first. They're just glad to be accepted into the program. Dr. Tehrani said you were an outdoor sports enthusiast."

"I am. I love just about any sport you can think of."

"Enough to tackle a three-day backpacking trip with these kids?"

"Sure, if I have the right equipment and the boys are ready."

Dax patted him on the shoulder. "Excellent. Let's see how things go. I'd like you to take them backpacking sometime during the last week if you think they're up to it. The first two weeks should give you plenty of time to get to know each one and help build the team skills they'll need. We've got a great program lined up."

"I assume I'll be bunking with the boys?"

"Yeah, at Red Feather." Dax walked over and pointed to a map mounted on an easel. "That's cabin six. Right here. Come on, I'll walk over there with you. The facilities are really nice. Dr. Tehrani's foundation didn't skimp on anything."

Ellen Jones sat in the musty morgue of the *North Coast Messenger*, experiencing both the sense of excitement she'd felt as a cub reporter and the weight of an almost impossible task. How foolish was it to think that something in these newspaper archives would tell her what the Ws spray-painted at the crime scenes meant? She felt almost foolish as she considered the odds of her finding the answer.

She'd been working on this most of the day and had gone back only as far as 1999. Though numerous incidents of racism had been reported, nothing was serious enough to end up on the front page.

The morgue had hard copies of the newspapers dating back to 1996. If she didn't find anything here, she would have to resume her search at the local library, which had all the newspapers on microfilm dating back to the 1920s.

She sensed someone standing behind her and turned around.

"Hello, Ellen," Valerie Hodges said.

"How did you know it was me?"

"Oh, just a hunch. I saw your name on the sign in sheet. It's nice to finally put a face to the name, but I never expected our first face-to-face to be here in the morgue."

"Is there something you want?" Ellen said.

"Look, I know you're mad at me for printing the threatening note the police found in your son's car, but the public deserved to know what was going on. The police chief isn't doing enough. Someone needed to push the envelope. I guess after this morning's incident, they'll realize how serious the threat is."

Ellen studied Valerie's eyes. "What incident? What are you talking about?"

"You haven't heard about the seven people who died in the black church that burned to the ground?"

"No, I've been here. I haven't listened to the news at all. What happened?"

"Someone torched Victory Chapel last night. The pastor, his wife, and their five kids perished in the adjacent parsonage. The notorious Ws were spray-painted on the church sign."

"Oh, no…" Ellen put her hands to her mouth and struggled to find her voice. "I worked with Pastor Jonah and his wife Jasmine at the shelter for Katrina evacuees. Did the authorities confirm they were the victims?"

"You know their names won't be released until their bodies are identified, but it appears there were two adults and five kids still in their beds."

Ellen blinked away the graphic image that popped into her mind and pictured instead the bright smiles that had always been evident on the faces of Jonah and Jasmine Delk.

"I *knew* something awful was going to happen," Valerie said. "The police chief should've made public what was in that note so people would've been prepared for the other shoe to fall."

"That's ridiculous. There's no way anyone could've known from what was in that note that the threat extended beyond Brandon and Weezie."

"Well, *I* sure did."

Ellen sighed loudly enough to convey her disgust. "No, Valerie, you didn't. But I'm sure you're going to take full advantage of the situation and let everyone in town believe you did."

"Forget about me. If you were a reporter and thought the police were wrong to withhold the note, would you have kept it quiet?"

"Well, I certainly wouldn't have…oh, think whatever you want. I need to get back to what I was doing."

"What are you working on?"

"A personal project that requires extreme *concentration*."

"Okay, I can take a hint. I've got to be at a press conference in twenty-five minutes anyway. But you should be thanking me for watching out for your son and all the other victims. Obviously no one in the police department was." Valerie turned on her heel and went upstairs.

Ellen sat motionless for a few minutes, glad to be rid of Valerie but stunned by the horrific news she had brought. Suddenly drained of energy, Ellen decided to quit for the day and resume her search tomorrow at the library, where she wouldn't have to deal with Valerie breathing down her neck.

She gathered her notes and went upstairs and out the front door of the *North Coast Messenger* building, more determined than ever to figure out what the Ws signified.

Ellen walked in the house, laid her briefcase and purse on the breakfast bar, went in the living room, and flipped on the TV. WRGL News was doing a live broadcast at the scene of the fire. Ellen turned up the volume.

"…and Police Chief Will Seevers has now called in the FBI and the ATF to assist in the investigation. The coroner's office confirmed that seven charred bodies were removed from the parsonage, which was actually an addition built directly onto the back of the church building some thirty years ago. Though authorities have not released the identities of the victims, Hattie Arnold, the pastor's sister and spokesperson for the family, told WRGL News that the family believes the autopsies will show that the victims were indeed the pastor, Jonah Delk, his wife Jasmine, and their five children, all under the age of eleven.

"Arnold also strongly cautioned the black community not to react with violence, but to unite and pray that God would help the authorities find the person or persons responsible. But as the news spreads of this unconscionable murder, one has to wonder how much longer public outrage can be contained.

"We go now to the press conference about to take place outside city hall…"

Ellen saw three men positioned behind microphones: Will Seevers standing in the middle; the FBI special agent she recognized from the Hamilton case on the left; and Sheriff Hank Martin on the right. She hoped no one thought it looked contrived that Will had an African-American on either side of him.

She went into the kitchen during the introductions and got a glass of lemonade, then sat on the couch just as the special agent started speaking.

"I'm Special Agent Bryce Moore of the FBI. Police Chief Will Seevers and Sheriff Hank Martin have asked me to take the lead in this case, not only because of its gravity, but because the FBI has experience in cases like this one, and we have resources available that may serve to hasten an arrest.

"At 7:05 this morning, an unidentified male called 911 to report a fire at Victory Chapel just off Hawkins Highway near Old Seaport. Emergency vehicles were immediately dispatched, but when police and fire officials arrived, they found only smolderin' remains of the church building. They also discovered seven bodies in the adjacent parsonage. And two white Ws spray-painted on the sign in front of the church.

"The fire marshal has confirmed that the outer walls of the structure had been doused with gasoline, and that the fire started sometime between 3:00 and 4:00 a.m. at the window to the left of the front entrance of the church and spread quickly.

"The bodies of the seven victims have not yet been positively identified, but members of Victory Chapel have confirmed that the pastor, his wife, and their five children lived in the parsonage.

"I want to state emphatically that the FBI is workin' concurrently with the Seaport PD, the Beacon County Sheriff's Department, and the Bureau of Alcohol, Tobacco, and Firearms and will do everything possible to get whoever is responsible for these tragic murders. It's not a matter of *if*, but *when*. I'll take a few questions. Yes…"

"Sir, when will you know for sure the identity of the victims?"

"The medical examiner's office is comparin' dental records and should be able to tell us somethin' in the next day or two. However, the smallest child may not have dental records, and the identification may take longer. Yes…the young man in the yellow tie."

"Can you tell us whether the white Ws spray-painted on the church sign match the letters found at the other crime scenes?"

Bryce nodded. "They do. Yes…the man in the blue sport coat."

"Sir, there have been reports of rioting and looting in areas of the black community. Can you confirm that?"

"I can tell you emphatically that's *not* the case. We've already met with city officials and leaders in the African-American community, both secular and religious, and assured them that endin' this reign of terror and bringin' the responsible party or parties to justice is our *number one* priority. I salute the black community for exercisin' restraint throughout this time of racial unrest and ask that it continue to support the efforts of law enforcement and resist the urge to retaliate. I think it's important that we all remember these unconscionable acts do not reflect the attitude of most of the citizens of Seaport. Yes…the woman in the green dress."

Valerie Hodges took a step forward. "Special Agent Moore, are you also taking the lead on all the hate crime cases associated with this one?"

"I am."

"Isn't it true, sir, that the Seaport police think the person who wrote the threatening note to the one Caucasian victim forms his Ws identically to whoever spray-painted the Ws at the crime scenes?"

"It's inconclusive, ma'am."

"But am I right that the police believe strongly it's the same perp?"

"I'll let Chief Seevers answer that." Bryce looked over at Will.

"Our handwriting expert says the Ws look strikingly similar," Will said. "But the strokes when using a pen versus a spray can are so different that it's impossible to say with certainty."

"But wouldn't you agree that if the contents of the threatening note had been released to the public sooner, people would have been more vigilant about the threat of violence?"

Will's eyebrows furrowed. "No, I think the motivation for the racial attacks perpetrated against Mr. Jones and Ms. Taylor were already obvious. The verbiage of the note actually confirms the threat was specific to them."

"I respectfully dis—"

"Let's move on," Bryce said. "Yes…"

"Sir, do you have any suspects at this time?"

"I'm not gonna answer that while the investigation's ongoing."

"But do you believe whoever is doing this is acting alone? Or do you think there are people from outside the community also involved?"

"We have no reason at this time to think that anyone outside the area is involved, but we can't discount the possibility."

"Should the community brace itself for more attacks?"

"Obviously, I can't know for sure. But from experience, I'd say that whoever is doin' this will keep on until we stop them. And that's exactly what we're gonna do. Thank you. That's all we have time for today."

Bryce stepped away from the mic and said something to Will Seevers, and then the three men went inside city hall.

The phone rang and Ellen put the TV on mute. "Hello."

"Mom, it's Brandon."

"Hi, honey. Were you able to find the camp okay?"

"Yeah, it's got great facilities, and the setting is really nice. Did you hear about the church burning?"

Ellen sighed. "Oh, yeah. From Valerie Hodges, no less."

"How'd that happen?"

"It's not worth rehashing. I'm just sick about the deaths. I knew

Pastor Jonah and Jasmine. I worked with them at the evacuee shelter. They were wonderful people. I'm pretty sure Weezie goes to that church."

"Really?"

"I'm not positive, but I think she does."

"Well, we got briefed on the whole thing because we're going to have quite a mixed bag at camp this weekend, and the camp director wants to be sure we're up to speed. Some of these kids may be really hurting or angry about it. We're going to have to be ready for that."

"Are you nervous about it?"

"No, not really. I haven't been around pubescent boys since I was one myself, and I'm sure the combination of that and all the racial unrest will make for an interesting week. Hopefully, they won't be exposed to any news while they're here. After a day or two, maybe we'll all forget the cares of the real world and just have fun."

Ellen glanced up at the TV images of the burned church. "If this thing gets any more intense, I may drive out there and join you."

28

William Seevers slammed down the phone and sent Tuesday morning's newspaper flying off the kitchen table with one broad sweep of his arm.

He got up and nearly ran headlong into Margaret as he passed through the doorway. "Sorry, honey. I've gotta leave. There's a gang of black teenagers turning over cars and vandalizing stores in the tourist district."

"Oh, no." Margaret Seevers heaved a sigh. "I was so hoping this wouldn't happen."

"Me too. The FBI already has agents on the scene, and they've asked that all available manpower head that way. The last thing we need is to sink all our efforts into keeping the peace instead of finding the scum that started this mess in the first place." He kissed Margaret's cheek. "I'll call you later and tell you what's going on, but something tells me you'll be watching it live on CNN."

Will went out the front door and to his squad car, aware that a layer of dark smoke had soiled the pastel colors of the morning sky. He got in his car and headed for Beachcomber Drive, wondering if Gordy knew what was going on. He took his cell phone off the clip and hit the autodial. It rang three times, and then someone picked up.

"Hello."

"Pam, it's Will. Is Gordy there?"

"Yes, he's sitting right here. Hang on…"

"Hey, Will. What's up?"

"Bad news. A gang of black teens is turning over cars and vandalizing stores down on Beachcomber. The FBI is on the scene, and I'm on my way."

"Any idea how close are they to the crab shack?"

"Six blocks. Hopefully we'll get this thing contained before they get that far. Stay home. I don't want you down there, but I thought you ought to know what's going on. I'll call you when I know something."

"Yeah, okay, Will. Thanks. Be safe, okay?"

"Always."

Will turned on his siren and sped across town, glad that the morning rush hour traffic wasn't heavy yet. He turned onto Sixth Street and then Beachcomber Drive and saw the FBI barricade up ahead.

Will got out of his car and walked over to Special Agent Bryce Moore and stood quietly for a few seconds, then said, "I guess we can forget being voted quaintest weekend getaway in Florida."

The corners of Bryce's mouth twitched. "This summer anyway."

Will put his binoculars to his eyes and looked down the street, where two blocks away officers were using tear gas to subdue an angry mob. The young people were shouting at police, breaking windows, and throwing what appeared to be produce, eggs, and bottles. In the distance it looked as though two motor vehicles had been overturned and were burning."

"Good thing you're here," Will said. "We don't have much experience with riot control."

"Unfortunately, when this kind of thing starts it usually runs its course. I have a feeling we've just seen the tip of the iceberg."

Will shook his head. "This didn't have to happen. How do we convince the black community we're on their side?"

"I don't know, Will. People can only get the short end of the stick so many times before they stop believin' in justice."

"That's a cheap shot. My department's been on top of this thing since day one, and we want justice as much as they do."

"I know. Don't take it personal. It goes way beyond what happened here. There's a ball and chain around the ankle of the black community that's never been unlocked. Whites don't want to deal with it. They just want to forget the past and move on."

"What's wrong with that? Seems pretty pointless to rehash our ancestors' mistakes over and over."

"Unless you're the one livin' with the reminders day after day. Much of the time blacks are tolerated merely because the law requires it, not because the rest of the population thinks we're legitimate members of the community."

Will turned the binoculars on police officers dragging several youths over to the paddy wagon. "You really think that's how white people see you?"

"Not me. I'm a big bad FBI special agent. They revere me. Fear me even." Bryce smirked. "Don't look so serious. I'm kiddin'…except for the part about feelin' tolerated because the law requires it. That's real. When I step out of these shoes, all that respect goes down the toilet and I'm just another black man. I'm treated completely different."

"So am I when people don't know I'm a police chief."

"Ah, but you're treated like just another *white* man. There's a big difference, no matter how uncomfortable it makes you feel to hear it." Bryce picked up his walkie-talkie. "This is Moore, over… How many…? All right, you know the drill. Bring them in and avoid talking to the media. Out." Bryce looked over at him. "Come on. I want to be at the station when they book these kids."

Ellen Jones sat in a corner of the public library, reviewing the microfilm of *North Coast Messenger* articles for 1997, thinking how foolish she was to have undertaken such intensive research with nothing more than initials to go on. She glanced at her watch. It was already 10:15. She was thinking that at the rate she was progressing, she'd be lucky to finish by Labor Day.

"Well, fancy meeting you here," a woman whispered.

Ellen turned around and looked up into the face of Valerie Hodges. She felt herself wince. "Why are you following me?"

Valerie sat in the chair next to Ellen and spoke softly. "Because I'm bothered by the hostility I sense from you. What will it take for you to let go of the past and believe I've changed?"

Ellen rolled her eyes. "Yes, I can see how much you've changed. You've already found the leak in the police department and used it to your own advantage."

Valerie looked at her hands for a moment and then at Ellen. "I know I handled the Hamilton case poorly. I admit I tweaked the story to advance my career, but don't forget I was almost positive that Ross was a killer."

"Well, *almost positive* nearly destroyed a family."

"I apologized to the Hamiltons."

"A little late, don't you think?"

Valerie nodded. "Yes, and if I could go back and change the way I reported on the case, I would. But it's not as though I'm the only one who thought Ross was guilty. You're the one who called me to pick my brain."

"Well, at least I didn't print my baseless opinion in the newspaper as fact." Ellen felt a twinge of guilt. *No, I just ran straight to the police chief with an earful of gossip. I'm no more righteous than she is.*

"Ellen, I can't undo past mistakes. But I want you to understand that I chose to reveal the threatening note because I believe there needs to be more public pressure on law enforcement, not because I wanted to get noticed. My source told me why Will Seevers withheld it, but I thought it was a bad call. It was wrong for the police not to let the public know how potentially explosive the racial situation really was—and all because some oddball *might* come forward and confess to a crime he didn't do. Can you honestly say if you were a reporter and someone had leaked this information to you that you'd have blown off your obligation to report the whole truth?"

Ellen studied Valerie's expression, surprised at how sincere she seemed. "I would've confronted the police chief privately instead of nailing him to the wall at a press conference."

"I called him multiple times and left messages. He never called back. So I went down to the police station and asked to see him for five minutes and was told that Chief Seevers would address the media only at scheduled press conferences. So what choice did I have?"

"I fail to see how that shows you've changed. You manipulated the situation until you got what *you* wanted."

"No, I did what I had to do to get the truth out. It's hard for me to believe you really think I was wrong to question the chief about a critical matter he wasn't addressing."

"What is it you want from me, Valerie?"

"Just the chance to explain myself." Valerie rose to her feet. "I don't expect you to instantly change your mind about me, but I wanted to tell you where I'm coming from."

"Why do you care what I think?" Ellen said.

"Because I respect you. Had I listened to your advice and not put my own spin on the Hamilton story, I might have saved this community a lot of grief. I learned a hard lesson from that situation, and time will prove that I've changed." Valerie bent down and picked up what appeared to be a gum wrapper off the floor. "I'm very sorry about Pastor Delk and his family. How well did you know them?"

"As well as you can know someone you work closely with for a few months. Jonah and Jasmine were wonderful people. Their commitment to the evacuees was an inspiration. They got the whole family involved."

"So you met their kids?"

Ellen nodded. "They brought their three-year-old with them all the time, and the other children when they weren't in school. They were well-behaved and played nicely with the kids in the shelter. It's so hard to believe they're gone, but it's comforting to know they never knew what happened. Have you heard whether or not things have calmed down in the tourist district?"

"Yeah, the police arrested about three dozen black teenagers who were breaking windows and throwing things. Two cars were overturned and burned, but no one got hurt. Those kids are just acting out the anger they've been stuffing for almost two weeks—or maybe a lifetime. Scary stuff."

Gordy Jameson came in the back door of the crab shack and saw Weezie Taylor looking out the front window, seemingly lost in thought. He coughed so he wouldn't startle her, then walked up and stood beside her. "You okay?"

"I will be. I'm sad. And mad. And disgusted." Weezie sighed. "It's bad enough that I just lost my pastor and his family. But what were those stupid kids thinkin', tearin' up stuff like that? All it did was shift the focus onto them and feed the fear whites already have of African-Americans." Weezie shook her head. "Any sympathy for what happened to Pastor Delk and his family just went up in smoke."

"I don't think so, Weezie. Most people are sympathetic to what's been goin' on. I'm just glad the police stopped the kids before they got this far, and nobody got hurt. But those shops havin' to close during tourist season is a big economic hit."

"Well, we can pretty much forget tourist season now," Weezie said. "Nobody in his right mind would wanna get in the middle of this."

Gordy was aware of the back door slamming and heavy footsteps on the wood floor, and then Billy Lewis standing between him and Weezie.

"I am sor-ry about your pas-tor and the child-ren. I am wor-ried about Lyd-ia and Sam-uel."

Gordy put his hand on Billy's shoulder, surprised that he'd made the connection between the black kids who perished in the fire and his Compassion kids in Uganda. "Aw, your two youngsters are safe, Billy. They live a long, long way from here."

"I'll tell you what, Billy," Weezie said. "How about when you've finished cleanin' those tables out back, you and I go e-mail a letter to Lydia and Samuel? Would you like that?"

Billy's head bobbed. "I will tell them to stay a-way from bad people! They will be safe."

"Of course they will." Gordy winked at Weezie. "They always listen to your good advice."

Billy went back outside, and Gordy stood for a moment in the quiet, feeling Weezie's pain and feeling helpless to do anything about it. "You wanna take the day off?"

"Heavens, no. Bein' around people will pick me up. I can hardly wait till the lunch crowd starts comin' in."

"Have the funeral arrangements been made yet?"

Weezie shook her head. "The relatives don't wanna do anything till little Gideon's body's been identified. Thank the Lord that child is runnin' on the streets of gold and doesn't know the medical examiner is diggin' through what's left of him." Weezie wiped a tear off her cheek. "Kinda strange feelin' joy and pain at the same time."

"I'm not so sure I would've found any room for joy if you'd died when your car was forced off the road."

"Goin' home to glory is somethin' to celebrate."

"I doubt the relatives will feel like celebratin'."

"Deep down they will, same as everyone who knows the Lord. We're gonna miss them, but we know where they went. It's not as though we're not gonna see them again."

"I know, but it's hard to get past the circumstances of *how* they died."

"It was tragic and a terrible injustice. No one's sayin' it wasn't. But God knew it was comin', and He had a place ready for them. They're never gonna know pain or sorrow or tears again. They're forever in His presence, right where they were made to be. It's not them we need to weep for, but whoever set that fire."

"I'm not wastin' my tears on those racist scumbags."

"We need to pray for them. Unless they let the Lord have their hearts, the kind of fire waitin' for them is never gonna go out."

29

Will Seevers went into his office, Al Backus on his heels, then shut the door and sat at his desk, his temples throbbing. "What a morning!"

"So how'd the feds do with riot control?" Al said.

"A lot better than we would've without them. But now the shop owners are in a lather over lost revenue from tourism. And the African-American community is yelling foul because we arrested three dozen black teenagers and not a single white person since this whole mess blew up a week ago."

Al rolled his eyes. "What'd they expect us to do—sit back and watch them trash Beachcomber Drive because we haven't arrested any white people?"

"They're not in the mood to reason, Al. They're mad and they're scared. Somebody torched seven African-Americans, and they want justice. If we don't make an arrest soon, they're liable to do a whole lot worse than we saw today! The last thing we need is a race war!" Will took out his handkerchief and dabbed his forehead. "All right, let's stay focused on what we've already got going. Did you question the employees on the list about the leak?"

"I haven't gotten to everyone yet, but I'm working on it."

"Anyone stand out?"

"Not really."

"All right, stay with it. Did you talk to Jessica Ziegler about our convicted felon who's driving a black or dark blue Ford truck?"

Al nodded. "We stopped by her apartment and showed her Beasley's picture. Says she's never seen him before. But the bartender at Big John's sure has and thinks Beasley may have been one of Jessica's one-night stands."

"Interesting that she would lie to you about knowing him."

"Well, the bartender wasn't positive about that. But he's sure Beasley's been in there a few times lately and thinks he's involved in some backroom high stakes poker games at The Cove. If Jessica knows that Beasley's involved in illegal gambling, it makes sense that she'd want us to believe she doesn't know him."

"Beasley still out of town?"

"Looks that way. We talked to his neighbors, and they don't know where he is or where he works. Say he keeps to himself. We showed his picture around all the art supply stores, too. No one recognized him."

"All right, go down to The Cove, and see what you can find out about Beasley, but try not to raise suspicion about him or the poker games. Not that we have anything on him, but I don't want him to run either. An ex-con is bound to be nervous with the police sniffing around."

Will heard a knock at the door. "Come in."

The door opened and one of the department secretaries, LaTeesha Johnson, stepped into the room, an envelope in her hand. "I'm sorry to interrupt you, but here's my letter of resignation. *I'm* the one who leaked the information to that reporter."

Brandon Jones carried his lunch outside the camp's dining hall and sat on the shady steps, savoring the scent of pine and glad for a moment alone. He couldn't stop thinking about the boys coming to Camp Piney Woods on Saturday and whether he'd be equipped to deal with any anxiety they may be bringing with them.

Dax Barnes had asked Dr. Tehrani to call in a sociologist to hold sessions on how to address racial issues and any hostility the kids might act out. So much for a fun and easy job that would help him get over his burnout. The thought that he might be dealing with angry adolescents day and night for three weeks was almost enough to make him back out of his commitment.

God, I'm a little overwhelmed. Did You open the door to this, or did I read into it?

"So how's the cheeseburger?"

Brandon turned and saw Dax coming down the steps.

"The cheeseburger is...well, campy." Brandon smiled. "Not exactly chopped sirloin, but it tastes pretty good about now."

"Yeah, it does," Dax said. "Mind if I sit with you?"

"Not at all. It's nice out here. I prefer fresh air to air-conditioning just about anytime."

"Yeah, me too." Dax sat next to Brandon on the step. "This may turn out to be more than any of us were counting on. Think you're up to it?"

"As much as anyone else. I'd feel better if we had a dress rehearsal."

"Yeah, that'd be nice. But when the kids start arriving, we're onstage till the curtain drops. And the racial issues may not amount to anything. I just wanted us to be ready in case."

Brandon nodded. "Smart move. Did you hear anything else about the riot this morning?"

"Yeah, just before I came out here. The police arrested about three dozen black teenagers, and things are quiet again. That doesn't mean it's over. Man, I wish the police would hurry up and arrest whoever's behind all the attacks." Dax was quiet for a moment and then said, "In case you were wondering, I'm aware of what happened to you and your girlfriend."

"Weezie's just a friend, not my girlfriend."

"Oh. I must've misunderstood. Well, I'm really sorry you were targets."

"Thanks. After hearing about that family dying in the church fire, I'd say we should count our blessings. It's hard to believe anyone would kill seven people just because they were black. It's going to be a long time before people get over that one."

"Yeah, it sure isn't going to happen by the weekend, so we need to be ready for anything. Did you find the sociologist's sessions helpful?"

"I think so. I guess I'll know if I learned anything when the time comes to put it into action."

"Come in here and sit down," Will said to LaTeesha Johnson. "At least give me the courtesy of explaining why you felt it necessary to undermine my authority."

LaTeesha sat in the chair next to Al Backus, her hands folded in her lap. "I was afraid. I didn't think you were doing enough."

"Afraid for yourself because you're African-American?"

"No, sir. Afraid of exactly what happened this morning. The black community can only take so much rhetoric before it blows."

"I see. And on exactly what do you base your penny-ante opinion that this department was dishing out *rhetoric*? Were you in the meetings we had? Were you out investigating crime scenes? Were you up night after night, racking your brain because the perps didn't leave enough clues for us to even bring someone in for questioning?" Will felt the blood rush to his face. "How dare you question this department's commitment to solving this case!"

"Sir, with all due respect," LaTeesha said, "if a white woman's car had been forced off the road, you wouldn't have waited to call in the FBI."

"Yes, I would! I don't call in the feds until I'm sure I need them. But I'm curious what you think the FBI would've done that we hadn't."

"Reassured the black community that you were serious about getting the perps."

"Since when is my word not good enough?"

LaTeesha looked at her hands and then at Will. "Actions speak louder than words. You should've made the note public. Every citizen had a right to know how calculated the attack on RuWeeza Taylor really was."

"The threat was directed at Mr. Jones, not Ms. Taylor."

"Yes, but Jones was threatened to stay away from the black widow or they'd step on him, too, which more than implies that they deliberately stepped on her and considered her no better than dirt. It's a wonder she wasn't killed. And now seven others have been. It's like the sixties all over again, and you can't even make an arrest!"

"You don't need to tell me how serious this situation is!" Will got up, his hands in his pockets, and walked over to the window, thinking he needed to calm down before he said something unprofessional.

"Chief, can I say something?" Al said.

"Go ahead."

"LaTeesha, how'd you get the note?"

"I spotted the file on your desk. I waited till you went to the men's room, then made a photocopy of the note and slipped it back in the file."

"Did you copy the note for Valerie Hodges?"

LaTeesha nodded. "She followed me to my car after work one day, asking all kinds of questions. One thing led to another, and I told her about the note and promised to get her a copy of it. I'm sorry if my actions seemed disloyal to you. But I had an obligation to protect my people, too."

Al rolled his eyes. "Your people, my people…are we ever gonna just be people, for cryin' out loud? Who else knows you're the leak?"

"No one, I swear." LaTeesha looked over at Will, her eyes both defiant and fearful. "I'd like to leave now. I already emptied out my desk."

"I'd appreciate it if you didn't talk to anyone on your way out of the building," Will said. *Good riddance, traitor.*

LaTeesha got up and left the office.

Will listened to the clicking of her heels as she walked down the hallway and out the side door. He went over to his desk and sat for a few moments, then picked up a plastic paper clip holder and threw it against the wall.

"At least we got rid of the leak," Al said.

"I'm fed up with the same old complaint that we don't act as quickly when blacks are the victims. I've never let race interfere with how I run this department!"

"Have you noticed how blacks only pitch a fit when the perps are white? When it's blacks killing blacks, they don't raise a stink." Al smirked. "On the other hand, when they're killing off each other, it does save us the trouble of cleaning up the hood."

Will glared at Al and shook his head. "Listen to yourself."

"What?"

"That kind of talk is totally out of line."

"I don't talk this way around them."

"If that's how you really feel, you can bet they pick up on it."

"You've never gotten on me for it before."

Will exhaled loudly. "Well, maybe it's time I did."

Will pulled into his driveway just after seven, his gut feeling as though he had swallowed hot coals.

Margaret met him in the doorway and put her arms around his neck, her eyes searching his. "You look beat," she finally said. "Want me to microwave your dinner?"

"Not just yet. I'd like a big glass of ice water."

Will followed her out to the kitchen. "Where's Meagan?"

"At play practice. She's so into this role she can hardly think of anything else."

"Good. At least *something* in this town is still normal."

Margaret filled a glass with ice and held it under the faucet, then set it on the table.

"Thanks. You probably should go do something else before I start ranting."

"Since when?" Margaret sat across from him, her arms folded on the table. "Tell me what happened. It's obvious you're upset."

"We found the leak." He told Margaret about the conversation he and Al Backus had had with LaTeesha Johnson.

"The woman's assessment is totally unfair," Margaret said. "You've never let race affect the way you do things."

"I never thought so, but I'm becoming aware of attitudes I don't like—racist remarks that I've let slide by." Will told her about Al's comments after LaTeesha left. "Al also made a few cutting remarks the other day about the mother of that biracial kid that got roughed up. I've always blown off Al's racial comments, maybe because I don't entirely disagree with him."

"Come on, you're no racist."

"I'm beginning to think all cops have racist feelings they didn't ask for and really don't want. It's easy to be cynical when we look at blacks from our side of the fence. But we've never been in their shoes. How do we really know what they think and feel—or why?"

"I think this case is getting to you."

Will glanced at the headlines on the newspaper at the end of the table. "Maybe it's a wake-up call to get my act together."

"What in the world are you talking about?"

"Look, honey, I admit I expect less from black people—except when it comes to crime, then I expect more."

"It's hard to argue with statistics."

"Maybe looking at black people as statistics instead of as people is part of the problem."

"Will, what's gotten into you? I've never heard you talk this way."

"Well, we've never had white racists vandalizing, running women off the road, burning innocent people alive before. How the heck did we end up in this mess? It's as though we're going backward instead of forward!"

Margaret took his hand. "It's just temporary. Things aren't that bad."

"I guess that depends on whether you ask someone who's black or someone who's white."

"Come on, Will, black people always think they're being put down, no matter how many times we tell them it's not true."

"How many black people have you discussed it with?"

There was a long pause. "None, I guess. I don't know any besides Weezie."

"Why do you suppose that is?"

Margaret shrugged. "I don't deliberately avoid black people. I'm just never around them."

"Right. Because the world we live in is primarily white."

"So? The world they live in is primarily black. People tend to gravitate toward others who are most like them. That's human nature."

"It's also how our thinking becomes so one-sided." Will took a sip of ice water, thinking what he really needed was a couple Rolaids. "It's not just Al and LaTeesha. Hank Martin suggested I put an African-American out in front of the media because blacks think the police are indifferent. And Bryce Moore made some offhanded remark this morning about blacks getting the short end of the stick only so many times before they stop believing in justice. I didn't expect to hear that from him. It's bothered me all day."

"You can't fight their battles for them, Will."

"Maybe what I'm really fighting is the truth. Maybe I *do* let race influence my thinking on some level. Maybe I would've responded with more passion if the victims in this case were white and if I didn't have to answer to the NAACP at every turn. I admit I resent blacks turning everything into a racial issue. But after Bryce's comment, I can't seem to let it go."

"I hate to see you so worked up over it."

"I'm just thinking from my gut. Bryce thinks that blacks are tolerated because the law demands it, not because anyone really thinks they're legitimate members of the community. I find that troubling. He said whites don't want to deal with it, that we just want to forget the past and move on. Maybe he's right."

"We didn't create the problem, Will. It started generations ago."

"So do we keep telling blacks to 'get over it,' or do we decide that enough is enough and we're going to settle it with this generation?"

"No one's been able to resolve it. It's naive to think you can do anything about it."

"Well, I can sure as heck change things at the Seaport PD. And it has to start with me."

30

Ellen Jones sat next to Guy on Seaport Beach, a cinnamon roll in one hand and a cup of coffee in the other. "I'm glad you didn't mind moving our Saturday morning tradition to the beach just this once."

Guy Jones zipped his Windbreaker. "This is nice for a change. I'm just surprised at how chilly the breeze feels this early."

"Have some hot coffee." Ellen licked her sticky fingers, then picked up another cinnamon roll and took a bite. "Mmm, these are good. I almost feel guilty enjoying anything knowing what the Delks' relatives and church family will be facing today. It's all so sad."

"At least the medical examiner was finally able to identify Gideon's body and the entire family can be buried at the same time. No one thought that was going to happen."

"Can you even imagine the media madness that will surround this?"

Guy shook his head. "No, and I'm glad the service is at the community center. If we go early enough, we might actually get a seat."

"I hope it doesn't turn violent."

"Security will be tight. Think we could find something more pleasant to talk about?"

Ellen sat quietly for a moment, then reached over and ran the back of her hand along Guy's cheek. "I missed you this week. It's kind of nice having the house all to ourselves again. Do you remember the first time the boys were away at camp?"

Guy picked up her hand and kissed it. "Uh-huh. It was like a second honeymoon."

"Yet we were the first parents in line to pick up our kids the day camp was over."

"Yeah, I remember us saying the house was too quiet and we missed the chaos." Guy chuckled. "Were we totally nuts?"

"No, we were just young—actually not that much older than Brandon is now. I wonder what time the campers will be arriving today?"

"Any time would be too soon for me. Signing up to be a camp counselor is not on my list of things I'd like to do."

"I sure hope that camp will help Brandon clear his head."

"If nothing else, working his tail off for two hundred dollars a week should cure his aversion to a corporate job."

Ellen studied Guy's profile and wondered why such an intelligent man found it so hard to accept that his son had different wants and needs. "I wouldn't count on it. He's been trying to tell you the conflict isn't about money; it's about finding significance in his work."

"He may change his mind about what's significant after he gets his fill of working for peanuts. Speaking of that, I'm really sorry your research has been a bust."

"So far, anyway. I've finished skimming *Messenger* articles back through 1938, and this town has certainly had its share of racial problems. But I haven't seen anything to connect the Ws."

"Sounds as if you had an amazing breakthrough with Valerie, though."

Ellen took a sip of coffee. "I wouldn't go that far. But I do sense something's changed in her. I'm just not ready to trust her this soon."

"How much more research do you have to do?"

"The library has microfilm of articles dating back to 1926. You know me. I'm not going to stop till I've exhausted my source."

Brandon Jones stood in the dining hall of Camp Piney Woods, his arms folded, his eyes fixed on the boys sharing a pizza at a nearby round table.

"So what do you think of *your* seven?" Dax Barnes said.

"They're great kids. We're going to have a ball."

"So they seem to be getting along?"

"I think so," Brandon said. "A couple of them seem shy and

content to let the others do the talking. I've got a few icebreakers planned after lunch."

Dax patted him on the back. "Super. By the way, Caedmon Nash's mom told me something you should be aware of. He's the boy who had his bicycle stolen and was roughed up by some white kids last weekend."

"Really? Cade's one of my quiet ones." Brandon glanced over at the table and noticed for the first time that Caedmon Nash was sitting between two Hispanic boys.

"His mom said he's been really withdrawn and angry since it happened. She almost cancelled his coming to camp, but he insisted he wanted to be here."

"I'll see what I can do to draw him out."

"Have you decided what you're going to do with them during your unstructured time this afternoon?" Dax said.

"Swim. Most of these boys have never even been in a pool. They learned to swim in the gulf." Brandon smiled. "I'll make sure they get the sand and salt off their swimming trunks before they jump in. To tell you the truth, I'm ready to get my mind off the situation in Seaport. The memorial service for that pastor and his family is today. I wonder if there'll be trouble."

"I wouldn't want to be there."

"My folks are going," Brandon said. "My mom knew the pastor and his family. They worked together at the shelter for Katrina evacuees. And my friend Weezie attended the church that burned."

"It's a sad day for Seaport, but let's put the bad news on hold. I don't want these kids exposed to anything that will distract them from having a great camp experience."

Brandon nodded. "I'm with you."

"Talk to you later." Dax started to walk away and then turned around. "It probably won't amount to anything, but there's another tropical depression forming. I'll keep an eye on it and keep you posted."

Brandon stepped out on the front porch of Red Feather and dialed Weezie's cell number, thinking he had about two minutes before the boys were changed and ready to race to the pool.

"Hello."

"Weezie…it's Brandon. I didn't really expect you to answer. I was going to leave a message. I'm so sorry about your pastor and his family. I can't get the whole thing off my mind. How'd the memorial service go?"

"It was hard seein' seven caskets laid out like that. But I kept focusin' on where they are now and not how they died. The eulogies were heartwarmin'. We all took turns. Your mother got up and said somethin' real nice."

"That took a lot. She's not big on public speaking."

"Well, you'd have thought she did it for a livin'."

"Was there any trouble at the memorial service?"

"Not inside, but the police had a few scuffles with some angry folks who wanted in. The place was packed out, and they finally had to turn people away."

"I'm relieved it went off okay."

"It did, but the black community's had the wind knocked out of it. People are scared. And angry. I'm afraid there may be more violence if the police don't arrest whoever killed those dear souls."

Brandon sighed. "What a vicious cycle. Have you given any thought to where you might go to church now?"

"My church family's gonna meet in the mornin' at Bougainvillea Park and have an outdoor service. I don't know how we're ever gonna rebuild because we didn't have insurance on that old building. But we're trustin' God to show us the way."

"I've been reading the Bible a lot lately, and I'm beginning to realize that trusting God is huge."

"Well, *God* is huge. Good thing He knows what He's doin' and I don't have to worry about it."

"Listen, I'm going to have to hang up any minute. I've got seven hyper boys that can't wait to get to the pool."

"So how're things out at Camp Piney Woods?"

"Good so far. It's got excellent facilities. The kids started arriving about nine this morning, and they were all moved into their cabins by eleven and chowing down on pizza by noon. Today and tomorrow are pretty relaxed, but then we're on a fast track."

"You feelin' confident?"

"I'd better be. You remember hearing about the biracial boy whose bicycle was stolen by some white kids?"

"I sure do."

"Would you believe he's in my group?"

The front door of the cabin flew open, and the boys came rushing out on the porch, whooping and laughing and jostling each other.

Brandon laughed into the receiver. "Hear that? Talk to you soon."

Will Seevers walked into his office and spotted Bryce Moore working at the table. "I wasn't expecting you back after the memorial service. Can I get you something to drink?"

"No, thanks. I'm fine," Bryce said. "I'm reviewing each of the hate crime files. The paint, the partial shoe print, and the bat chip are so universal that they're basically useless without a suspect to match them to."

"Don't remind me. We're still trying to locate an ex-con named Mick Beasley who lives in Seaport and drives a truck consistent with both the eyewitnesses' description and the tire tracks found at the other church."

"I saw that in the report. Do you have any reason to suspect him other than that he's an ex-con and drives a black Ford truck?"

Will shook his head. "Not really. But it seems just a little too coincidental that the bartender at Big John's says Beasley and Jessica Ziegler know each other, yet she denies it. He also claims Ziegler borrowed a cell phone and called someone right after my detectives questioned her about the drunks who harassed Jones and Taylor. She denies that, too. The bartender also thinks Beasley's involved in illegal poker games going on behind closed doors at The Cove. We've decided to leave that alone till we locate him. We don't want to scare him off."

"How hard have you leaned on Ms. Ziegler?"

"We've questioned her a couple times—once at home and once at work. If we make too big a stink, she may alert Beasley and he'll run."

"How do you know he hasn't already done that?"

"We don't. But judging from dates on the newspapers piled up on his front lawn, he hasn't been home since two days before the church burning. Could be a smoke screen."

Bryce's eyes widened. "Or he could be on vacation."

"Look, I know it's weak, but it's all we've got. It's not that far-fetched that if he *was* involved, he'd stay with someone else so it would look as though he was out of town at the time of the fire. Unfortunately, his neighbors don't know anything about him, not even where he works. But even that's suspicious."

"Then I suggest it's time we find out whether or not he's been around lately for those poker games you mentioned."

Brandon tossed a volleyball to one of the boys in his group and then got out of the pool and walked over to where Cade lay on a towel. "Hey, don't you want to play?"

"I'm tired," Cade said. "I didn't sleep last night. Guess I was excited about comin'."

Could've fooled me, Brandon thought. "Okay, go ahead and rest. But let me rub sunscreen on your back. Your mom's not going to be happy with me if you go home blistered."

"I hardly ever burn," Cade said. "It's one of the advantages of bein' a skunk."

"What?"

"A skunk—half black and half white."

Brandon squeezed sunscreen on his palm and rubbed it on Cade's back. "I think a better term is biracial. Why don't we go with that?"

"Doesn't matter what *you* call me. That's still how they think of me."

"I doubt that, and I don't want you putting yourself down. Nobody here is better than anybody else. Each of us is different and special in his own way. It would be boring if we were all alike."

"For you, maybe."

"Cade, turn over and look at me."

Cade rolled over on his back, his hands shading his eyes, and looked up at Brandon.

"I know about the boys who took your bike and gave you a hard time."

Cade winced. "Oh, man. Who told you?"

"Your mom told the camp director, and he thought I should know. Don't worry, no one else knows. But you and I need to have an understanding: We're all here to have fun. We're a team. We need each other. No one is going to put you down."

"You can't stop it."

"Of course I can."

Cade rolled his eyes. "Whatever."

"Has someone here said or done something that hurt your feelings? Because as far as I can tell the other boys have tried to include you in everything. You're the one who's been standoffish."

Cade turned over on his stomach. "I told you I'm tired."

Brandon looked down at the long, skinny twelve-year-old and decided to let him be for now.

Ellen sat on the couch with Guy, knitting a sweater for Annie and only vaguely aware that the six o'clock news was coming on. The memorial service was replaying in her mind, and she couldn't shake the awful image of seven caskets lined up according to size. It was unconscionable that these vibrant lives had been swallowed up in the flames of racial hatred. The quiet weeping of family and friends had seemed to her more powerful than all the demands for justice.

The voices of the Victory Chapel choir coming from the television brought Ellen back to the present.

"…More than a thousand mourners filled the Seaport Community Center this afternoon as this dazed city said good-bye to all seven members of the Delk family, who perished in the parsonage of Victory Chapel after an arson fire destroyed the church early Monday morning.

"The memorial service lasted almost two hours as friends, family members, and community leaders offered eulogies for the victims and condolences for those still trying to make sense of this terrible loss. Mayor Dickson was the first to take the podium."

A short clip followed with the mayor vowing to do everything possible to ensure that tragedies like this would never happen again and to find ways to foster respect for racial differences.

"Mayor Dickson went on to say that donations coming in from private sources have already more than covered the burial costs for the Delk family, and any money left over will be given to the Victory Chapel rebuilding fund.

"Some of the most stirring words in today's service came from RuWeeza Taylor, a member of Victory Chapel and the African-American woman whose car was forced off the road last week by who police now believe were white racists."

The camera zoomed in on Weezie, who stood somberly at the podium, outfitted in a black dress and a floppy, wide-brimmed hat.

"There aren't words to describe how our hearts ache for the loss of this precious family. We've laughed and cried and prayed and sung with them. We've played and worked alongside them. We've welcomed them into our homes, and the littlest ones into the world. But the last thing we ever expected to do—was bury them, Lord have mercy. The day my car got run off the road, Pastor Jonah reminded me that the only thing stronger than hate is love. He said that when I'm tempted to hate whoever did it, choose to love instead. And when I feel like strikin' back, pray a blessin' on my enemies. If he were standin' here, he'd tell us to act like children of the light and not be overcome by evil, but overcome evil with good."

"Also represented at the service were sixty-eight of the more than seven hundred Katrina evacuees who now make their home in Seaport…"

Ellen closed her eyes and pictured Jonah Delk walking the aisles of the evacuee shelter with his family, offering comfort and encouragement to everyone he met. She wiped a tear off her cheek. The absence of this peace-loving family was more of a loss to the community than most people realized.

She also wondered if those eager for justice would rise to Weezie's challenge—or if more violence would follow.

31

On Monday morning, Ellen Jones sat out on the veranda, her Bible open in her lap and her thoughts on Brandon. She wondered how he was doing but had determined days ago that she wouldn't call and risk embarrassing him.

"Okay, honey, I'm heading out." Guy Jones came out on the veranda dressed in a dark olive Italian suit and yellow tie.

"You look sharp, Counselor."

"Thanks. Let's hope the jury is as impressed as you are."

"What time do you have to be in court?"

"Ten. I have some things to do at the office first, so I'm leaving a few minutes early. You never know what the Tallahassee traffic is going to be like." Guy picked up her cup and took a sip of coffee. "Since Sunday's Father's Day, would you pick out a gift for Dad—maybe a couple really nice long-sleeve shirts? He said something about the air-conditioning making him chilly."

"I'd be glad to. What do you think about us inviting Owen and Hailey and the kids to join us for brunch? I'm sure your dad could handle it for a few hours. We haven't all been together since Daniel's birthday."

"Sounds like fun. Seems a shame with Brandon so close that he can't be here, too."

"I know. I imagine he'll call."

Guy lifted his eyebrows. "I'm not counting on it."

"Don't assume he's avoiding you. He was on a fast track to get ready for camp with only twenty-four hours notice."

"You don't have to spare my feelings, honey. He could've found sixty seconds to call me if he'd wanted to."

Ellen slipped her hand in his. "What would you like me to fix for your Father's Day brunch?"

"I'd love something spicy, but Dad won't. How about pork tenderloin and those little potatoes with parsley? And maybe that vegetable dish you made at Christmas—the one with yellow squash and carrots and sour cream? Everybody went nuts over it."

"Okay. Why don't I add sourdough rolls and a tossed salad and strawberry cheesecake for dessert?"

"That'd be great. My mouth's watering already."

Ellen squeezed his hand and let go. "You'd better get on the highway before the traffic gets heavy."

"Okay, honey. See you Wednesday night." He bent down and pressed his lips to hers. "I love you."

"I love you, too."

Brandon Jones sat on the wood steps at Red Feather, the boys still asleep inside the cabin, and listened to the damp morning breeze whistling through the pines. The room had seemed closed-in with seven other bodies breathing the same air, and he had tossed and turned all night, thinking he would've done much better under the stars.

Cade hadn't slept well either. The boy was fidgety for hours and finally got up and took what appeared to be a stack of comic books and a candy bar out of his drawer and tiptoed into the bathroom. He had been in there over an hour when Brandon finally drifted off to sleep. No telling when he went to bed.

Brandon stood, his hands on his low back, and stretched. The sky visible between the tree branches was flaming pink, and he wondered if his mother was out jogging on the beach and if his father had left for Tallahassee.

Why hadn't he just forced himself to call his dad over the weekend? The longer he avoided doing it, the harder it was to know what to say. At least he had a legitimate excuse not to be there for Father's Day.

He went up on the porch and leaned against the railing and thought about last Father's Day. Kelsey had invited him to a Hartman family reunion and showed him off to all her relatives—long before he'd even been offered the big promotion. How he missed her being proud of him!

He wondered if things really had been as awful at Mavis and Stein as he remembered them, or if his dad was right, that his expectations were too high.

Brandon heard the squeaking of the door and saw Cade standing in the doorway, already dressed for the day.

"Can I come out?" Cade said.

"Sure. Did you ever get to sleep?"

"After I read for a while. I do that at home."

"Have you always found it hard to go to sleep?"

Cade shrugged. "Not always."

"Well, everything's new. Maybe it's just going to take a few days for you to adjust." Brandon glanced at his watch. "I hope you're not starving because they won't be ready for us in the mess hall for another forty-five minutes."

"That's okay. I'm not hungry when I first get up." Cade came over and sat on the railing, his skinny legs dangling.

"You an early riser?"

"Not when I have school. But in the summer and on weekends I am. I like bein' outside. Sometimes I ride my bike down to the marina and talk to the fishermen when they're riggin' up for the day. They let me borrow their light tackle so I can fish there on the dock."

"Catch anything?"

Cade smiled for the first time since he'd arrived. "Tarpon. The small ones school up under the dock—ten, maybe twenty pounds. It's so cool when they bust the top water baits. You like to fish?"

"I did when I was younger," Brandon said. "My granddad used to take my brother and me stream fishing all the time. But I've never fished saltwater."

"I'm savin' up to go out on a group boat and fish the wrecks, but I can't tell my mom or she'll freak. She'll just say it's a waste of money. All she ever does is worry about payin' bills."

"What else do you like to do?" Brandon said.

"Read comics. Ride my bike. Explore things."

"What's your favorite thing to explore?"

"The Jackson Caves. Someday I'm gonna stay out there at night."

"Do you have camping gear?"

Cade shook his head. "No, but there's this really deep cave I could sleep in. All I'd really have to take is energy bars and bottled water and stuff like that."

"So what's stopping you?"

"Mom won't let me go by myself—you know, in case somethin' happens."

"What if you took a couple buddies with you?"

Cade's eyebrows came together, and he swung his legs a little faster. "Nah, they're all chicken."

Brandon sensed there was more to it than that. He slapped Cade on the knee. "Well, if I can get you boys whipped into shape, we're going to take a backpacking trip the last week of camp."

"Really?"

"If we learn to work together as a team. Think you can do that?"

"Yeah, if the other guys'll let me. I don't exactly fit in."

"Are you kidding? You're just the one I need to fine-tune this outfit. You willing to set the example for the others?"

Cade turned and stared at him blankly. "Me?"

"Absolutely. I can already tell you're a natural leader." *I can't believe I just said that.*

Gordy Jameson stood outside the crab shack and welcomed the steady stream of lunch customers. His weekend sales were way down, and he hoped the trend wouldn't continue. He saw Eddie Drummond walking across the pier and waved. "Hey, good to see you."

"What's the special?" Eddie said. "I'm starved."

"Grouper: fried, grilled, baked—you call it. Pam just pulled some fruit pies out of the oven."

"Man, let's get after it. The other guys here yet?"

"That looks like them now." Gordy cupped his hands around his eyes and saw Captain Jack and Adam Spalding starting across the pier "Let me go tell Pam I'm eatin' with you guys. I'll meet you out on the deck."

Gordy went out to the kitchen, the aroma of warm pies wafting under his nose. Pam was standing with her back to him. He walked up behind her and put his arms around her, his chin on her shoulder. "How's my favorite bakery chef?"

"Plenty busy trying to replenish my freezer stash of pies. Seems as though I can hardly keep up with the demand anymore."

"Maybe I should hire you a helper."

"Weezie would love *that*. She hasn't given up on the idea of marketing 'Pam's Blue Ribbon Pies' to the grocery chains."

"If we do that, we're gonna have two businesses to run. You willin' to give up any more free time?"

"No, but I wouldn't have to actually make the pies that we sell elsewhere. We could hire someone for that, and I could keep doing what I'm doing. It might be fun having a little business of my own that ties in with the crab shack."

Gordy kissed her cheek. "Okay, let's talk about it some more later. Can you handle things while I eat with the guys?"

Pam turned around in his arms, the corners of her mouth twitching. "With one hand tied behind my back."

Gordy chuckled. "You're even startin' to *sound* like Weezie."

"Go. I can handle it."

Ellen finished reading through the microfilm of *North Coast Messenger* articles for May of 1937. She stopped and slowly rolled her neck in a circle, thinking her tight muscles had more to do with Saturday's memorial service than the tedious work in front of her. The image of those seven caskets kept intruding on her thoughts like a pop-up ad on the computer, making her feel more determined than ever to connect the Ws to the past.

There had been plenty of racial tension here, especially during the fifties and sixties, and she'd found numerous articles that she planned to get hard copies of. She did n't see any significant articles about racial issues in the forties, possibly because of the war.

She started skimming articles again, her eyes stopping on a story that appeared in the *Messenger* on June 3, 1937.

NEGRO RAPIST SHOT AND KILLED
AFTER ESCAPING FROM JAIL

A twenty-one-year old Negro man, Sampson Harper, broke out of the Beacon County Jail yesterday and was pursued by three deputies, including Ernie Lloyd, who shot and killed him.

The Negro had been jailed the night before after unlawfully entering the home of a white couple, the parents of four young children, and sexually assaulting the wife after locking the husband in the bathroom.

According to Sheriff Joe Quentin Raynor, the Negro escaped from jail after grabbing the pistol from the sheriff's holster and waving it in the air, threatening to kill anyone who tried to stop him. The Negro then fled on foot.

Lloyd and three other deputies pursued the escapee into a wooded area near the warehouse district and ordered him to stop and put down his weapon. But when the Negro turned around and began shooting, Deputy Lloyd discharged his weapon and the escapee fell to the ground.

County coroner Slidell Pickens confirmed that the Negro died of a gunshot wound to the chest despite allegations made later by the Negro's mother that deputies laughed in her face and said they made up the story about the jailbreak and had taken her son out to the woods and lynched him.

Judge John Bailey Williams said the allegations are preposterous and indicated he would not order an investigation into the matter.

Ellen's heart sank. How many times throughout the nation's history had incidents like this occurred? She added the article to the list of those she planned to request hard copies of and then continued reading through the microfilm.

Gordy walked through the dining room and out onto the back deck and saw Eddie Drummond, Captain Jack, and Adam Spalding sitting at a round umbrella table. He flopped in the empty chair next to Adam. "So what'd I miss?"

Eddie popped a hush puppy into his mouth. "We were just talking about the race riot. I sure hope the blacks don't decide to tear up another part of town. It's so stupid. I mean, what did they accomplish by making whites mad? Who's gonna feel sorry for them now? Every time blacks don't get what they want, they start burning and looting and acting like a bunch of savages."

"Come on, Eddie. A very small percentage of black people are involved in riots—and not all that often."

"So that makes it okay?"

"Of course it's not okay!" Gordy said. "But I think we have to realize that desperate people sometimes do desperate things."

"That's a lame excuse!" Eddie threw his hands up. "If more blacks would speak out, they could stop stuff like this from getting out of hand."

"Right. Like you and me and other whites speakin' out could stop the racist scumbags who started this whole thing."

"It's not the same, Gordo."

"Yeah, it is. You can't blame all people for the actions of a few."

Eddie's eyes narrowed. "And you can't deny that blacks have this thing about destroying stuff when they're ticked."

"I won't deny that *some* blacks destroy *some* stuff *some*times. But that's a far cry from what you said."

Eddie leaned his head back and exhaled. "Why do I bother arguing with you? I can never win."

"Did you go to the memorial service?" Adam asked.

Gordy shook his head. "Nah, I covered for Weezie and Pam so they could go."

"How's Weezie handling it?"

"A lot better than I would. Anybody see her on the news?"

Captain nodded. "I thought she handled it well. And for your information, Eddie, Weezie did ask her church people not to react with violence."

"Yeah, well, I have a feeling it isn't the church people who are out stirring up trouble."

32

Will Seevers heard footsteps coming down the hall and folded Tuesday's issue of the *Messenger* and set it to one side of his desk. A few seconds later, Bryce Moore came through the doorway.

"What's in the sack?" Will said.

Bryce walked past Will's desk and set the sack on the table. "Coffee and sausage biscuits. I didn't figure you'd eaten this early."

"You figured right." Will got up and went over to the table and sat across from Bryce. "I'm hungry. Thanks."

"No problem. I think I still owe you about a dozen of these from the last time we worked together. I thought it would be good to wolf somethin' down before we start another long day."

Will sat quietly and savored the buttery taste of the sausage biscuit, wondering how many fat grams he was consuming. He could almost imagine Margaret popping up next to him, her palm out, demanding that he hand it over.

"What are you grinnin' about?" Bryce said.

"That I'm enjoying the taste of *real* food. My wife's trying to get me healthy, and I haven't had one of these in a while."

"I figure all this protein is brain food. I'm just not a granola kind of guy. I need somethin' substantial that sticks with me all morning."

"You're also a lot younger than me and probably never had your cholesterol checked. Sometimes ignorance is bliss."

There was a knock on the door. Will turned and saw Al Backus standing in the doorway.

"Come in, Al. What'd you do, work all night?"

Al came over and stood at the table, his hair disheveled, a dark shadow covering the lower half of his face. "Yeah, Beasley finally showed up at his house about 12:15 this morning. Said he'd been at his girlfriend's for over a week and came back to check his mail, pitch his newspapers, and pick up some things. He didn't seem to mind talking to us."

"That's a strange hour to be doing errands."

Al pulled out a chair and sat, his arms folded on the table. "He worked the three to eleven shift at the tire plant, ate dinner at IHOP, then dropped by his house on the way to his girlfriend's. It all checked out."

"Who's the girlfriend?"

"Some chick named Tonya—a barmaid at The Cove. For all practical purposes they've been living together for a couple weeks. He's been slowly moving his things over to her place before his lease runs out at the end of the month. We talked to the girlfriend, and she corroborates his story. Plus, the bartender at The Cove confirmed it."

"Can Beasley account for his whereabouts between midnight and seven the morning of the fire?"

"Says he was cozied up to Tonya. Obviously, no one can prove whether he was or wasn't. She says he was. Oh…and he wears a size eleven shoe, though he and the girlfriend both said he doesn't own a pair of Performas. Or a Louisville Slugger."

"Can he draw?"

"About like my six-year-old. I asked him to draw a flaming cross. I don't think someone with artistic talent could fake being that bad."

"Unless he deliberately drew it with the wrong hand. Which hand did he use?"

"The left. But I noticed he'd picked up his glass with his right hand, so I asked him about it. Told me he's ambidextrous. I had him write a sentence with his right hand, and then the same sentence with his left hand below it. I couldn't tell much difference. I gave the note and the picture to handwriting analysis."

"What about the poker games?" Bryce said.

Al shook his head. "They're all playing dumb on that one. Denied knowing anything about it—didn't even flinch."

"Well, I didn't expect them to freely admit to illegal gambling,"

Will said, "but I hope you didn't push that button too hard. I really don't want Beasley to disappear."

"What are you thinking?" Bryce said.

Will shrugged. "Just a feeling. I'd rather not close the door on Beasley just yet."

"Well I doubt our gamblers will be holding the games at The Cove now," Bryce said. "Why don't I put a tail on Beasley and see if he leads us anywhere."

Brandon Jones sat on the front steps of Red Feather, his Bible open in his lap, a flashlight in his hand. He pondered the words of Psalm 139 for few moments, and then held the beam of light on the page and reread verses thirteen through sixteen:

> For you created my inmost being;
> you knit me together in my mother's womb.
> I praise you because I am fearfully and wonderfully made;
> your works are wonderful,
> I know that full well.
> My frame was not hidden from you
> when I was made in the secret place.
> When I was woven together in the depths of the earth,
> your eyes saw my unformed body.
> All the days ordained for me
> were written in your book
> before one of them came to be.

Brandon looked up at the first streaks of morning and tried to fathom the magnitude of those words. God knew him before he was born and had already planned out his days. There it was on the pages of Scripture. It was true. He didn't have to take anyone else's word for it.

"This is amazing," he mumbled.

"Who're you talkin' to?"

Brandon jumped at the sound of Cade Nash's voice behind him.

He closed the Bible and patted the step. "Come sit. How'd you sleep?"

"Better. Were you talkin' to yourself?"

"Yeah. I was amazed by something very cool I just read in my mom's Bible."

"Oh. My mom never reads hers. She blames God because my dad left."

"I'm sure that was really hard for both of you."

Cade shrugged. "Not me. I was only two. My dad's a real loser. I'm glad he's not around. Is your dad still alive?"

"Yeah, he's only fifty-nine."

"My *grandpa's* younger than that, I think."

"Do you see him much?"

"No. Mom says I remind him that she was married to a black man. Grandpa hates my dad."

"Do you?"

"Not really. I don't even know him. But if I did, I probably would. Are you close to your dad?"

"Not as close as I'd like to be. I have a lot of respect for him, but we're nothing alike."

"Do you fight?"

Brandon smiled. "What's with the all the heavy talk? We're here to have fun."

"I *am* havin' fun."

"What's your favorite thing so far?"

"Soccer. I'm better and faster than the other guys."

"I noticed they've nicknamed you *Flash*. But it's not about being the best or the fastest. Teamwork's the name of the game."

"I know, but I'm still faster."

Brandon reached over and ruffled Cade's already unruly curls. "Come on, let's go pry their lazy bones out of bed. The dining hall will be open in fifteen minutes."

Ellen Jones sat in the public library, reading through microfilm articles, surprised and appalled at the frequency of racial incidents in the late thirties. She went back and reread the most disturbing article, which appeared in the September 7, 1937, issue of the *Messenger*:

JUDGE GIVES NO CREDENCE TO ACCUSATION THAT COLORED GIRL WAS HELD AGAINST HER WILL

Neither Judge John Bailey Williams nor Beacon County Sheriff Joe Quentin Raynor would comment today after the judge's ruling that there was insufficient evidence to bring a case against Mr. and Mrs. Harvey Ledbetter for allegedly holding a colored girl against her will at the couple's rural estate.

Last Friday, traveling salesman Arthur Phillips was leaving the Ledbetter's property and was confronted outside his car by a Negro girl about fifteen years old, who told him she was being held there against her will.

The girl, known only as Mariah, alleged that she had been taken to the estate by a stranger, a white man who abducted her from a dry goods store when she was about five. Since that time she had been forced to cook, clean, and do other domestic chores for the Ledbetter family.

The girl said the Ledbetters told her that her parents and siblings had died in a fire and that the Ledbetters were going to take care of her. She told Phillips she had never been allowed to leave the estate and has had no contact with the outside world, does not know how to read or write, and doesn't remember her last name or her birth date. She thinks one sister's name may have been Martha. She also said Mr. Ledbetter had made many uninvited visits to her bedroom.

Phillips went straight to the Beacon County Sheriff's Office and reported what the girl had said.

Sheriff Raynor questioned the Ledbetters at length, and they emphatically denied that the girl was brought to them illegally. They said the girl's parents had worked for them for a few months and then came to them and said they were moving up north with relatives to look for work. They begged the Ledbetters to let their daughter stay with them until they came back for her, which they never did.

The Ledbetters told the sheriff that they had given the girl room and board in exchange for domestic duties and are crushed by her misrepresentation of both their generosity and their good name. They asked the sheriff to remove the girl from their home, which he did. It is unknown at this time exactly where the girl is living, but Sheriff Raynor indicated she is with "her kind" and will no longer present a problem to the Ledbetters.

Judge Williams has ordered no further investigation into the matter.

Poor Mariah. How could the judge have dismissed something so obviously suspicious merely on the word of the accused?

Ellen looked at her growing list of articles to print out and decided that she wouldn't give up on this project until she had read every remaining article back to 1926.

Ellen sat at the breakfast bar eating an order of popcorn shrimp she had picked up at Gordy's when the phone rang. She reached over and grabbed the receiver.

"Hello."

"It's me," Guy Jones said. "Sounds like I caught you with your mouth full."

"That's okay. I'm glad you called. I've been at the library all day looking through microfilm. You can't believe all the racial problems that happened here in the thirties. It's appalling."

"Did you find a link to the Ws?"

"No, but I'd like to go back in time and give Judge John Bailey Williams and Sheriff Joe Quentin Raynor a piece of my mind." Ellen told Guy about Mariah, the young black girl who had been held against her will, and the young black man Sampson Harper, who had allegedly been lynched by sheriff's deputies, and several other incidents that had occurred over a five-year period involving Judge Williams and Sheriff Raynor.

"I'm sure they weren't the only ones covering up racist activity back then."

"I finally had to quit for the day. I couldn't take any more."

"How far did you get?"

"Only back to 1936. I've got a ways to go."

There was a long moment of silence.

"Hi," Guy finally said.

Ellen chuckled. "Hi, yourself. So how was *your* day?"

Brandon Jones sat up and swung his legs over the side of the bunk, his eyes wide and his mind racing. He pulled on a pair of cargo shorts, then tiptoed across the wood floor of the cabin and slowly opened the door and stepped outside.

The air was warm and thick, and the darkness alive with the sound of crickets. The moon was a glowing crescent and the stars like glitter sprinkled across the heavens. If only he could pitch a tent out here, he'd have no trouble falling asleep.

He sat on the top step, his senses filled with the sights and sounds and smells of night. He pushed the button on his watch and brought it closer to his eyes: 11:20.

He looked up at the moon and wondered if Kelsey was still awake and if she could see it, too. Maybe he would have the courage to call her after camp was over. Maybe after a few more weeks of being apart, she'd relent and agree to work things out. Brandon felt a twinge of sadness. Who was he kidding? As long as he had nothing to offer her, why would she even consider getting back together?

"Can I come out?" someone whispered.

Brandon turned around and saw Cade Nash's silhouette in the doorway.

"Sure. I hope I didn't wake you."

"No, I can't sleep either." Cade quietly closed the door and sat on the step next to Brandon. "Maybe we're part werewolf or somethin'."

Brandon poked Cade in the ribs with his elbow. "We can't be sure till the moon is full."

Cade laughed. "You know about werewolves?"

"Hey, I was a kid once. So how come you can't sleep?"

"I don't know. I'm not used to goin' to bed early."

"You a night owl?"

"Yeah. Mom says I need time to wind down."

"What do you do on school nights?"

A mischievous grin spread across Cade's face. "I read under the covers with a flashlight."

"Anything besides comic books?"

"I've read a whole stack of old James Bond novels I found in the shed."

"That stuff's got some pretty trashy parts. Does your mom know you're reading them?"

"No, but I'm not a little kid. I know about sex."

"Yeah, well. You should stick to comics for the time being."

"Do you have kids?" Cade asked.

"No, I'm not married."

"My mom isn't married anymore, but she's got me."

Brandon nodded. "I've never been married *or* divorced."

"Do you have a girlfriend?"

"Not at the moment. What's with all the personal questions?"

Cade shrugged. "Just curious."

Brandon sensed the boy had a deeper question he hadn't asked. "What's really on your mind?"

"Nothin'."

"I thought we decided to shoot straight with each other."

Cade sat for a few moments, cracking his knuckles, and then said, "You ever date a black woman?"

"Can't say that I have. Why?"

"I saw you on the news. I know what those guys did to your car and the black lady you were with."

"The lady's a friend. We weren't dating. But somebody obviously wasn't happy about us being together. It wasn't the first time either. Someone hit her in the head with a rock that same morning."

"Did you see who did it?"

"Yeah, we reported it to the police. It was a kid about your age and build…" *With tanned skin, curly hair, and who ran like the wind! Why didn't I see it before?* Brandon turned, his mind replaying the scene on the beach, his eyes searching Cade's. "I can't imagine why a boy would do such a thing. Can you?"

Cade looked down and started cracking his knuckles again. "Will they throw him in jail if they catch him?"

"Not unless he did something a whole lot worse than throw a rock at my friend. I'm guessing he didn't."

Cade got up and stretched. "I'm feelin' sleepy now. I think I'll go back to bed."

"Okay. Maybe we can discuss this case again sometime."

Cade pulled open the door and went back inside.

Brandon was thinking that if Caedmon Nash wasn't on the beach that morning, he must have a twin.

33

Ellen Jones sat in the public library on Wednesday morning reviewing the microfilm of *Messenger* articles for 1936 when an article dated March 6 caught her eye:

SHERIFF JOE QUENTIN RAYNOR DENIES TIES TO WHITE SUPREMACISTS

Allegations that Beacon County Sheriff Joe Quentin Raynor is linked to a secret society of white supremacists known as White Wash were dismissed today after a committee appointed by Judge John Bailey Williams submitted their findings following an investigation into the sheriff's background.

The committee found no evidence to support allegations made by Pastor Oliver Slade of the First Missionary Baptist Church in Seaport that Sheriff Raynor has strong ties to White Wash or that such a society even exists.

Further investigation into the sheriff's job performance revealed that he has been fair and lawful in his dealings with Negro lawbreakers.

Sheriff Raynor's badge was returned to him, and he was reinstated with apologies of the court.

Ellen's heart pounded so hard she was sure the man sitting next to her could hear it. *White Wash!* She marked this article on her sheet with a big star and continued reading.

"Hello again."

Ellen turned and looked up into the face of Valerie Hodges and felt the blood rush to her own. "Valerie…what are you doing here?"

"I'm checking out a book," Valerie said, "but I'm curious why you're still looking through microfilm."

"I haven't finished the project I told you about."

Valerie lifted her eyebrows. "That was days ago. Must be pretty important."

"It's just something my husband wanted me to get involved in."

"Oh, that's right. He's an attorney, isn't he?"

Ellen forced a smile. "Yes, he is."

"I saw you at the memorial service. I appreciated your eulogy."

"Thanks. Pastor Jonah and his family made a big impression on me at the evacuee shelter."

"Sounded like it. By the way, did you hear that the tropical depression is now a tropical storm and expected to be upgraded to a hurricane some time today?"

"No. Is it a threat to us?"

"Too early to tell. Well, I've got to get back to work. I just wanted to say hello."

"Have a nice day," Ellen said.

She watched Valerie walk down one aisle and disappear around a corner. She looked at her watch and decided to stick with this until noon. That should give her time to get hard copies and decide what to do with the information.

Will Seevers sat at the table in his office with Bryce Moore and Hank Martin, discussing whether to hold another press conference.

"People are going to be mad when we remind them we still haven't arrested anyone," Will said.

Bryce turned a pencil upside down and bounced the eraser on the table. "Regardless, it's better if we keep the lines of communication open. I think we should make a strong plea for people to be vigilant and report any suspicious activity."

"We've already done that," Will said. "Hasn't reaped anything."

"Can't hurt to do it again. It's good for the community to feel a sense of bein' involved."

"We better be addressin' the black community," Hank said. "I live right in the heart of it, and I'm tellin' you this thing is so close to turnin' violent it scares me."

"What do you think we should do?" Bryce said.

"I think we should stop concentratin' on talkin' to the media and get out there and talk to the black community leaders. Reassure them that we're workin' our fool tails off to figure out who's responsible. Give them our full attention and let the media report it from the periphery."

Bryce nodded. "Not a bad idea. What do you think, Will?"

"I'm totally open. I'm about the least popular guy in town at the moment, and the last thing I want is more rioting."

Will heard his administrative assistant's voice on the intercom. "Chief, Ellen Jones is here to see you, and—"

"Tell her I'm in a meeting."

"Sir, I did. She insists she has information pertinent to the case that you'll want to know about right away."

"Hold on a minute." Will looked at Bryce and then Hank. "Ellen's a friend of mine who used to be a newspaper editor. Her son Brandon is the kid who got the threatening note. She wouldn't bother me if it weren't important. You want in on this?"

"Sure," Bryce said. "I need to check in with some of my people, but it can wait a while longer."

Hank nodded. "Let's hear what she has to say."

"Okay, go ahead and send Ellen to my office." Will pushed back his chair and walked over and opened the door and stood with his arms folded. "I can't imagine what she's got that's so important."

A few seconds later, he saw Ellen coming down the hall toward him and met her halfway. "Special Agent Moore and Sheriff Martin are in my office. I'd like them to sit in on this, if that's okay with you."

"That's fine. I only need a few minutes to explain what I've got here."

"All right, come on."

Will escorted Ellen into his office, introduced her to Bryce and Hank, and then seated her at the table. "Okay, we're all ears."

"My curiosity has been on full tilt ever since the Ws started to appear at the crime scenes," Ellen said. "I decided to research old hate crimes and see if I could make a connection." Ellen handed Will a stack of papers. "I don't know if anything there will shed light on this case, but on March 6, 1936, an article appeared in the *Messenger* that made mention of a secret society of white supremacists called White Wash."

"Really?" Will skimmed the article, and then read it aloud to the others. "It's certainly uncanny, though I don't see a connection."

"I don't either," Ellen said. "But look through the other articles. Two names appeared over and over during the 1930s: Judge John Bailey Williams and Sheriff Joe Quentin Raynor. You'll have to judge for yourself, but these articles made me wonder whether the judge and sheriff were in cahoots to cover up gross injustices against black people. It may have absolutely no bearing on this case, but it was just too coincidental to ignore."

"Thanks for bringing it to our attention, Ellen," Will said. "We'll look into this."

"You're welcome." Ellen got up and left the office.

"Raynor…?" Will said. "Raynor…? Where have I heard that name recently?"

He walked over to his desk and thumbed through the file on the Caedmon Nash case till he found what he was looking for.

"Interesting…two of the kids who roughed up the Nash boy had the last name Williams and Raynor." He walked over to the table and laid the file between Hank and Bryce. "How weird is that?"

"Those are old names in this town," Hank said. "There're a bunch of them."

"That may be," Will said, his finger pointing to Reese's father's name on the page, "but how many *Quentin* Raynors do you suppose there are?"

Brandon Jones stood on the sidelines and watched Cade Nash hit a stand-up triple, thinking the kid was an amazing athlete.

"Looks like your boys are having a good time," Dax said.

"Yeah, they're a great group of kids. Really starting to work as a team. I think they'll be ready for that backpacking trip we talked about."

Dax sighed, his hand on Brandon's shoulder. "I hate to be the bearer of bad news, but that tropical depression I had my eye on has developed into a category two hurricane—Hector. It's expected to intensify when it crosses open water, and right now the projected path is somewhere along the panhandle, with landfall late Saturday or early Sunday. We're going to have to send these kids home."

Brandon shook his head. "I can't believe this."

"Yeah, it's a real bummer. A few nervous parents have already called, and Dr. Tehrani has volunteers making sure each child's parents are contacted."

"When do we tell the kids?"

"I'll announce it during lunch. But these kids are used to hurricane warnings, so I'm not expecting much of a reaction other than disappointment because we're closing down. Parents can start picking them up anytime. The governor hasn't issued a mandatory evacuation order yet, but that may come later, depending on the storm's path. A lot of these kids live in mobile homes. They'll need to stay in shelters or move inland."

Brandon looked up at the bluebird sky. "I heard somewhere that Seaport's never taken a direct hit."

"It's not like we don't get slammed pretty hard, but the worst of it always seems to miss us."

"That's good, right?"

"Yeah, but it also means we're due."

Will followed Bryce into Quentin Raynor's office at Q & R Appliances and sat in a gray vinyl chair.

Quentin leaned on the front of his desk, his arms folded. "What's this about?"

"Special Agent Moore and I are trying to tie up some loose ends," Will said. "We wanted to ask you some questions."

"My boy already told you everything he knows, and if that Nash kid told you otherwise, he's a liar."

"Mr. Raynor, are you related to Joe Quentin Raynor who used to be sheriff in Beacon County back in the 1930s?"

"He was my grandfather. Why?"

"Are you aware that he was accused of being tied to a secret society known as White Wash?"

Quentin's eyebrows came together. "Really? I didn't know that. What kind of society was it?"

"White supremacists," Bryce said. "It was a matter of public record. The *North Coast Messenger* made mention of it in an article in March of 1936."

Quentin shrugged. "That was a long time before I came along. My folks never mentioned it."

"Are your parents still alive?"

"No. What does this have to do with Reese?"

"Is it possible that your son knew about White Wash?"

Quentin shook his head. "How? I didn't even know. Reese has never said anything to me about it. What are you implying?"

"We're not implyin' anything," Bryce said. "We're just tryin' to establish whether the Ws found at the hate crime scenes could mean that this secret society has resurfaced."

"Not at my house it hasn't."

"It could explain where Reese got the idea to torment Caedmon Nash."

"Reese already told Chief Seevers he was just trying to look cool with the other guys. That Drummond kid was the ringleader."

Bryce nodded. "I'm familiar with your son's statement, Mr. Raynor."

"Then why are you embarrassing me by coming into my store and questioning me like some criminal?"

"Sir, do you frequent a local tavern called The Cove?"

"Yeah, I'm there a couple nights a week. I like to have a few beers and watch ESPN."

"Ever play poker in the back room?"

"What?"

"We know there've been some high stakes games going on down there. You ever ante up?"

"No, I don't gamble."

"Do you know a guy named Mick Beasley?"

"No."

"So if we check your phone records we're not going to find that you've called his number?"

"Absolutely not! Who's Mick Beasley? What's going on? Do I need a lawyer?"

"I don't know, sir. Do you?"

Quentin took out a handkerchief and dabbed his forehead. "I have nothing to hide. Why are you asking me all these questions?"

"There're just some coincidences we'd like to put into perspective," Bryce said.

"Like what?"

"Like the fact that your grandfather was often mentioned in news articles with Judge John Bailey Williams."

Quentin shrugged. "Is that important?"

"It might be if your son's friend Dakota Williams and his father are related to the judge."

"I seriously doubt that. Williams is a common name."

"But if it turns out the Williamses *are* related to the judge, it could seem like more than a coincidence that your sons were involved in terrorizin' a biracial kid."

"With all due respect, Agent Moore, I don't see that what happened generations ago has anything to do with Reese."

"So how did a couple twelve-year-olds learn to hate African-Americans?"

"You think it's just these boys?" Quentin said. "All they hear about is blacks stealing, raping, murdering, looting, rioting. They have to deal with racial conflict and threats all day at school. What'd we expect when we took in all those Katrina evacuees? Kids aren't blind."

"Just so you'll know, Mr. Raynor," Will said, "the crime stats have hardly changed this past year. Some categories are actually down."

"Well, the schools have a lot more dark faces and a lot more trouble. The racial tension's so thick you can cut it with a knife. I pay taxes so my kid can go to school to learn math and science, not how to defend himself."

Bryce got steely quiet and stared at Quentin, his jaw set. "Reese was hardly defendin' himself when he and his buddies beat up on Caedmon Nash."

"In his mind, he was defending his neighborhood against undesirables. He's twelve, okay? That's the way he saw it."

"All right, let's talk about Dakota Williams's father. Are the two of you friends?"

"Yeah, Jesse and I are neighbors. Our families cook out once in a while. What does that have to do with anything?"

"Are you friends with the Hall and Drummond boys' fathers, too?"

"No, I hardly know them."

"So if we ask your wives, they're going to tell us the same thing?"

"You think I'm lying? Go ahead, ask them. While you're at it, maybe you can explain to them why you're treating me as if *I'm* the criminal. This is harassment!"

"No, Mr. Raynor, this is a hate crime investigation. If you don't have anything to hide, you have nothin' to fear. But if you're involved in these hate crimes or know who is, you'd better start talkin' while we're still in the mood to cut a deal."

"I told you I don't know anything."

Bryce stood and handed him a business card. "Here's my number. I suggest you think real hard about it. There's bound to be a loose cannon out there. And whoever talks to us first gets the deal."

Will followed Bryce out of the building to the parking lot.

Bryce stopped and glanced back at the front of Q & R Appliances. "Raynor knows somethin'. Let's subpoena his phone records—here and at his home. Cell phone, too."

Brandon sat on the cabin bunk next to Cade, his hands between his knees. "I know you're disappointed we had to cancel camp. I am, too. We were all starting to click."

"The stupid hurricane'll probably not even hit us. I get so sick of this."

"I know, but we can't afford to take chances."

"So what am I supposed to do till my mom gets off work?"

Brandon glanced at his watch. "Why don't we go hiking? I discovered a trail through the woods that leads down to a swamp. I saw an alligator there."

Cade slid off the bed onto his feet. "Cool."

Brandon walked out of the cabin and headed up toward the main lodge, Cade on his heels.

"Why are we going up there?" Cade said.

"Remember Rule Number One? As a safety precaution, always tell somebody where you're going."

Brandon bounded up the steps and pushed open the door, surprised that the big reception hall had cleared out and nearly all the kids were gone. He saw a couple other counselors, but didn't spot Dax.

"Come on, let's leave the director a note."

Brandon went down to Dax's office and tore a piece of yellow paper off a ruled pad on his desk. He said the words out loud as he wrote them, "2:40 p.m. Dax, I took Cade Nash hiking on the swamp trail. His mother is coming to get him at 5:30, and we'll be back before then. The other six boys in our group have been picked up. Brandon."

Brandon taped the note on Dax's door. "That should do it. Why don't we grab a couple soft drinks to take with us? And maybe a handful of those M&Ms cookies we had at lunch."

Will paced in front of the window in his office, wondering which weighed more heavily on him: another hurricane threat or the thought that White Wash might have resurfaced.

There was a knock at his door and Sheriff Hank Martin and an FBI agent Will had met earlier came in and sat at the table with Bryce. Will went over and joined them.

"We questioned Jesse Williams, Dakota's dad," Hank said. "I could tell right off that he didn't much like havin' to answer to a black sheriff. He admitted that Judge John Bailey Williams was his great-uncle, but says he never heard of White Wash. Says he doesn't hang out at The Cove, doesn't know Mick Beasley or how to play poker."

"Did he know his great-uncle and Quentin Raynor's grandfather were tight?" Bryce said.

Hank shook his head. "Said he had no idea. Bottom line: We got nothin'."

"Was he cooperative?"

"Seemed to be. Didn't act like he had anything to hide."

"Did you tell him we could check his phone records to see if he made calls to Beasley or The Cove?"

"Yeah. He said to knock ourselves out."

Bryce sat back in his chair and exhaled. "I hate it when I smell a rat but can't trap it. Let's go question Josh Hall and Abel Drummond's dads. Also find out if Raynor and Williams have alibis for the nights of the crimes. We need to push this thing into high gear and find out as much as we can before we have to shut it down and deal with Hurricane Hector."

34

Brandon Jones eased down the sloping trail that cut through a forest of pine, palm, and hardwood trees. He looked up at the holes in the green canopy and caught glimpses of blue sky. "Listen…hear that sound?"

"All I hear is a bird," Cade Nash said.

"Hear how crisp and clear he sounds? It's a cardinal. See him way up there on the edge of that limb? There're so many of them around here I'm wondering if that's where our cabin got its name." Brandon reached down on the ground and picked up a red feather and handed it to Cade.

"You already spotted those two woodpeckers and a nuthatch. How come you know so much about birds?"

"I've been hiking a lot and I pay attention. I usually have a bird handbook with me so I can identify life birds."

"What're those?"

"Birds I'm seeing for the first time. I keep a running list." Brandon continued walking. "Ah, there's the swamp down at the bottom. See it?"

"Yeah. Can we squish our toes in it?"

Brandon smiled. "Not unless you want them to be some alligator's dinner." He eased his way down to the bottom of the trail and stood facing the swamp, Cade standing on his right.

"Not much to look at, is it?" Cade said.

"But it's teeming with life." Brandon pointed to a half dozen white birds picking at the ground. "Do you know what those birds are called?"

"Yeah, those are ibis. I see them all over the place."

"What about those?" Brandon nodded toward some tiny little shorebirds.

"I didn't see them before. What are they?"

"Lesser yellow legs."

Cade laughed. "Very funny."

"I'm dead serious," Brandon said. "I'll show you in my book when we get back." He climbed up on a smooth boulder and pulled Cade up next to him. "Watch the surface of the water for a pair of eyes sticking up."

Cade turned to Brandon, the corners of his mouth twitching. "Did you really see a gator down here, or were you just kiddin'?"

"I really saw one. Must've been four feet long."

For the next forty-five minutes, Brandon sat with Cade and helped him spot thirteen species of birds, including a well-camouflaged night heron, plus a bobcat and an alligator.

"This is so cool," Cade said. "I wish camp didn't get cancelled."

"Me too, sport."

"I guess I'll never see you again after this." Cade looked out over the swamp and seemed to be bothered by something. Finally he said, "I need to tell you somethin'. I'm the one who hit your lady friend with a rock and kicked you in the ribs."

"I know. Thanks for having the courage to finally admit it."

"So you *did* figure it out… Why didn't you ask me about it?"

"I thought you'd tell me when you were ready. I'm curious why you did it."

Cade shrugged. "I saw a white man with a black lady, and it just reminded me how sick I am of bein' half-and-half and not fittin' in. I was mad that you might have a kid that would have to go through what I'm goin' through. It was stupid. I'm sorry if I hurt her."

"I think her feelings were hurt more than her head. Sometimes she gets put down because of her race. Sounds like you can relate to that."

"Are you gonna tell the police?"

"Only so they know it had nothing to do with the hate crimes. It might be nice, though, if you'd apologize to my friend."

Cade sighed. "Okay, but I'm not tellin' my mom. She gets upset anytime I act sad about being biracial."

"It's best not to have secrets from your mom."

"Well, there's stuff I can't tell her."

"Can't or won't?"

"She doesn't understand what I'm goin' through. She has no idea the stuff I have to put up with every day. And she'd freak if she knew how much I wanna get even with those stupid white kids who call me skunk and treat me like dirt."

Brandon debated whether he should continue this conversation but decided it would be unwise to shut Cade down when he was venting his feelings. "What would you do to get even?"

The expression left Cade's face. "Steal a rifle and shoot them all. I used to think about it every day...but I don't anymore. Now it just makes me depressed."

"Why do you think that is?"

"Because I know it's wrong. I would never really hurt anybody. I'm just so mad." Cade quickly brushed a tear from his cheek. "I shouldn't be talkin' to you about this."

Brandon put his hand on Cade's shoulder. "Yeah, you should. You're a good kid caught in a trap. There has to be a way to fix this."

"Well, there isn't. My mom never should've had me."

Ellen Jones put the weather channel on mute and went out to the kitchen and dialed Guy's cell number.

"Hello," Guy Jones said.

"Where have you been? I called and left messages."

"I was just about to call you back."

"How close are you to home?"

"About an hour away. I've been on the phone with Ross Hamilton. He's picking up the supplies we need to board up the house. He'll bring them over in the morning before they pick up Blanche and head for Meridian."

"Yeah, Julie called and told me." Ellen glanced across the hall at the TV. "You should see the mob at Wal-Mart and Home Depot. I can't believe we're going through this again."

"Well, not to worry. We're getting to be pros. Did you go see our dads?"

"Yes. Mine didn't have a clue what I was talking about. I'm not sure he even recognized me. The staff is already preparing to evacuate all the patients to the Alzheimer's center in Adelville. Same as last time."

"Good. That's a load off."

"Your dad, on the other hand, was his usual sweet self. He's ready to go when we are."

"Thanks. Once we get the house boarded up, we'll go get him and head for Tallahassee. Owen and Hailey can meet us at the apartment. I've got it stocked with everything we'll need. If the hurricane center predicts Hector will pose too big a threat there, we'll drive up into Georgia. Did you get a hold of Brandon?"

"No, and I'm starting to get worried that he hasn't called me back. Surely he knows what's going on."

"Honey, get on the phone and call Ali and find out."

"I really don't want to embarrass Brandon by going to Ali."

"Well, maybe he'll start thinking about someone besides himself. Were you able to finish your research at the library?"

Ellen smiled. "I thought you'd never ask." She told Guy about the article she had discovered that mentioned the secret society called White Wash. "I took copies of that article and several others straight to Will. Sheriff Martin and Special Agent Moore were in his office when I arrived. They were all ears."

"I'm proud of you, honey."

"I don't know that it means a thing, but it was satisfying just finding it. Oh, and get this, Valerie Hodges came up behind me while I was reading the article. Said she was there to check out a book and was curious why I was still reviewing microfilm. I told her I wasn't finished with the project my husband wanted me to work on."

Guy laughed. "Well, that's true."

"But you know what? She was really nice. I discovered it's not as much fun to win when I'm the only one playing the game."

Brandon Jones walked down the steps of the main lodge and over to a white Ford Escort. He held the door while Cade's mother got in on the driver's side, then walked around to the passenger side and leaned on the open window.

"Why such a sad face?" Brandon said. "Your mom said we could get together after the hurricane blows through."

Cade sat twirling the red feather with his thumb and forefinger. "What if I'm stuck in a shelter and you can't find me?"

"Then I'll hunt you down. There's no way I'm going to lose track of you. I promise."

"You're just sayin' that."

Brandon smiled. "You kidding? You know where the tarpon hole is. I thought maybe I could figure a way to scrounge up a couple of fishing rods and you could take me to the fish."

"Cool!"

"Maybe we can do some camping out at the Jackson Caves, too. You've talked so much about the place that I'm anxious to see if I've got it pictured right."

"But we get to sleep in the cave, right?"

"Sure. It's all part of the experience."

Brandon looked over at Angel Phelps and decided Cade had her eyes. "Are you going to stay here in a shelter or are you heading up north?"

"It's too far to Shady, Alabama, where my daddy is," Angel said. "I'm not sure this old car would make it that far. I expect we'll stay in a shelter like last time. What about you?"

"I'll go wherever my folks go," Brandon said. "I haven't had a chance to talk to them yet."

"Well, you have our address and phone number. It's nice you wanna stay in touch with Cade."

Brandon nodded. "You two stay safe. I'll call when the dust settles."

He stepped back and watched the Escort rock and bounce along the uneven gravel road, then disappear behind the trees, leaving a haze hanging phantomlike over the road.

He went back to Red Feather and started packing up his things, his mind echoing with conversations he'd had with Cade Nash. The kid had seemed relieved after he confessed to throwing the rock at Weezie and having entertained thoughts about shooting the boys who tormented him. Brandon didn't believe this kid was capable of violence. But he sensed there was something Cade was still holding onto—something he didn't feel he could tell anyone.

Lord, I'm worried about him. He seems to be reaching out to me. If I'm supposed to help him, show me what to do.

Gordy Jameson sat on a wood bench in front of Gordy's Crab Shack and wondered how many times this season he'd have to board up the place. He heard someone whistle and looked up. Eddie Drummond was walking across the pier.

Gordy glanced at his watch and wondered what he was doing here at 3:20 in the afternoon.

"Looks like Hector may give us heck," Eddie said.

"Yeah, I could do without that. What's up with you?"

"I'm so ticked off I can hardly see straight. You're not gonna believe what just happened." Eddie sat on the bench beside Gordy. "Will Seevers and Special Agent Moore paid me a visit at work. Talk about embarrassing!"

"What'd they want?"

"That's just it. I'm not really sure. They asked all kinds of questions about the dads of the boys Abel got in trouble with. They wanted to know if I ever see the other dads socially or if I drink with them at The Cove or play high stakes poker in the back room. Like *I'm* supposed to know poker games are going on there? They asked about some guy named Mick Beasley, who I never heard of. Then get this: They wanted to know if I've ever heard of a secret society of white supremacists called White Wash."

Gordy's eyes locked on to Eddie's. "So they think that's what the Ws stand for?"

"I was hoping you could tell me. Didn't Will talk to you about it?"

"If he did, you know I couldn't say anything." Gordy sat quietly for a moment, his mind racing, and then said, "But he didn't."

"Well, something's going down. They asked if I would mind if they check my phone records, which I agreed to but resent. And they wanted to know where I was at the time each of the hate crimes was committed. Like I'm supposed to remember right off the top of my head. Why would they come at *me* with this?"

"I'm sure they're just turnin' over every rock, Eddie. The black community's a time bomb after the deaths of that pastor and his family."

"Well, I didn't have anything to do with it! Don't I have any rights?"

"Did they tell you to get a lawyer?"

"Only if I think I need one."

"Do you?"

The lines on Eddie's forehead deepened. "How can you even ask me that? We've been friends a long time. We don't always agree on things, but have I ever lied to you?"

"Not that I know of."

"Then you've gotta trust me on this. I'm really getting scared that the cops and the FBI think I'm involved in this thing. I'm not! And I don't know who is, I swear."

Brandon pulled out of Camp Piney Woods onto the highway and hit the autodial on his cell phone.

"Hello."

"Mom, it's Brandon."

"Why didn't you call sooner? I've been worried sick about you."

"Sorry. It got pretty hectic trying to get the kids sent home and the place shut down. Camp's been cancelled."

"Where are you?"

"On my way to your place. Are you and Dad going to board up the house?"

"Yes, our friend Ross Hamilton already purchased the supplies for us so we wouldn't have to fight the crowd at the stores."

"What's the latest from the National Hurricane Center?"

"Hector is expected to be upgraded to a category four within the next few hours. The projected path puts us in the cone at the moment. We'll prepare for the worst and hope for the best. It's nerve-racking, but we always seem to escape the worst of it."

"I'll help dad board up the house."

"Thanks. He'll appreciate that. Owen's got his hands full doing his own house."

"Is he going to ride it out?"

"No, he won't chance it with the kids. We'll all stay at your dad's apartment in Tallahassee."

"Well, if this thing decides to come straight at us, Tallahassee could get hit hard, too."

"We'll watch the reports. We can always drive up into Georgia and find a place to stay."

"I'll bet you're sick and tired of running from hurricanes."

Ellen sighed. "Yes, but we don't dare chance riding it out. As close as we are to the beach, a good storm surge would wipe our house off the map."

35

Brandon Jones opened his eyes and for a few seconds thought he was still at camp, then recognized the striped wallpaper in the guest room at his parents' house. He turned over and looked out the window, glad to see the sun filtering through the massive live oaks. He heard hammering and threw back the covers. He slipped into shorts and a T-shirt and went downstairs to the kitchen.

"Good morning, sleepyhead," Ellen said.

"Why didn't Dad wake me? I told him I wanted to help board up the house."

"He wanted to get an early start, and when he's focused on something, you know how he is. I was about to come get you."

"What's the latest on the hurricane?"

"Still a category four, but they think it'll be a five before afternoon. It's really getting scary. They're talking as though it might make landfall between Port Smyth and Seaport."

"That's not good news." Brandon glanced down at Thursday's headline: *Hector Threatens Panhandle.*

"It would certainly be the end of life as we know it. I keep seeing those awful images of the devastation in Biloxi and Gulfport."

"When will they know for sure?"

"These things change from hour to hour. Right now, they're predicting landfall around noon Sunday. The whole waiting-it-out process is enough to set your teeth on edge."

Brandon poured himself a cup of coffee. "What's the evacuation plan?"

"The governor hasn't issued a mandatory evacuation order yet, but we've decided to leave tonight for Tallahassee. I assume you're coming with us."

"I'd go nuts just sitting around the apartment. Why don't I hang out here and drive up Saturday afternoon?"

"The traffic will be atrocious."

"I know, but I may never be this close to a hurricane again." Brandon lifted his eyebrows and tried not to smile. "I don't want to miss all the excitement."

"This is a serious situation."

"I know, Mom. That's part of the thrill."

"Not to me."

Brandon put his hands on his mother's shoulders and looked her in the eyes. "Maybe it's the adventurer in me, but I'd like to hang out here and live the experience until it's time to hightail it out of here. You know I won't take any chances."

"I don't care what their phone records show," Will Seevers said. "These dads are connected. I feel it."

Bryce Moore set his pencil on the table. "None of them called Mick Beasley, and he never called them. And any calls made from one of their residences to the others could easily have been made by the boys."

"Some of them were made late at night," Hank Martin said.

"So the kids were up late. Still doesn't prove anything."

"Darn this hurricane!" Will said. "I don't want to lose momentum on this case! There's something here. I just can't get hold of it yet."

"We could always go back to the dads and make them believe we're close to makin' an arrest," Bryce said. "See if one of them starts squirmin'."

Will's administrative assistant's voice came over the intercom. "Chief, Angel Phelps is on the phone, the mother of the biracial boy who—"

"I know who she is. Tell her I'm in a meeting."

"She says it's an emergency. She's crying and refuses to hang up."

Will sighed. "All right. Put her through." He got up and picked up the phone as soon as it rang. "Hello, Ms. Phelps."

"Cade's gone! I heard angry voices! I don't know where he is, and we have to evacuate! You gotta do somethin'!"

"Slow down, ma'am. Tell me what you know."

"I heard Cade arguin' with someone during the night. I thought I was dreamin'. But when I woke up, his bedroom window was open, and he was gone. He didn't leave me a note! He always leaves me a note!"

"Not always," Will said. "He snuck out of the house the night he went to Abel Drummond's to get his bike back."

"But he was actin' strange before he went to camp and wouldn't talk to me about it! I asked him if those bullies were still givin' him a hard time, and he just stared at me like his mouth was wired shut. His eyes looked scared, like he was terrified of somethin'. But he wouldn't talk to me! Somethin's goin' on! Please, you have to help me find him."

Brandon nailed the last piece of plywood over the windows in the widow's watch and then climbed down the ladder. "Okay, Dad. That's it."

"Thanks for your help," Guy said. "That didn't take long."

Ellen came outside on the veranda. "Brandon, Will Seevers and Special Agent Moore are here to see you."

"Really? Okay, I'll be right there."

Guy put his hand on Brandon's shoulder. "I wish you'd reconsider and follow us to Tallahassee tonight."

"I'll be fine, Dad. I'll be up there by Saturday night. I'd better go see what gives. It's not every day the FBI pays *me* a visit."

Brandon bounded up the back steps and went inside where he saw Will Seevers and another man talking with his mother.

"Brandon, this is Special Agent Moore," Will said.

Brandon nodded. "I recognize you from TV. What can I do for you?"

"Why don't you three sit here in the living room," Ellen said, "and I'll get you some lemonade."

Will and Bryce walked over and sat on the couch. Brandon sat in the love seat across from them.

"I've got disturbing news," Will said. "Cade Nash is missing."

"Did he run away?"

"We don't know. His mother thinks she heard him arguing with someone in the middle of the night. She thought she was dreaming, but when she got up this morning, Cade was gone. His bike, too. There's no sign of a struggle."

Brandon exhaled. "How can I help?"

"Since you probably spent more time with him in the past few days than anyone else, we were hoping you'd give us a heads-up on how he seemed to you."

"Cade's a great kid. Fast runner. Fantastic athlete. I think he's mixed up right now about being biracial and is really mad at the kids who've been bullying him. But I was surprised at how quickly he adapted to our group. He was really starting to be a team player."

"Did he ever seem distracted?"

"More like standoffish. I kept encouraging him to get involved, and once he did, there was no stopping him. After I watched him run relays a few times, I noticed this uncanny resemblance to the kid who hit Weezie with the rock. I suspected Cade had done it. He admitted it to me yesterday on his own. Even apologized."

"Why didn't you tell the police?"

"I was going to call you today. I'm convinced the incident isn't related to the hate crimes." Brandon explained why Cade had reacted so strangely to seeing a white man with a black woman. "Like I said, he's mixed up about himself right now. Truthfully, I don't think he has a mean bone in his body."

Will got steely quiet for a moment and then looked at Brandon. "You're not running this investigation. It wasn't your call. You should've reported it."

"Sorry, I've barely had time to breathe since I got home. Do you think Cade's in some kind of trouble?"

"We don't know for sure. His mother's frantic. She asked us to talk to you and see if you could tell us anything."

Brandon ran his finger along the couch seam. "Cade did confide something in me. I hate to break a confidence, but I guess this warrants it. He mentioned that he used to think a lot about stealing a rifle and shooting the boys who've been harassing him." Brandon held up his palms. "But in the next breath, he said he doesn't think that way anymore, that he knows it's wrong, and he wouldn't really hurt anyone."

Will closed his eyes and shook his head. "And you believed him?"

"Actually, I did. I'm a pretty good judge of character. It took guts for him to admit that to me. I don't think he would've if he still had those thoughts."

"Unless he was crying out for help. Maybe he wanted you to stop him."

Brandon's mind raced back through the conversations he'd had with Cade. "I didn't get that sense at all. But he did seem troubled about something. I always got the feeling there was something he wanted to tell me but couldn't."

"Listen, Brandon, I need you to think carefully. Did Cade say anything that might suggest someone wanted to hurt him?"

"You mean other than the kids who were bullying him?"

Will nodded.

"Not that I picked up on. But like I said, I always got the feeling there was something he wanted to tell me but couldn't."

"Funny, his mother said the same thing."

Will walked into his office behind Bryce Moore and saw Hank Martin sitting at the table eating pizza.

"Come join the party," Hank said. "It might be the most fun you have for a long time. Hurricane's been upgraded to category five. Sustained winds at 163 miles an hour, gusts to 190. Governor's called for a mandatory evacuation along the panhandle. Looks like we're finally gonna get creamed."

Will flopped in his chair, his thoughts suddenly on Margaret and Meagan. "Darn! We need to find Cade Nash."

"He'll probably show up on his own," Bryce said. "We should go back to the dads and turn up the heat before they have time to regroup."

"I doubt they're thinking about anything other than getting out of Dodge," Will said. "Which is what you should be thinking about.

You guys need to get home to your families. We can pick this up after the hurricane."

Hank looked at Bryce and then at Will. "Well, if we get hit with a category five, there may not be anything left to investigate."

Brandon stood on the front porch and waved good-bye to his parents as they left for Tallahassee. He looked up at the bluebird sky and tried to comprehend the magnitude of the approaching hurricane.

He took out his cell phone and dialed Angel Phelps's number.

"Hello?"

"Angel, it's Brandon Jones. Any sign of Cade?"

"No. Did the police talk to you?"

"Yeah, they did, but I don't know that I was very helpful."

Angel began to cry. "What am I gonna to do? The hurricane's comin', and no one knows where he is! The governor's issued an evacuation order! I'm not goin' to no shelter without Cade!"

"I'm coming over there, okay? Stay put."

Brandon disconnected the call. He went in the house and got the directions Angel had given him the day before. He locked the front door, got in his SUV, and headed for Harbor Drive.

Lord, You know where Cade is. Show us how to find him.

Brandon drove down Seaport Parkway, his mind replaying over and over the conversations he'd had with Cade. Had he missed something? Was Cade's admission that he'd thought about shooting the boys who'd hassled him really a cry for help? Brandon didn't know what to think anymore. He just knew that someone had to find Cade before the weather made it too dangerous to try.

He looked at the directions in his hand and turned right on Morton, and then left on Blake, and then right again on Harbor Street, where he saw the rusty sign at the entrance to the Harbor Street Mobile Home Village. He turned in and drove to J Street and spotted the white Ford Escort parked in the space out front. Before he could get out of the car, Angel Phelps was standing at the driver's side window.

"I'm so glad you're here." She dabbed her eyes, her face red and swollen. "I don't know what I'm gonna do if the shelter fills up before we can get there."

"Where have you looked for Cade?"

"I've driven up and down the streets here in the park and asked neighbors if anyone's seen him. Nobody has. I went to all his favorite places and didn't see him. I don't understand why he didn't leave me a note."

"Is it possible Cade didn't leave on his own—that he was co-erced?"

She shrugged. "I don't know. The police dusted the window in his room for prints but didn't find any but his and mine. I thought I heard him arguin' with someone last night, but I was half asleep. Maybe I imagined it."

"Describe what you heard."

"Male voices. Angry. More than one. They sounded muffled."

"Men or boys?"

"Men, I think. Maybe both. I'm not sure."

"Has anyone questioned the boys who've been harassing Cade?"

"Chief Seevers and that FBI agent did."

"Have you ever the met the boys?"

"No. I'd probably strangle them."

"Do you know where they live?"

"All of them live on Shady Lane by that Methodist church—the one with pretty stained-glass windows."

"Can you tell me their names?"

"No, but they're on the police report. Come in. I'll get it for you."

Brandon followed Angel into the mobile home and waited at the front door. A minute later she brought him a copy of the police report.

Brandon perused it. "Looks like Reese Raynor, Joshua Hall, Dakota Williams, and Abel Drummond."

"Are you gonna talk to them?"

"What have we got to lose? You want to come?"

She shook her head. "It's probably better if I don't."

"Okay, I'll be back in a little while." He took an old business card out of his wallet and wrote his cell number on it. "Call me if Cade comes home. And please don't leave without letting me know where you are. We haven't got time to waste trying to keep track of each other."

Brandon turned onto Shady Lane and saw several people boarding up their houses. He drove slowly until he came to a two-story stucco home with a green metal roof and the numbers 385 on the front. He pulled over to the curb and got out. A man and a young boy about Cade's age were in the garage on hands and knees, sorting out sheets of plywood. He walked toward them.

"Mr. Raynor?"

The man looked up. "Yeah."

"I'm Brandon Jones."

"And I'm busy. This is a heck of a time to be selling something."

"I'm not. I'm looking for someone."

Mr. Raynor hollered over his shoulder. "Reese, put those nails in the pouch and get a couple hammers out of the toolbox. So who're you looking for?"

"Caedmon Nash."

Mr. Raynor stopped what he was doing and looked up, his eyes searching Brandon's. "He doesn't live in this neighborhood."

"I know. But his mother's looking for him, and I thought your son might know where he is."

"You thought wrong." Raynor's eyebrows came together. "Why would you come here looking for that trailer trash?"

"Mind if I ask Reese if he's seen him?"

"He hasn't."

"I'd like to hear him say it."

"Look, buddy, I'm busy. Think you could give me a break here?"

"Actually, no. Cade's missing. A hurricane's coming. And his mother's worried sick. So how about you giving *me* a break?"

Mr. Raynor rose to his feet, his arms folded. "I already told you, we don't know where the kid is. What's your interest in him? You dating his mother? Is she into white guys now?"

"I was Cade's camp counselor."

"Camp? How'd she afford that?" He rolled his eyes. "Let me

guess. The People's Clinic gave her a handout. Really burns me that I can't afford to send my kids to camp. They're not poor enough or black enough to qualify for a scholarship."

Brandon decided he wasn't leaving until he got a straight answer. "Hey, Reese!"

The boy turned around.

"Where's Cade Nash?"

"How should I know?"

"You saw him last night, didn't you? What did you say to him?"

Reese's face went blank. He looked at his dad and didn't say anything.

Mr. Raynor walked up to Brandon and stood nose-to-nose. "How dare you come on my property and harass my son! I told you we don't know where that half-breed trailer trash is. Now get off my property before I throw you off."

"Fine, I'll go talk to Dakota Williams. Maybe he'll tell me where Cade is. Or maybe Joshua Hall knows. Or Abel Drummond."

"Go ahead. Nobody around here knows or cares where that kid is."

"Well, the police do."

Mr. Raynor took a step back and flashed a phony smile. "Then ask them. I've got work to do."

Brandon shook hands with Will Seevers and then sat in a chair next to his desk. "Thanks for seeing me. I wasn't sure if you were even here."

"My wife and daughter have evacuated, but I'm staying," Will said. "We're setting up a makeshift police department in Palm City, where we'll be safe from the storm surge but close enough to get back in here quickly to maintain order. What about you?"

"I'm driving up to my dad's apartment in Tallahassee on Saturday. Most of my family will be there."

"So what's on your mind?" Will said.

"Reese Raynor and his dad. I went to see all the boys who'd been hassling Cade. Since Angel thought she heard him arguing with someone, I thought maybe they were bothering him again."

"How'd you know where to find them?"

"Angel showed me the police report."

"I see. So why are Reese and Quentin Raynor on your mind?"

"Because the kid's dad was a total jerk. Wanted to know why I was looking for trailer trash in his neighborhood. He totally ran interference. The only way I was able to ask Reese anything was just to shout it out." Brandon relayed the entire conversation to Will. "I think the Raynors are hiding something."

Will's eyes seemed to be probing. "Did your mother put you up to this?"

"What do you mean? She's on her way to Tallahassee. She doesn't know I went over there."

"Ellen didn't talk to you about the old newspaper articles?"

"No, did she find something?"

"Brandon, look. You're getting into something much bigger than you know. You need to back off and let us handle this."

"You expect me just to back off when they might know where Cade is? He needs to be in a shelter."

"You think I don't know that?" Will sighed. "Look, we questioned each of the boys and their fathers earlier today. They didn't give us any reason to suspect they were involved in Cade's disappearance."

"That doesn't mean they weren't! They're hiding something. I can feel it. What if they've hurt him?"

"There was no sign of a struggle at the house," Will said. "Why would Cade go with them willingly?"

Brandon raked his hands through his hair and let out a sigh of exasperation. "I don't know."

Will got quiet and seemed to be deep in thought. Finally he said, "Reese's dad was a real jerk, huh?"

"Yeah, he assumed I was dating Angel and made some sarcastic remark about her being into white guys now. I wanted to punch him."

"Do you think he recognized your face from the news?"

"I hadn't thought about that. Maybe."

"Have you ever seen his face before?"

"Not that I know of. What are you getting at?"

Will folded his hands on the desk. "This is an FBI investigation, and I can't get into details. But I don't want you having any more contact with the boys or their families. I'm serious about this."

"Okay, but I'm not going to stop looking for Cade."

"Neither are we. But once we start to get slammed by the outer bands of this hurricane, we'll have to pull all law enforcement personnel off the street till this thing is over."

36

Brandon Jones laid Friday's newspaper on the breakfast bar and picked up the phone and dialed his father's apartment in Tallahassee.

"Hello."

"Mom, it's me. Did you have any problem getting there?"

"No," Ellen Jones said, "but it took us a lot longer than we anticipated. It was exhausting for your grandfather. The traffic was horrible. I called Owen and Hailey and told them not to wait till noon to leave, so they're on the way. I wish you were. So is your prehurricane adventure all you hoped it would be?"

"Truthfully I've been too busy to give it much thought. I spent all yesterday afternoon and evening trying to find Cade."

"You mean that child hasn't come home yet?"

"No, and Angel's beside herself. She refuses to go to the shelter without him. The police have an APB out, but he still hasn't been spotted."

"So you've just been driving around, looking for him?"

"No, I went to talk to the boys who'd been harassing him. I figured if Cade had been arguing with someone, it might be one of them. Reese Raynor's dad turned out to be one of the biggest jerks I've ever met. You wouldn't believe the racist comments he made." Brandon told his mother about his unpleasant exchange with the Raynors and about his suspicion that they were hiding something. "Mom, you there?"

"I'm here. Is Reese's last name spelled R-A-Y-N-O-R?"

"Yeah."

"Do you know his father's name?"

"Quentin, I think."

"Oh, dear…"

"Why do I get the feeling I'm the only one who doesn't know what's going on? Chief Seevers asked me if you'd put me up to talking to the boys and if I knew about the old newspaper articles. Do you know what he was talking about?"

"Brandon, did one of the other boys have the last name Williams?"

"Yes. Would you please tell me what's going on?"

"I think you should ask Will."

Brandon exhaled loudly. "I'm asking *you*. I don't have time for this! I need to find Cade before this monster storm hits. Would you just tell me what you know?"

"All right. Go into the master bedroom. In the nightstand you'll find copies of articles I got from the library and gave to Will, Special Agent Moore, and Sheriff Martin. Read the one dated March 6, 1936, that mentions a secret society of white supremacists called White Wash. Then read the others and notice how many times the names Sheriff Joe Quentin Raynor and Judge John Bailey Williams are mentioned together—and in what context."

"Mom, just give me the bottom line."

"I'm only guessing, of course. But I think the *W*s at the crime scenes were meant to give credit to this secret society, which probably means it's active again."

"Why didn't you tell me?"

"I wasn't sure. I couldn't find a connection between the past and present. The boys' names were never released, and Will never mentioned them to me. I didn't know one was a Raynor and one a Williams until just now."

Brandon sat on a barstool. "So you're saying the Raynors and the Williamses are involved in White Wash and the hate crimes?"

"Let's just say a huge red flag just went up."

"No wonder the chief wants me to stay away from them."

"Did he say that?"

"Yeah, he said it's an FBI investigation and I need to stay away from the boys and their families."

"Then you have to," Ellen said. "Or you'll get charged with impeding an investigation."

"What if Cade knew something and they decided to shut him up?"

"I'm sure Will's thought of that. Why don't you go back and talk to him again. Once he realizes how much you know, he may be more open to sharing what he knows."

Gordy Jameson held a piece of plywood over the front window of Gordy's Crab Shack while Billy Lewis drove in the last nail. "Good job. We're done."

"I will go now," Billy said. "I will nail ply-wood on my mom and dad's house."

Gordy patted him on the shoulder and slipped him a fifty-dollar bill. "Thanks for your extra help the past couple days. You deserve this."

"Thanks, Mister G!" Billy flashed a crooked smile, his eyes moving from side to side. "I did an ex-cel-lent job!"

"Yeah, you did. Your mom and dad said you and Lisa are gonna evacuate with them."

"We are go-ing to stay in a mo-tel and play cards with the flashlight on."

Gordy smiled. "I have a feelin' we're gonna be doin' the same thing. See you as soon as the storm passes. You be safe now."

Gordy turned and saw Pam standing on the pier, looking up at the sky. He walked over and stood next to her and held her hand. "Hard to believe that beautiful sky is about to turn dangerous, isn't it?"

"I'm scared," Pam Jameson said. "If we get hit with a five, not a board of this place will be left standing. Our home either. This town, for that matter."

"Well, it's never happened before."

"But how long can we beat the odds?"

"Oh, darlin', most of the time the darn hurricanes take a turn, and we miss the worst of it. Hector's probably gonna do the same thing."

"I don't know. I have a bad feeling about this one."

Gordy wasn't about to tell her that he did, too.

"There you are!" Weezie walked out of the crab shack and over to the pier. "I should've known I'd find you two out here makin' goo-goo eyes at each other."

"It's a great stress breaker. Can't you tell?" Gordy rolled his eyes toward Pam.

"Well," Weezie said, "I'm not gonna prance out here and pretend I'm cool as a cucumber, but I'm prayin' for the best. I appreciate you and Billy helpin' me board up my house. It'd been a long time since I'd been out there. It was like meetin' up with an old friend."

"You'll be back in there soon. What time do you girls wanna close? We can stay open through today if you want and take off for Georgia in the mornin'. Or we can shut her down anytime and leave today."

Pam turned to him. "I thought we agreed to stay open so we could be here for the community?"

"I was just checkin' in case you had a change of heart. The traffic's gonna get worse the longer we stay."

"I vote to wait," Pam said. "People who're still boarding up need a place to eat."

Weezie nodded. "I'm in."

Pam wiped a tear off her cheek and then another and another.

"Darlin', don't go worryin' yourself sick over somethin' you can't control. What will be will be. We'll deal with it."

Pam put her head on his shoulder. "I just can't imagine this place not being here."

Will Seevers sat with Hank Martin at the table in his office and looked up, surprised to see Bryce Moore standing in the doorway. "I thought you were driving back to Tallahassee to be with your family."

"I did. I changed my mind and sent them up to Macon to stay with my folks. They'll be safe there no matter what this storm does. I think I'm needed here." Bryce smiled. "My wife says I need my head examined."

"A category five is no joke," Will said. "You should listen to your wife."

"What? And let you guys get credit for solving this one?"

Will tried to hold back a smile. "Hank and I were just discussing the case. I doubt there's much more we can do until after Hector runs out of steam. But Brandon Jones had an interesting encounter with Quentin and Reese Raynor yesterday afternoon." Will told Bryce what Brandon had told him about Quentin Raynor's answering for Reese, and his racist remarks. "Brandon thinks the Raynors are hiding something."

"Very astute of him, but he had no business sticking his nose into it."

"He doesn't know we suspect Raynor and Williams of being involved in the hate crimes. He was just trying to find Cade Nash. Frankly, I'm glad he's out looking. None of our people have spotted the kid."

There was a knock at the open door.

"Come in, Al. Did you get your family squared away?"

Al Backus walked in and nodded a hello to Bryce. "Yeah, they're on their way to Columbus, Georgia. We've got friends there." Al held up a plastic evidence bag with a folded sheet of paper. "This oughta make your day. Mick Beasley's *ex*-girlfriend Tonya just dropped this off. Apparently the lovebirds have had a falling out. The paper contains the names and addresses of twenty guys, including Quentin Raynor and Jesse Williams, who supposedly were involved in backroom poker games at The Cove. I checked to be sure, and Beasley's prints are all over this paper. And it's his handwriting."

"Williams and Raynor emphatically denied they knew Beasley," Will said. "And that they played poker."

A grin spread across Al's face. "So why'd they lie?"

Brandon paced in the waiting area at the police department. He glanced at his watch, thinking he should be out looking for Cade instead of wasting time waiting to talk to Will Seevers. He walked over to the receptionist. "Excuse me, has Chief Seevers come back yet?"

"No, sir. I'll let you know as soon as he does."

Brandon resumed pacing and felt his phone vibrate. He took it off his belt clip and hit the talk button. "Hello."

"It's Mom. I've been trying to get through for twenty minutes.

The phone lines must be jammed. Would you talk to Annie for a minute? Owen and Hailey just arrived, and she's been driving us all crazy asking about you."

"Yeah, sure."

"Hi, Uncle Bwandon."

"Hi, Annie. What're you doing?"

"I'm waiting for the hurry-cane, but it's taking too long."

Brandon smiled in spite of himself. "I'll be there tomorrow night. Maybe we can play games or something."

"I like Go Fish and you know what else?"

"What?"

"Piggyback rides!"

"Well, then, I'll just have to save up a few for when I see you."

"Okay. Gwandma wants to talk to you. Bye."

"Thanks, honey," Ellen said. "The kids are stir-crazy from the long drive. Did you talk to Will?"

"No, I'm going nuts. I've been here at the station waiting to talk to him for over an hour. Like I have time to waste? It's all I can do not to go back to the Raynors and grab that jerk by the collar and—"

"Don't you dare!"

"I won't. But I'm really concerned that creep's done something to Cade."

"Didn't Will tell you there was no sign of a struggle? Cade must've left on his own."

Brandon sighed. "Yeah, but it doesn't make sense. I can't imagine he'd just take off and put his mother through this, especially with a category five hurricane on the way."

"He may not realize it's that big a threat, especially since we've had so many false alarms."

"Well, I guarantee you people here are taking it seriously. It's starting to look like a ghost town."

"Let's just pray that cold front they're talking about gets here in time to push the storm to the east, though I feel guilty wishing it on anyone else."

"Mr. Jones?"

Brandon glanced up at the receptionist. "Mom, hang on a second." He put his hand over the receiver. "Yes?"

"The chief is back and will see you now."

Brandon nodded. "Mom, Chief Seevers is back. I've gotta go."

"Let me know what you find out."

"I will."

Will looked over at Hank and Al, then set his eyes on Bryce. "How honest do you want to be with Brandon?"

"There's no reason to pull him into this," Bryce said. "Even if Beasley *has* split, we're gettin' close."

Will nodded. "Okay, it's your show. But I think he knows just enough to be dangerous."

"Well, here's our chance to find out," Bryce said.

Will got up and opened the door to his office and saw Brandon approaching. "Come in. I'm sorry you had to wait."

Brandon walked into the office, and Will seated him at the table with the others.

"I think you know everybody."

Brandon nodded. "Thanks for seeing me. I spoke with my mother this morning about my frustration with the Raynors. I'll cut to the chase. After she heard me say the name Raynor, she started asking questions and made the connection between Judge Williams and Sheriff Raynor and White Wash."

"So she told you about the articles?" Will said.

"Mom wasn't going to say anything, but I laid a guilt trip on her. I told her I was scared that Cade knew something and Raynor shut him up. She told me about the articles and said I should come talk to you again."

"But I already told you we didn't find any sign of a struggle," Will said. "No indication that Cade didn't leave of his own accord. There were no fingerprints on the window or the casing other than Cade's and his mother's. The Raynors and Williamses claim they were home sleeping, and there's nothing to prove they weren't. No evidence. No witnesses. What more do you think we should do?"

"Go back and lean on Quentin Raynor till he tells you where Cade is! The guy's lying! There's no way you don't suspect him of being involved in the hate crimes. Who knows what he's capable of?"

Bryce held up his palm. "Okay, Brandon. Calm down and listen to me. We just got back from the Raynors' and the Williamses'. Their houses are boarded up. They've already evacuated. So there's no way to talk to them right now."

Brandon threw his hands up. "Why didn't you do something sooner? Cade could die in this storm if he's not in a shelter!"

"We know that. But like Chief Seevers said, he left on his own. He could be anywhere."

"We have another problem," Will said. "We just got word that the hurricane has picked up speed, and they're now predicting landfall by 7:00 a.m. Sunday. We're under a mandatory evacuation, and I need to utilize all available law enforcement personnel to help get people out of here. We have thousands of lives to protect. We can't zero in on one boy. The smartest thing you can do right now is get in your car and head up to Tallahassee."

Brandon walked into Gordy's Crab Shack at 8:00 p.m. on Friday night, famished and exhausted and glad no customers were waiting to be served. The place appeared to be only about a third full.

Weezie was talking with a young couple and acknowledged Brandon with her eyes. A few seconds later, she patted the woman on the shoulder and said something, then walked over to Brandon and hugged him.

"What're you doin' here?" she said. "I assumed you went to Tallahassee with your folks."

"They drove up early. I'm supposed to meet them there tomorrow night."

"I hope you're leavin' early in the morning," Weezie said. "The traffic's really backed up, and it's liable to take you all day to get up there."

"Yeah, I know. You're not staying here, are you?"

"No, we decided to stay open tonight for the people who're still here. Gordy, Pam, and I are headin' up to Georgia in the mornin'. Poor Pam is havin' a heck of a time. She's so afraid there won't be anything left when she comes back."

Brandon lifted his eyebrows. "She might be right."

"Well, I just can't allow myself to think that way. So where would you like to sit? Any place but the deck. We've got the back door and windows all boarded up."

"A booth's fine. I'm starved. I've haven't eaten all day."

"Well, that's no good." Weezie seated him in booth two and handed him a menu. "What made you decide not to drive up with your folks?"

"You mean besides the fact that my parents, grandfather, brother, sister-in-law, niece, nephew, and their cat and dog are all going to be cooped up in a one-bedroom apartment?"

Weezie laughed. "Oh, boy."

"I'll be a basket case, especially if we lose power. I'm not in a big hurry to get up there. But there's something else going on. Remember the biracial boy in my group at camp—the one I told you about? He's missing. I've been trying to find him since yesterday afternoon."

"Missing? Do the police think he was kidnapped?"

"No, it's more complicated than that." Brandon glanced up at the entrance and saw two more customers coming in. He lowered his voice. "I shouldn't talk about it here. You need to get to work."

"Not really. We've got plenty of help tonight." Weezie slid in on the other side of the booth. "I can see this has really got you down."

Brandon nodded. "The boy's name is Cade Nash. Want to hear something really weird? He's the one who hit you in the head with the rock and kicked me in the ribs."

Weezie leaned forward on her arms. "How do you know?"

"The kid runs like a deer. Between that and his body build, I began to suspect him early on. He finally admitted it."

Brandon told her about the conversations he'd had with Cade at the camp and everything that had happened from the time Cade disappeared until Brandon went back a second time to talk to Will Seevers. He also told her about the newspaper articles and what his mother had discovered.

"I probably shouldn't even be telling you this," Brandon said, barely above a whisper, "but I don't know what to do. The police didn't find any sign of foul play. The Raynors and Williamses have already evacuated. Cade's poor mother won't go to the shelter without him. And I need to get on the road soon."

Weezie sat with her hands folded, seemingly trying to process the barrage of information he had just dumped on her. Finally she looked up at him and said, "Well, the Lord sure knows where Cade is. We need to ask Him to show you."

"How in the world did I get in the middle of this?"

Weezie's dark, penetrating eyes held his gaze. "It was a divine appointment if I ever saw one. Surely you realize it's not by chance you got to know this boy."

"What's a divine appointment?"

"Somethin' that was meant to be—set up by God Himself."

"I doubt that. Of all the people in the world, why would God pick me to help Cade?"

"Why not you?"

"Because that kid needs someone a whole lot more qualified than me to help him."

"But God brought him to *you*. Just look how he opened up. He obviously trusts you. For a kid like him, that's huge."

Brandon's heart sank. "What if I can't find him? If I don't leave in the morning, the traffic may be so thick I'll get stuck on the highway."

"I know one thing: If God wants you to find Cade, you will. Don't go guiltin' yourself. Do what you can and let God do the rest. It's up to Him."

Brandon opened the menu but didn't read a word of it. He closed it again and looked up at Weezie. "I want you to know how much being able to talk to you has meant to me."

"I'm glad. I've enjoyed it, too."

"I've thought a lot about the things we talked about. And I've been reading my Bible a lot. Have you ever read Psalm 139?"

Weezie's half-moon smile appeared and disappeared. "A time or two."

"It kinda sums up everything you and my mom have been trying to tell me about God having a plan for my life. All this time I thought life was about me, but it's really about Him, isn't it?"

"All the way."

"Well, I just wanted to thank you. If this hurricane leaves Seaport in shambles, it may be a long time before I see you again. I'm glad our paths crossed. I guess that wasn't by chance either."

Weezie reached over and touched his hand. "Before you order your dinner, let's go back to Gordy's office and pray for Cade."

37

Brandon was aware of a loud buzzing sound and realized it was the alarm clock. He groped for the button and turned it off, then threw back the covers and sat on the side of the bed, his hands rubbing his eyes. He reached for his cell phone and dialed Angel Phelps's number.

"Hello."

"Angel, it's Brandon. Sorry to call so early, but I thought of something last night before I finally crashed and didn't want to waste any time."

"You didn't wake me up. I'm just sittin' here worryin' about Cade."

Brandon heard her sniffling.

"I'd like to come over there and look through Cade's room myself, if that's okay. Maybe you missed something."

"I thought you were leaving for Tallahassee?"

"I could probably wait till noon. That would give me another six hours to keep looking for Cade."

"All right, come on over. Would you like breakfast?"

"No, thanks. Last night's dinner feels like a lead weight in my stomach. I'll see you in about a half hour."

Brandon got up and quickly showered and shaved, then put on a clean T-shirt and pair of shorts. He went downstairs and out to the garage and grabbed his father's old backpack down off the shelf. He went back in the house and filled the backpack with the bottled water, cereal bars, trail mix, an apple, a pear, and carrot sticks his mother had left for him. He also packed a flashlight and extra batteries, a pouch with a rain slicker, his Bible, packets of Advil, and the directions to his father's apartment.

He paused for a moment, then sat at the breakfast bar and closed his eyes. *God, I feel so helpless. If it's not Your will for me to find Cade, at least keep him safe.* Brandon's mind replayed the images he'd seen of Biloxi and Gulfport after Hurricane Katrina. *Be with my family and with Weezie, Gordy, and Pam. Help me convince Angel to go to a shelter and to know when it's time for me to leave.*

Brandon picked up his backpack and went out on the front porch. He locked the beveled glass door, then nailed a sheet of plywood over it and went out to his car.

The sky was streaked with pink and gold, and he wondered what it would look like tomorrow morning when the ominous threat became a reality.

Ellen Jones lay on the couch in the living room of Guy's apartment, watching the weather channel, the sound on mute. Guy and his father were asleep in the bedroom. Owen, Hailey, and the kids were sacked out in sleeping bags on the dining room floor. Snickers the dachshund was curled up next to her, and Stripey the cat was busy batting around a Q-tip that must have fallen out of someone's bag.

Ellen saw that a hurricane update was coming on. She turned up the sound.

"At 7:00 a.m. eastern daylight time, the National Hurricane Center downgraded Hurricane Hector to a category four, but the storm is still packing sustained winds of 145 miles per hour with wind gusts to 170 miles per hour. Hector continues to pick up speed and is moving in a north/northeasterly direction at thirteen miles per hour and is expected to make landfall in Seaport around 4:00 a.m. Sunday, bringing with it a storm surge of eighteen to twenty feet.

"The increased speed of this hurricane makes it unlikely that the cold front sweeping down from the northwest will arrive in time to push this powerful storm eastward, which is bad news for the panhandle and good news for residents on the upper west coast of Florida."

"I guess we're finally going to get it."

Ellen was suddenly aware of Owen standing next to the couch. "I'm afraid so," she said. "The projected path shows the eye wall passing directly over Seaport. And we're going to feel it here in Tallahassee, too—100-mile-per-hour wind gusts, power outages, and tornadoes."

Annie Jones got out of her sleeping bag, a well-worn teddy bear under her arm, her pink nightgown almost dragging the ground. She stumbled over to the couch and crawled up in Ellen's lap. "Is the hurry-cane here yet?"

"No, sweetie, it won't be here until tomorrow."

Annie wrinkled her nose. "Why do they call it a hurry-cane when it's so slow?"

"We'll just have to find something fun to do while we wait. Why don't we take Daniel to the park with the giant red slide?"

Annie nodded, seemingly content at the moment just to cuddle.

Ellen looked over at Owen. "Why don't you call your brother and see if he's on his way."

Brandon Jones strolled around Cade Nash's room, surprised that it was as neat as it was. "My room looked like a trash heap when I was twelve. Drove my mother crazy."

"Cade's always been neat," Angel said. "But he shoves his dirty dishes under the bed, and we tangle over that sometimes." She sat in the chair at Cade's desk and let out a loud sigh. "There's nothin' here that gives a clue where he is. I've already looked."

Brandon opened the closet and looked up on the shelf at a pair of leather sandals and a pair of reef runners, but didn't see the black high-tops Cade had worn to camp.

"What's in the plastic containers?" Brandon pointed to four Tupperware containers stacked one on top of the other.

"Shells. He saves them."

"Mind if I look?"

"Go ahead."

Brandon picked up the plastic containers and set them on the bed and took off the lids. "Wow, quite a collection."

Angel stared at the shells, her face forlorn. "There's nothin' here that's gonna tell us where he is."

Brandon looked up at the closet and then at Angel. "Maybe it's not what's here, but what's not here that will tell us something. We know he's wearing his black high-tops, his Camp Piney Woods shirt, and his cargo shorts because you said they're missing."

"Right."

"Is there anything else missing?"

Brandon's phone vibrated, and he took the phone off his belt clip. "Hello."

"Brandon, it's Owen. Mom wants to know if you've left yet."

"I've left the house, but I haven't left town yet. I'm at Cade's mother's house. We're still trying to find him."

"Are you aware the hurricane's supposed to make landfall at 4:00 a.m.?"

"No, why'd they change it?"

"It's picked up speed. It's a strong category four storm now, but they're talking about a storm surge of twenty feet. You and everybody else in Seaport need to get out. Last I heard they were evacuating everyone up to ten miles inland. The flooding's going to be the worst of it."

Brandon glanced over at Angel. "I need to get Cade's mother to a shelter."

"Well, step on it. The freeway's jammed packed. If you leave now, it's going to take you at least fifteen hours."

"Okay, Owen. I'll talk to you when I'm on the road. Tell Mom not to worry."

"All right. Don't do anything stupid."

"I won't."

Brandon put the phone back on his belt clip and noticed Angel was rooting through a small treasure chest on the desk. "What're you looking for?"

"The red feather you gave Cade. It's not here. I saw him put it in this treasure chest when he got home."

"Maybe he moved it."

Angel rummaged through all the drawers. "It's not here." She turned to Brandon, a spark of hope in her eyes. "What if he went back to the camp? Maybe he's hiding there."

"The camp's completely boarded up. There's no place for him to hide. And it's a long way to ride a bicycle. " Brandon glanced at his watch, his mind racing, Angel staring at him with those pleading eyes. "All right, what have we got to lose? It's not even eight o'clock yet. We've got time."

Gordy Jameson nailed a piece of plywood over the front door of Gordy's Crab Shack, then put the hammer back in the toolbox. "Between me and my dad, I wonder how many times we've done that in the almost sixty years this place has been here?"

"Weezie and I finished packing the car," Pam Jameson said.

"I guess we oughta hit the road then. Sure don't like thinkin' about that storm surge. Will said even the cops are movin' inland. Sounds like it's gonna be pretty bad."

"I just hate to leave."

Gordy put his arm around Pam and looked up at the crab shack. "I wouldn't take a million bucks for the memories I've got of this place. Whether it's still here when we get back or whether we have to start from scratch, it's what's inside our hearts that'll bring this place back."

"I like the sound of that." Weezie Taylor came over and stood next to them. "I wanna leave with positive thoughts."

Pam reached over and took Weezie's hand. "So do I, but you two have been here a lot longer than I have. I just don't know if I have enough of it yet to let it go. I was just starting to feel as though I had contributed something."

"You mostly certainly did." Weezie was quiet for half a minute and then belted out a laugh. "Whooeee! I can see it now. Pam's Blue Ribbon Pies *delivers* to reconstruction sites. There's gonna be thousands of workers down here puttin' the city back together. They're gonna be missin' all that home cookin', and your fruit pies are just the ticket."

"They are?"

"Leave everything to me—Weezie the wise and wonderful. I'll do all the marketing. And I *will* deliver. All you need to do is keep crankin' out the pies."

Gordy chuckled. "Where you gonna get power to keep the ovens goin'?"

"Hmm…I haven't figured that out yet, but I will."

"Well, come on, girls. Let's hit the road. We've got a lot of time to think about it."

Gordy followed Pam and Weezie toward the car, Weezie chattering incessantly, the way she always did anytime she felt overwhelmed.

He stopped and looked back over his shoulder, a wad of emotion forming in his throat. He memorized the scene: the bright blue sky, the blue-green waters, the gray shingled building that held so many precious memories of his parents, his childhood, his marriage to Jenny—and now Pam.

Stand strong. I'll see you soon. He blinked several times to clear his eyes, knowing full well that all the wishful thinking in the world wouldn't enable the crab shack to withstand what was coming.

Brandon jogged back to the locked gates at the entrance of Piney Woods Camp and squeezed through the slats in the fence and then helped Angel do the same. Tears were running down her cheeks.

He put his hands on her shoulders and looked her in the eye. "I have to get you back. There are only so many buses taking people inland to shelters, and with the storm surge they're talking about, no one's safe staying."

"I was so sure Cade was here."

"I'm really sorry, but we have to go. You have to think of your own safety now."

He walked over and opened the passenger side door, and Angel climbed in and sat listless as a rag doll.

Brandon went around and got in the car, his heart racing, wondering what he was going to do if she refused to get on the bus. He glanced at his watch: 9:40.

He pulled onto the highway, amazed at the bright sunny morning, and turned on the radio as if he expected the news to have suddenly changed. It hadn't. Seaport was going to take a direct hit, and there was nothing anybody could do about it.

Neither he nor Angel said anything on the drive back to town.

Brandon pulled into the mobile home park and noticed a couple and their three children loading suitcases into the trunk of their car. He pulled up in front of Angel's house and sat for a moment, then turned to her and said, "I'll help you get your things."

He got out and followed her inside. Angel disappeared into her bedroom, then came out, shouldering a green vinyl bag. She brushed past him and went outside, the note she had written earlier falling to the floor.

Brandon picked it up and read it.

Cade,

It's 7:55 Saturday morning. Brandon and I went to Camp Piney Woods looking for you. If you come back while we're gone, STAY HERE until we get back. There's a category five hurricane approaching, and the whole town is going to flood. This is the real thing. We have to evacuate!

I love you,
Mom

Brandon tossed the note in the trash can and wrote another one.

10:25 a.m. Saturday

Cade,

I'm taking your mother to the high school, where she's going to catch a bus to a shelter. She's worried sick about you. You have to evacuate. You're in danger. Go to the high school and ask someone to help you. The hurricane is going to hit by 4:00 a.m. Sunday, and it's going to be catastrophic. You won't survive unless you get out.

Brandon

He laid the note on the table by the front door, the gravity of the words paralyzing him for a moment. He went out to his SUV, where Angel sat in the passenger seat, shoulders limp, eyes vacant. He didn't try to ease her pain. How could he? What words even existed that could comfort a mother who was forced to flee to safety, leaving her child to die?

Brandon started the car and drove out of the Harbor Street Mobile Home Village, thinking that by this time tomorrow, it would no longer exist.

38

Brandon Jones stood leaning on the open door of his car and watched as Angel Phelps boarded a yellow school bus bound for the civic center in Palm City. He couldn't remember ever seeing a more desolate look on anyone's face. The poor thing was too dazed even to argue about leaving, and some kind older couple had promised Brandon they would look after her.

As the bus drove off, an unexpected wave of emotion flooded over him. He got in his car and sat for several minutes, feeling as though he were going to lose it. He fought the emotion till it passed, then started his car and drove toward the evacuation route. If Owen's assessment of the traffic were correct, he probably wouldn't make it to Tallahassee until well after midnight—if he didn't run out of gas first.

Brandon pulled in to the first gas station he saw and started filling his tank, still bothered by the missing red feather. The last time he had seen Cade, the kid was sitting in the front seat of his mother's car, twirling the feather with his thumb and forefinger.

"Why such a sad face?" Brandon had said. *"Your mom said we could get together after the hurricane blows through."*

"What if I'm stuck in a shelter and you can't find me?"

"Then I'll hunt you down. There's no way I'm going to lose track of you. I promise."

Was it possible that Cade would pull a stunt like this just to see if Brandon really would go to the trouble to find him? But if he wanted to be found, why didn't he follow Rule Number One? Brandon's pulse began to race, and then race faster and faster, thinking maybe that's exactly what Cade had done!

He put the nozzle back in the holder, tore off his receipt, and climbed in the Xterra. He pulled onto Seminole Boulevard and made a U-turn, his tires squealing, and drove in the opposite direction toward the Jackson Caves.

Ellen Jones turned off her cell phone and dropped it in her purse.

"What's the matter, honey?" Guy Jones came over to the park bench and sat next to her.

"I can't get through to Brandon's cell phone. All I get is a busy signal."

"I'm sure he's on the highway and headed this way."

"I'd feel better if knew that for sure."

"Try not to worry. Brandon's smart enough to stay safe. Remember this is the same son who taught wilderness survival and white-water rafting and mountain climbing—and probably leaps tall buildings with a single bound."

"Well, not even Superman is a match for Hector."

"Gwandpa, Daniel wants you to push him!" Annie said. "Look how high I can swing all by myself. Did you see my toes almost touch those bwanches?"

Guy smiled. "The princess calls. It's nice to have a diversion."

Brandon entered the Old Seaport city limits and didn't see any cars on the road. Or people. Everything had been boarded up. He did see the frozen custard stand that Cade had said was shaped like an ice cream cone. He drove six streets beyond it and turned right down a road that started out as asphalt and soon turned to gravel.

Brandon realized this area wasn't far from the gulf and was a dangerous place to be during a storm surge like the one that was predicted. He continued driving until the brushy fields became wooded, and he spotted a massive live oak with a rusty Old Seaport Dairy sign nailed to the trunk—just as Cade had described.

He pulled over to the side of the road and reached in the glove box and took out a roll of duct tape and a hunting knife, then got out of the car. He put on his backpack and trudged through the high weeds toward the tree with the rusty sign, the beeping of his watch reminding him that it was already one o'clock and too late to consider driving to Tallahassee.

When Brandon reached the tree, he discovered a red feather secured to it with clear fishing line that had been wrapped around the trunk several times. He cupped his hands around his mouth and yelled, "Cade, it's Brandon! Where are you? Cade…?"

His mind reeled with the implications, and he was at the same time relieved, angry, and apprehensive to discover that his hunch had been right.

He stepped around to the other side of the tree and looked deep into the woods. Cade had talked about how to reach the Jackson Caves but had never pinpointed the location of his favorite cave—or even how many caves there were. The search for the boy suddenly seemed daunting. Brandon had been warned that low-lying escape routes might be cut off by rising water three to five hours before the hurricane hit. Even if he found Cade, would there be enough time to evacuate?

He rested his foot on a log and pondered his circumstances. If he committed to being back at his car with or without Cade no later than 9:00 p.m., he should still be able to make it out of Seaport and up to Palm City before the water made it impossible. Was it worth the risk? He decided it had to be.

God, I'm really scared. But if I leave Cade out here, he'll never survive. You're the only compass I've got. Please help me find him.

Brandon entered the woods, which seemed strangely void of bird life, well aware that he had just broken Rule Number One.

Ellen Jones picked up seven KFC dinner boxes filled with chicken bones and greasy napkins and dumped them in a trash bag. "Owen, would you put this in the dumpster next to the clubhouse?"

"Sure." Owen Jones took the bag from Ellen and put his arm around her shoulder. "Mom, Brandon's fine. It's just going to take a long time to drive up here."

"Why do I have such an uneasy feeling about him?"

Owen kissed her cheek. "Because you're his mother."

Ellen was aware of Owen going out the front door and Guy wrestling with the grandkids in the living room. She turned on her cell phone and hit the autodial for Brandon's cell and got only static.

She glanced up at the kitchen clock and went in and turned on the TV to the weather channel. "Could I get you three to put all that energy on hold for just a minute? There's supposed to be an update at seven."

Annie let out a piercing shriek. "Gwandpa's tickling us!"

Daniel squealed with delight and crawled up the easy chair and started jumping up and down, Snickers running in circles and yapping.

Ellen looked over at Guy, one eyebrow raised. "Maybe the *instigator* needs a time out?"

Guy smiled and came over and sat next to her. "Sorry. I guess we could go outside and run off some steam. Turn up the volume."

"At 6:45 p.m. eastern daylight time, the National Hurricane Center reported that Hurricane Hector is following the same north/northeasterly path and is now moving at a brisk 20 miles per hour. It continues to be a strong category four storm, packing sustained winds of 150 miles per hour and gusts up to 187 miles per hour. We expect the storm to weaken slightly as it gets closer to the Florida panhandle, but by all indications, Hector will be a category four when it makes landfall in Seaport around 3:00 a.m. Sunday and will bring with it a storm surge of eighteen to twenty feet.

"The only good news is that Hector is a fast-moving storm, so the affected areas will not be pounded for a long period of time with those powerful winds. However, the storm surge continues to pose the worst threat, and the Florida governor has issued a mandatory evacuation order for residents living in coastal areas of the panhandle.

"Areas within one hundred miles of the center of the storm can expect five to eight inches of rain and hurricane force winds. And tropical storm force winds will be felt up to two hundred miles from Hector's center.

"It's unlikely that the cold front sweeping down from the northwest will arrive in time to push the storm eastward, but residents along the upper west coast of Florida remain under a hurricane watch…"

Ellen sighed and put the TV on mute. "Darn! Tallahassee's going to get the outer bands. I guess we need to go over to the clubhouse and get away from these windows."

Guy put his arm around her. "On a positive note, the storm is moving really fast and should pass quickly."

"What if Brandon gets stranded on the highway? What if he can't get out of the worst of it?"

"There are shelters in every town along the evacuation route. If the traffic stalls, the authorities aren't going to leave those people out there unprotected. But as long as he's out of Seaport, he's out of the worst of it."

Brandon squatted at the entrance to another shallow cave, this one cluttered with crushed beer cans and cigarette butts. He dropped his backpack on the ground and sat next to it. He took out a bottle of water and a cereal bar, then glanced at his watch: 8:05. Now that the sun had moved to the west, only diffused light came through the cracks in the leafy canopy, and it was getting harder to see. He had twenty-five minutes to find Cade before he had to head back to his car.

He was tempted to doubt everything he had recently come to believe. How could a loving God's plan for his life include this impotent search for Cade and putting Angel on a bus headed for a bleak future? Maybe it was too good to be true that God knew every step Brandon would ever take and had actually planned it out ahead of time. Maybe Gary the homeless guy was right after all.

He stuffed the last of the cereal bar into his mouth and chugged down the water, then took the flashlight out of his backpack. He got on his feet and pulled on the backpack and continued walking.

"Cade, it's Brandon!" he called. "Are you out there…? Cade…?"

He trudged about fifty yards up a gradual slope and discovered another empty cave. How many was that—seven, eight? He was suddenly aware that the trees were swaying. Fear seized him. There was no way he was going to find Cade in time. The smartest thing he could do now was go back to his car and get to shelter while he still had time. He pushed the button on his watch and the face lit up blue: 8:35.

God, I've given it everything I've got. It's not enough. If You don't help me, it's all over for Cade.

From somewhere deep inside him, Brandon felt persuaded to keep going. *I can push it thirty more minutes,* he thought.

The wind split open the canopy, and he noticed that the evening sky was a peculiar shade of white. How he wished he could snatch what was left of the daylight and focus it on the densely wooded area. How many caves could there be?

Brandon cupped his hands around his mouth and shouted, "Cade, it's Brandon! I need to find you *now*, or I'm going to have to turn back and leave without you!"

The only reply was the wind whipping the trees.

Ellen sat curled up on the couch in Guy's apartment, hugging a throw pillow and only vaguely aware of Hailey reading Annie and Daniel a bedtime story.

Guy Jones sat on the couch next to Ellen and took her hand. "How're you doing?"

"I'm so worried about Brandon that I keep praying the same prayer over and over: 'Lord, keep him safe.'"

"I know. Me too."

"Surely he's on the way up here."

"Of course he is. The kid's smart. And he's got a healthy respect for nature. He's not going to take any chances."

Owen came in the living room, carrying a giant bowl of popcorn. "Anybody hungry?"

"How can you even think of eating when your brother is out there somewhere?" Ellen said.

"My going hungry isn't going to get him here any faster, Mom. Stop worrying. Brandon could probably wrestle an alligator with one arm tied behind his back. He's a resourceful guy. Even if he runs out of gas, he'll figure out what to do."

"If that was meant to be comforting, it wasn't." Ellen felt someone touch her arm and turned her head. Two round blue eyes framed in blond curls looked up at her.

"Gwandma." Annie Jones wagged her tiny index finger. "You

hafta twust Jesus to take care of Uncle Bwandon."

"I know, sweetie. You're right. But since I'm Brandon's mommy, I would just feel better if he was safe here with us."

"Are you afwaid the hurry-cane is going to blow him away?"

"I just want the whole family together right now. Would you like to pray for Uncle Brandon?"

Annie gave a firm nod and reached for Ellen's hand and then Guy's and bowed her head. "Jesus, You can see weally, weally far. Help Uncle Bwandon get here before the hurry-cane. And help Gwandma not be scared. Amen."

Ellen smiled. "That was a nice prayer, Annie. Thank you."

"Okay, princess," Owen said. "You need to crawl into your sleeping bag."

"Me and Daniel are camping in there." Annie pointed to the dining room. "If you get afwaid, Gwandma, wake me up and I will pway with you."

Ellen pulled Annie close and kissed her soft cheek. "I feel much better already. I love you. Sweet dreams."

Annie went into the dining room and crawled into the sleeping bag next to Daniel's.

Ellen held tightly to Guy's hand, wishing she had Annie's child-like faith. "What time do you think we should go over to the club-house?"

Guy glanced at the muted TV screen. "Let's just keep an eye on the weather. I doubt we'll get much wind and rain before dawn. When it looks like the outer bands are getting close, we can carry the kids over there. In the meantime, they might as well sleep here where it's quiet."

Brandon held his flashlight so it illuminated the ground in front of him. The forest floor was uneven and rocky, and it seemed as though he'd been walking slightly uphill for some time. Without the sun, it was hard to maintain a sense of direction. He pushed the button on his watch: 10:07. He should have been on the road over an hour ago.

Lord, if You really are directing my steps, this would be a good time to point me in the right direction because I really don't want to die out here for nothing.

Brandon sat on a tree stump and held the flashlight so he could see the treetops being thrashed by the wind. He moved the beam of light back and forth across the canopy.

"Cade!" he shouted. "It's Brandon! Can you see my flashlight on the trees? If you can, say something or make a noise…"

Was that a voice—or just the wind?

"Cade, whatever you did, do it again."

All he heard was the wind bashing the trees.

Brandon suddenly felt foolish and angry and panicked. "For crying out loud, Cade, we're both going to die out here unless I get you to shelter right now! Can you hear me? Stop playing games!"

There! He was sure he heard a muffled voice.

"Cade, where are you?" Brandon held the flashlight in front of him and slowly turned 360 degrees and saw no sign of Cade. He turned the flashlight up to the canopy and waved it back and forth. "Cade, do you see the light?"

There was the muffled voice again!

"I hear you, buddy! I hear you! I'm going to move the flashlight around. When the light gets close to where you are, holler out. Don't make a sound until it's close."

Brandon's pulse raced so fast his hand was shaking. He pointed the beam of light up on the trees and imagined it at twelve o'clock and listened for Cade's voice. Nothing.

He moved it to one o'clock. Nothing. Then two. And three. He kept moving the light and listening intently. Had he imagined the voice? Was he so desperate he was hearing things? He continued to move the light with no response—until he came to nine o'clock.

That was a muffled cry. He was sure of it.

"Cade? I hear you, buddy! I hear you! I'm heading your way! Give me some kind of a sign where you are… Holler or throw something."

Brandon slowly lowered the flashlight, his eyes peeled for any sign of the boy. "Talk to me, Cade." He heard someone calling, but couldn't tell where the voice was coming from.

Brandon moved quickly toward the imaginary nine o'clock position. "Cade, am I getting close? Can you see the flashlight?"

There was the muffled voice again!

Brandon picked up his pace, his pulse racing and his hope renewed. "Cade, am I getting close? Say something, buddy. Stay with me."

"I'm over here."

"Where?"

"On the ground. I see the flashlight comin' toward me."

39

Brandon Jones kept moving toward the voice and spotted a red Camp Piney Woods T-shirt—and the boy wearing it lying on his back on the ground.

Brandon hurried over to Cade and knelt beside him. "Are you hurt?"

"I think I busted my left arm and leg," Cade Nash said, his face tear-streaked, his voice shaking. "I climbed that big tree behind me and lost my footing. I fell on my side. It hurts like crazy when I move."

Brandon gently examined Cade's arm and leg, relieved to see no bones had pierced the skin. "At least they're not compound fractures. When did it happen?"

"I don't know. Seems like a long time."

"I've been out here searching for you since one o'clock. Didn't you hear me calling?"

"I—I couldn't tell it was you till you got close. I thought Reese's dad had followed me." Cade's eyes suddenly welled with tears. "H—he swore they'd kill me if I told anyone what they did! Said they'd skin me alive and then lynch me—that I was nothin' but a useless half-breed nigger and he'd be doin' the world a favor. I was scared! I didn't know where to go, so I came here." In the next instant Cade clutched Brandon's arm and started sobbing. "I was hopin' you'd find me! I was afraid you wouldn't."

"Why didn't you tell your mom what happened and let her call the police?"

"Reese's dad said they'd kill her if I told her! That they'd do awful things to her first!"

Brandon took the handkerchief out of his pocket and wiped the tears off Cade's face. "Shhh. Don't try to talk about this right now. Your mom's safe, and you're safe with me. I need you to tell me how you're feeling. Are you cold? Hot? Feeling shaky? Sick to your stomach?"

"No, I'm hungry."

"Well, that's a good sign." Brandon picked up Cade's wrist and took his pulse. "Heart rate's normal. Skin doesn't feel clammy. Pupils aren't dilated. It's a pretty safe bet you're not in shock."

"What's that?"

"Oh, just a bad reaction to trauma. But I think you should hold off eating or drinking anything for a while till I'm sure. We need to figure out how to move you. It's too late to try to get you out of here before the water starts flooding the low-lying areas. We're going to have to find shelter and ride out the hurricane. Any idea how far above sea level we are here?"

"Not really, but it's uphill all the way to the caves once you get to the rusty sign."

"Where's the cave you told me about?"

"Behind you."

Brandon turned around and directed the light across a moss-covered rock formation until he spotted Cade's bicycle on the ground and the entrance to the cave. He went over to the opening and guessed it to be about five feet high. He ducked to get inside, then walked hunched over for about twenty feet to the back, pleased to see that the ground was dry.

He went back outside and knelt beside Cade. "It's probably our best option. I've got food and water and one rain slicker we can share. I have a feeling we're going to need it when those hurricane winds start throwing the rain around. Right now, I need to figure out a way to make a splint for your arm and leg and get you inside."

"Guy," Ellen Jones whispered, her hand gently shaking him. "The hurricane has slowed, and now they're saying there's a chance the cold front may push it eastward."

Guy Jones opened his eyes wide and blinked several times, then captured a yawn with his hand. "Now that's a twist I didn't expect. What time is it?"

"One o'clock. Hector's only moving five miles per hour now and is expected to make landfall much later than originally projected. That gives Brandon a lot more time to get up here."

"I'm sure he's listening to the weather reports." Guy raked his hands through his hair. "Sounds like Seaport might not take a direct hit after all. And maybe we won't get anything worse than strong winds here."

Ellen nodded. "Praise God! But those poor people on the west coast…they're going to get pounded

Guy looked at the TV. "Turn up the sound, honey."

"…communities you see in the cone are currently in the projected path, but Hector's unanticipated slowdown increases the chances that it will collide with the cold front and get pushed off to the east, posing the greatest risk to the upper west coast of Florida. The National Hurricane Center has suggested a mandatory evacuation of low-lying areas from Bradenton north to Cedar Keys and urges residents in that part of the state to prepare for the worst. We will have an update for you at the bottom of the hour."

"Well, that's the first sign of hope we've had," Guy said. "I've had visions of Seaport getting wiped off the map."

"I hate the waiting." Ellen linked her arm in his. "I have trouble imagining that beautiful old house of ours destroyed, especially since it's managed to stand up to hurricanes for over half a century."

"Well, we're not out of the woods yet. If Hector picks up speed again, this collision with the cold front may never happen. We could still get slammed."

Brandon placed his hands underneath Cade's arms and dragged him ever so gently to the far end of the cave and sat him against the wall. "How're those splints working out?"

Cade fought back the tears. "Okay. It hurts a lot, but I couldn't stand to move at all till you put them on me."

Brandon set the flashlight on the ground so the light shone up on the roof of the cave.

"Pretty cool splints," Cade said. "Looks like whittled tree branches and duct tape. Where'd you get the tape?"

"I never go hiking without it. The splints aren't ideal, but they should do the trick as long as you don't try to move too much. Let me give you a couple Advil."

"It really hurts," Cade said, his eyes brimming with tears.

Brandon reached in his backpack and took out two Advil and gave them to Cade with a bottle of water. "You should probably drink the whole thing, but just a little at a time. Did you bring any provisions with you?"

"Just a couple Cokes and some Pop-Tarts, but they were gone yesterday."

"Here, eat this cereal bar. I've got some fruit, too, if that doesn't fill you up."

"Thanks."

Brandon sat next to Cade and glanced at his watch. The wind was blowing, but it didn't seem as though it had increased in hours, which seemed odd if there was a hurricane approaching.

He noticed Cade had already devoured the cereal bar. "Here, eat the apple. I haven't listened to the news since noon, but last I heard this thing was supposed to hit by 4:00 a.m. That's less than two hours from now. I'm surprised we're not feeling it more."

"The stupid hurricanes never do what they say."

"Well, I'm not taking any chances. I'll go move your bike someplace where the wind won't pick it up and sling it right into our faces."

Brandon went outside the cave and stood Cade's bike upright and rolled it several yards away and wedged it between two trees. Then he went back inside the cave and sat next to Cade, his mind reeling with questions.

"Feel better now that you've got something in your belly?"

"Yeah, thanks."

"You feel up to telling me everything you know about Quentin Raynor and anyone else who threatened you?"

Cade was silent for a moment. Then he picked up some small rocks and tossed them against the wall of the cave. "The man who came with Mr. Raynor and Reese was Mick something. I remembered seeing him on Reese's screened-in porch the night I heard them talkin' about burnin' down that church."

"Who're *they*?"

Cade shrugged. "There were lots of men, but I only recognized Mr. Raynor and Mr. Williams, Dakota's dad. I knew the one guy's name was Mick because someone called him that."

"I'm not following you. Why were you at the Raynors'?"

"The night after I got my bike back I went over there to spray-paint Reese's house to get even for him painting the Ws on ours. I saw him do it, but I didn't tell the cops. Anyway, it was real late when I got there, but a bunch of cars were parked out front, so I snuck up next to the house. I went around to the side and peeked around the corner of the bushes. That's when I saw the men sittin' on the screened-in porch, laughin' about how stupid the cops were. Mr. Raynor said it was time to send a stronger message by burnin' down a *nigger* church."

"Did he say who was going to set the fire?"

"He and that Mick guy. They started jokin' about runnin' your lady friend off the road when someone tapped me on the shoulder and nearly scared the pants off me. It was Reese. Before he could say anything, I shoved him and ran like crazy back to my house."

"And you didn't tell your mom or the police?"

Cade shook his head. "I was scared. But if I'd known anybody was gonna get killed, I would've. I swear."

"Did Reese realize how much you heard?"

"I don't know, but the next day he came to the trailer park and found me ridin' my bike and asked what I'd been doin' at his house. I played dumb. I told him I'd gone there to spray-paint it like he did mine but changed my mind because his parents had company and I didn't want to get caught."

"Didn't he even ask you if you'd heard anything?"

"No. He called me a stinkin' skunk and told me to stay on my own side of the tracks, and then he left."

"That was Monday afternoon, and you left for camp on Saturday, right?"

Cade nodded. "Then the night I got home from camp, I woke up and heard someone knockin' on my window. It was Reese. I opened it, and the next thing I knew, Mr. Raynor grabbed me by the arms and squeezed really hard. He told me that Reese said he found me snoopin' around their house. And whatever I thought I heard, I didn't. And that if I ever told anybody, they'd...well, you know."

Brandon noticed the bruises on Cade's arms and the fear in his eyes. "Hey, it's okay. No one's going to hurt you or your mom. As soon as you tell Chief Seevers and Special Agent Moore what you heard, they'll put Raynor and his racist cronies behind bars and throw away the key."

Cade sat silent, tears trickling down his face. Finally he said, "Do you know where my mom is?"

"I put her on a school bus headed for the civic center in Palm City. She's fine, but she's worried sick about you. This hurricane is coming straight for us. It's a dangerous situation."

Brandon heard what sounded like a fast-moving freight train and then felt something shake the ground. He opened his eyes and saw only darkness. For a few seconds he was confused, then remembered he was in the cave with Cade. He groped for the flashlight and felt a spray of water slap him in the face. He looked beyond the entrance and saw daylight. It looked as though a tree had fallen just a few yards beyond the cave, but it was difficult to see. Rain came down in sheets, the fierce wind twirling it like a lasso and flinging it into the cave.

He reached in his backpack for his rain slicker. "Cade, wake up. Looks like Hector finally made it. We need to put this slicker over us so we don't get soaked."

Cade opened his eyes and looked outside. "Wow, I've never been this close to a hurricane before. We always had to evacuate."

Brandon sat next to Cade and held the slicker over both of them, the wind whipping the bottom. He glanced at his watch. "It's after nine. I can't believe we slept that long. I didn't hear a thing until now." Rain came swirling through the cave and slapped him in the face. "This isn't going to work. Hold on."

Brandon got up and turned around and sat facing Cade, his back to the entrance of the cave. "I'll wear the slicker and try to be a wall between you and the blowing rain."

Seconds after Brandon put on the slicker, he felt rain splatter his back, but Cade was mostly untouched by it. "That's better. You hungry?"

Cade shrugged. "I can wait."

"You don't have to. My mother bagged a ton of trail mix for me. Want some?"

"Okay."

Brandon opened a jumbo baggy of trail mix and offered some to Cade, then poured a small mound of the mix into his wet palm and popped it into his own mouth. "This is my first hurricane. Any pointers?"

The corners of Cade's mouth turned up. "Yeah, don't believe anything the weatherpeople tell you."

Brandon remembered that the storm surge was supposed to be eighteen to twenty feet and wished he could see outside. Was it worth getting drenched and battling the wind to take a look? What difference did it make? He and Cade were trapped. If the water rose, where could they possibly go?

Ellen Jones paced in the living room of Guy's apartment, all too aware of the tropical storm outside. "If Brandon had left when he said he was going to, he'd have been here by now."

"Not necessarily," Guy Jones said. "He probably went to a shelter. Seaport's only expected to get category two winds now. That's the best news I've heard since this whole thing started."

"Well, I'd hardly pooh-pooh hundred-mile-per-hour winds, especially if Brandon's caught in it."

"I'm not. But it beats the heck out of 155-plus. Have a little faith in him. He has a healthy respect for nature."

Brandon sat facing Cade—rain, leaves, and twigs pelting the back of his slicker, the overspray wetting Cade's face and hair and dripping off his chin. The two of them had to yell to be heard.

Brandon reached in his backpack and handed Cade a T-shirt to wipe his face. "Sorry I can't stop the rain from getting you wet."

"That's okay. I'm just glad I'm not still out there in the middle of it. I thought I was gonna die."

"If you'd been lying out there when that tree fell, you would have."

Brandon didn't miss the sadness in Cade's expression. "I'm sorry about the threats Reese's dad made and the name he called you. Try not to think too hard about it or let it make you feel bad about yourself. The guy's twisted. You just have to consider the source."

"There're a lot more people like him than you think. I hear put-downs from both sides. Whites don't accept me because I'm part black. And blacks don't accept me because I'm part white. I don't fit anywhere."

"Sure you do."

"Where?"

"At camp, for starters. All the guys liked you."

"They just acted nice because you made them. They'd treat me like dirt if we were at school."

Brandon studied Cade's face. Such a handsome kid. Smart. Athletic. What a shame he didn't see himself that way. "Have you always felt like you don't fit?"

"What do you think? Even my own dad doesn't want me."

"Just because he's absorbed with himself doesn't make you less of a person. It's his problem."

"Well, I don't care if today *is* Father's Day, it doesn't mean anything to me."

Father's Day. Brandon felt ashamed that he was glad to have a legitimate excuse not to have to deal with it.

"What did you get your dad?" Cade said.

"To tell you the truth, with everything I've had going on, I didn't have time to buy him anything." Brandon was thinking it was tedious having to yell to be heard.

"Weren't you even gonna take him a card or somethin'?"

A thunderous, almost explosive sound outside caused Brandon

to duck, then another surge of rain and debris slammed his back. "I think the storm's intensifying. This wind is really something."

Cade tapped him on the arm. "If I had a dad who cared, I'd sure remember him on Father's Day."

40

Brandon Jones had started to nod off when he felt something whack the back of his neck and realized the wind had turned an empty aluminum can into a missile. He pressed his fingers on the spot, relieved not to see blood. How much longer could this thing last?

God, please get us through this. Help me get Cade back to his mom.

Brandon felt his stomach rumble and glanced at his watch: 12:35. He had decided to save the cereal bars and fruit for Cade, and eating a handful of damp, mushy trail mix had little appeal at the moment.

Brandon's neck and back were starting to knot up after hours of sitting cross-legged, his back to the wind and rain, trying to protect Cade from flying debris. He wondered if Gary the homeless guy was hungrier than he was—and if his home under the bridge ever got this wet.

He glanced up at Cade's sleeping face, and it finally sunk in that he really had saved this boy's life—not that turning back without him had been an option once he discovered the feather tied to the tree. How could he have lived with himself if he'd left a twelve-year-old at the mercy of a hurricane?

His last conversation with Weezie came rushing back to him…

"It was a divine appointment, if I ever saw one," Weezie had said. *"Surely you realize it's not by chance you got to know this boy."*

"What's a divine appointment?"

"Somethin' that was meant to be—set up by God Himself."

Brandon pondered the implication and remembered the words of Psalm 139 that had given him a whole new perspective. *When I was woven together in the depths of the earth, your eyes saw my unformed body. All the days ordained for me were written in your book before one of them came to be.*

There was no doubt in Brandon's mind that the Lord had wanted him to find Cade and had been his compass for getting it done. After nine agonizing hours wandering in the woods around the Jackson Caves, he knew he'd failed. It was only an unexplained nudging deep inside that had kept him searching beyond the cutoff time he had set for his own safety. This was a God thing.

It also occurred to him that if he'd never met Weezie, he wouldn't have applied at the camp or met Cade. And if he hadn't met Gary and been stumped by the man's probing question of what life was all about, he wouldn't have been drawn to Weezie and may never have realized that the same question that plagued Gary was the one he himself needed to answer. The whole chain of events seemed like a divine setup.

All of a sudden Brandon sensed God's presence as he never had before, and a shiver crawled up his spine. He closed his eyes, his heart pounding, and just rested in the moment.

Ellen Jones sat looking out the living room window of Guy's apartment, praying for Brandon and grateful that the worst was over. Tallahassee had never lost power, and she had been able to watch the weather channel and follow the progress of the hurricane as the outer bands moved through Seaport and Port Smyth. According to the National Hurricane Center, the winds in Seaport were sustained at 98 miles per hour, gusting to 110.

"Ellen, did you hear me?" Guy Jones said.

"No, sorry. What'd you say?"

"I said the eye wall's passing over Sandal Bay Harbor, just south of Cedar Keys. And Hector's been downgraded to a category three."

Ellen went over and stood next to him, her eyes fixed on the TV screen. "At least Tampa/St. Pete didn't take a direct hit."

"Yeah, looks like they're just getting the outer bands."

"I feel so sorry for the people who're getting the storm surge. It could've just as easily been us."

Guy kissed the top of her head. "Thank the Lord, it wasn't.

Seaport is still getting tropical storm force winds, but they expect the storm to be over soon. The early damage reports are encouraging. As soon as we get the all clear, we can go home if you don't mind being without power for a few days."

"Hey, wake up. The rain's stoppin'."

Brandon opened his eyes and saw Cade's face. It took a few seconds before he was awake enough for the words to sink in. He turned around and looked out the entrance of the cave and saw that the rain and wind had died down considerably and that the floor of the cave was cluttered with tree branches, mud, leaves, rocks, and trash. He glanced at his watch.

"It's five o'clock. Looks like we weathered the worst of it." Brandon raised his hand and gave Cade a high five. "That ought to be worth a badge of some kind."

"Yeah, this was harder than a backpackin' trip, huh?"

"You got that right." Brandon took his thumb and forefinger and peeled his soggy socks away from his skin. "The two of us look like a couple drowned rats. You cold?"

"Yeah, but I'm glad we made it."

"Me too. You should take some more Advil. You still hurting?"

"Not as much. Could we eat somethin'?" Cade said.

"Sure. How about a cereal bar and an orange?"

"What'll you eat?"

Brandon gestured toward the soppy backpack in his lap. "There's plenty of trail mix left. I'm thinking we need to stay put till morning, then try to figure out how to get you out of here. Even if my car survived and I'm able to get it started, it'd be risky moving you from here to the road by myself. I think everyone and his dog evacuated Old Seaport, so I may have to go a long way to get help—assuming the lowlands aren't flooded and I can get through."

There was a long pause, and then Cade said, "I still can't believe you found me."

"I'm not sure *I* did. I think we should give God the credit."

"You didn't say that last night."

"I know, but the more I've thought about it, the more I realize it's the only logical explanation. I was out of ideas, and He was the only compass I had. He obviously wanted you found."

Cade's eyes turned to slits. "You really believe in God?"

"Absolutely. And I've had a lot of time to think about you and me and how we met. I think God set the whole thing up."

"Come on, even if there *is* a God, I'm sure He doesn't waste time thinkin' about a kid like me."

"A great kid like you—and I think you'd be surprised. Did you know that before you were born, He knew every step you would ever take?"

"What do you mean?"

"God knew you when you were still in your mother's womb. And He has a plan for your life."

Cade rolled his eyes. "No way. I was an accident. My parents had to get married."

"That may be true, but you were no accident. God knew you long before your mom was pregnant."

"Says who?"

"Says the Bible." Brandon tilted Cade's chin and looked into his eyes. "You know what else? God's your heavenly Father, and it was *His* will that you were born. You're not inferior to *anyone,* because what gives you value comes from Him."

"What is it?"

"You're made in His image, Cade. You were made to have a relationship with Him."

"I was?"

Brandon nodded. "And your worth as a person has nothing to do with race, social class, who your parents are, when or how you were conceived, or what anyone else thinks of you…it has to do with your being His. You're here because He wants you to be."

There was a long pause, and Cade seemed to processing. Finally he said, "Are you sure? Sounds too good to be true."

"Yeah, but it *is* true. I wouldn't lie to you."

"How do you know all that stuff?"

"I've been doing some soul-searching, and I've learned a lot from my friend Weezie and my mom. But it's all in the Bible. And the Bible is God's own Word. Everything in there is true."

"So where does it say God knew me in my mother's womb?"

Brandon smiled. "I was hoping you'd ask me that since I recently discovered it myself. As soon as I can get my hands dry enough to pull my Bible out of this backpack, I'll show you."

41

Late Monday afternoon, Ellen Jones walked out on the veranda of her home and looked out over the rain-soaked backyard strewn with leaves and twigs and trash. One of the branches of the live oak had broken and was hanging on the ground, and all her flowers had been flattened. But the gazebo was completely intact, right down to the shingles on the roof.

Thank You, Lord! I'll never take any of this for granted again.

She sensed someone standing in the doorway.

Guy Jones came outside and stood next to her. "I checked out the house, and it seems fine. This old place is a fortress. Guess I'd better get busy and get the plywood off the windows. Are the phones working yet?"

"No, and we don't have power or water either. I'm just so thankful we have a house to come home to. I really thought we were going to get wiped out this time."

"I think we all did. I'm sure Brandon will call as soon as he can get through."

"He'd better."

"I'll go out to the car and get the cooler. Good thing we picked up food and ice before we headed home. Hard to say when they'll get the power back on. I'll bring in the porta-potty from the garage." Guy smiled wryly. "You remember how to camp, don't you?"

"We were a lot younger then, but you won't hear me complain. I'm just glad to be home. I'm anxious to hear if Owen and Hailey had any damage, though I doubt it since Port Smyth didn't get the wind we did."

"Anybody home?" said a familiar voice behind her.

Ellen turned around and saw Gordy Jameson's burly silhouette standing in the open front door. She hurried to him and gave him a hug. "Did you stay here during the hurricane?"

"Nah, me and Pam and Weezie hung out in Georgia. We were really sweatin' it, but our house is still standin'. I still can't believe we escaped the big storm surge. We've got a little water damage from a couple leaks, but nothin' serious."

"What about the crab shack?"

"The sign was ripped off and blown clear out in the parkin' lot, but other than that it's fine." Gordy chuckled. "Pam got down on her hands and knees and kissed the pier, and Weezie shouted a 'Thank You, Jesus' that I'm sure they heard in Miami. We never thought we'd see it again."

"What about the inside?" Guy said.

"Just like we left it. Billy and I had it boarded up tighter than a tick. All we need is power and water, and we're back in business."

"That's wonderful," Ellen said.

"Weezie wanted me to ask if Brandon ever found the kid he was lookin' for."

Ellen lifted her eyebrows. "We don't know. Brandon was supposed to meet us in Tallahassee but never got there. We assume he either decided to stay in a shelter or was forced to because of stalled traffic. Our phones and cell phones aren't working yet, so we haven't heard from him."

"Well, when you do, let us know. Weezie's been prayin' he'd find the boy."

Brandon Jones pushed open the door to the Palm City Civic Center and stepped into a large, bustling room filled with rows of cots and what he guessed to be several hundred people. An elderly man dressed in pajamas and slippers and pushing a walker nodded at Brandon and shuffled toward the men's restroom.

Off to one side, three little boys were fighting over a beach ball, and a young woman sat on the floor, reading a storybook to a little girl about Annie's age, seemingly oblivious to the toddler throwing a tantrum not ten feet away. Brandon wondered how long anyone could stand to live in these conditions.

A silver-haired lady holding a clipboard approached him, kindness in her eyes. "I'm sorry. This shelter is at capacity, but there's still room down at the elementary school."

"I'm not looking for shelter," Brandon said. "Can you tell me if a lady by the name of Angel Phelps is staying here? She and her twelve-year-old son were separated before the hurricane hit, and she has no idea that he's all right. I'd like to tell her."

The woman slipped on her half glasses and scanned the list of names on the clipboard, then flipped the page. "Here we are…Parker, Pearlman, Pembrooke, Perkins, Peterson, *Phelps*. Yes, there's an Angel Phelps on aisle two, third cot on the right."

"Thanks."

Brandon walked toward aisle two and spotted Angel sitting on the side of her cot, her elbows on her knees, her chin resting on her palms. He squeezed past a young couple holding a tiny baby, then reached down and tapped her on the shoulder. "Ready to get out of this place?"

Angel glanced up and gave him a double take. "Brandon! I thought you were in Tallahassee."

"Never made it there." Brandon felt a smile overtake his face. "I know a soggy twelve-year-old who's anxious to see you."

"You found Cade!"

"He's got a broken arm and leg, but he's going to be fine." Brandon reached for her hand and pulled her to her feet. "Come on. I'll tell you the whole story while I take you to the emergency room."

Brandon walked in the wide open front door of his parents' home and stood in the entry hall. "Hello…? Mom…? Dad…?"

"Brandon, is that you?" said a muffled voice.

Ellen came running out of the kitchen and Guy from down the hall. It was impossible to tell who was hugging whom.

"We've been worried sick about you," Ellen said, the look on her face telling him she had just noticed how disheveled he looked.

"Where in the world have you been? How'd you get all those cuts and bruises?"

"Would you believe I rode out the hurricane in a cave with a twelve-year-old?"

"*I* would." Guy rested his arm on Brandon's shoulder. "You smell like a wet dog."

"As well I should. Cade and I got hammered for eight hours with blowing rain and debris. It was incredible."

"So you did find him," Ellen said. "Gordy came by and said Weezie was wondering if you had."

"Yeah, I found him at the Jackson Caves around ten Saturday night. His left arm and leg were broken, and it was too late to evacuate since they kept talking about the danger of high water in the low-lying areas. I couldn't leave him there alone."

"Of course you couldn't," Ellen said. "But I am curious why you were still in Seaport ten hours after you were supposed to leave."

"It's a long story. Let's go sit outside where there's a breeze, and I'll tell you everything." Brandon turned to his dad and shook his hand. "Happy Father's Day a little late. Sorry I didn't have a chance to get you anything."

Guy smiled and pulled him into a one-armed hug. "Having you home safe and sound is better than any gift you could've bought me."

Brandon sat out on the veranda and gave his parents a detailed account of all the events leading up to his finding Cade, as well the details of the harrowing hurricane ordeal and Cade's terrifying encounter with Quentin Raynor.

"I talked to Chief Seevers right after I dropped Angel off at the hospital," Brandon said. "He and Special Agent Moore were anxious to get Cade's statement. He said they could get a warrant and search the Raynors' house, even if they had to pull off the plywood first. And if he had anything to say about it, Quentin Raynor would never sleep another night in his own bed."

Ellen shook her head. "That poor child. Thank God you were there for him. Can you imagine how frightening it must have been for him being stuck out there alone and thinking Quentin Raynor had come after him?"

"You have such a healthy respect for Mother Nature," Guy said. "I'm kind of surprised you didn't talk yourself out of it—especially with the storm surge they were predicting."

"I can't explain it," Brandon said. "But as time went on, finding Cade was more important than saving my own neck. When I found the red feather tied to the tree, I was sure he was out there. I wasn't going to leave him to die."

"No, you could've *both* died." Guy held Brandon's gaze, and then gave a slight nod. "I'm proud of you, son. It took a lot of courage to do what you did."

"I'm just glad I didn't know anything about it," Ellen said. "I was a nervous wreck as it was. So how'd you manage to get Cade out of there?"

"I hiked back to the road and was surprised it wasn't flooded. I found my car right where I'd left it, drove back to Old Seaport, and found three guys who'd just taken the plywood off a convenience store and were loading it into a pickup. I asked if they'd help me move Cade from the cave to the car. We nailed three sheets of plywood together and made a pallet. Then they followed me out there and we carried him out. No sweat."

Guy smiled and glanced at Ellen. "Told you he was resourceful."

"I drove Cade to the ER at Seaport Community and left him there while I went to find Angel. It was the best feeling in the world being able to bring him back to her alive."

"Where is he now?"

"Checked in at the hospital. He's dehydrated and will have to learn how to function with a cast on his left arm and leg. Can't imagine how he's going to manage in a shelter." Brandon glanced at his watch. "There's more to the story, but I'll have to save the best part for later."

"What best part?" Ellen said, a smile stretching her cheeks. "You're not going to just leave us hanging, are you?"

"Sorry, but I promised Cade I'd be back at six to see his casts and find out how his meeting went with Chief Seevers and Special Agent Moore."

Brandon stood leaning on the wall in Cade's hospital room, his arms folded across his chest. "I'm proud of you for having the guts to tell the authorities everything you know about Quentin Raynor."

Angel brushed the curls off Cade's forehead. "I don't feel good about him testifyin' against that monster. It's gonna be painful havin' to listen to those awful racial slurs and threats repeated in a courtroom full of people. I don't know that I wanna put him through all that."

"I can do it, Mom. Prejudice is his problem. I'm not gonna make it mine." Cade glanced over at Brandon, the corners of his mouth twitching. "I just need to do the right thing."

"Why, Caedmon Robert Nash," Angel said, "where on earth did *that* come from? I've never heard you talk so grown up before." She looked over at Brandon and held his gaze. "Cade said you wanna buy him a Bible."

"I'd like to. I hope you don't have a problem with it."

"Why would you do a thing like that?"

"Cade and I had some interesting conversations while we were riding out the storm. He has a lot of questions, and the Bible has a lot of answers."

"Yeah, did you know Brandon and me have the same Father?" Cade said.

"Excuse me?"

"The One in heaven, Mom. Did you know that He knew me before I was born, and I wasn't an accident? That I'm just exactly the way He wanted me to be?"

Angel moved her eyes from Cade to Brandon with an I-get-what-you're-trying-to-do look on her face. "If talkin' about God bein' his Father will help Cade accept that he's biracial, I'm all for it. Just don't expect me to get involved in readin' the Bible with him. I gave all that up years ago."

"Do you mind if I read it with him? I'm kind of into it right now."

"I guess not. I can never thank you enough for all you've done."

"Listen, finding Cade alive and being able to bring him home was the greatest experience of my life. You have no idea what it's meant to me. Which reminds me…" Brandon went over and stood next to Cade's bed. "There's something I want to write on your casts."

"Cool!"

"I'm not sure I've even got a pen," Angel said.

"Not to worry." Brandon reached in his pocket and pulled out a black marker. "I brought just the tool for this momentous occasion." He pulled up a chair next to Cade's bed. "Which do you want me to sign first: your arm or your leg?"

"Arm."

"Okay, here goes."

"What are you gonna write?"

"You'll see." Brandon wrote the words he'd prayed about as he drove over to the hospital, not even worried that they might sound corny. "Okay, done."

"It's upside down," Cade said. "Read it to me."

"It says, 'This was no accident. It was meant to be. I'm proud to be your brother for all eternity. Brandon.'"

Cade's smile would have melted an iceberg. He gave Brandon a high five, then looked over at Angel. "What's wrong, Mom?"

Angel's eyes brimmed with tears, and her chin quivered. It was several seconds before she found her voice. "You got saved, didn't you?"

Cade stared at her for a moment. "How'd you know?"

"Because I recognize the joy that's all over your face. I got saved at church camp when I was fifteen."

"Then how come you never told *me* about Jesus?"

Angel plucked a tissue out of the box on the rolling bedside table and wiped her cheeks. "I don't know, Cade. I guess I got disillusioned with life after your daddy left. I was bitter about raisin' you alone and felt put down because I brought a biracial kid into the world." She reached over and stroked his cheek. "I've *never* been sorry that I had you. But I felt guilty because people had a hard time acceptin' you, and I was mad at God for not doin' somethin' about it."

"It wasn't God's fault," Cade said.

"But I needed it to be someone's fault besides mine. It hurt so much…" Angel's voice trailed off, and she covered her face with her hands.

"It's okay, Mom. I just wish I would've known a long time ago that God had a plan for my life. This changes everything."

Will Seevers sat at the patio table, drinking a warm Diet Coke and hoping the power would be restored before Margaret and Meagan drove home tomorrow from Valdosta. His cell phone rang, and he grabbed it before it could ring a second time. "Seevers!"

"Oh, good, your phone's workin'," Bryce Moore said. "We arrested Raynor the minute he and his family pulled into the driveway. You should've seen his face. It was the most satisfying 'I gotcha' I've had in years. We're on our way to the station. I'm bringin' his wife and son in for questioning. We should be able to get at least one of them to crack. The kid's gonna end up in juvy. We'll see about the wife."

"Did Raynor confess to anything?" Will said.

"Not outright. But we found the Louisville slugger in his garage. And his handwritten notes from White Wash meetings at The Cove over the past couple weeks and a set dated the night Cade claims he heard them plannin' to burn the church. Raynor didn't deny writin' the notes, but swore on his grandmother's grave he didn't know Victory Chapel had a parsonage. That's practically an admission that he set the fire."

Will stood and walked inside the house. "I'll see you in a few minutes. Does Raynor know Cade talked to us?"

"No, and if we can get him to confess, we may not even need to involve the boy. I led Raynor to believe that we arrested Beasley and Williams, and the first one to talk gets the deal. I have a feelin' he's gonna spill his guts before the night's over."

42

Brandon Jones parked his car in front of his parents' home and waltzed up the porch steps and through the house out onto the veranda, feeling as though his feet were barely touching the ground.

Ellen and Guy were sitting in cane rockers, the blazing sunset the only source of light, the night air thick with humidity and the scent of mosquito repellent.

"There you are," Ellen said. "The water's back on, but still no phones or power. How'd it go with Cade?"

"Great. Unbelievable really. It's been an amazing day."

"Did he tell Will and Special Agent Moore what happened with Quentin Raynor?"

Brandon nodded. "He did. And he even seems confident about testifying if it comes to that."

"Being a witness for the prosecution can be tough," Guy said. "He's going to need a lot of support to get through an ordeal like that."

Ellen fanned herself with what appeared to be a manila envelope folded in two. "Go ahead and finish telling us your story. You said you were saving the best for later."

"Okay, but I'm going to give you the punch line first because it just got better, and I'm totally blown away by it: Cade accepted Christ this morning, and Angel recommitted her life to Christ about an hour ago."

Ellen looked at Guy and then at Brandon and seemed unable to find her voice.

"I know," Brandon said. "I can hardly believe it myself. The most amazing part of all is that God used *me* to bring it about. Like *I* know anything."

"Well, you must know something," Guy said. "People don't make a profession of faith out of the blue. I've never led anyone to Christ."

Brandon shrugged. "It's the last thing I ever expected to do. Weezie told me I had a divine appointment with Cade. I'd never heard of such a thing, but she said it wasn't by chance that God brought us together."

Ellen reached up and took Brandon's hand. "This is so exciting. Sit down and tell us everything."

"I think God was preparing me for it before I left Raleigh. I had this weird encounter with a homeless guy named Gary who got me asking myself if there's a reason we're all here—if life has any real purpose."

"This was a stranger on the street?" Guy said.

"Yeah. He asked me for money so I bought him lunch. He was about your age, Dad. He'd quit his job as a vice detective years ago because it was depressing always seeing the bad side of people. When he couldn't get motivated to do anything else, his wife took the kids and left him. Ever since, he's been roaming the streets, trying to figure out a reason for all the craziness. He said that far as he could tell, life's pretty pointless—that after we're born, the strong prey on the weak, and if we survive, we get old and eventually die."

"Talk about cynical," Guy said. "What'd you say to that?"

Brandon shook his head. "Absolutely nothing. After burning out at Mavis and Stein and losing Kelsey, I could relate to what the guy said. Life didn't make sense to me either."

"Didn't you even broach the subject of God?" Ellen said.

"Sure, but he said that if there is a God, He's sleeping on the job—at least the one the Salvation Army was trying to sell him. What was I supposed to say to that?"

"So how'd you finally part ways?" Ellen asked.

"Gary finished eating and started to leave the café, then turned and gave me the most desolate look. He said if I ever figured out what the heck life is all about to come find him, that he was living under the Twelfth Street Bridge."

"Goodness." Ellen stopped rocking. "That must've been sobering."

"It was. And it got me thinking about my own circumstances. I sure didn't want to hit bottom the way he did. Maybe that's why I was instantly drawn to Weezie. She seemed excited just to be alive. I wanted to understand what it was that kept her going. We had some of the best conversations. I've come to the conclusion that the quality of a person's life all boils down to *perspective*."

Brandon relayed to his parents bits and pieces of his conversations with Weezie, including her perspective on her worth in Christ.

"If I hadn't listened to Weezie tell me how she learned to value herself because she's God's child, I would never have known what to say to a twelve-year-old biracial kid who'd been abandoned by his father." Brandon smiled. "It really does seem like a divine setup."

"So what *did* you say to Cade?" Guy asked.

"We talked about it being Father's Day. It had been obvious to me from the first day I met Cade that he was starved for a father's love and a sense of belonging. One thing led to another, and I shared Psalm 139 with him. Finding out that God knew him before he was born and planned him exactly the way he is was about the most exciting news he'd ever heard. We talked about that for a while, and then I told him about how sin separates us from God and that Jesus' death on the cross paid the price so we could have a relationship with the Father again. Cade told me he felt guilty about all the ways he'd thought about getting even with the boys who badgered him. He asked me if he could be forgiven and have a relationship with God. I never thought I'd be leading anyone to Christ, least of all a kid…" Brandon's blinked the stinging from his eyes. "It was amazing."

"I'm proud of you, son." Guy reached over and gave his arm a gentle squeeze. "I'm sorry I was so negative about you working at the camp. I was thinking of your financial future and honestly never gave a thought to the possibility that God might have a purpose for you being there."

"It's a major rush, but it was humbling to be used that way." Brandon stood. "Listen, if it's okay with you two, I think I'd like to be by myself for a while and let all this sink in."

Brandon lay on the bed in the upstairs guest room, his hands clasped behind his head, his mind processing all he had learned in the past couple weeks. He was suddenly aware that the lights had come on and the ceiling fan was moving. A few seconds later, air was blowing out of the vents.

He got up and showered and shaved, then put on his last pair of clean shorts and a T-shirt, aware of footsteps on the staircase. Seconds later his mother appeared in the doorway.

"The phones are back on," Ellen said. "Kelsey left three messages—all on Saturday morning."

"Rats! I was out of here at the crack of dawn and went to help Angel look for Cade. What'd she say?"

"That she wants you to call her. She'd been following the hurricane reports and knew Seaport was supposed to get the worst of it. She sounded really scared."

"Well, since Hector didn't amount to much, she may not be so eager to hear from me."

Ellen lifted her eyebrows. "Are you willing to pass up a chance to find out?"

"No way. I'll call her right now. Are your cell phones working, too?"

"Uh-huh."

"Good, then I can use mine."

Ellen smiled. "Okay, I'm leaving. And, of course, you'll come downstairs and fill me in?"

Brandon laughed. "As if I had a choice."

"Go on before you talk yourself out of it. Just be your lovable self." She turned and went back downstairs.

Brandon flopped on the side of the bed and turned on his cell phone and noticed a new message waiting. He played it back.

"Brandon, it's Kelsey! It's 11:15 Saturday morning. I tried reaching you at your parents' house and kept getting the answering machine. I've been following the hurricane. I hope you're not planning to ride it out. I'm worried about you. Call me!"

Brandon sat for a moment, absorbing the sound of her voice

and trying to let his pulse calm down. She didn't say she wanted to rekindle the relationship. Just that she was worried about him. Could he handle that? He decided it was better than nothing. He hit the autodial and let it ring.

"Hello."

"Kelsey, it's me."

"Brandon! I've been so worried about you! Where are you?"

"At my parents' house. The power just came back on, and I got your messages. I'm fine. We're all fine. Mom and Dad, my grandfather, and my brother and his family all went to Tallahassee to get out of Hector's way."

"What about you?"

"I ended up staying, but it wasn't something I planned to do. Anyway, I'm fine. As it turned out, we only got category two winds here. Sorry you were worried. I called as soon as I got your messages."

There was a long, agonizing stretch of dead air.

"I miss you," Kelsey finally said.

"I miss you, too. But you already knew that."

"So what've you been doing?"

He smiled without meaning to. "Oh, the usual—trying to discover the way to significance." He waited for her to sigh or make some wisecrack.

"And have you?"

"You know, Kel, I really think I'm starting to."

43

At nine o'clock Tuesday morning, Will Seevers sat in his air-conditioned office, his feet on his desk, his hands clasped behind his head.

"This has been quite a ride, hasn't it?" Will said.

Bryce Moore nodded, the flecks of gray on his unshaven face enhanced by the fluorescent lighting. "Yeah, thanks to our collective efforts, White Wash is history—*again*. I had a feelin' that once Raynor confessed to everything, the other members would fold. He was a moron to keep the meeting notes at his house. I mean, the guy's handwriting matches the note found in Brandon Jones's car. This was just too sweet."

"Do you think he's telling the truth about not knowing that the church had a parsonage and that the pastor and his family lived there?"

Bryce shrugged. "That's for the jury to decide. He doesn't have a history of violent behavior, and he didn't kill Cade when he had the chance. But Raynor seemed more upset over goin' to prison than over the fact that he'd torched seven human beings. I didn't sense he had any real remorse—certainly not for any of the vandalizin' or for runnin' Ms. Taylor's car off the road."

"Beasley didn't either. It's amazing how cold these guys are."

"Made me wanna puke the way Raynor kept pattin' himself on the back for doin' what he says his old man never had the guts to do. Some family legacy."

Will shook his head. "It's not like it took a lot of brains either. The entire operation was piecemeal, right down to his going back and adding the Ws to the crime scenes after the fact."

"Well, they stumped us for a while, but we should be through processin' these paltry losers before the day's over. I'm confident we got them all. When this hits the evening news, there should be a sigh of relief in the community. Too bad it won't bring back the pastor and his family."

"No, but the African-American community will sure sleep better now. Thanks for your help, Bryce. We made a good team."

"What are you smilin' about?"

"Can you imagine how mad Raynor must've been that he was arrested in front of his neighbors by a *black* FBI agent?"

Bryce chuckled. "Poetic justice, I'd say."

Brandon Jones went downstairs and to the kitchen, where his mother was sitting at the breakfast bar, reading the newspaper. "Morning, Mom."

"Well, well, well…the boy finally rises," Ellen said. "Did you have trouble falling asleep?"

"No, I crashed. Felt great having air-conditioning again." He walked over to the coffeepot and sensed his mother's probing eyes. "I didn't come down and talk to you after I hung up with Kelsey because I needed space to think."

"And…?"

"And what?"

"Oh, come on, at least give me a hint," Ellen said. "I could hardly sleep wondering what you and Kelsey said to each other!"

Brandon carried his coffee to the breakfast bar and sat on the stool next to his mother. "I guess the bottom line is we're miserable without each other."

"I find that encouraging, don't you?"

"That we still love each other, sure. But our relationship was never the problem. It was my obsession to find a job with significance that split us up. From everyone else's perspective, I had it made. But it wasn't enough. That hasn't changed."

"Well, something has. I've never seen you more confident."

Brandon took a sip of coffee. "Actually, what's changed is my perspective. I guess I'm realizing that life isn't about getting what I want. It's about God and what *He* wants for me. He's the one with the game plan."

"I couldn't agree more."

"So I suppose just about any career path could be significant if I do it to please Him. He can use me anywhere, just like He used me at the camp to reach Cade. That opens up a whole new set of possibilities."

"Indeed it does." Ellen smiled and put her hand on his. "Did you explain all this to Kelsey?"

"Yeah, for two hours."

"What'd she have to say?"

"She was surprisingly supportive. Totally blown away by everything that's happened since I got here. Apparently she's done a lot of soul-searching, too, and decided she was insensitive to my struggle to find significance in what I do. She thinks it's important that I settle this."

Ellen lifted her eyebrows. "Sounds like a breakthrough to me."

"I think what surprised her most was that she could hear joy in my voice. She thinks that maybe God's been trying to show me what I'm best at and I should start researching career opportunities at Christian camps."

Ellen's eyes widened. "Kelsey said that?"

"Yeah, do you believe it?"

"So…is there any hope for a future together?"

"I don't know, Mom. I'm afraid to think that far ahead. Right now, I just need to get my act together and see where it leads. But Kelsey sure didn't close the door on the possibility."

44

Gordy Jameson sat in his office, reading Wednesday's issue of the *North Coast Messenger*, thinking how odd it was having two major stories dominating the front page. He glanced at his watch and thought he'd give it another twenty minutes and then go out front and greet the lunch customers.

He heard footsteps and then looked up and saw Eddie Drummond standing in his doorway.

"Can I talk to you?" Eddie said.

"Yeah, sure. Come in and take a load off. Glad to see you made it through Hector in one piece. I'm anxious to have lunch with you guys and swap hurricane stories."

"I wanted to catch you before the other guys get here." Eddie sat in the chair next to Gordy's desk and looked at the newspaper out of the corner of his eye. "I want you to know that I didn't have a clue about White Wash. I couldn't believe it when I found out who the ringleaders were. Murderers—right there in my neighborhood. Made me sick."

"I can see why."

Eddie shook his head and stared at his hands. "I'm telling you, Gordo, it was a wake-up call. I don't want Abel ending up like that. I'm gonna get him into counseling if I have to work two jobs to pay for it."

"Did Abel know about White Wash?"

"No, none of the boys did, except Reese Raynor. But the hate sure filtered down. It's not gonna be easy to reprogram Abel's thinking, but I'm committed to it—even if it means moving out of Seaport."

Gordy looked into Eddie's eyes. "You'd be willin' to leave?"

"If that's what it takes to save my kid. Let's hope it doesn't come to that. I know one thing: I've gotta clean up my own act. I can't keep making cutting remarks about the blacks I work with and not expect my kids to pick up on it." Eddie cracked his knuckles and seemed to be pondering something. "What do you think about me volunteering at the People's Clinic? I'm thinking I should lead by example."

Gordy stared at Eddie and tried to find his voice. "Well…I'd say that's about the smartest thing I've ever heard you say." Gordy rose to his feet and patted Eddie on the shoulder. "Come on, let's go find the guys and swap hurricane stories."

Brandon Jones drove past the old-fashioned Mobil gas station and spotted the red, white, and blue mailbox with the name Taylor painted on the side. He turned into the gravel drive, maneuvering carefully to avoid downed tree limbs, and finally spotted a small blue frame house. He pulled his car in front and turned off the motor. Weezie Taylor waved from the window.

Brandon got out and met her halfway to the door and gave her a hug. "Can you believe it's over?"

"I haven't stopped praisin' the Lord since Chief Seevers told me about the arrests. Between that and Hector takin' a turn to the east, it's been somethin' to celebrate."

"I'll bet it feels good to be back in your own house, too."

"Whooooeee, it sure does!" Her laughter filled the front yard.

Brandon chuckled. "Well, I've got good news, too."

"Come in outta the heat and have a Coke. I never get tired of hearin' good news."

Brandon followed Weezie inside and out to the kitchen. He sat in one of two chairs at a small table in the corner.

Weezie brought him a glass with ice and a can of Coke and then sat in the other chair. "Your eyes are smilin'. What's up?"

"Something else happened that I didn't want to tell you on the phone. Cade accepted Christ before we left the cave."

Weezie put her hand on her heart. "I just *knew* the Lord had somethin' special for that boy!"

Brandon gave her details of what had happened after he and

Cade started talking about Father's Day, up to Angel recommitting her life to Christ in Cade's hospital room. "You were right about it being a divine appointment. But how'd you know?"

"Don't know that I can answer that," Weezie said, wiping the tears off her cheeks. "It was just somethin' I felt deep inside."

"Well, it blew me away. Cade and Angel are going to church with me and my folks Sunday."

Weezie shook her head from side to side. "Mercy me, if that's not somethin'."

"We're thinking of asking them to come stay with us till their mobile home gets replaced. I'm just concerned that Cade's going to have a big hassle trying to negotiate my parents' front steps with an arm and a leg in a cast. I'm sure we'll figure out something, though."

There was a long pause, and then Weezie said, "Cade and his mom are sure welcome to stay out here. I've got two extra bedrooms, and I'm hardly ever home. No steps to worry about either."

"That's an awfully generous offer, especially since you've never even met them."

"But I feel like I have. And I sure know what it's like not bein' able to go home. I'd be more than happy to share what I've got."

45

Six weeks later…

Brandon Jones sat on Seaport beach, the August sun a fiery red ball above the horizon, the gulf a blue-gray sea of glass. The sound of gulls echoed across the expanse, interrupted briefly by the blast of a distant freighter. Along the wet sand, tiny shorebirds scurried to and fro. And overhead a majestic frigate bird hung like a kite without a string.

Brandon slowly filled his lungs with the damp morning air and then let it out. As ready as he was to go back to Raleigh, it was hard leaving the place where he had stood at a fork in the road of his spiritual journey and found the path to real significance.

He sensed someone standing behind him and turned. "Hi, Mom."

"Mind if I join you?" Ellen said.

"Not at all. How was your run?"

"Invigorating. Of course, you know I really come out here for the sunrise."

Brandon smiled, thinking how much he would miss their talks.

"You were really quiet at dinner last night," Ellen said, her eyes seeming to probe his thoughts. "You're thinking of leaving, aren't you?"

"Yeah, I can't stand being away from Kelsey anymore. I'm driving back to Raleigh in the morning. I've arranged to stay with an old friend of mine and swap out yard work for rent."

"Does Kelsey know you're coming?"

Brandon nodded. "You know how we've been exploring job opportunities at Christian camps? Well, Kelsey just found out that

Three Peaks Christian Camp and Conference Center in Colorado is looking for a new camp director, and she thinks I'd be perfect. She went to college with the administrator and has been on the phone with him singing my praises. He wants me to send my résumé as soon as possible."

"What do *you* want to do?" Ellen said.

"Whatever the Lord wants me to do. Kelsey and I have been praying about it for weeks, and then this position opened up. The job sounds terrific. We'd have to learn to live on a lot less money, but lodging's included, and I can't imagine a better fit for me. Plus Kelsey loves the mountains. I guess I just need to turn in my application and see if the Lord opens the door."

Ellen turned to him, her eyes as animated as Annie's. "Then you and Kelsey *are* getting back together!"

A grin took over Brandon's face and he laughed out loud. "Yes! I can hardly wait to slip her engagement ring back on her finger. I'm not sure where the future's going to take me, Mom. But I'm absolutely sure that Kelsey's supposed to be with me."

Brandon picked up Cade Nash from Seaport Middle School and drove toward Weezie's house. Cade talked with excitement about his new teachers, two new friends he'd made, and the doctor giving him the okay to go out for the track team.

"It's so great to see you excited about school, Cade. And the track team? Wow! As soon as you get back in shape, I fully expect you to break the state record. One of these days, you may be competing at the Olympics."

"Yeah, maybe if I work at it. I'm pretty fast. How come you look so serious?"

Brandon pulled up in front of Weezie's house and turned off the motor. "Let's go inside. There's something I want to talk to you about."

Cade got out and reached under the mat for the key and opened the front door.

Brandon followed him out to the kitchen and got two Cokes out of the fridge. "I talked to your mom today. Your new mobile home is being delivered next week. Looks like you won't be needing a ride to and from school anymore."

"Good, I like ridin' my bike. Plus I miss havin' my own room and my own stuff. Mom said when we get settled, I can have sleepovers with Jeff and Gabe. They're both goin' out for track, too."

"That's so great. I knew God would help you have a better year at school. Listen, you know how I've been talking about missing my fiancée and having to get really serious about finding a job?"

"Yeah."

"Well, I feel it's time for me to go back to Raleigh. I'm leaving in the morning."

Cade's face fell. "That soon?"

"Kelsey wants me to come back, and there's a job opportunity at a Christian camp that I might have a crack at."

"You'd be super at it."

"Thanks. We'll see if that door opens. But whether it does or doesn't, I really need to see my lady."

"I'll miss you." Cade's eyes suddenly welled with tears.

Brandon reached across the table and wrapped his fingers around Cade's wrist. "I'll miss you, too. We've had something really special…" Brandon stopped to let the emotion pass. "You're going to do great now. And it's not as though I won't see you again."

"Then you'll come back to visit?"

"Absolutely. But preferably *not* in hurricane season." Brandon grinned at the same time Cade did. "So are we cool?"

"Yeah, we're cool. Have you told Weezie?"

Brandon shook his head. "I'm on my way to the crab shack right now to tell her."

Brandon sat with Weezie at an umbrella table on the back deck of Gordy's Crab Shack, waiting for her to react to the news that he was going back to Raleigh.

"Whoooeee, the man's finally come to his senses!" she finally said. "You'd better invite me to your weddin', that's all I can say about it."

"I haven't asked Kelsey to marry me yet."

"Well, she sure didn't ask you to come back so she can refuse your proposal."

"You're right." Brandon smiled and wondered if he was blushing. "I'm pretty fired up about the possibility of being on staff at a Christian camp, too—especially in Colorado. And I never would've expected Kelsey to be even more excited than I am." Brandon paused to collect his thoughts and then said, "I'm really going to miss this place—and you."

"We've sure been through some stuff, haven't we?"

"We really have." Brandon took a sip of limeade and looked out at the gulf, hoping he could say what was on his heart without it sounding schmaltzy. "I'm not going back to Raleigh the same man, you know. I have you to thank for that."

"Me? What'd I do?"

"You helped me see that significance is found in belonging to God and living each day for Him. I was trying to find it by altering my circumstances, but my premise was wrong. It's not the circumstances of my life but Who I'm living it for that gives me purpose."

Weezie shook her head from side to side. "Well, listen to you. I never said it quite that way."

"But you modeled it that way," Brandon said. "I see now that if I try to please God in everything I do, my life *will be* significant, even if things don't happen the way I want them to. This life isn't about what I want, but what He wants for me. The rewards come later."

Weezie eyes brimmed with tears. "So help me, I don't know how you got all that from hangin' around me."

"Well, I've been reading the Bible, too. It started to make sense after I studied your reactions to things and listened to your explanations. I thought you should know that God really used you."

Weezie wiped a tear off her cheek and reached across the table and squeezed his hand. "Mercy me, before I get to blubberin' over here, I wanna wish you the Lord's very best. You and Kelsey are gonna be in my prayers every day."

46

As the morning sky turned the color of molten lava, Brandon carried the few belongings he'd brought from Raleigh out to his SUV. His father came down the front steps, still clad in his bathrobe, and walked up next to him.

"Need any help?" Guy said.

"No, that's it."

Guy put his hand on Brandon's shoulder. "I want you know I support what you're doing. If there's one thing I've learned from all this, it's that the Lord, and not your dad, needs to direct your life." He shook Brandon's hand and then pulled him into a bear hug. "Call us when you get there, okay?"

"I will, Dad. Thanks for everything."

Brandon saw his mother walking toward him and didn't know if he could handle an emotional good-bye.

"I love happy endings," Ellen said. "I never gave up on the idea of Kelsey being part of the family."

Brandon smiled. "Just like I never gave up on you getting back into the newspaper business. Tell me again when you start."

"A week from Monday. I'm sure I'll love being a feature writer for the *Messenger*, though I haven't been this nervous since I was a cub reporter."

"You'll do great, Mom."

Guy nodded. "Indeed she will."

"Did you get the snacks I left on the counter?" Ellen said.

"They're in the car. Thanks. Be sure to tell Owen and Papa I'll call them when I get settled." Brandon put his arms around his mother and held her a little tighter than usual. "I don't think I'll ever see a sunrise again without thinking of you. Thanks for all the great talks we had and for always being a cheerleader. I love you."

"I love you, too. Now go home and ask that sweet girl to marry you. I want details."

Brandon reached for the car door, blinking rapidly to clear his eyes. He caught his father's gaze and exchanged an "I love you" without saying the words, then climbed up in the front seat and started the car. He pulled away from the curb and waved a final good-bye as he caught a glimpse of his parents in the rearview mirror.

He drove down the hill to Beach Shore Drive and stole one last look at the gulf, then turned onto Seaport Boulevard with its glorious old mansions and magnificent live oaks, remembering the first time he had driven down this street, feeling empty and lost and homeless.

It suddenly occurred to him that perhaps another divine appointment awaited him in Raleigh—that somewhere under the Twelfth Street Bridge, a lost soul named Gary needed to be convinced that life wasn't meaningless and random.

Brandon made the final turn onto Seminole and drove out of the Seaport city limits. He pushed the autodial on his cell phone, his pulse racing and his heart overflowing, thinking Kelsey would surely forgive him for calling so early on a Saturday morning.

"Hello," said a sleepy voice.

"Kelsey, it's me, honey. I've left Seaport. I'm coming home!"

Afterword

*Many are the plans in a man's heart,
but it is the LORD's purpose that prevails.*
PROVERBS 19:21

Dear friends,

Even Christians can sometimes struggle with the feeling that this time on earth has little meaning and that when all is said and done, their feeble existence won't have mattered much. But God created each of us with a specific purpose in mind, and we've touched more lives and influenced more situations than we can possibly know this side of heaven. Even if we haven't been endowed with extraordinary abilities, God has planned all of our steps for His purpose and His glory. *Every* person matters. Each has a part to play.

And regardless of what role God has assigned to us in His Master production—whether we're onstage or backstage—we were created first and foremost to be in relationship with Him. Just the humble realization that He loves each of us and desires a personal and unique relationship with us is reason enough that we should value our existence.

But a life truly rich with meaning is one that is sold-out to God, regardless of how it lines up with the world's idea of success. Pleasing Him in everything we do should be the heart's desire of every believer, and it's the only way to find real significance. Brandon finally got it right when he said, "This life isn't about what I want, but what He wants for me. The rewards come later."

Whether we're drawn to the mission field, the ball field, or the cornfield, our true purpose is fulfilled in seeking to please God and bring Him glory in every situation, regardless of our circumstances.

Goodness, can you believe we've come to the end of the Seaport Series? I have often wished it were possible for me to walk into the pages of my stories and talk with my characters. But never more than at this moment, when my head and heart are reeling with the reality that I have to say good-bye to Ellen and Guy. They've lived in my imagination for the past five years, and have come to life on the pages of nine novels—five Baxter Series books and four Seaport Suspense novels. Their family struggles have caused us to empathize with their doubts, failings, and sorrows—and to celebrate their epiphanies, victories, and joys. Such an intimate association has made for a bittersweet, albeit satisfying, farewell.

But though we're leaving Seaport, we're not cutting all ties with the Joneses. Join me in book one of the Phantom Hollow Series, and find out if Brandon and Kelsey ever tied the knot. The setting for this series is the town of Jacob's Ear, Colorado, where the influx of tourists during all four seasons keeps it a hub of bustling diversity—ripe with possibilities for suspense and intrigue!

I so enjoy hearing from my readers. You can write to me through my publisher at http://fiction.mpbooks.com or directly through my website at www.kathyherman.com. I read and respond to every e-mail and greatly value your input.

In Him,

Kathy Herman

Discussion Guide

1. Define in your own words God's purpose for creating us.

2. Do you think it's possible for someone to have a *false* sense of significance? Do you think famous people, such as movie stars, sports heroes, rock musicians, CEOs of Fortune 500 companies, have cause to feel significant? Is significance based on achievement?

3. Can believers have a false sense of significance? Do you think that any person who loves his or her profession should feel significant? Is how a person *feels* a good indicator of whether he or she has value? If not, what do you think is a good indicator?

4. Explain what you think Weezie meant when she said (in chapter 7), "I've had to learn that it's not who you are but *whose* you are that matters."

5. Do you think the very nature of racial discrimination can cause victims to feel insignificant? Have you ever been the victim of racial discrimination or known someone who was? Do you think people can nurse quiet prejudices they wish they didn't have? If so, can you identify a few reasons why that might happen?

6. Have you ever been made fun of for how you look or think or feel? Or been put down or demoralized through verbal, physical, or sexual abuse? Have you been humiliated by an

employer or a teacher or someone else in authority? Did the experience leave you feeling bad about yourself? If your answer is yes, can you explain why?

7. Do you think it's possible to be so secure with who we are in Christ that we are no longer burdened by the insensitive, cruel, or misguided actions and remarks of others? Explain your answer. Be honest.

8. Did you feel compassion for Cade Nash? Have you ever sat in judgment (even silently) of someone who chose to bring a biracial child into the world? Do you believe that every child was planned by God? Do you think God prefers one race of people to another? Do you think that spiritual roots are more important than ethnic roots? Do you think every person is of equal value to God? Should they be of equal value to us?

9. Explain what you think Galatians 3:28 means: "There is neither Jew nor Greek, slave nor free, male nor female, for you are all one in Christ Jesus."

10. On a scale of one to ten, one being the least and ten being the most, where would you place yourself on the significance scale—and why?

11. Who was your favorite character in this story? If you could meet that person, what would you like to say to him or her?

12. What did you take away from this story?

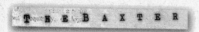